THE BIZARRE APPARITION IN THE DOORWAY WIDENED ITS GRIN . . .

"How did you like my tape, Doctor?"

Helzer's mouth felt stuffed with cotton "It . . ." His throat pinched off the rest of the sentence.

Perry raised the crystal until it was level with his own face. Again his eyes stared into it as he focused the full intensity of his hatred in Helzer's direction. The psychiatrist tried to look away, but the shimmering, lustrous crystal held him mesmerized.

A searing ruby beam as narrow and concentrated as a powerful laser bored into Helzer's forehead. Hell was no longer an abstract concept as the terrified man realized the contents of Harlan Perry's mind were being projected into his own. His inner eye was assaulted with vile images—bloody guts leaking from spongy corpses, infected brain matter that resembled a squirming, convoluted mass of fat white gelatinous snakes trying to swallow each other. He saw the beloved city of his birth lying in a carpet of smoldering ashes like the aftermath of Dresden, and with disbelief felt his own body willing itself to die.

Other Leisure Books by J. Edward Ames:

THE FORCE

THE DEATH CRYSTAL

J. EDWARD AMES

LEISURE BOOKS　　NEW YORK CITY

A LEISURE BOOK®

November 1990

Published by

Dorchester Publishing Co., Inc.
276 Fifth Avenue
New York, NY 10001

Copyright © 1990 by J. Edward Ames

Printed in the United States of America.

PROLOGUE

BONES THE COLOR OF CREAMY MOONLIGHT GLIM-mered all around him in the dim, cavernous room.

Harlan Perry leaned the push broom against a glass exhibit case and used his free hand to unhook a passkey from his belt. The other hand clutched a can of Lysol disinfectant spray. Now the vast Permanent Exhibits gallery, with its collection of dinosaur skeletons, receded behind him as he entered a hallway illuminated only by a red, flickering EXIT sign at the far end.

He paused in the middle of the corridor to stare into empty space.

"The pretty *bitch* called me a freaky *glitch*," he intoned absently. The rhyme was intoned mindlessly by now, as automatic as a pop tune nagging at one's subconscious.

Perry carried his disinfectant past the walls, corners and lintels, spraying only the steel knob of a door marked STORAGE FACILITY 'A.' Finally satisfied it was safe to touch, he unlocked the door and opened it cautiously. He switched on a light, then descended a flight of unpainted concrete steps into the museum's basement. In the wavering fluorescent light his face was the bleached, naked white of a puppy's belly.

Halfway down the steps he stopped to turn on the Walkman cassette player bouncing against his left hip. As Perry eased the headphones over his ears, he smiled and listened to his shrill, whiny voice begin its apocalyptic message, an ominous warning about universal social sickness and the pressing need for a new cosmic chemotherapy.

His voice also spoke about the lies the U.S. Government psychiatrist had invented to stop him years ago and about his inexorable campaign against infection and sickness. It was the voice of health and strength and hope for the future, a voice that had been made more powerful by a secret hidden in his closet at home.

True, that secret concerned a dead man, except that the so-called dead man had miraculously defied a brutal death and was now somehow bonding with him, using him, directing him through some awesome kind of spiritual entry.

The dead man had called himself—Johnny Law.

Absorbed in the tape's message, he descended the rest of the steps like a man sleepwalking.

The immense basement storeroom was a motley hodgepodge of low priority artifacts and donated memorabilia which the museum directors could not strictly classify as natural history. Covering the wall at the foot of the steps was a huge, dusty *trompe l'oeil* oil painting, its bold vermilion and ultramarine colors depicting a hustling, 19th-century port city panorama of barges and fully rigged schooners. The janitor ignored it, just as he ignored the intricately scrolled Regency chair stored in front of it.

With his voice still exhorting its messianic message in his ears, he wandered toward a far corner of the basement. He was passing a tier of metal storage shelves when something on a middle shelf, something covered with a black velvet drop cloth, caught his eye.

He paused, stopped the cassette and moved closer to the object. It was flanked on one side by a book with a buckram cover, on the other by an exhibit placard typed in neat capital letters.

Perry reminded himself that he came down here often to edit his message tapes. He knew everything down here, as well as every exhibit upstairs in the museum. Despite its settled-in appearance, whatever the hell this was was definitely a new arrival.

He frowned as he read the title of the book flanking the velvet-draped object: *The Tuaoi Stone; The Story of the Terrible Crystal*.

He shifted his attention to the other side and flicked the placard a few times with one fingernail, scattering spiral swirls of dust motes, then sprayed it lightly with Lysol before picking it up—no telling who had touched it last. He read it, his lips moving soundlessly as they tried to keep up with his eyes:

THERE STILL EXIST MANY DEVOTEES OF THE LEGEND OF ATLANTIS, AN ISLAND OR CONTINENT SUPPOSED TO HAVE EXISTED WEST OF GIBRALTAR AND TO HAVE SUNK INTO THE ATLANTIC OCEAN. THE MYTH CLAIMED EVEN MORE INFLUENTIAL ADHERENTS WHEN SPIRITUALIST LUMINARIES SUCH AS EDGAR CAYCE AND MADAME BLAVATSKY WERE ALIVE TO PROMOTE IT.

ACCORDING TO LEGEND, THE ATLANTINS POSSESSED A CRYSTAL STONE FOR TRAPPING AND USING THE SUN'S RAYS. THIS TUAOI STONE OR TERRIBLE CRYSTAL COULD BE DIRECTED FOR GOOD OR EVIL. SOME CLAIM IT WAS THE TUAOI, HAVING FALLEN INTO THE WRONG HANDS, WHICH SUPPOSEDLY WROUGHT THE DESTRUCTION OF ATLANTIS.

EARLY IN THE 20TH CENTURY, A CRYSTAL CLOSELY RESEMBLING DESCRIPTIONS OF THE TUAOI STONE WAS RUMORED TO HAVE SURFACED IN THE AZORES ISLANDS, WEST OF PORTUGAL, AND SEVERAL POTENT INCIDENTS WERE ATTRIBUTED TO IT. THAT CRYSTAL SUBSEQUENTLY DISAPPEARED; SINCE THEN, HUNDREDS OF CLEVER FAKES —SUCH AS THE PRESENT EXHIBIT—HAVE FLOURISHED.

Perry was so curious he forgot to use the disinfectant, quickly brushing the black velvet cloth aside. His breath suddenly caught in his throat like a kernel of unchewed popcorn.

The replica looked like a fist-sized chunk of clear, brilliant, transparent quartz. But the longer he stared at its dazzling facets, the more perfectly its surface planes harmonized with and replicated the internal structure, like holding a mirror in front of another mirror and watching the reflections march off to infinity.

He reached for it with one hand, felt the cool surface and picked it up.

He was about to replace it when the quartz abruptly turned warm in his hand and made his fingers tingle numbly, as if they had gone to sleep and blood was just now rushing back into them.

He was still too surprised to drop it before a pencil-thin, ruby-red light beam emanated from the crystal and punched through his forehead.

It left no mark and caused no pain—but now he saw the city in flames, devastated, a wasteland of smoking ruins and rotting corpses. He heard the hellish screams of the dying and saw that the levees and dams had all burst. The river was flooding the cemeteries. Their bloated dead floated everywhere, released, skulls grinning in death rictus and some still trailing grave cerements like wakes of putrescent mold. But beyond it all, the grating backdrop of his voice on the tape exhorted the theme of blessed destruction and regeneration, preaching hope for his diseased and dying civilization.

Now the vision altered, shifting from a premonition to a terrible moment from his past. Perry saw himself in a behemoth, tiled laboratory, high-tech instruments blinking and clacking and recording; he was backing away in numb horror from the pretty girl in the starched white coat. Doctor . . . Doctor . . . He always forgot her name, some little boy's name.

"But it must be a mistake, Mr. Perry." She was coaxing him, holding the wildly erratic tracings of an EEG brain scan in front of her as she drew nearer. "Some electrical freak, a glitch in the equipment. Just let me run some more tests to see if—"

"No!"

He was screaming, his terrified eyes seeking the door. Then, right before he bolted out of the lab, his stare became fixated just below the delicate bones at the hollow of her neck and froze on the long, thin white proof that she, too, had been implanted with infection. "No! I know what you're doing! You're poisoning my brain!"

Now the crystal raised a clattering echo in the basement as it tumbled from his fingers and fell back onto the metal shelf. Harlan Perry uttered a half-smothered cry of protest and backed away as if his hand had just been licked by a flame-thrower.

He stood rooted for several minutes, waiting for his heart to stop scampering around inside his chest cavity like a frenzied animal in a cage. The painful pressure was back deep inside his head. Fizzling and tingling the back of his neck, it was the carcinogen that bitch had planted inside him years ago.

He had waited so very long to neutralize her and all the other vested interests who were trying to stop him. They were now also trying to stop Johnny Law from using him—teaming up with him from beyond the grave—to salvage the still healthy remnant of the human species. But that was before the Fates had sent him—this.

Perry glanced briefly at the crystal. It was an omen. The tide of battle was finally shifting in his favor.

He slowly drew near the shelves once more but kept his gaze averted as he recovered the Tuaoi Stone with its velvet cloth.

Perry turned the Walkman back on.

Then cautiously, ever so slowly, like a man sneaking past a sleeping snake, he reached for the book beside the Terrible Crystal.

CHAPTER ONE

DOCTOR LYDELL HELZER JABBED THE TAPE RE-
corder's stop button with a trembling index
finger, then quickly poured himself a generous
shot of Crown Royal and tossed it down neat.

"How could I have missed it?" he muttered
before rewinding the tape.

He poured another whiskey and stepped
through the open French windows onto a
wrought-iron balcony. Though it was nearing
midnight, the New Orleans summer night remained hot and sultry, the reluctant breeze a
moist, warm breath tickling his eyelids. Nervous
sweat glued a thin batiste shirt to his back.

He nursed the shot, an alcohol-induced glow
of optimism soon beginning to suffuse his body.
There was still time to get his files caught up this
very night and make an official record and

written diagnosis of the strange liar who was masquerading under the name Benjamin Davis. Then he would be in a position to report the case or at least cover his own ass if something happened.

He knew from nearly three decades of clinical experience that most psychotics kept their aggression verbal. Even so, he was sure that the man who made that tape was now close to the edge—perhaps already over it.

Helzer's office suite was located in a half-deserted commercial section along the city's East Bank, occupying half the third story of a garish and peeling Victorian stucco. He could see the Mississippi two blocks straight ahead, but a cloudy night muted its reflection. Beyond the artificial levee a dimly lighted dredge, diesels chugging, was taking advantage of the slack in river traffic to remove sediment. He could just make out the dark peninsular mass of the Algiers District jutting out from the far bank of the river. Damp tendrils of humidity still thickened the air. In the anemic penumbra of the street's mercury-vapor lamps, purple-leaved bougainvillaea vines hung as limp as the faded chintz curtains behind Helzer.

He tried to clear his head with a series of deep breaths, but the humid air only seemed to tighten his throat. Helzer finished the drink and returned to his office. The cassette tape recorder Davis had left earlier during his session sat in the middle of a badly pockmarked, rolltop desk.

The back of his neck tingled for a moment. He

thought he heard someone on the stairs leading to his landing. Then he remembered that the man from the janitorial service often worked late on Wednesdays.

He punched rewind and listened to the tape whirr hypnotically. When it clicked to a halt, he depressed the play button. The sudden voice was eerie in the late stillness of the office, high-pitched and whiny, the cadence so shrill at times that it pierced his eardrums with a grating sting.

"All people are merely cells in the great body of civilization. That body is now sick, diseased, decaying with age, with slimy cancerous growths and bloodsucking parasites. *I* alone am a strong cell, and *I* alone can regenerate the diseased body. But first the rotted, pulpy, infected portions must be scraped away and de-*stroyed* at my command!"

There was a pause in the tape, and somewhere along the borderland of awareness Helzer thought he heard a board creak outside the door.

"Come to me," continued the insane bray on the tape. "Gather around me, you who have suffered so! Soon I will begin to eradicate the parasitical cells among us. Believe in me, my poor little maggot-riddled soldiers for—"

Helzer clenched his jaw hard in disgust and stopped the tape. He couldn't, wouldn't listen to the rest again.

Benjamin Davis had exhibited no obvious signs of psychosis during their initial session— or was I simply too booze-fogged to notice them, the psychiatrist wondered. He had readily agreed to meet Davis at 7:30 P.M. twice weekly, especially when the younger man hesitantly asked if cash would be acceptable. And booze hadn't kept Helzer from feeling sorry at first for the supposed veteran. That was two weeks ago. He had meant to start a file, record a diagnosis and recommend a regimen of psychotherapy. Without such a file, he knew the state could come down hard on him for malpractice—assuming, of course, that Davis was or soon would be over the edge and actually try to somehow "eradicate the parasitical cells." And assuming he would mention that Helzer was his psychiatrist, a link Helzer felt his patient was intelligent enough to establish even if the doctor flatly denied it to the authorities.

Helzer rewound the "real me" tape, as Davis had called it. This raving megalomaniac might be the real man, but in fact he could not be Benjamin Davis, former U.S. Army corporal with the 61st Infantry, as he claimed. Helzer knew that for sure now.

The psychiatrist had first become suspicious last week when Davis' war memories began to take on the boastful cinematic proportions of a barroom bull session. Since it hadn't cost Helzer much valuable drinking time, he had tapped a few familiar channels he knew from his days as a screening psychiatrist at the Armed Forces Examination Station downtown.

It turned out that the only Corporal Benjamin Davis who had served with the 61st, in the exact area and during the time Helzer's patient mentioned, was a black man from Chicago. This real Benjamin Davis had filed no VA health claims whatsoever, meaning he had never requested treatment at a Veterans Hospital, as the fake Davis maintained, for post-traumatic stress disorder. Where and how he got hold of that name and unit Helzer didn't know, but—

The crack under the door leading to Helzer's reception area abruptly filled with yellow light. A moment later something thunked against the filing cabinet in the outer office, presumably the janitor's dustmop. Helzer snatched up the bottle of Crown Royal and returned it to its drawer.

He ejected the cassette and stood for a moment with it balanced on his palm, staring at it and pondering. At first after running the VA records check last week he had concluded that his budding hunch was right. Whoever this client really was, he was suffering from a harmless, if vivid, delusional neurosis. This neurosis perhaps afflicted, in some measure, many other American men in their thirties and forties. From such a therapeutic perspective, the masquerading Benjamin Davis of those first few sessions was nothing but one more harmless Walter Mitty enjoying his ego-bolstering fantasies, albeit at a slightly more exaggerated level.

But that rosy perspective was worthless now. The psychotic who made this tape had undeniably projected a schizoid alter ego onto it—a possibly dangerous alter ego that was close to taking possession of the man's psyche.

Helzer had settled himself at the rolltop desk and was about to start a postdated patient profile on Davis when his office door groaned slowly open.

The apparition watching him from the doorway looked like a cross between a mad doctor and a playground flasher. He wore a gauze surgical mask, thin latex gloves and an unbuttoned forest-green military raincoat. His left hand was hidden behind his back; the right hand clutched a scalpel, its razor-sharp blade glinting cruelly in the light pouring over his shoulder.

Only the pastry border of skin which had eluded the surgical mask identified the intruder as the self-proclaimed Benjamin Davis. That identity was confirmed when he pulled the mask down and grinned at the psychiatrist.

All Helzer managed to stammer was a foolish-sounding, "Mr. Davis, may I —may I help you?"

The bizarre apparition in the doorway widened its grin, revealing stained and decaying teeth too small for the mouth. "Try Harlan Perry, Doctor. Does *that* name ring a bell?"

Again the voice clawed along Helzer's spine. He tried to swallow the hot, painful lump in his throat and finally shook his head without a word.

For the first time Helzer noticed that his patient was guarding something in his left hand, something covered with a black velvet cloth. Perry slid the cloth away, and Helzer stared at a brilliant chunk of what looked like clear glass. But since gazing into its shifting, melting, shimmering lines and surfaces brought on a bad case of vertigo, Helzer turned his face away.

18

"Let's refresh your memory, Doctor."

Perry glared at the crystal. In just seconds the dull flat discs of his pupils were gleaming like chips of radioactive obsidian as they absorbed its coruscating brilliance. Helzer's heart palsied in terror at the sound of the oh-too-familiar voice which next emerged from the psychotic.

"I'm sorry, Mr. Perry, but that's my final determination based on your test results. As head of this board, I declare you unfit for military service due to mental incompetence."

The voice was 17 years younger but unmistakably Helzer's—not a clever imitation but Helzer's own.

"You bastard!" screamed Harlan Perry, but his, too, was the voice of a younger man, the younger Harlan Perry who had uttered those same words before being escorted out of the Armed Forces Examination Station back in 1969. "You cruddy goddamn quack! I'll kill you if it takes the rest of my life!"

Now Perry tore his gleaming eyes away from the crystal and fixed them on Helzer again.

As memory returned, the psychiatrist felt his armpits and groin break out in frigid sweat. The blood pressure roaring in his ears was like angry surf. "*You*?"

"That's an affirmative. *Me!*"

Harlan Perry stepped further inside and shut the door softly behind him.

"I remembered your name. When I spotted your sign in my own neighborhood, I figured you must have hit the skids. At that first meeting you were so hungover you didn't know your ass from your elbow. I knew a broken-down alcoholic quack like you would agree to night sessions. That way I avoided your receptionist. Nobody's seen me here but you."

He crossed halfway to the desk and stopped. Helzer shrank into the chair.

Again Perry exposed his decayed teeth. "How did you like my tape, Doctor?"

Helzer's mouth felt stuffed with cotton. "It—" His throat pinched off the rest of the sentence.

Perry raised the crystal until it was level with his own face. Again his eyes stared into it as he focused the full intensity of his hatred in Helzer's direction. The psychiatrist tried to look away, but the shimmering, lustrous crystal held him mesmerized.

A searing ruby beam as narrow and concentrated as a powerful laser bored into Helzer's forehead. Hell was no longer an abstract concept as the terrified man realized the contents of Harlan Perry's mind were being projected into his own. His inner eye was assaulted with vile images—bloody guts leaking from spongy corpses, infected brain matter that resembled a squirming, convoluted mass of fat white gelatinous snakes trying to swallow each other. He saw the beloved city of his birth lying in a carpet of smoldering ashes like the aftermath of Dresden and with disbelief felt his own body willing itself to die.

And in the last moment before Helzer's heart dutifully surrendered life in a final, violent stomp against his ribs, he was forced to preview the ugly mutilation Perry was about to perform on his corpse with the scalpel.

A minute later, when Perry had finished leaving the one useful clue he had decided to give the police, he wiped the scalpel's blade on Helzer's trousers and returned it to the pocket of his raincoat. Careful not to touch anything else, he popped the cassette tape back into the player and looped the portable unit around his right shoulder. No one needed to know his plans yet. They'd find out soon enough. The whole city would, including the pretty Scar Baby who tried to infect his brain.

He was not who they thought he was, not anymore, and soon, after studying the book more, he would be ready. Goddamn all of you, he would be *ready*!

He carefully wrapped the crystal in its velvet cloth and tucked it into the other pocket of his Army surplus raincoat. He still had to return the Tuaoi to the storage shelf before the museum opened. His final act was to remove a small white card from his shirt pocket and lay it on the desk beside Helzer's slumped head and the growing pool of blood staining the blotter.

Perry gazed at his handiwork one last time as he snapped the gauze mask back into place—no telling what kind of airborne germs were drifting around in a city as decadent as this one. He didn't bother to turn off the lights when he left the office.

The neatly printed, linen-finish card proclaimed in florid scarlet capitals: JOHNNY LAW RULES!

CHAPTER TWO

"THE POSSIBLE OUTCOMES OF AN ATTACK MUST BE faced from time to time as part of your training. You may be killed. You may be raped. You may be maimed for life, or your children raped, injured, or killed. Or you may be fortunate and escape, surviving with nothing but the trauma of the memory."

The woman speaking to the all-female class was barefoot and wore white cotton pants and a loose matching jacket, tied with a sash. She was somewhere in her late 20's, rather tall, with a severely pretty, fine-boned face. Her movements suggested the grace and flexibility of a dancer.

"Sometimes any of these may happen whether or not you choose to fight back. Other times it clearly might be better *not* to fight back," continued Stevie Lasalle.

"The point of your training thus far is not that you must lash out like an automatic machine. The objective is simply to provide you with a repertoire of effective self-defense skills so you are able to fight back if you choose to do so or have no other option."

The women in the class ranged from 18 to their early 50's and wore a motley array of exercise garb—sweatshirts, t-shirts, cotton workout suits like Stevie's, tights, gym shorts and stretch shorts. They listened attentively, most of them obviously nervous; after three weeks of mat practice in the South Central College Intramural Gym, they were now about to experience their first exercise in simulated attack situations.

Today's male guests—husbands, boyfriends, brothers, even one father-in-law—had volunteered to be the aggressors and sat at the opposite end of the bleachers. One, a stocky, aging, hippie type, was politely attentive. Others fidgeted and looked bored, amused, or ill-at-ease.

"Remember, too," Stevie said, "that you are not trying to pawn yourself off as Hollywood's version of the Kung-fu killer. Rely on the basic stock of kicks, stomps, jabs and well-timed feints that we've practiced; concentrate on breaking chokes and holds and getting out of the attacker's striking range. Your life is on the line. Don't be squeamish and waste time aiming at so-called clean targets. A man who attacks a woman, especially if he's a stranger, is not thinking about a clean fight. He's a ruthless animal who

24

gives up his human rights the moment he attacks you."

"*If* you decide to fight, commit yourself 100 percent. Be totally aggressive and follow through. Do not rely on one blow—kick, kick again, jab, punch, stomp. You're a woman, and he expects you to be passive. Surprise him. Go straight for his kneecaps, his solar plexus, his throat, especially his groin."

There was a ripple of nervous laughter from the male side of the bleachers.

"Don't worry, guys."

Stevie smiled, walking toward the volunteers and surveying them. Most of them already knew that her graceful movements in fact resulted from five years of dedicated training in aikido and karate. Those with the best memories for headlines could even recall the incident that had impelled her dedication.

"I've been teaching this class for three years now, and we haven't put too many men out of commission—so far."

Laughter came from both ends of the bleachers.

"Okay then!" Stevie clapped her hands once sharply, the sound echoing in the corners of the huge gym. "One last reminder, victims and attackers. You may practice any move we've discussed with the exception of a blow toward the eyes. That option is too simple as well as too dangerous to warrant practice. It's retained for real attacks only."

"Victims, take a few minutes to warm up on

25

the mats. Attackers, please remain seated. I'd like to have a word with you."

While the women performed jumping jacks and stretches at the far end of the gym, Stevie addressed the volunteers.

"Gentlemen, thank you sincerely for agreeing to help us. I know that some of you may have studied hand-to-hand combat or martial arts in the military or elsewhere. Your first impulse might be to laugh when some of these women make their initial attempts at being physically aggressive. Please don't. We can and will criticize them more bluntly later, but for now help them build some confidence by taking this seriously. Growl and swear. If they make a pretty good move against you, then go ahead and stumble a little, even fall down. Help them out. Correct them without belittling them."

She had lowered her voice and moved in closer to the bleachers. Her huge gray eyes confronted the outside world frankly and confidently, if somewhat mistrustfully. The thick hair was the color of roasted coffee and grew in a widow's peak on her forehead. It was pulled into a tight, efficient knot on the back of her neck. When she wasn't teaching this volunteer class or lecturing on brain pathology at the South Central College Medical Center, Stevie usually let it cascade over her shoulders.

"I assure you," she continued, "I am no raving, man-hating feminist. But I think you can agree with me that women have endured too long a history of vulnerability to male attacks. Your patience now might save their lives later, or"—she paused to swallow, her voice becoming a little more self-consciously forceful—"or even help them save the life of someone else very close to them."

Stevie had placed her hands on her hips as she spoke, the movement parting the lapels of her cotton jacket wider. Now she was close enough for some of them to notice the long, livid white scar just below the fine bones at the hollow of her throat. The attention level of her audience abruptly soared.

"You may also be helping to reduce their fear levels so they can function better from day to day. I hope you'll agree these are worthwhile goals. May I count on your cooperation?"

A muscular towhead in jeans and tank top, sitting down front, flicked his eyes away from her throat.

"I'll cooperate," he assured her in a firm voice. The rest echoed their assent.

"Thank you. Now, to make this exercise more realistic, please attack women you don't know. We'll run through the safety procedures one more time, then if there are no further questions I'll turn you hoodlums loose."

Fifteen minutes later Stevie was circulating among the struggling couples on the mats, making suggestions, correcting techniques, offering compliments when a woman made a good defensive move. The enthusiasm remained high, but everyone adhered to the safety rules. At one point she was forced to bite back a smile as she took the blond in the tank top aside and whispered, "You don't have to fall on your can every time she looks at you, Gary! You want her to start thinking she's Wonder Woman?"

After class Stevie showered and changed into a cool shirtwaist dress and ankle-tie espadrilles. She stopped by the Medical Center to check her mailbox, then made the eight block hike from campus to her apartment downtown. The dampness of early afternoon heat clung to her skin. To the north, over Lake Pontchartrain, she could see the dark, boiling spume of a thunderhead.

About a block from her apartment, she felt a sudden chill on the back of her neck. She spun around and hastily scanned the sidewalk behind her, but no one was watching. The city went on about its business, mercifully ignoring her.

Her building was a new high rise made of steel, glass and gleaming white marble. She stopped outside the foyer to read the headline glaring at her from the *Times-Picayune* box:

"POLICE STYMIED IN BIZARRE DEATH OF CITY PSYCHIATRIST."

Before she could push the double glass doors open, the building's security guard scuttled forward to hold them for her.

"Thank you, Duncan."

Duncan Hilliard, an elderly mulatto with bristly white chin whiskers and a smile full of gold crowns, gave her an approving glance. He made a point of knowing all the residents by name and always had a friendly word or a corny joke for each of them.

"Lookin' good, Miz Lasalle."

Her lips pursed in an ironic smile. "I might

28

be flattered if I didn't happen to know you're the most notorious flirt in the building."

He winked at her. "Practice makes perfect."

Stevie crossed through the potted palms of the lobby to the elevator and pressed the button for the 11th floor. Again she congratulated herself on discovering this place. Since deciding against medical school here in New Orleans and instead opting to complete a Ph.D. program in physiological psychology at the Sorbonne, Stevie was rapidly acquiring the status of a highly sought expert on the anatomical malfunctions of the human brain. She lectured thrice weekly to interns and third-year medical students at South Central College, and her new apartment was close, convenient, and —above all—secure. A guard remained on duty in the lobby until 11 P.M., contacting residents by house phone when they had visitors. All residents had keys to both the main entrance and the elevator. The ground level, behind the foyer and the elevator, was a well-lighted parking deck; it, too, was patrolled regularly by the security guard until 11, then by city police until Duncan came on again at 7 A.M.

Stevie was thinking of her afternoon lecture as she fished the key out of her purse and slipped it into the lock of apartment 11-B. She didn't hear the faint rustling noise behind the door as she swung it open.

A streaking motion caught the corner of one eye. Stevie hissed as she caught her breath.

They held her down while the steel pipe gleamed dully in the moonlight. It lashed down over and over, turning her brother's head into a battered melon.

Keith no, oh no no no, please God no . . .

Her will clenched like a fist before the rest of the terrifying images were allowed to surface in conscious memory. A moment later her heart crawled down out of her throat, and she was laughing with embarrassed relief.

"You dummy! That's what happens when you fall asleep behind the door."

Her pet tabby, Mr. Cat, watched her reproachfully as he resettled under the coffee table. She'd had him for nearly five years now, since she'd returned from graduate school in France, and he'd proven to be a good though somewhat aloof friend. He was also finicky and comically dignified. Other cats announced their touchy moods with yowling, growling, mewing and spitting; Mr. Cat, however, confined himself to a little chittering complaint when he was malcontent. Otherwise it was the silent treatment.

"I beg your pardon, your Highness."

Stevie closed the door and pushed the deadbolt home. Despite the building's ultra-modern exterior, the spacious living room boasted a beautiful solid oak floor with a Persian rug. The huge north window looked out over City Park and Lake Pontchartrain; its mate on the east wall offered an excellent view of the Mississippi and the new suburbs mushrooming beyond the expressway on the far bank. The apartment's antique motif continued in her bedroom with a tall, ornately carved, cheval glass that had belonged to her great-grandmother, as had the ivory-inlaid vanity table. The spare bedroom was kept closed against Mr. Cat and had been converted into a mat-lined area for daily practice of different martial art forms which kept her fine-tuned between full-contact sessions with her instructor.

The rest of the apartment was decorated simply, a few tastefully selected paintings and sculptures rather than a confusion of bric-a-brac. Stevie was not a saver, her drawers and shelves were not cluttered with postcards or play programs or coupons or old telephone numbers.

Some visitors found her apartment impressive but a little cold, a little hostile, not the kind of place where you lightly kicked off your shoes and laid back—"a carefully controlled environment," as one thwarted romantic hopeful had cracked sarcastically on his way out for the last time.

And he was right, she thought now, her eyes rotating toward the photo on the smoked-glass coffee table in front of the sofa. The youth smiling back at her was barely in his 20's when this final picture had been taken, but the huge, wary, gray eyes and finely etched cheekbones left little doubt that he was Stevie's twin brother.

For a moment she did something she rarely did in public. She touched the thin, hard, white ridge of scar tissue below her neck.

Not just her apartment but her entire life was going to be a carefully controlled environment. She had made that decision eight years ago

31

when she crawled back from the brink of Hell and reconstructed the fragments of a broken life.

Deep inside her a warning sounded, and she shifted mental gears from past to present. She decided to check the message machine for calls, then prepare her notes for the three o'clock lecture.

Three people had called that morning while she was teaching the self-defense class. The first was her New York editor, his harried tone reminding her that the deadline for the next chapter of her textbook revision was rapidly approaching. She winced when she recognized the sonorous voice of the second caller as Charles Wright, a prominent M.D. on South Central's Medical Center staff.

"Stevie, why are you avoiding me? It won't work—not after what happened between us last weekend. That was special, and you know it. Please return my call. I'll be waiting."

No, she *didn't* know it was special, Stevie thought with a quick flush of irritation. She had been half-heartedly dating Wright since last winter, carefully keeping the relationship platonic despite his obvious desire to make it something very different. Then last Saturday night, for reasons she still hadn't quite figured out— maybe too much claret, maybe a moment of vulnerability during which she could no longer deny her body's physical needs—she had slept with him. Now he was acting possessive, protective, patriarchal, adopting a new tone of intimacy that was starting to exasperate her.

He would find out as the others had that no one was going to control her life but Stevie Lasalle. One night of naked groping and mutual sexploitation hardly constituted a contract.

The third caller's voice was unfamiliar.

"Doctor Lasalle, Neal Bryce here. I'm a detective with the Algiers Precinct's Bureau of Special Investigations. I wonder if you'd kindly return my call at your earliest opportunity? It pertains to the death Wednesday night of Doctor Lydell Helzer. My office number is two-five-five, two-seven-nine-seven, extension three-three-three. Home phone, two-seven-seven, four-eight-one-two. Thank you."

The answering machine clicked off. Stevie stared at it and smiled, in spite of her puzzled curiosity, at the man's pronounced Texas drawl. The headline she'd spotted earlier now drifted back: "POLICE STYMIED IN BIZARRE DEATH OF CITY PSYCHIATRIST." She glanced at her Omega and saw it was almost 1:30. I'll call after the lecture, she decided.

But during the next 15 minutes she found she couldn't concentrate on her notes. Curiosity competed with irritation at the unwelcome interruption, so she called the detective's office.

She let the phone ring five or six times and was about to hang up when there was a brief click as someone picked it up. The first thing she heard was a faint strain of symphonic music. My God, I'm on hold and the police have resorted to classical Muzak, she thought incredulously. Then above the plaintive wail of rising violins, she heard a voice.

"Neal Bryce speaking."

"Yes, this is Doctor Lasalle returning your call."

The music abruptly stopped.

"Thank you for getting back with me so soon." The voice was lazy and slow and Stevie imagined a plump, good-natured redneck wearing boots and sporting perpetual half-moons of sweat under his armpits.

"I confess I'm curious as to my connection with a murder case. Tell me, Mr. Bryce, am I a suspect?"

"No, but I was hoping you might help us find one."

"Isn't that your job?"

The man at the other end ignored the question. "Are you familiar with the Lydell Helzer case?"

"Just the headlines."

"This case is an odd one. Helzer was discovered by his receptionist yesterday morning, slumped dead at his desk. The Medical Examiner places time of death somewhere between eleven P.M. Wednesday and one A.M. Thursday. His left ear had been amputated and apparently taken from the scene by his attacker. Even more bizarre, Helzer was not otherwise physically harmed. Autopsy shows massive heart failure as probable cause of death, and the body tissue was abnormally stiff with adrenaline, suggesting that he was literally scared or shocked to death."

"It's all very lurid and gruesome, Mr. Bryce, but what do I have to do with it?"

Patiently, he continued as if she had not spoken. "We have only one possible clue, and it's not too meaningful at present. We're examining Helzer's files, which are a shambles, and interrogating his receptionist. We're also running checks on all his recent phone calls. All we know about his personal life is that he was a divorced alcoholic with few friends beyond casual drinking acquaint—"

"Mr. Bryce, please. Exactly what do you want from me?"

His gently reproving sigh suggested that *some* people had no appreciation for life's little gallery of criminal curiosa. Bryce's manner became more businesslike.

"Last year you published an article called 'Organic Brain Disorders and Criminal Motivation' in the *Review of Neuropsychiatry*. A less technical summary of that article, written by a professor emeritus of criminology at Baylor University, subsequently appeared in the *Journal of Forensic Science*."

"Yes, I remember a Professor Moran requesting my permission to do that article. He sent me a copy."

"He sent me one, too. Moran was my advisor when I was a student at Baylor. He—*we're* interested in your conclusion that the most sensational and unusual crimes tend to be committed by people with a particular type of malignant tumor in the cerebral cortex. In the field of criminology your work is becoming known as the 'festering brain' theory of shock crimes."

"I see," Stevie said. "And amputating an ear

definitely qualifies as *National Enquirer* fare."

"Right. That, and whatever might have caused massive heart failure and so much adrenaline in Helzer's system. That man was more than just frightened. He was psychologically totaled."

"I'm pleased that my work has drawn the attention of professionals outside of medicine—I truly am—but how can I help you further? You've said you already read my article. If my hypothesis is correct, then there's a good chance the man you're looking for has a malignant brain tumor—so?"

"You're an expert on this type of offender, Doctor Lasalle. According to your article you interviewed and studied nearly a dozen of them at the Shreveport State Mental Hospital. You know what, if anything, distinguishes them from other psychotics. Would you be willing to act as a resource person for me in this investigation? We're talking something as simple as jotting down your impressions of these so-called festering brain criminals. Any ideas you have might give me a working personality composite of the type—how they reason, think, formulate their grudges, whatever. I admit that right now I can't find a handle on this case."

"I'm not a forensic psychiatrist, Mr. Bryce. I'm a researcher. Besides, you're only assuming organic brain disorder here. I understand that amputating ears was a common atrocity during Vietnam on both sides. Your criminal could be a disturbed Vietnam veteran with organic brain damage, but considering the special nature of that war, he's just as likely to be a vet suffering purely psychological problems. Wouldn't local Vietnam veterans with histories of mental illness be the logical first line of investigation?"

"Maybe," Bryce conceded, though not too enthusiastically. "We're checking into that angle." He cleared his throat with diplomatic politeness. "Well? Could you possibly help us?"

There was an awkward pause, and he added, "You'd be paid for your time, of course. I'm authorized—"

"Money isn't the chief consideration here, Mr. Bryce. I have research projects to supervise, lectures to prepare, and a textbook to revise by September or my editor will boil me in red ink. I also teach a volunteer class which I consider too important to neglect. I simply don't have the time."

During another long pause, they both listened to the vague static rumble of the telephone company's bowels. Bryce said, his tone heavy with resignation, "I understand. By the way, that textbook you're revising. Wouldn't happen to be *Organic Dysfunctions of the Human Brain*?"

Stevie was mildly surprised. "Yes, it is. It's a series of highly technical monographs aimed at medical students and practitioners specializing in brain pathology. I wouldn't have guessed that a"—she paused, uncertain what to call him—"that a law enforcement official would be aware of it in its present form."

"That's another reason why I hoped we could get together sometime. I had a medical consultant translate parts of your book into layman's language for me. I was fascinated by the chapter on physiological factors in criminal behavior."

Stevie's lips pursed against the mouthpiece. "You're a charming manipulator, Mr. Bryce. Now that you've mentioned my article and complimented my book, you're confident that I'll feel compelled to help you."

"Do you?"

"No, Mr. Bryce, I don't. I sincerely wish you luck in your investigation, but I won't be part of it. Good-bye."

But even as she hung up, Stevie experienced the uncomfortable suspicion that she would eventually cooperate with Bryce. Worse, she suspected he already knew she would. This man was used to cleverly controlling others.

The thought triggered another hot flush of irritation—and something else a little more difficult to label.

CHAPTER THREE

THE MAN IN THE PRUSSIAN BLUE CUTLASS SUPREME had to cruise the Decatur Street sleaze strip twice before a parking space opened up.

He maneuvered into a tight slot between a Silverado pickup and a Harley Sportster, killed the engine and popped Vivaldi's *Four Seasons* out of the tape player. With practiced dexterity he slipped a pair of remarkably long legs around the steering column and unpacked his six-foot-five frame from the Olds. He was in his late 30's, the normally dark-complexioned face even duskier from a few days of beard. A slight paunch was just beginning to protrude under the beige summerweight sport jacket.

To his left was the row of neon-winking sailors' bars which gave this stretch of the Vieux Carré its seamy reputation with tourists; to his right, a coppery confusion of railroad tracks was followed by the dark smooth hump of a levee, then the river. In the fading sunlight the sluggish water was a metallic gray, a dingy, turgid ribbon of molten lead twisting and looping through the city. The sun was setting, and already the moon illuminated one jagged edge of a cloud high above the water.

For a moment he smelled a thick familiar smell that itched in his nostrils like the musty odor of ropes soaked in creosote. Why did it always make him think of faraway places and naked women and more recently of Stevie Lasalle and death?

Neal Bryce abruptly turned his back on the river and crossed Decatur in a few springing bounds. He was grateful for the pulsing music and the garish light that leaked through the clubs' slatted jalousies and zebra-striped his jacket. He walked half a block, then paused in front of a two-story stucco which proclaimed itself RUDY'S TAHITIAN PALACE in green, glowing letters. The two I's of TAHITIAN were shaped like palm trees bowing in a typhoon.

It was impossible to ignore the flamboyant four-foot poster pasted beside the front entrance:

SEE THE INCREDIBLE SHONEEN, THE IRISH FAKEER WHO FEELS NO PAIN! TWO SHOWS NIGHTLY, 7 AND 9! NO COVER FOR LADIES!

Bryce grinned at the crude drawing of a man lying on a bed of nails while he swallowed a flaming torch. It was a bad likeness of the person he had come to see, but no doubt it was McKenna himself who insisted that the posters not resemble him.

"Stayin' for the show, Cap?"

Bryce nodded at the sleepy, bored bouncer seated at a folding card table. He dropped a trio of dollar bills into the cigar box and made a loose fist so the other man could stamp him. The Friday night was still young, and the Palace was only about a third full with the usual mostly male clientele—merchant marines on liberty, local dock workers, a few adventuresome tourists looking to score dope or absorb the seediness that even Bourbon Street didn't offer. Overhead fans revolved slowly, pushing great clumps of stagnant, smoky air around. A skinny black kid in a New Orleans Saints t-shirt was pecking out some blues at a badly tuned piano. Bryce knew he was only providing background noise until The Incredible Shoneen, one of the hottest new acts on the riverfront, came on. Ironically for the publicity-shy McKenna, his local fame had been assured from that day last month when he turned down a bid to appear on the Johnny Carson show, a refusal that even the wire service tickers had picked up on.

"Bryce! Hey, Neal Bryce!"

Wade McKenna was waving to him from the bar. Bryce raised a hand in greeting and joined him.

"I work in this septic tank," McKenna greeted him. "What's your excuse?"

"Came to see you."

"See me on stage or in person?"

Bryce shrugged one shoulder. "Actually, both. I'll take a draft," he added as the bartender leaned across the gleaming mahogany bar to take his order.

"Give him your cleanest glass and me another Remy Martin, Lance." McKenna's tone was laced with mock reverence. "I'm drinking with a man who turned down an offer to play pro basketball so he could get his ass shot at in Vietnam."

"It was semiprofessional ball," Bryce said, trying to find room for his knees, "and I've told you at least twice now that I never saw combat when I was in Nam. I was with CID in Danang."

McKenna was too drunk to register the correction. He was 40, but until recently most people were startled to learn it. A boyishly beardless face was too ordinary to call handsome; his hair was darker by several shades than the explosion of freckles on his muscular forearms.

"Yeah, that's all right, Bryce. All-American jock, bigtime war hero, supersleuth. Always gets his man—"

"Knock it off," Bryce said, though his tone revealed no irritation. "You want me to leave, just say so. Nobody's coercing you."

"Steady on, boyo. You here to talk business?"

Bryce nodded.

"Okay. But let's go up to my room. I go on in thirty minutes, and Rudy pisses blood if I hang around while the crowd's building. You can bring that swamp elixir with you," he added, nodding toward Bryce's beer glass and signaling okay to the bartender.

Bryce also palmed a salt shaker with his free hand as he lifted his glass. Then McKenna led them past a ratty chenille curtain at one end of the bar and up a narrow staircase that reeked of Pine Sol. His tiny room at the end of the landing, though neat and recently scrubbed, was doomed to permanent dinginess by the deeper smudges and stains accumulated through decades of transient boarders.

"This penthouse comes with my three-month contract," McKenna said. "Here, take the seat of honor." He pointed toward a lopsided recliner in the middle of the room. A cot was set up against the back wall, paperback books stacked neatly underneath according to category.

Bryce opted for a sturdier straight chair near the door. He had just settled in when someone out in the hall discreetly rapped on the door.

"Lena?" The voice was a husky whisper.

"Go back one to your left!" McKenna shouted. He raised his palms toward Bryce in supplication. "Sorry. She has a lot of visitors, if you catch my drift. Sometimes they get lost."

"Don't worry. *Miami Vice* has copped the Southern market on hookers and nose candy."

"So," McKenna said, "how's the kid?"

"Ornery as ever. Passed his citizenship test a while ago. Says he's saving up his paper route money to buy a motor scooter."

McKenna aimed a significant glance at the cracked Baby Ben alarm clock on the floor near his cot, then finished a third of his drink in one long sip. "Okay, so much for the civilities. What brought you here? Wait, don't tell me. It's this so-called van Gogh slasher the papers are whooping up?"

Bryce nodded before tasting his beer.

"Yeah, I was thinking you might show up. What's the pay?" McKenna demanded.

Bryce ignored the question while he salted the beer and watched it grow a new head of foam.

"This case has an added wrinkle or two. The shrink, Helzer, was known for offering cut-rate therapy. Spell that easy prescriptions for Demerol and Dilaudid. Since all the prescriptions are on file, the list of potential suspects is easy to trace on paper, but it's costing us a lot of man hours trying to track them in the real world."

"Yeah, right, my heart goes out to you and New Orleans' finest. The pay, Bryce? The green backs?"

Unruffled, Bryce set his beer down and slipped an English Corona from his coat pocket, snapping open its tube. He made no further progress toward lighting it, but instead began to reflect as if McKenna were not in fact on the other side of the room, staring at him with impatience. At first Bryce had hoped the calling card the attacker had apparently left behind would yield something, but the paper stock and ink were traced back to a Wisconsin toy company which mass-manufactured miniature printing press kits. An estimated quarter-million of the kits had been marketed nationally, including chain stores throughout New Orleans and Louisiana. So far the name 'Johnny Law' was proving equally worthless. It could mean anything—a punk rock group, a motorcycle gang, a mocking reference to the police themselves. Nor was there any proof Helzer's attacker had even left the card.

McKenna finished his drink and pretended to rattle nonexistent ice cubes. "Bryce, watching that erotic look on your face when you start thinking cop stuff is disgusting. Look, I go on in twenty minutes. Do we strike a bargain or not?"

"Same terms as last time," Bryce responded promptly. "Fifty bucks per diem special consultant's fee, beginning today. Plus another seventy-five every time we actually employ your services."

"Employ my services. Jesus, I like that." McKenna discovered for the second time that his drink was empty and grimaced. Something in the way the tall cop was eyeing him made him turn his face away.

"What's the matter, lieutenant? You can't get used to the idea of a spiritual mercenary?"

Bryce finished lighting his cigar and said nothing.

"I suppose you figure that a higher plane also means a higher morality? Well, meet your first psychic sleaze, old sleuth. Just the bucks, ma'am, just the bucks." McKenna's voice tightened with bitterness.

Bryce, who knew the man's history better than most people in town, smoked his cigar and said nothing.

"Look," McKenna said, "I have to dress for my first gig. Why don't you hang around downstairs and fill me in after the show?"

This had been precisely Bryce's plan, but now he carefully gauged the volatile McKenna's mood and decided it wasn't the best time to brief him. During Bryce's six years with the NOPD's Bureau of Special Investigations, the BSI had recorded its highest percentage of solved cases. The Bureau perpetually received the weird, the bizarre, the impossible assignments, the cases cops hate and newspaper publishers love. His success did not usually depend on hunches or intuition; in fact, it was just the opposite. When it was possible, he played cop like he had once played basketball—conservatively and methodically, a team player, not a star, usually winning even when it didn't look too pretty. But he was also known for occasionally blowing the game wide open, much to the chagrin of the police department's brass.

Like most of his peers, Bryce relied on the usual network of paid informers. But he had also carefully cultivated an especially diverse pool of contacts he referred to as 'resource people,' ranging from unusually perceptive high school dropouts working down on the docks to world-famous academics at New Orleans' Tulane, Dillard, and Loyola Universities. As a result his special consultant fees were the chief subject of Precinct Captain Lucien Milo's tirades. But Bryce was also the cop most likely to be on top of a new angle, opening a door where others had only seen a blank wall. The Texan knew he enjoyed the favorite brat status of an upstart who had compiled a winning record, a record which had brought the department national recognition in law enforcement circles.

"Tonight's not a good night for me," he finally said, looking for a place to butt his cigar. "I'll drop by again in the next couple days."

Again there was the discreet rat-a-tat-tat on the door.

"Back one door to your left, dammit!"

For a moment, exhaustion obvious on his face, McKenna let his head drop forward and massaged his forehead with his fingertips. Then a grin split his face.

"Yeah, stop by soon. My act'll kill you, boyo."

Harlan Perry reluctantly paused along Decatur Street, unable to resist reading the crude poster which assaulted him like an aggressive panhandler.

The Incredible Shoneen. What garbage!

Perry stuck both hands into the pockets of his forest-green military raincoat and lumped them into angry fists. Another foreign parasite was spreading infection and ripping off the delta hicks and local scumbags. Perry's thin, bloodless, disgusted lips peeled back from gums that looked like strips of raw meat. In the lurid neon twilight his face seemed a very convincing wax replica of a corpse.

He hurried through the evening's gathering crowds, making sure none of them brushed their germs against him. As he crossed Fulton

Street his eyes automatically flicked about half-way down the block to the wrought-iron second-story balcony draped in bougainvillaea. Seeing the balcony made him think of the newspaper accounts of his mission last Wednesday night, and a thin hot geyser of gastric acid erupted up his esophagus.

The lying civilian media! Count on them to distort war news so the victor looked bad. Like Helzer they all had wormy rot for brains.

Suddenly self-conscious, convinced someone somewhere was drawing a bead on him, Perry barely restrained himself from running. He continued following the river for two blocks until a stretch of abandoned wharves yawned into view on his left. To the right was the sprawling East Bank ghetto which included his upstairs efficiency. One block over, out of sight from this side but a familiar view from his only window, was a tacky commercial stretch dominated by junkfood palaces and a K-Mart mall with colored plastic flags curling in the humidity.

Perry tried to appear bored and unhurried as he climbed the cement steps leading into the pre-World War II four-story redbrick at 421 1/2 Arno Street. He encountered no one on the stairs or the landing, fumbling nervously trying to peel his key apart from the knotted confusion of garbage bag twists he used for a key chain.

His upper lip and forehead were shiny with nervous sweat by the time he'd locked the door of unit 2-C behind him. He turned, his face cautious and suspicious, to scrutinize the apartment for signs of infiltration.

He flicked the light switch and a naked 60-watt bulb in the middle of the ceiling spilled its dirty yellow light. The gauze mask and latex gloves were still neatly displayed at the foot of his metal-frame bunk, where he had left them after his recent mission. The walls were covered with health-information fliers and late 1960's and early 1970's recruiting posters. THE SEVEN WARNING SIGNS OF CANCER and COMMON CARCINOGENS IN THE WORKPLACE alternated with TODAY'S ARMY WANTS TO JOIN YOU and THE MARINES DON'T PROMISE YOU A ROSE GARDEN.

And centered on the cheap Formica kitchen table a huge one-gallon jar he had purchased last Thursday at the K-Mart across the street. In it, he located what he was looking for, drifting lazily like a wrinkled and bloated potato chip in the hazy formaldehyde solution—the first of Johnny Law's soon-to-be-expanded collection of war trophies.

Everything appeared to be in order within his apartment. It was past six now, and he was due at work by seven. Tomorrow was Sunday when the museum opened early for the family crowd. Perry knew it wouldn't be such a good idea to borrow the Tuaoi tonight, but he could at least be near it for a few more hours and study the book some more.

He rummaged through the cupboards and refrigerator, slapping together a hasty supper of stale cheese curls, flat cola and the remainder of a can of fruit cocktail that had gone mushy and pungent from sitting open in the fridge for at least a week. He sat on an upended footlocker, using his scalpel to pry the lid of the can out of the way. Perry stirred his syrupy fruit with the point of the blade, then felt anger churn deep in his guts.

Dammit, there was no cherry.

He was sure there hadn't been a cherry either in the half he'd already eaten. The sudden fury made his scalp sweat. What right did these goddamn maggot-riddled corporations have to treat him like a second-class consumer? The bitching slut of a can said there were cherries, didn't it? Where the hell were they?

Well, certain individuals could muck him around before he had the crystal, maybe, but soon they were going to find themselves up to their asses in shit.

He began pacing the buckled linoleum, too angered and excited to eat. Outside, across Arno Street, he heard a familiar explosion of crackling static. Rage prickled his skin. It was that damn drive-thru speaker at the junkfood restaurant kitty-cornered from the K-Mart. Some nights it clamored until 2 A.M., pandering ptomaine trash to every loudmouthed drunk on the East Bank.

"Welcome to Burger Boy," a teenage girl's nasal voice whined, "May I take your order?"

The customer's voice, amplified on an evening breeze, boomed back. "Gimmee two Bodacious Boy Platters, one Baby Boy Basket, hold the onions, two—"

Snarling, Perry charged toward his open front window, elbowed the dirty Venetian blind out of

50

the way and screamed shrilly, "Order it in Hell, bastard!"

There was a long startled silence, as if the entire city were holding its breath before a hurricane. Perry's bloodless lips creased in a smile of self-satisfaction and revealed the tiny, moss-rimmed teeth. That shut the sonofa—

"Fuck you, dogbreath!"

The hearty male taunt from below was followed by a woman's laughter and her clearly audible shout. "Wimp!"

It was happening again. The inside of his skull was fizzling like nothing was in there but ice water and a couple dozen Alka Seltzers. An invisible hand laid a strip of red celluloid across his vision. Now the voice was rising up out of him in a deep, powerful bray so unlike his own shrill whine, rising up to split the stillness of his room.

"Lissenup, people," barked Johnny Law, *"and don't ever forget. The shit rolls downhill!"*

His waxen face now almost serene, he turned away from the window, returned to the table and examined the label of the fruit cocktail can until he had found what he wanted. Then he crossed to a tiny corner closet and dug out a vinyl U.S. Army-issue handbag.

He began removing its contents, paying little attention to the plain black journal whose gold-embossed letters said simply PERSONAL RE-CORD. He likewise ignored the dull, silver beads of the military dog tags wrapped around it, taking special care not to read the name on the tags. He resolved once again to replace that name with his own. A moment later Perry had begun yet another perusal of a three-hole spiral notebook labeled in militarily precise block letters: KNOWN AND SUSPECTED POLITICO-CARCINOGENIC AGENTS (PCA'S).

He turned to the first blank page and entered The Tradewinds Fruit Company, San Jose, California in his neat printing. Perry flipped back a few pages and stopped at a glued-in page whose letterhead had official Air Force seal.

"Dear Mr. Perry: This agency regrets to inform you that your application for enlistment . . ." The letter was dated June 1, 1969, and signed by Lydell Helzer, M.D.

To the opposite page was taped a recent statement of account from a nearby dental clinic. Perry's tongue probed experimentally at the still tender gap where—they claimed—his root canals had abscessed. But they lied! Root canals my ass, Perry told himself with bitter indignation. They were attempting to infect him; that was why they shoved the needles so far up inside. Then there had been the blatant lie about how root canal therapy had been too late and he would have to lose the crown anyway.

Unlike the rest of the things in the handbag, the notebook had been his own brainchild years before. One of the first pages was reserved for a classified ad clipped from the March 4, 1981 *Times-Picayune*.

WANTED: Adults between 18–65 to participate in a study of electrical changes within the human brain. Participants will receive $5 for approximately 40 minutes and will be monitored by a painlessly attached EEG (electroencephalograph) machine while they view films varying in level of fantasy. For further information contact project coordinator Stevie Lasalle at South Central Medical College, ext. 6500.

Stevie Lasalle. Stevie. A boy's name for the pretty, stuck-up bitch with the scar. Perry's right cheek twitched for several seconds. She was the agent who planted the poison in his brain, using that machine. But now he was sure he was destroying the foreign growth. The battle raged inside his skull, but he was winning.

The last page he turned to was the most recent passage he had copied from *The Tuaoi Stone; The Story of the Terrible Crystal.*

"A supposed occult power, the Tuaoi or Terrible Crystal was most feared for metempsychosis —the projection of the mind and will into the body of others. As the Tuaoi master perfected his skills, he could eventually direct the crystal's power as a wave in the universal psychic ether, eventually affecting larger and larger groups of people."

"The road to Hell," whispered Johnny Law's voice inside him, *"is paved with bones."*

CHAPTER FOUR

MARTIN FISCHLER RUBBED A CRUMB OF SLEEP
from the corner of one eye, paying little attention to the almost nonexistent six A.M. traffic
dotting Perdido Street.

On his right the Louisiana Superdome swelled
up out of the drowsing city like the undisputed
king of the Jiffy Pops. As always when he passed
it, Fischler thought the same rankling thought.
That huge monstrosity, built mainly to piss
Texans off, had lined the pockets of certain local
politicos with millions of dollars in graft.

He turned right at the next side street, guiding
his Mercedes 380 SL toward the heart of the
familiar East Bank ghetto where he had practiced dentistry for nearly three decades. Each
time he spun the steering wheel to the left, the

charcoal-gray jacket and long-sleeved shirt rode up a few inches on his right forearm, revealing faint blue traces of the numbers which had been tatooed there more than 40 years earlier.

The empty K-Mart plaza, less garish in the steely morning light, slid by on his right. Next came the A-frame Burger Boy where he had imbibed too many hasty burgers and greasy fries between back-to-back emergency root canals. He was uncomfortably aware of the drab redbrick tenements hovering on his left, though he seldom let himself glance toward them; he sensed their looming presence like giant, angry beasts waiting to pounce if he ever made eye contact. He actually felt a weight lift from his chest as he nudged into the right-turn lane and put more distance between himself and the tenements.

He parked in his reserved slot behind Riverside Medical Suites, a no-frills brown stucco spattered with bird droppings. The building's one concession to aesthetics was a long window box around front, flamboyant with huge red and white and yellow mums. Fischler hesitated a moment beside the flowers to fish out a few limp cigarette butts, a Chicken McNuggets container and a mildewed *Watchtower*.

He dropped them into the huge nearby trash container and slipped his key into the blue metal-plated door of Suite 13.

He was still swinging the door open when a man lunged at him from the far side of the reception room.

"Shalom."

Fischler always spoke in Hebrew when he greeted his own reflection in the full-length mirror behind the coatrack.

There were very few mornings in his long career when Fischler had failed to arrive first at the office. He had discovered long ago that a fanatical attention to detail was the best antidote for the terror and sadness and unnameable fears which invaded his idle moments. Consequently, he always came in early to clip crisp new napkins to the chairs, lay out his equipment, double-check the day's appointments and look up the relevant x-rays and charts if they were former patients. This allowed him to save money on payroll hours, a savings he passed on directly to his most indigent patients—though of course he had once heard a disgruntled customer remark "the old Jew is tighter than a fat man's fart."

He straightened up the tatty issues of *People*, *Newsweek*, *Redbook*, and *Sports Illustrated*, then noticed that the chart demonstrating the proper way to brush was drooping at one taped corner. He made a fist and hammered it back up. It wasn't until he turned away from the wall that he spotted the card.

It was lying just inside the door—a white business card with scarlet letters he could almost make out from where he stood. He must have stepped right over it as he came in.

Maybe a salesman called yesterday after the office closed. So why was there this queasy churning of gears deep in his gut? Fischler crossed the cool tile floor and picked up the card. The eight all-capital words made tiny globules of sweat pop out on his upper lip.

WAR IS OUR BUSINESS AND BUSINESS IS GOOD!

He turned the card slowly and found two more lines of all-capital print on the back. One was upside down. The one that wasn't asked:

WHAT'S THE DIFFERENCE BETWEEN A PIZZA AND A JEW?

For a moment Fischler felt like he was riding a furiously whirling merry-go-round and had just lost his grip. Spinning, flying, he struggled for control. His temples throbbed as he slowly won the battle to retain equilibrium, then turned the card upside down and read the punchline: A PIZZA DOESN'T SCREAM WHEN YOU PUT IT IN THE OVEN.

The dentist's fingers trembled for a moment, but only a moment, while rage and pain and disbelieving shock flared within him. He glanced at the telephone on the reception counter, but quickly decided against calling the police. Why bother? What did they care about one more anti-Semitic *shikse* in a world full of them? He was familiar with such sick humor by now.

Martin Fischler, who seldom found time to read a newspaper or watch TV, ripped the card into a dozen little pieces and dropped the last possible chance to save his life into the trash.

Bryce stood under the streaming hot water until it finally started running lukewarm. He cranked the cold up for a few seconds to shock himself awake, then shut both spigots off just as a violin shrieked Paganini's name to the heavens.

He winced when the ghetto blaster's loud volume, no longer competing with the splashing water, demolished the Monday morning quiet of the bathroom. Grunting as he folded his long naked body under the shower curtain rod, Bryce hustled through billowing clouds of steam and turned the Panasonic down.

Four days.

The thought recurred as he vigorously snapped the towel across his back. Four days since Helzer was found dead and mutilated. Captain Lucien Milo and others at the precinct were beginning to voice hopes that Helzer's assailant was not a pattern killer on some sort of psychotic vendetta. Bryce knew he had no real evidence to the contrary, and though it was not his style to have funny feelings about a case, the thought had been annoying him since Thursday that Helzer was not going to be an isolated incident.

He finished drying off, examined his face in the steam-blurred mirror and decided he'd rather shave than listen for the millionth time to Milo's "Texas flytrap" joke. After feeding his Schick a new blade and shaving so close his cheeks went numb, he slipped into cotton slacks and a short-sleeved shirt.

The pendulum clock at the bottom of the stairs was nearing eight A.M.. Knowing Sonny would have gotten up long ago to prepare to deliver his newspapers, he bypassed the kitchen doorway. He smelled the rich, drifting aroma of perking coffee and heard an occasional angry murmur in Cajun dialect as Kyla, their part-time housekeeper, prepared breakfast while arguing with a radio commentator who advocated casino gambling for the city. A moment later Bryce was peering through the kid's open doorway.

"*Qué* pasa, hombre?" Sonny said. He had gotten an A in Spanish last semester and liked to strut his stuff.

"*Nada de nuevo, chico*," Bryce replied in his drawling Tex-Mex.

He waded into the room's cluttered confusion. Son Minh Nguyen, his Vietnamese foster son, sat on the edge of the bed lacing a scuffed white Pro Wings hightop. Sonny was slight and short by American standards for a home-grown 12-year-old, with long black bangs that threatened to conceal his handsome eyes.

Bryce glanced around. Mounted over the bed were full-color posters of Luke Skywalker and Darth Vader. Car and motorcycle magazines lay scattered everywhere like a tossed deck of cards. The corners of the room were precariously stacked with games and toys and sports equipment Son had outgrown or worn out but insisted on saving. He saved everything his foster father or anyone else had ever given him, including the chrome-and-black 16-inch Roadmaster bike beside the dresser, training wheels still attached.

Bryce was trying to gently wean him from this pack rat obsession, but he found it too easy to understand. The boy had been born aboard a refugee boat drifting in the South China Sea toward the end of the Vietnam War. His parents either died or deserted him, and he eventually became part of a group that was resettled in a refugee camp near Corpus Christi. Bryce now considered him thoroughly Americanized, but he also knew it would be a long time before Sonny learned he could let possessions out of his sight, at least in his own home, without necessarily losing them.

Bryce nudged a couple of magazines with the toe of one shoe. "You could at least organize this mess a little, partner. Kyla's gonna have kittens when she comes in here."

"Yeah," Sonny said ambiguously, not committing himself to any promises until coerced to do so.

Thoroughly Americanized, thought Bryce again. He noticed his old basketball scrapbook lying on the bed beside Sonny. The boy saw him look at it and said, "Neal, how tall were you when you were twelve?"

Bryce considered. "I'm not sure, but I'd say I was probably about six inches taller than you."

Sonny's face collapsed in a frustrated scowl. "But you know what else?"

Bryce nodded in the direction of the garage behind the house. By tacit agreement, he let Sonny use it as a workshop, parking the Olds instead in the port-cochere attached to the river side of the house. In addition to Sonny's woodworking equipment, the garage currently housed a completely assembled, mechanically perfect 50cc. Honda engine. Using his own paper route money, Sonny had picked it up in far from running condition for five bucks at a flea market, then completely disassembled and rebuilt it for another 20 bucks.

"That engine of yours. I envy you. Even when I was seventeen I couldn't tell a spark plug from a condenser. Every time my old Chevy conked out I had to bribe one of my mechanical friends into fixing it. If they wouldn't, I was stuck without wheels."

"God, that would bite," Sonny said. His tone implied that he himself never went anywhere without his Porsche Targa. He stole a quick glance at Bryce and bent to lace his other Pro Wing as he added, eyes averted, "Did your dad come to your games?"

Bryce didn't expect the question, much less his inability to answer it immediately. It was a given, of course, that his old man would come to every home game he could and follow the road contests on radio or TV. Then he would constructively criticize his every mistake in cassette tapes which were always sent via registered mail. After all, it was the old man who pushed him into going out for basketball, after first swallowing the hard reality that Bryce was too light to excel in college football as he had in the prep leagues. Just as the old man had tried to decide everything else, he had even interfered when Bryce finally rebelled and signed up for Army OCS after college instead of accepting a position in his father's petroleum firm.

The old man's money and influence couldn't keep his determined son out of Vietnam against the young lieutenant's will, but they had made sure he was kept out of front line combat, in spite of Bryce's repeated efforts to stay with his airborne unit when it rotated to the bush. Thanks to the old man's meddling, his boy remained behind, an untested soldier at the rear in Danang. His comrades fought and killed and died while he searched state-bound troop planes for drug caches. He would toss sleeplessly on his cot, listening to the distant sounds of nighttime fighting reach him in a flurry so fuzzy and muffled it might have been cheap fireworks out at nearby China Beach.

Dimly, Bryce was aware of the telephone ringing out in the living room and heard Kyla's aggressively cheerful, "Bryce residence."

"Yeah," he finally answered Sonny's question, "he hardly ever missed a game. But for him going was a duty, not a pleasure."

"Mr. Bryce!" Kyla was bellowing up the stairs, thinking he was still in his bathroom. "Telephone! It's Mr. Baptiste."

Bryce winked at Sonny and covered the 20 feet from the bedroom door to the telephone in five strides, startling Kyla. "Morning, Dell."

Delbert Baptiste, head of the Algiers Precinct's Records and Identification section, didn't believe in wasting time on salutations. "Possible break in the Helzer case."

Bryce's pulse quickened.

"I got some feedback from the check of his telephone records," Baptiste continued. "On 21 June Helzer called an old acquaintance of his in the regional VA records center in Houston, psychiatrist named Owen Jeffries. Said he was counseling a real loony tune who claimed he was a Vietnam vet and had served with the 61st Infantry. Called himself Benjamin Davis. Helzer wanted to verify that the guy had been treated by the VA for combat-related injuries and stress."

"So spare me the dramatic pauses. Was he?"

"No way. Jeffries has access to national VA files, and he checked. A Benjamin Davis did serve with the 61st in Nam during the time period Helzer mentioned. This Davis is a decorated front line vet, but he was never wounded and has only the usual VA transfer-discharge file. Also, the dude is black, and Jeffries insists he clearly remembers Helzer saying this loony was a white local. And get this—the real Benjamin Davis has owned and managed a popular seafood restaurant in Chicago for the past six years. Place called the Sou'wester."

"You've verified all this?"

"Through the Shytown PD before I called you. Davis was born in that area. Outside of two years in the Army, he's never lived anywhere else. He's a family man, a scoutmaster, active in the local Baptist Church, sponsors an exchange student each year."

Bryce blinked with rapid, stupid irritation, unable to make this new information gel into anything substantial. "Same name, same unit, same period in Vietnam," he mused, almost to himself. "It means something, all right, but not necessarily anything useful."

"What'd you say?"

"Nothing, just muttering. At least we know we

might be looking for a white local. Anything else?"

"Just the usual. Milo's teed off and threatening to demote your butt to Vice for putting that psychic on per diem—again."

"He'll get over it."

"Only after he makes life hell for me, buddy. Oh, yeah—you also had a call from some female named Sheila Lasalle."

"Stevie, not Sheila."

"Stevie? Stevie Lasalle, huh? Damn, that name rings a bell."

"Maybe," Bryce said, "you're thinking of Stevie Nicks, the chick who sings with Fleetwood Mac?"

"Could be. I don't like that rock shit, though. I like—"

Bryce cleared his throat impatiently. "So what'd she want?"

"Wondered when you'd be in this morning. She said to tell you she changed her mind."

Baptiste added, "This little gal look as good as she sounds?"

"Couldn't tell you. I've never met her. Listen, I'll be in by nine. Leave me a bio sheet on Davis."

"Never met her, yeah, right. And I've never had hemorrhoids, either."

"In your case," Bryce said, right before hanging up, "just call hemorrhoids a migraine."

The morning air was already thick with humidity when Bryce backed his Cutlass out of the porte-cochere and looped around the asphalt of the cul-de-sac.

He and Sonny lived on the West Bank near the expressway, a suburb of refurbished double bungalows and narrow Caribe-style houses with louvered doors and floor-length windows. Bryce had chosen the neighborhood because it was in a good school district and only ten minutes by car from precinct headquarters in New Orleans' Algiers sector.

He could see tourists already milling around the dock of the Canal Street ferry when he flashed past, Dvorak's *New World Symphony* throbbing from the car's speaker system. A mammoth cargo ship flying the Japanese flag nosed its way up the river; in the murky morning light, the water parted before the ship's bow like a dirty column of mercury. Bryce rounded the tip of the Algiers peninsula and parked behind a drab, top-heavy house with its main floor elevated against flooding. This building housed the NOPD's Bureau of Special Investigations. As the result of some city planner's grim sense of irony, it also sat near the spot which had been one of the first U.S. ports of entry and homes for the Mafia.

He paused for a moment after he locked his car door to stare across the Mississippi. Beyond the levee, Decatur Street's bars and warehouses fronted on the opposite bank. The familiar scene faded like a light show mirage as fourteen scarlet letters abruptly seared themselves onto the screen of his mind:

JOHNNY LAW RULES!

66

Bryce took the steep wooden steps two at a time. He was less than five seconds into the main office area when he was accosted from a side door.

"Bryce, you fucker! You think we're runnin' a goddamn soup kitchen for unemployed carnies, or what?"

The speaker was a short, chunky, swarthy man with bright little suspicious eyes and a fat neck that formed a spare tire around his collar. Precinct Captain Lucien Milo, whom a Yankee reporter had once mistaken for a prominent Latin American dictator, still clutched the bargain-rack polyester jacket he had just squirmed out of.

"What are you whining about now, Milo?"

"I'll give you 'whining,' cowboy. I'm talking about putting that smartass medium on fee again, that's what."

"Wade McKenna is legit. I've checked him out."

"He's shit! What good was he on the Folger kidnapping case?"

During this exchange Bryce was aiming purposefully for the stairs which spiraled up to his office, the shorter man dogging his heels like an angry pit bull.

"That psychic mumbo jumbo," Milo continued, "is for faggots and vegetarians."

Though the tough little cop hadn't messed with a street creep since being promoted to his present desk job, he still wore a snub-nosed .38 in a spring-clip holster under his left armpit. He followed Bryce up the steps, puffing slightly and angrily shaking the folded newspaper in his right hand.

"Show you what I mean. Catch my horoscope for today: 'Your day is here, but don't wait passively for your opportune moment to arrive. Seize it!' "

Milo crumpled the newspaper in disgust. "Bunch of horseshit! If McKenna is so damn insightful, why did he marry that hot little wife—*ex*-wife—of his? I hear she's been down with everything but the Nautilus. How come he couldn't use his power to stop her from filing for divorce and marrying that hotshot tax lawyer?"

By now Bryce had reached his office. Milo followed him in and watched as he crossed to the wooden jalousies and tugged them open. The gray sky had partially cleared, and now weak yellow slivers of sunshine made dust motes glitter and mellowed the pecan veneer of Bryce's desk. Not until he had popped a Proko-fiev tape into the stereo cassette deck, making sure the volume was turned low, did he deign to look at Milo and answer him.

"So what? Yours divorced you, too. All four of them."

"Yeah, but that's different. I *wanted* to get rid of 'em. And don't get so damn smarmy, high pockets. You're not back home in San Antonio spending the old man's oil money to dazzle the cheerleaders. We don't need to turn this Helzer case into a goddamn freak show. I got enough problems with the media as it is. Wait'll they hear we're payrolling the same spook who turned down Johnny Carson."

"Life is tough and then you die," Bryce sympathized, adding, "Don't let me keep you from your demanding PR work downstairs."

Milo shot him a murderous look.

"I mean it, Bryce. You're really starting to chap my ass. I've got half a mind to deny your budget request. I don't know what kind of hoity-toity college boy crap you're up to now, but I'm dropping the hint only one more time, Tex. You better start with the outpatient psycho ward at the VA hospital. Mark my words. What happened to Helzer was the work of some boony who went batshit in them Asian jungles."

"I told you I've got Patterson and Rohr checking that angle. Personally, I think it's too obvious. It was meant to look that way—psychological feint, the crazed-Viet-vet syndrome."

Milo snorted. "The crazed-Viet-vet syndrome, huh? That's rich. Where'd *you* learn about combat stress? While you were feeding those marijuana dogs in air-conditioned Danang?"

Bryce paused in the act of pulling a tubed English Corona from the supply in his top desk drawer. For a few seconds his cheeks glowed like they had after shaving too closely earlier that morning. He was doubly angered—first, that Milo had succeeded in driving one of his cheap barbs home, and second, that the captain's cream-licking grin showed that he fully realized he had struck a rare, raw nerve.

"Okay, Milo." Bryce didn't bother to blunt the machete edge of his tone. "Everybody in the office knows you're a badass ex-Marine who kicked butts in Korea. We've all seen your old vintage GI Zippo that's painted black to cut reflection. I'm duly impressed. I really am, okay? No shit. But this isn't combat, so quit squawking and let me handle this case my own way. Got it, boss?"

Milo, still grinning from his victory, decided he could afford to let the matter ride for now. He edged toward the door, his voice oily with insincere good will.

"Jeez-us! One polite request to keep a lid on your spending, and you turn on me like a rabid animal. You insult the moral conduct of my mother. You—"

Milo was rudely interrupted when, turning a split second too late as he left, he collided hard with the doorjamb. He stared at it accusingly for a moment, as if it had deliberately moved a few inches while his back was turned. He was about to spin back around and finish his roasting of Bryce when he suddenly froze, staring out into the hallway.

"Excuse me," said the tall, pretty brunette in the nylon knit dress. Her huge gray eyes looked down into and held Milo's beady little black ones. "I'm Stevie Lasalle. You must be Neal Bryce?"

Milo registered the long, curving calves. The cowled neckline of her dress was conservative, and Milo couldn't realize it barely concealed a livid five-inch scar below the caramel hollow of her throat. He boldly apprised the swell of her breasts, noting with satisfaction that she was definitely the kind of woman who would jiggle at even a slow trot. Thus distracted he didn't immediately recognize the last name.

Opting for his most politely lecherous grin, he said, "In your case I'll forgive the insult."

He pointed toward the desk. *"That's* Neal Bryce. I'm just his lowly little treasurer."

Milo invited Stevie into the office with a gesture somewhere between a slight bow and an elaborate wave. He enjoyed another visual helping of her body, called out an ambiguous, "Take 'er easy, Bryce," then disappeared down the hallway.

The tall detective had scrambled to his feet when Stevie entered. When their eyes met, she couldn't hide her embarrassment at the mistaken identity; Stevie recovered quickly, assuming the easy but confident professional mien she found most comfortable with men.

"Mr. Bryce." S e offered her hand across the desk. Stevie noticed she was reaching up as well as out.

"Doctor Lasalle. This is a pleasure. I admire your work—as far as I understand it, of course."

Bryce also admired her tropical flower perfume but kept that thought to himself. He only held her hand for a second or two, but it was long enough to feel the combined impression of fine-tuned delicacy and impressive reserves of strength.

Bryce turned the music off and offered her a chair. "Coffee?" he added. Immediately he noticed that neither the secretaries nor Delbert

Baptiste had bothered to switch on the Mr. Coffee which sat on a metal trolley near the window.

She declined, handing him a manila folder.

"I've changed my mind about helping you, Mr. Bryce. This is a Xerox of the raw data and primary sources I used for the article you read on tumor-influenced criminal pathology. I've also included a very general description of a possible personality complex for this type of individual."

Bryce flipped open the folder and began examining the crisp neat photocopies.

"Are you familiar, Mr. Bryce, with the behavioral disorder known as megalomania?"

He nodded. "Delusions of grandeur, right? Wealth, power, etcetera?"

"Exactly—especially power. Megalomania isn't limited to brain tumor cases, and often its manifestations aren't even exaggerated enough to label 'psychotic.' But there is a much higher incidence of the condition in certain brain tumor patients, especially when the tumor is located in the cerebellum or parietal lobe. I'd say acute megalomania, often combined with extreme paranoia, is the single most common psychological trait of the brain tumor-influenced psychotic. The material I'm giving you goes into complete detail about the physiological factors involved."

She was interrupted by two quick raps on the door.

"Excuse me, Lieutenant Bryce," Baptiste said, sliding his eyes over Stevie as he entered.

"Here's that bio work-up you wanted on Ben Davis."

Bryce picked up a folded sheaf of computer printouts from one corner of the desk. "You already dropped it off, remember?"

"Huh! I'll be jiggered. Patterson must have delivered it without telling me."

The R & I section chief was still staring at their female visitor, and Bryce realized that Milo must have just tipped him off.

"Well, say, you two carry on. Don't mind me. I'm just gonna start a pot of coffee, then I'll be out of your way."

Baptiste crossed to the Mr. Coffee, sneaking sidelong glances at Stevie. Bryce sighed and locked glances with the pretty researcher.

"Doctor Lasalle, in your opinion what would it take to literally scare a person to death?"

At her puzzled frown he explained. "We didn't go into all the clinical details with the press, but Helzer's body showed signs of extreme autonomic nervous system shock. The muscle tissue was almost crystallized with surplus adrenaline. His bladder and bowels had emptied simultaneously just before death."

"I'm afraid I can't help you there, Mr. Bryce. Scaring people to death is not my specialty. I've never read the man, but I hear some Englishman named Ramsey Campbell is pretty blood-curdling. You might try one of his books."

Bryce easily ignored Delbert's snort from the back of the room, but the woman's mildly derisive tone had put him on the defensive.

"What I mean, Doctor Lasalle, is that your

interest in the criminal mind is motivated by clinical curiosity. You're as close as a person can come in my business to a purely objective perspective. You've studied in great detail the type of criminal who might be Helzer's killer. What you think could prove very valuable."

At that moment Stevie was sure she would hate Neal Bryce if she ever had the misfortune of getting to know him. It was something in that smug, boyishly egotistic face and 'Gee whiz' attitude that made it seem as if all this were purely experimental to him, as if crime itself was merely a chance to pit his superior wits against the cosmic forces of darkness.

What did he know about her objectivity, her clinical curiosity? His Southwest accent was strong, and she suspected he was a relative newcomer to the city. For a moment she was tempted to lay it on him, calmly and clearly, in the same detached tone she might have used in explaining to a class the step-by-step vivisectioning of a brain lobe.

Bryce admired objectivity, did he? Well, she would narrate it as objectively as a news caster. She would give a dispassionate account of the attack, shirking nothing—not even the part when they took turns raping her, slamming their stinking unwashed bodies into her over and over and grunting like men in pain as they ejaculated, defiling her. Her eyes had remained fixed on the broken, pipe-bludgeoned, mutilated heap that she could no longer call Keith. His eyes—what was left of them—had stared back at her as if pleading, begging her to never forget

74

this night. And no horror before or since could ever match her realization that he had still been alive, dying but aware, his last impression that of seeing the animals who killed him now rooting and plunging on his sister.

Stevie abruptly tasted the salty tang of blood and realized she was biting her lower lip. She said quietly but firmly, "I'm not the neutral observer you think I am, Mr. Bryce. My work in brain pathology reflects a sincere desire to eliminate the worst of the criminal lowlifes—the repeat rapists, kidnappers, child molesters, murderers—from society. Eliminate them efficiently and permanently."

Delbert Baptiste cleared his throat. Suddenly losing interest in brewing a pot of coffee, he made a point of avoiding eye contact with Stevie as he sauntered toward the door.

"See you later," he threatened Bryce. His offended tone suggested that he hated like hell to find flaws in quality merchandise.

Bryce watched the back of the other man disappear down the hall. "Delbert shares your view, but he doesn't approve of women with strong opinions," he explained. "It has something to do with his rigid toilet training."

"I'm sure Delbert's toilet training is a fascinating subject." Stevie glanced down at her Omega. It was almost time to meet with the self-defense class. "Unfortunately I have other obligations."

Bryce stood up when she did. "I hope, Mr. Bryce, that this data I'm leaving helps you. My time is limited, but please call if I can clarify something for you."

He thanked her, then, thinking with delayed embarrassment about the gaucheries of his two cohorts, he said, "I apologize if you found the atmosphere around here . . . ahh, less than gracious."

"I found it about as I would have expected."

She didn't need to add—for a police station.

She smoothed her dress with both palms, bade him good day and was on her way toward the door. Bryce never did quite figure out what inspired his parting shot—flirtatiousness, her plantation-missy haughtiness, battle-of-the-sexes hostility, maybe a hybrid of all three—but he was as surprised as she when it came blurting out.

"We get a little nervous around beautiful women. Contrary to academic rumors, cops are human, too."

When she turned around, the gray eyes were huge and brimming with offended dignity.

"Don't, Mr. Bryce."

He wasn't quite as innocently surprised as he pretended to be. "Don't what?"

"Don't try to hustle me. You're wasting my time and yours."

Bryce realized he was breathing a little quicker and getting just a tad pissed. He respected this woman for her intelligence and her education, and she was beautiful into the bargain. But she had been playing the snotty uppity bitch and putting him down since she had arrived.

"No ego problems here, I see. I suppose the response has become automatic. After all, every man finds you irresistible and immediately falls in love with you, right?''

Anger didn't prevent his noticing the abrupt trembling of her chin and the flaring of her delicate nostrils.

"Don't you dare analyze me! I hardly think someone in *your business*"—she emphasized the words as though he ran a whorehouse for school kids—"is qualified to judge my attitude toward men."

"Of course not, I'm just a dumb gumshoe, and no doubt you've got some fancy scientific word for your condition. I'd call it a fairly standard case of man-hating."

Her eyes beamed pure scorn at him. "How original! A form of thinly disguised penis envy, I presume?''

"Maybe. Or . . . penis fear."

She was still trying to compose a suitable response when she saw Bryce's eyes focus on the door behind her. She spun around. The man she had earlier mistaken for Bryce stood in the doorway, grinning, eagerly waiting to hear more.

Milo stared from one to the other and said with grudging admiration, "You don't waste time, do you, cowboy?''

Martin Fischler was still about 20 feet away from his car when he spotted the object. Something reddish and about half the size of a man's head was centered on the hood of the Mercedes.

At 15 feet he felt the first sickening suspicion;

at ten feet that suspicion congealed into a numbing certainty. He stopped near the left front fender, his vision momentarily dimming until the car wavered as if seen through heat shimmers.

Someone—some sick, disgusting sonofabitch, he thought in disbelieving shock—had placed a chunk of raw pork smack in the middle of the 380 SL's almond-beige hood.

Care for a snack, yid?

Fear laid a cold hand on the back of his neck. He was intensely aware of the apron of murky, early evening shadow which half-engulfed the Riverside Medical Suites. Straight ahead, the back of the long stucco professional building was frustratingly windowless. To Fischler's right was a row of huge unsavory dumpsters, then the high, graffiti-cluttered adobe wall which separated the medical plaza from the Delta Terrace apartment complex next door. Behind him, beyond the asphalt parking lot webbed with cracks, was an expanse of weeds rising to meet the Napoleon Freeway. To the left a redwood fence marked the boundary between the professional building and the fast food restaurant.

A nice little spot with a future, the realtor had called it 15 years ago.

"Welcome to Burger Boy," crackled a drive-thru speaker even as Fischler nervously glanced about him. "May I take your order, please?"

The jarring teenage voice suddenly converted his fear into blurry anger. Fischler made a tight fist and whopped the offending meat in a powerful blow, watching it land on the asphalt with a splat and roll several feet. It came to rest in the middle of an amoeba-shaped oil leak; bits of dust and gravel clung to the gleaming pink skin like crystals of brown sugar.

This time he had to call the police. Obviously, leaving the card hadn't been enough for the sicko who was persecuting him. No telling what the next prank might escalate into. Fischler cursed himself for ripping the card up this morning. Maybe he could still salvage the pieces. Had one of the girls emptied the trash? And the meat—he realized now he shouldn't have disturbed it.

He was halfway back to the office when it registered that one of the other two cars in the lot was a dark green Toyota Celica. He had almost forgotten that his new part-time hygienist, Dotty with the D-cup tits, was finishing up a late cleaning appointment. If she heard him calling the police, his troubles would be broadcast all over the East Bank by tomorrow.

He turned back toward his car. He could call from a pay phone at the nearby K-Mart mall. If the police said they were coming out to look around, which he doubted they would offer to do, he could drive back the few blocks and meet them. Dotty should be gone by then.

He had one hand on the door and the other in his front pocket, reaching for his keys, when he heard the quick skittering rustle moving close behind him.

Fischler's legs were suddenly gum rubber, failing him, and he was forced to grip the door of the Mercedes harder. Something infinitesimally light brushed the cuff of his gray wool slacks. He made an involuntary little whimpering noise and jerked his eyes toward the ground near his foot. A bright-red Kit Kat wrapper was nudging his heel, still fluttering slightly in the puff of evening breeze which had blown it into him.

He was so grateful he almost picked it up and tucked it into his pocket. Fischler reminded himself, as his trembling fingers coaxed the key into the lock, that he was too old to let his heart start hammering like this.

He was taking long, disciplined breaths by the time he'd gotten in, locked his door and slipped the key into the ignition.

For a second he noticed a vague smell like disinfectant spray, but he ignored it.

His heart was slowing down. This *goy* bastard wanted to scare him senseless, but he would deny him the pleasure.

This thought made him realize he could be under observation at that very moment, and he was grateful for the car's tinted windows. Now the parking lot lay three-quarters in shadows, and Fischler imagined someone watching him from nearby.

He was on the feather edge of turning the ignition switch when he remembered he hadn't checked the lock on the passenger's side.

The door was unlocked, and he couldn't seem to get the mechanism to catch. Why? Why was it moving up and down like a worn-out light switch instead of catching with its usual precise metallic click? Unless . . . unless it had been . . .

The car rocked slightly, and he heard a noise like snakes slithering on silk as someone rose from the floor behind him.

"Doctor, with so many people starving in Africa you really shouldn't throw away good meat."

Hot urine stabbed along Fischler's left thigh, as the voice scraped down his spine like a rusty razor. The other man's breath was damp and hot on the back of his neck. Besides the briny smell of his own piss, the dentist smelled something bitter and rotten and putrid, some foul poison festering.

Fischler thought, *I'm going to die*, and then he slowly rolled his eyes toward the rearview mirror.

For a moment he thought the intruder had a bandage on his neck. A second later he recognized the gauze mask, which had been pulled down. The eyes met his, the man smiling a stiletto-thin smile. His bloodless lips and gums immediately made Fischler think of the corpses he used to practice on in dental school.

"Please turn around, Doctor. Under Geneva Convention regulations you have the right to face your executioner."

An invisible hand seemed to grip the back of Fischler's head and revolve it until he was looking back over his right shoulder. He was too incoherent with terror to recognize his one-time patient or even to notice the long military rain-coat or the razor-fine scalpel protruding from his gloved right fist. He only had eyes for the black velvet cloth and whatever it was concealing in the man's left palm.

He knew that whatever was under that cloth was going to kill him, but it was impossible to look away.

"Let's get to know each other," whispered his executioner, breaking into a giggling whinny.

The velvet cloth slid away as the man shook harder and harder with laughter. Fischler was forced to squint in the shimmering, glittering, melting confusion of brightness that was revealed. He could not tear his eyes away and slide toward one of the doors. He was a madman staring into an eclipse, deliberately scalding his retinas, refusing to avert his glance even when the dazzling crystal released a slender red beam that bored painlessly through his skull.

For an eternally long second before Fischler went insane, he realized his soul had just been destroyed by that hellish beam. He was now a spiritless parasite, sharing the thoughts of the insane creature in the back seat, the poison throbbing in his own brain, a giant abscess ready to burst.

"No! Please, oh please God, no!"

Harlan Perry's giggles rose to a hiccuping shriek as he watched the concentration camp survivor thrash around on the front seat in a fit worse than a *grand mal* seizure. Whatever Fischler was experiencing, he was somehow convinced it was real in the present moment and that it was located in his eyes, not his mind. He was literally trying to claw them out, ripping, gouging and tearing. Fischler might have emptied the sockets completely, Oedipus howling to the gods while blinding himself, if several cerebral arteries had not suddenly erupted, mercifully killing him almost instantly.

Perry covered his precious Tuaoi and the giggling immediately ceased as his urgency to escape took over. Some cunning, still unravaged piece of his brain reminded him that his powers with the crystal were only in the late fetal stage. He had taken out two key polluting pigs, yes, but from the point of view of martial effectiveness, it had merely been like stepping on two ants. And ants were everywhere. An effective offensive would eventually stomp them out on a massive scale.

Fischler had died with one hand thrown over the back of the front seat. Perry's smile was almost affectionate as he threaded his scarlet-lettered calling card through three of the corpse's fingers. Fischler would literally be handing the cops their clue.

A moment later he snapped the gauze mask back into place over his mouth and raised the scalpel. Then he leaned forward, his expression pious as he prepared to make the victor's cut.

CHAPTER FIVE

"HEY! THE GIRL OVER THERE IN THE LYCRA shorts. Yeah, you by the jukebox. You got just the kind of legs us religious mystics like—feet at one end and pussy at the other!"

Rudy's Tahitian Palace erupted in a chorus of polyglot shouts, whistles, hisses and catcalls. It was Monday night, but like several of the former barrelhouse joints along the waterfront of the Vieux Carré, the Palace was a crowded, neon-dappled barroom scene from a French Impressionist's decadent period.

One end of the dance floor was a raised bandstand now serving as a stage.

"Nice set of spirit knockers, too," added the man on stage, cupping both hands in front of his chest and pretending he was bobbling a pair of cantaloupes. "I wonder if she approves of *aural* sex?"

The crowd erupted again. The Incredible Shoneen was barefoot and wore sequined turquoise tights. They glittered like sunlit fish scales in the glare of the portable footlights. He was naked to the waist, swirling curlicues of red hair carpeting his chest. The performer had painted his nipples purple and the surrounding aureoles a sheening Aztec gold. Perched at a rakish angle on his head was a gaudy red fez with a black tassle hanging down to his navel.

"Thank you. You're very drunk—I mean, kind. And now . . ."

Right on cue, the skinny black kid who played piano between acts now trilled a snare drum just offstage. The hubbub lowered a few decibels.

"Think I'll crap out for a while if you folks don't mind."

Wade McKenna capered over to a thick, brick-supported plywood bed through which had been driven a man-shaped grid of widely spaced three-inch nails. He lifted one side and slanted it toward the audience so they could inspect it, then lowered it again. Effortlessly, backwards, like an agile dancer leaning lower and lower under the limbo stick, he eased himself down onto the nails until all his weight was off the floor and supported on the sharp points.

Whistles and applause were followed by somebody screaming, "It's a trick! They do it with mirrors!" McKenna slowly lifted his left hand and gave the anonymous bitcher the finger. Another sputter of laughter exploded.

A sailor down front who had been getting steadily blitzed all evening shouted, "But what if you score and the woman wants to be on top?"

"So what's the problem?" McKenna retorted, still squinting into the overhead spotlights. "It's just a few more nails digging into your back."

With practiced timing he waited only long enough for the laughter to subside before adding one of his standard backup gags for the few drunks who always missed each one-liner. "Besides, I've always got the poor man's harem—imagination and the palm of my hand."

This joke bombed, and McKenna reminded himself to scrap it. He'd have to rotate his material more, too many regulars caught his act nowadays.

He slapped the stage with one hand, freckled biceps flexing as he deftly used the arm as a pivot for dismounting the nails.

He knew what they were waiting for.

"All right," he shouted, "huzzah, huzzah, huzzah! Let's play with *fire*!"

No apparent cause of death.

Bryce ignored the roar of the Monday night regulars as they cheered McKenna's "play with fire" comment. Some other night he might have enjoyed a perverse snigger or two at the man's cynical, tacky, yet occasionally funny self-abasement. But not tonight. Not to a backdrop image, only hours old, of Martin Fischler's corpse splayed out in the front seat of his Mercedes, eyes half-clawed out and only a bloody stump of gristle where one ear should have been.

The fingers had been clutching that card, the calling card of the mad slasher. It matched the pieces of the joke card he and Patterson had sifted out of the office trash and duly transferred to a glassine envelope.

No apparent cause of death.

There was just a corpse whose fingernails were clotted with its own eyeballs, whose clothing was soiled with piss and shit, whose face was a frozen mask of unnameable terror.

The corpse had a full head of distinguished white hair which, according to the hysterical employee who had discovered Fischler, had been salt-and-pepper only a half-hour earlier.

McKenna's blustery stage voice cut into Bryce's thoughts like an intrusive radio signal. "Listen, folks, I'm telling you that once you've swallowed your first hot one, you'll never again be intimidated by Linda Lovelace."

Bryce tried to concentrate as the sleazy Shoneen fired up a balsa stick that had been dipped in lighter fluid. He capered around with it like an enraged Caliban, inviting anyone in the audience to try swallowing it or "even giving it a little kiss." No one rushed to take him up on the offer.

No apparent cause of death.

Bryce knew what the Medical Examiner's report would eventually be—massive nervous system failure similar to that induced by curare drugs. But in this case the failure would be brought on by undetermined causes, just like Helzer's death.

Tomorrow Fischler's gruesome fate would be

played big in all the city papers. The local AP and UPI bureaus would scent a serial attacker and feed the story to their national and international tickertapes. Tonight's 10 P.M. TV news, less than a half-hour away, would pander the gory details to the city and tease it with the promise of more splatter and gore to come.

Bryce idly shook some salt into his lager and watched the streaking columns of tiny bubbles froth into a momentary head. He was only dimly aware of the sudden chorus of "oooooooo's " and "ahhhhhhhh's" and "far fucking out's" as McKenna swallowed his flaming baton.

The cop reminded himself he should be paying closer attention. He was, after all, the only person in the audience who knew that McKenna wasn't somehow deceiving them with drugs or props or sleight-of-hand.

His tired mind lost the thought like a dream image fading. By default everything was coming down to the elusive Ben Davis. What was his connection, if any, to the even more elusive Johnny Law? Bryce had two men working Milo's VA Hospital angle, and a list of the names of disturbed veterans with histories of violence was on file. But so far nothing linked any of them with the two victims. Maybe they'd hit paydirt later when the names were matched with those in Fischler's patient files. If none of Bryce's efforts panned out soon, he was toying with the idea of flying to Chicago and visiting the real Ben Davis unofficially, not as a cop. He knew he could seek the cooperation of Illinois officials and have Davis questioned as a potential material witness, but experience told him that volunteers were usually more enthusiastic to help.

Now McKenna was prancing around on stage, long needles pierced through several of his fingers. A woman shrieked in delighted disgust as he slowly pushed another through the web of flesh between his left thumb and index finger. There was no blood. He looked like a giant voodoo doll practicing on itself.

The snare drum trilled as Bryce sighed and tried to fold his legs under the table so the hustling waitress would quit glowering at him. He glanced at McKenna and hoped this pathetic act would end soon.

"Stick it to me, big boy!" McKenna taunted, inviting the nearest drunk onto the stage to poke the next needle home. "Pick a toe, any toe, and ram that sucker home. The Incredible Shoneen is the human pin cushion who feels—no—pain!"

The entertainer seemed almost ridiculously ordinary now that he'd changed into Khaki twill trousers and a faded t-shirt. He watched the tall detective salt his beer and stare at the sudden foam.

"That's only going to make you thirstier, old sleuth. My ex was smarter about her nervous habits. She had this harmless little fake yawn."

McKenna, still hyper from his performance, didn't expect or wait for a reply. "You ever been married?" he added.

Bryce shook his head.

"Ever even been close to it?"

"Once, right after college. I was engaged."

"What happened?" McKenna demanded. "Wait, don't tell me. She waited till you were ordered overseas, then fucked you over?"

"You'd see it that way, maybe, what with your charitable attitude towards women. But I think a sociologist would call it a mutual contract between significant others to cool out."

"Right, sociologists. You *are* in a blue funk tonight, boyo."

McKenna drained his vodka and tonic and raised a finger to catch the bartender's attention. "Another spot of the giant killer, Lance."

The two men occupied the final pair of stools at the end of the gleaming mahogany bar. The crowd had thinned out after The Incredible Shoneen's final act, and now the black kid was thumping out an old tune at the piano. Near the opposite end of the bar two drunk, glassy-eyed mailmen, still in uniform, wolfed down sandwiches and stared at the Zenith color TV bracket-mounted at a slant over their heads. The volume was turned completely down, but they seemed to enjoy *Hart to Hart* better in mime.

McKenna was always jittery after his act. Now, as he began to numb in a warm alcohol buffer zone, he took a closer look at his companion. Whatever he saw or felt made him turn quickly away and drain half his glass. His voice was cold sober when he said, "I just snapped on. This is definitely a business call. Who'd the slasher jump today?"

Bryce showed no surprise. Speaking quietly

91

and concisely, he filled McKenna in. He had just finished when, almost as if timed to follow and verify his narration, the 10 p.m. news flashed on the Zenith and the words VAN GOGH SLASHER STRIKES AGAIN paraded across the screen. There was a brief sequence of a hunched-over, hustling team of paramedics and a blanket-covered body in a wheeled litter being loaded into the back of an ambulance.

The next clip showed Bryce ducking several reporters who seemed to be trying to beat him with their microphones.

"Jesus Jumping Christ! The next stop is the *National Enquirer*." McKenna glanced around nervously, as if to see if anyone else had recognized Bryce. He added grimly, "Money I love, but publicity sucks. My involvement stays quiet, right?"

"Right, but that means first we have to get you involved."

"I'm sure you have some thoughts in that direction."

Bryce searched for the right tone, knowing how volatile McKenna became when his psychic abilities were the topic of conversation.

"I want to take you to Helzer's office tomorrow. Fischler's car, too, when the lab crew is finished with it. And I want you to—I don't know—hold something I guess. Handle a couple objects the slasher might have handled. See if anything comes to you."

McKenna seemed intensely interested in the texture of his bar napkin.

"You pay the piper, I dance to the tune, Bryce.

Long as you keep the bucks coming in I don't care if you tell me to crap in my hat and say a Pater Noster over it. But I'm not like what you're thinking."

"Like what?"

"Like Peter Hurkos. He's the clairvoyant who solved a murder case by handling the murderer's discarded coat or something. I'm not like that," McKenna said. "I don't think I can do that."

"What *are* you like?"

"What are *you* like?" McKenna shot back.

"If you keep taking me personally," Bryce complained wearily, "how am I supposed to exploit you so you can hate me like you hate everyone else?"

McKenna evaluated the remark and decided he liked it. "You're good people, Bryce. I'm trying to cooperate. Look, I'm just saying I'm no good at this business of describing past or future events. No psychic whodunits. You've read that university report on me. I'm mainly limited to what the parapsychologists call aural sensitivity and fairly extensive powers as a fakeer."

Bryce had already ruined his beer. All he could do now was add more salt to it. He said quietly, a bit deferentially, "The Stanford report was incomplete. We both know they left something out."

McKenna twisted and untwisted his napkin. "Okay. I also have limited—a very hit-and-miss —ability as a channeler."

"So that's what you call it when you can put the living in contact with the dead?"

Bryce's tone was genuinely curious, but McKenna glowered as if he had just been hazed by a sadistic bully.

"I didn't do what you're thinking, Bryce. I told you that when you first approached me. I was used against my will."

That incident two years ago had triggered the break between McKenna and his wife. At that time he was an anonymous but well-paid legal researcher for the D.A.'s office, a lucrative private practice already in the planning stages. Judith and a few of his closer legal associates had already learned, one way or another, that the young attorney had mild psychic abilities, a trait (he sometimes reminded them defensively) he shared with approximately two percent of the general population. Usually his gift was the subject of good-natured ribbing about which horse to bet on or what stocks to float. But one night he learned, to his utter mortification, that his ability went far beyond mild psychic predisposition.

Owen Bannon, a local politico with formidable finances, had hosted a sundowner for the D.A.'s staff and their spouses, the usual goodwill gesture which preceded some profitable Louisiana venture in graft. Bannon was in his sixties, but his beautiful, poised, Sarah Lawrence graduate of a wife was only mid-twenties. Like most people present that night, McKenna knew that the Bannons' two-year-old daughter had died a few months earlier. A horrible tragedy in the family swimming pool, local papers had commiserated. Colette Bannon had been hysterical with self-recrimination. She should have checked the baby's playgate more carefully, she shouldn't have stayed on the phone so long, she never should have given nurse the day off, etc.

Of course no one questioned the coroner's ruling of accidental death.

No one did so, that is, until the day of the sundowner when an unknown staff mole named Wade McKenna went into a spastic seizure sometime between the apertif and the lobster thermidor.

And spoke in a child's voice, a little girl's voice, a voice that sang in tones so hideous it could only be Death's proxy. He kept singing over and over, dozens of times, before someone finally knocked him out with a heavy glass candlestick:

> *"She held me under the water.*
> *And now she'll go to Hell!*
> *She held me under the water,*
> *And now she'll . . ."*

It was Judith who finally told him, only weeks before she filed for divorce, that it had taken six men to pry him out of Colette Bannon's lap. He had sat on the shrieking woman, jabbing an accusing finger into her Ivory Snow cleavage as he sang his horrid little ditty over and over. Several witnesses swore they heard the hysterical woman confess she had drowned her own child in a momentary fit of anger that had gone further than she intended. But of course she retracted the statement the next day, claiming McKenna had made her temporarily insane with grief.

Since no actual crime had been committed on Wade's part and Owen Bannon was anxious to contain further publicity, the politico had no option but to let the incident pass—publicly. But certain rumors were carefully planted and nurtured in high places—Wade McKenna was a certified psychotic, Wade McKenna was a spurned contender for Colette Bannon's ample charms, and others equally damning. Of course his legal career was destroyed, along with his marriage. A former debutante like Judith could not be expected to link her destiny with that of a freak whose exploits were reported in cheap tabloids. Even McKenna had not questioned that.

McKenna now became aware that Bryce was looking at his hands, looking for holes and blood from the needles.

"Did you ever," Bryce said, "call about that teaching job I mentioned? Or do you plan on wallowing in self-pity and booze forever?"

Faintly, muffled by the curtain behind the bar, the ritual knocking and hoarse plaintive whispering reached McKenna from upstairs. He recognized it, and suddenly his rage found voice before he could stop it.

"Just say it, Bryce! 'Be a man.' Well, I can't be a man. When are you going to snap to that fact? I'm a freak!"

McKenna slammed his glass against the bar and a few loaded patrons at the nearest table glanced at the two curiously.

"Watch," McKenna muttered. He swiveled his stool toward the drunks and forced eye contact with the biggest one.

"You know what, sailor? Your face reminds me of something I once scraped off the heel of my shoe."

The bearded, burly merchant marine slowly lost his affable grin. He made the first move to scoot his chair back when a buddy leaned across the table and said something to him, pointing at McKenna and gesturing excitedly. The dull anger smoldering in the big sailor's eyes turned to startled recognition.

"I ain't gonna mess around with that little spook," he announced to his companions. "He'll turn my balls into Easter eggs, then hide 'em."

The group around the table roared with appreciative laughter. One of the sailors signaled the bartender and Lance brought the pair at the bar a fresh round of complimentary drinks.

"See what I mean?" McKenna said, revolving back around to face Bryce again.

Before Bryce could reply, an even louder flurry of knocks from upstairs was followed by an urgent, "Lena? Are you there?"

McKenna, his eyes wild with an emotion Bryce couldn't label, almost snarled as he slid from his stool. He tore the curtain aside and screamed up the stairway, "Back one door to your left, you stupid slobbering asshole. Your goddamn *left!*"

It was 9:45 P.M. when Harlan Perry paused among the shadows to listen.

From well behind him, toward the river and Decatur Street, the tense, fast rat-a-tat-tatting of a drum roll reached him on a sudden breeze. It was followed by a brief scattering of drunken laughter and applause.

"The pretty *bitch* called me a freaky *glitch*," he intoned rotely.

Both hands protecting the lunch pail tucked under his left arm, Perry hurried on through the poorly lit, half-deserted warehouse district which flanked this side of the Municipal Museum of Natural History. For a change the June night was clear and cool, less humid. The sky was endless folds of black satin studded with pinpoints of starlight. Now and then the wind moaned in a nearby alley.

Perry noticed none of this; he only scurried on toward the huge stone and timber building looming dead ahead that housed the museum. He bent forward slightly when he reached the first tier of steps out front, taking them two at a time. In the multicolored glow filtering through the stained-glass fanlight over the front entrance, he could just make out some of the latest graffiti it would be his duty to expunge.

"Howzit goin', Perry?"

The Brinks security guard nodded at him as he nudged the carved door open for Perry with one hip.

The janitor nodded curtly back, making sure he avoided contact with Wally Cruz and his germs as he edged past him into the foyer. Perry had removed his military raincoat when he entered. He wore baggy gray chinos several sizes too large, so it looked like he had no butt or waist. His blue work shirt proclaimed HARLAN in red script stitched over the pocket. The shirt was left over from his brief stint as a custodian at Houston International Airport more than 15 years ago.

The security guard eyed the black lunch pail as he let Perry into the staff room to punch his timecard. Perry shifted it to his other arm, trying to make the movement look casual.

"Decided to start bringing some chow, huh?"

Perry nodded. His back was suddenly cold with nervous sweat.

"Good idea," Cruz said affably, whumping his own ample gut with both hands. "Skinny little fellah like you. Hell, you don't wanna catch that anorexia nerveeosa. Girl I use to know in high school? She's got it. They say she's down to sixty-some pounds now. Just lays there like a vegetable, practically, 'cept to rip the IV's out. It's a damn shame. Say, ain'tcha gonna leave your lunch pail here?"

"I like to nibble during my shift," Perry explained. He tried to edge away from the guard and toward the huge double oak doors leading to Permanent Exhibits.

"That's not good for you," Cruz warned. "Keeps too much acid in your stomach. That old gastric acid, boy, she's a bitch. Not that I don't

J. EDWARD AMES

pig out once in a while between meals myself."

He wasn't quite halfway to the oak doors when Cruz said authoritatively behind him, "Perry!"

Perry's head throbbed like it was in a vise as he halted and turned around slowly. Discipline, he reminded himself. Don't look toward the lunch pail.

"Lissenup, people," barked the mental voice which Perry had one day realized was Johnny Law, *"If taken prisoner you are not required to call the enemy's attention to any concealed weapons."*

"Be on the watch," the guard said, "for bums sleeping back in some of them storage rooms. Sometimes they slip in and hide right before closing. I chased one out earlier. Some burned-out dipshit of a hippie that smelled worse'n a beer fart. Christ, don't you wonder sometimes what their underwear must look like? Assuming they wear any."

"Parasites," the janitor spat out. His face was ugly and twisted with contempt, but Cruz wasn't paying close attention.

"Howzat? Sure, you got it. Parasites. Know what they oughta do with those hippie street bums? Round the sonsabitches up and sterilize 'em. All that free love crap, they breed just like rabbits."

Cruz was surprised when, instead of his usual unenthusiastic grunt, Perry uttered more words than the guard had ever heard him say at one time.

"There's two types of people in the world—

100

the producers and the parasites, the healthy cells and the slimy, cancerous growths. But when I . . . ''

Perry realized he was being indiscreet and cut himself off. His sallow cheeks were mottled red with suppressed emotion.

Cruz narrowed his eyes and examined the other man until the silence finally made the guard nervous. ''Sure. That's it, right on. Producers and parasites.''

At least, Perry noted with satisfaction, his little outburst had driven the blabbing guard away. He watched the portly blue-clad figure scuttle toward the east staircase. Cruz had apparently decided it was time for an impromptu inspection of the fossil and rare map display areas on the second floor.

Harlan Perry tensed his back and shoved one of the heavy, noiseless doors open. Inside, only the exit signs and a few small display lights were lit, leaving the cavernous Permanent Exhibits gallery glowing in dim confusion like a room just after a flash bulb goes off. Perry could easily have elbowed the light switch beside him, illuminating the familiar chamber with its beamed ceiling and oak-paneled walls, the tall, varnished walnut cases housing the Indian artifacts collection, but his destination was the storage area behind this wing. Besides, he knew the floor plan too well to require the overhead fluorescent lights.

He always tried to avoid bright lights. The chronic pain in his head, like an earwig drilling through his brain, usually eased in the dark.

Perry's crepe-soled shoes were silent on the tile floor. He ignored the velvet ropes that marked the exhibits—The Story of Human Evolution, The Acadian People, Recent Acquisitions —with the contempt bred of long familiarity. Likewise he ignored the thirteen-foot Hairy Mammoth skeleton on the central dais, excavated from the swamps near Bogalusa, its tusks J-curved like a pair of giant candy canes.

His heart started thumping when he left the gallery and turned right, down a concrete hallway marked STAFF ONLY. A feltboard sign over the door at the end said STORAGE FACILITY A. He unlocked the door with his passkey and, flicking on the lights this time, descended into the basement.

The underground vault was a veritable graveyard for dead and retired natural wonders— dust-laden display cases of rocks and minerals, a collection of stuffed birds, a jagged meteorite which had crashed into a local levee on Mother's Day 1918. Perry threaded his way through the helter-skelter confusion. He stopped before a terrace of metal shelves against the back wall, setting his lunch pail carefully beside *The Tuaoi Stone; The Story of the Terrible Crystal*. He had not taken the book with him this last time.

For an uncomfortable moment the book reminded him of the journal at home in his closet, of the handwriting that was not his. But he was quick to remind himself that Johnny Law had chosen that journal as the route of entry to his psyche.

He flipped back the narrow little volume's cover and read the first passage his eye landed on.

"According to Jung, in the collective unconscious of any race are certain patterns of imagery, archetypes whose ultimate meanings cannot be absolutely interpreted because they represent sacred, inexpressible, deep-rooted needs of the human soul—flight, rebirth, motherhood, etc. The legend of Atlantis maintains that the Tuaoi Master could convert these patterns into their corresponding negative archetypes through a massive mental perversion, a pure concentration of hatred, afforded by the Terrible Crystal. The legend refers to these altered longings as 'nether archetypes.' Thus, for example, Jung's *anima* archetype, symbolizing the very love of life and beauty itself, is transformed into a morbid compulsion, a craving for death and ugliness."

Perry closed the book. His smile was so broad it triggered a quick stab of pain in his sore gum. But *that* score already had been settled.

He glanced back over his shoulder, then opened the lunch pail and removed his Walkman cassette player, setting it down on the shelf. Next he reached into the pail and removed the velvet-enshrouded crystal, placing it carefully beside the book where he had discovered it.

For a moment, before he let go of the crystal, he noticed a luminous aura around the fingers holding it. He had read about that weird glow in *The Story of the Terrible Crystal*. It was an electromagnetic penumbra called the "etheric double," and all genuine psychics, or any person holding the crystal, supposedly gave off one. It was a psychic sheen which could be seen only by other psychics or the few Tuaoi Masters.

Perry had noticed, while fondling the Tuaoi in his apartment and watching passers-by below in the street, an occasional blue-glowing etheric double surrounding someone in the crowd. Sometimes it was barely visible, other times a lustrous, glowing band projecting a full six inches around the person. But he had noticed not all the auras were blue; just as many were amber. And a few people had infrared penumbras surrounding them like a radioactive trace, almost the same deep ruby red of the Tuaoi beam and his own sheen. These people would begin to fidget and glance about as they passed his apartment, some even slowing down, stopping for a moment and glancing at his tenement.

He knew his powers were being honed sharper every day. Again Perry thought of the pretty, stuck-up scientist with that livid scar—Stevie Lasalle, one of their cleverest and most lethal PCA's. Hadn't she almost destroyed him with her cancer-planting machine?

No doubt she thought her unlisted home phone number was a clever idea, but it had been easy enough to locate her office at the medical school and follow her home one day. Unfortunately the building she lived in had no outside directory and was huge and well-secured.

He glanced at the velvet-covered Tuaoi and smiled again. Correction: The building had been well secured before the Terrible Crystal became his.

Again Perry checked over his shoulder as he slipped on the Walkman's earphones. Then he poked the play button. His own metal-grinding voice assaulted the musty quiet of the basement.

"All people are merely cells in the great body of civilization. That body is now sick, diseased, decaying with age, with slimy cancerous growths and bloodsucking parasites. I alone am a strong cell, and I alone can regenerate the diseased body. But first the rotted, pulpy, infected portions must be scraped away and destroyed at my command!"

Memories. Sometimes they only come out at night.

Moonlight slanted in through the bedroom's dormer windows and laid a sterling path across the couple sleeping in the queen-size bed.

Ben Davis muttered something incoherent in his sleep and snuggled closer against his wife's bare, warm coffee-colored skin. His face was blank, still and peaceful, but after several minutes his right eyeball began twitching rapidly when he passed into REM sleep.

Outside, the wind bumped angrily against the window panes; inside, the dreaming man descended yet once again into the belly of the dragon.

First day in the boonies and he still hasn't mastered walking in that motherfucking elephant grass. It grabs at his legs and claws him down, and the other soul brothers are laughing, calling him

Cherry Boy the virgin who can't keep up. The stinging sweat, the stinging insects, the godawful banging humping weight of the radio strapped to his back, and cold lead chunk of fear deep in his guts because, hey Cherry Boy, old Charlie always aims for the radio humpers first . . .

KA-WHUMPF!

It takes a long shocked moment to realize that the shiny white airborne snakes wrapped around his neck are the guts of the man who'd just been walking next to him, oh Lord God no . . .

KA-WHUMPF!

Oh no no no, someone screaming at him, ambush Cherry Boy, cover your ass, but can't move, oh God no, can't move . . . rounds zwipping through the elephant grass, a big bellowing fifty-cal pounds, dirt and guts and shards of bone into his face, the air acrid with cordite, sticky with the sweet steaming smell of blood, the platoon dying screaming being ground into suet all around him . . . the voice again screaming, take cover Cherry Boy, you stupid crazy fucking nigger, you want to die you want . . .

The enemy grenade whunks into the dirt at his feet and Cherry Boy screams at God to have mercy on his soul. . . .

"Shhh! It's okay now, honey, it's o-kay."

Yolanda Davis hugged her husband's trembling body even closer, rocking him in bed. "Shush now, hon, it's okay. You're never going back there anymore. It's only a dream."

She was still half-asleep and didn't quite catch what Ben mumbled back. But the last two words sounded something like "law duels."

Or maybe, "law rules."

Memories. Sometimes they can be fought to a standoff.

Stevie Lasalle lay naked between the satin sheets. She slept on her side, the silver sheet outlining a sweeping plunge from her hip to her waist. One arm was tucked under her head, the other across the firm swells of her breasts. Hair the color of ground cocoa beans lay fanned against the pillow like a tangled, windblown mane. In sleep the pretty, normally vigilant and wary face seemed almost fey.

Though the rest of her apartment was practical and modern, Stevie had learned during her student days in France that the boudoir is where you pamper yourself. The bulb still burned in a hand-painted blue porcelain lamp on the nightstand. Its fluted shade softened the glare and highlighted the delicate Chinese motif of the room's wallpaper. Mr. Cat lay in a curled ball of fur at the foot of the bed.

A vellum-bound book titled *Advanced Movements and Meditations for Bushido* lay sprawled open on the bed beside Stevie. Unlike Ben Davis, she was not usually vulnerable to nightmares and would sleep uninterrupted—soundly, if not quite peacefully—until precisely 7:20 a.m., when an internal alarm would waken her.

But her invulnerability did not come easily, especially tonight. Since catching the 10 P.M. news, she had been plagued with the image of that blanket-covered corpse being lifted into an ambulance and Neal Bryce swatting downward at microphones, his face a mask of grim patience.

That's why Stevie's voice—calm, detached, monotonous—could now be clearly heard though she was sound asleep. It emanated from the tape recorder on the floor beside the bed. There were long pauses between sentences, the self-repeating tape making a soft fuzzy sound like an open phone line.

"Only the present moment can touch you."

Stevie stirred restlessly in her sleep. The sudden movement startled Mr. Cat, who swatted indignantly at her foot. Then the two of them sank back down into sleep.

"The past is a dead thing," droned the voice on the tape, quoting from the book which lay beside Stevie. "Leave it alone . . . leave it alone . . . leave it . . ."

CHAPTER SIX

"YEAH, THIS IS BRYCE. PUT ME THROUGH TO LAB."

While he waited Neal Bryce gazed through the half-open drapes without bothering to focus his eyes, which were still too puffy with sleep to respond well. Dimly, he was aware that it must be well before 8 A.M. Sonny was outside on the cul-de-sac, straddling the front wheel of his bicycle to remove the huge gray canvas pouch he had just hauled his morning *Times-Picayunes* in.

"Yankee Stadium, third base. May I help you?"

Time constraints had forced Bryce to skip his usual cold rinse this morning, but Victor Arnett's snappy, alert voice shocked him awake in its place.

"Don't you ever go home and sleep, Arnie?"

"Speed freaks don't sleep. Especially when"
—the lab chief lowered his tone significantly—
"certain individuals are showing up at six A.M. to piss and moan about the slackasses around here."

No further hints were necessary. Bryce could hear Milo's voice bullhorning in the background. The detective sighed and gave up any hope for it being a fruitful day. "What about the car?"

"We turned it inside out, Neal—practically zilch as far as any concrete leads. We found metal shavings around the busted lock mechanism. Tempered steel. Probably a strong screwdriver was used to force it."

Bryce grew impatient during the ensuing pause. "That's all?"

"No." Arnett's tone was mildly resentful. "I just figured I'd begin at the beginning."

"Sorry," Bryce said. "Haven't had my morning coffee yet. What else did you turn up?"

"Well, it's possible the attacker wore military fatigue-type trousers and hid on the floor in the back. Spectral analysis showed recent concentrations of minute green cotton fibers on the rear carpet. The color was derived from a dye used almost exclusively by clothing manufacturers under contract to the Defense Department. The two heaviest concentrations are about the size of a grown man's kneecaps, suggesting someone crouched near the backseat for awhile."

Bryce heard but didn't deign to comment. After all, it was unlikely that the assailant would have hidden in the glove compartment. Of course Milo would gloat about the military fatigue fabric.

Arnett added, "You were right. The M.E. says cause of death was massive autonomic nervous system failure. And Fischler's ear was definitely amputated with a sharp, non-serrated blade. Just like Helzer."

"Anything outside the vehicle?"

"Zip."

"No prints at all?"

"Except for Fischler's, that car was cleaner than the Pope's conscience."

"Dammit!"

Bryce paused until the sudden flush of irritation had passed. He worked with the best forensics lab crew in all of Louisiana, and he knew it. It wasn't their fault he could only spin his wheels while a psycho terrorized the city and made a mockery of the law.

"All right. Thanks, Arnie. Let me know if anything else turns up."

Bryce hung up and dialed Baptiste's extension at Records and Identification.

Delbert Baptiste answered and reported few results in the comparison of Fischler and Helzer's patient files. His voice testy, he reminded Bryce that both victims had seen literally thousands of patients over the years. Not only did each name have to be checked against the other set of records, it was necessary to cross-check each address in case an alias had been used to visit one or the other doctors. Besides, he added pointedly, it was only speculation that a mutual patient was the criminal.

Bryce apologized for the second time that morning. Then he remembered Milo's harping and asked Baptiste to include in his search the recently compiled names of potentially violent disturbed veterans living in the area. Though Helzer had been a nominal Episcopalian, Bryce recalled the circumstances of Fischler's death and reminded Baptiste to scan the vets' files for any possible signs of an anti-Semitic angle.

He was about to hang up and scavenge some breakfast (Kyla worked only three mornings a week) when Baptiste remembered something.

"Bryce, you still there? Hey, have I got some news for you concerning that foxy Lasalle babe."

Bryce tightened his grip slightly on the receiver. "What about her?"

"Hafta stow it for now, ace. Here comes the King Kong of the Cajuns, and that man do look pissed."

An explosion hit Bryce's ear as the phone at the other end crashed into something hard.

Then he heard, "Bryce, you fucker! Are you out of your mind? What's with this memo about you taking Wade McKenna around to Helzer's office and Fischler's car this morning? You were just on the tube! Those media bozos lay eyes on him, just once, mister, and we're up shit creek."

"They won't see him."

"What, he makes himself invisible, too? Listen, you know who called me up last night and ruined the measly three hours of sleep I had coming to me?"

"Let me guess. Nobody makes house calls anymore, so it was either Tinkerbell or the Tooth Fairy."

"I'll tinker your bell, high pockets. It was Reno Morgan."

Bryce reclassified the day from "badly flawed" to "total wipe out." Reno Morgan was Chief of Operations at the FBI downtown. The man was vicious and vindictive, but he was also resourceful and ambitious. He was aware of the Bureau of Special Investigation's—and Bryce's—reputation and hated them both accordingly. His hatred was not unrequited.

"He says," Milo continued, "that he hopes we'll 'liaise' with him on this slasher case. Meaning the sleazy rodent is looking for any excuse he can find to take over the whole damn ball of wax himself."

"So make sure you don't give him one."

Bryce added quickly, before Milo could insert another complaint, "Have you got men guarding Fischler's car and Helzer's office like I asked?"

"Yes, goddamnit! But mark my words, Bryce, you better bag this appointment with the swami before you make nationally broadcast asses outta all of us. You get the City on my back, Tex, and I'm gonna unscrew your head and shit in it!"

"Yeah. Well, *you* have a nice day, too," Bryce said sweetly, hanging up.

The spare room Stevie used for practicing her *katas* was simple and clean in the style of a *dojo*, the typical martial arts school or training room —mat-lined floor, plain walls, an unadorned bamboo screen over the only window. An unframed full-length mirror was for monitoring her form. There could be no extraneous decorations to distract the pretty woman in belted white cotton from achieving the blessed condition of *mushin*—

no-mindedness, the ultimate weapon and the ultimate solace of the martial artist.

Her feet made hard decisive slaps as she progressed along the mats, performing the practice defensive movements with a fluid grace that looked deceptively easy—front snap kick, side thrust kick, middle section reverse punch, high section reverse punch, midsection punch, conclude the set with a spinning back fist. She was a lethal marionette being controlled by precise invisible strings.

Under the thin cotton *gi*, her buttocks formed taut concaves as she crouched, chambered to kick, kicked, instantly rechambered and snapped off another kick. Stevie's face showed relaxed but total concentration. She was not thinking about her movements or psyching up. Her mind was free of anger and pain; it felt clear and clean and strong.

Because of this superior ability at total concentration to free her mind, Stevie had advanced rapidly through the levels of expertise in karate and aikido. She had recently progressed to a higher level of physical and mental techniques, deadly techniques it would be a sacrilege to actually use outside of practice, except in the ultimate struggle to protect life and dignity.

But it was only here in the sterile loneliness of her training room or in a competition *dojo* practicing full-contact discipline with a capable partner that she achieved the condition of *mushin*. And already *mushin* was receding as her internal clock told her the *katas* were finished for today. Consciousness returned, and with it came the oppressive weight of her mortality.

She showered, changed into a full wine-colored skirt and a crepe de Chine blouse. Today was Tuesday, and her only obligation was office hours on campus. She didn't have to lecture at the med school or teach her self-defense class, so she didn't bother to pin her hair into its usual efficient knot. Instead she simply brushed it vigorously, then gathered it behind her ears and fastened it with silver barrettes.

It wasn't until she was in the kitchen, preparing Mr. Cat's breakfast, that she recalled what she had felt upon waking.

She had sensed it rather than realized it intellectually—the foreboding sense that she must be prepared for an ultimate contest with a force a thousand times more evil and more destructive than the thugs who killed her brother. This force would test her mind and her will even more than it would test her body.

115

Even now it was only a hunch, too insubstantial to call a thought. It passed like a brief sensation of *deja vu* the moment Stevie felt Mr. Cat sweep impatiently against her ankles, demanding to be fed.

"Mornin', Miz Lasalle. Sleep good?"

Duncan Hilliard's glance appraised her frankly. He added, "You must have. You sure *look* good."

Stevie paused in front of the double glass doors leading to the street. Outside, passing cars burst into flames as their windshields caught the early morning sun.

"I slept fine, Duncan, thank you. Any messages for me yesterday? I forgot to ask the night guard."

"Matter of fact—" Duncan turned to the wall of pigeonholes behind his wide polished counter.

Stevie guessed the visitor's identity even before Duncan handed her the note torn from a prescription pad with Wright's urgent scrawl: "Call me!!" For some reason the two exclamation marks irritated her. How could men file such an emphatic claim on the basis of one night of lust?

"This gent was mighty anxious to see you." Duncan flashed a glittering, gold-studded smile. "*Mighty* anxious, I'd say. To the tune of twenty bucks if I was to just let him slip on up for a few minutes."

Stevie flushed slightly. "I wasn't home anyway, but thank you for being incorruptible."

"Oh, they say every man's got his price, Miz Lasalle, even iffen it's a lady involved. But when that lady's as pretty as you, it's a heckuva high price. More'n *he* offered."

Stevie was circumnavigating the last potted palm and heading toward the doors. She looked over her shoulder and smiled with mild irony. "Then I guess it's a good thing you don't think I'm homely, isn't it?"

As soon as she reached the sidewalk, sticky cobwebs of humid air brushed against her face. She was too slow to avoid the religious zealots who always congregated before her high rise as if waiting to convert residents of this modern Tower of Babel.

"Woe, woe, woe to the inhabitants of the Earth!" shouted a man wearing a giant badge that said I'M GOING STEADY WITH JESUS. She jutted past him, clutching the Swiss briefcase which held the day's work. "One woe is past and behold, there come two more woes hereafter!" he screamed at her retreating figure.

For a moment, his words reverberating behind her, it felt like someone was tickling the back of her neck with a feather.

"Sorry, old sleuth. Much as I hate to say it—looks like you better cross me off the payroll."

Safely anonymous again behind the dark-tinted windows of Bryce's Cutlass, McKenna removed the Nikon aviator-style sunglasses and slipped them into his shirt pocket. It had been business as usual at the Riverside Medical

117

Suites, and the sunglasses had proven necessary. The uniformed cop on guard, the cordoned-off Mercedes, the TV news last night and today's papers had ensured a larger than usual crowd of gawkers and thrill seekers. But McKenna had risked press exposure for absolutely nothing. He had sat in the car for 45 minutes and held every item in the glove compartment. Just as he expected, it had been useless.

The slow throbbing of a Mahler symphony filled the car. Bryce turned the volume down a tad, checked traffic in the rearview mirror, then glanced over at McKenna.

"You hear me complaining? I'm thinking positive. We'll hit paydirt at Helzer's office."

McKenna doubted it but said nothing, moodily watching Lower Canal Street flash by in a kaleidoscopic pastiche of colors and architecture.

McKenna said, "I've lived here all my life, and I still don't want to leave. But what attracts a rich Texan?"

Bryce glanced at him and looked away as he swung around a city bus plastered with advertisements.

"I'm not rich. My old man is."

"Okay. So what attracts a not-so-rich Texan?"

Bryce shrugged one shoulder. "Before I moved here I was a rookie investigator in Houston. This was right after I got out of the Army. My precinct supervisor got this bright idea that he was going to send me to law school at UT and groom me for some community relations administrative post within the department."

"I take it he knew who your old man was?"

Bryce nodded. "He knew. And it pissed him off royally when I turned down the offer. After that there was no chance in hell for anything but shitty assignments under him. I started watching the position-vacancy memos, and when I saw a slot open up here I went for it. It was just me and Sonny, anyway, so why not?"

"Hell, 'why not' is my motto." McKenna fell silent for a minute, brooding. He shook his mood off and said, "So how's the kid, anyway?"

"Great. He still talks about that show you put on for his party."

During the nadir of his post-divorce daze, McKenna had farmed himself out to an agency that provided entertainment for various party functions. Bryce arranged for the same agency to supply a magician for Sonny's 12th birthday party. The cop had recognized McKenna immediately from the recent publicity. McKenna might easily have been offended by Bryce's blunt request after the party to become one of his resource people, but Bryce made it matter-of-factly, so clearly devoid of any fright or disdain or morbid curiosity. Besides, McKenna knew he would need the potential income; just as matter-of-factly, he had accepted.

"I like that kid," Wade said now. "He's had some tough breaks without copping an attitude problem."

"Yeah." Bryce kept his eyes on the road. "Maybe kids are more versatile."

Abruptly, McKenna changed the subject. "Is anybody else consulting on this case besides me?"

"Sure, but she's not as purely mercenary as you are. Better looking, too."

"She? If it's a female, it's a mercenary. My ex didn't just leave me, Bryce. She had to rub my nose in it by dumping me for a securities lawyer, highest paid profession in the country these days. So who is she?" he added.

"Stevie Lasalle. Doctor Stevie Lasalle, as in Ph.D. She's a research expert in brain physiology and brain pathology. Writes highly specialized medical texts and teaches at South Central Medical School."

"Well, lah-dee-fucking-da," McKenna said. "Another female version of the yuppie success story. Not some on-the-skids goofball like me, right?"

"You asked, so I told you."

McKenna repeated the name. "Lasalle . . . Stevie Lasalle. Damn, why does that name seem to ring a bell?"

"That's twice now somebody's said that," Bryce mused out loud, thinking of Baptiste.

Bryce signaled and turned right on Fulton Street. His passenger fell silent, stewing in the juices of his foul mood. Today for some reason —maybe the gawking crowds earlier— McKenna was especially embittered by all the psychic frauds who promised to expand consciousness. In contrast to them, he knew he was desperately seeking to narrow his. The glib hucksters always glorified the supposedly positive aspects of possessing a third eye. If they ever, he thought, experienced a true moment of psychic insight they'd probably shit in their pants.

Lost in gloomy reverie, he was surprised to realize that Bryce had parked in front of a peeling three-story Victorian stucco.

"Well," Bryce said, ejecting his Mahler tape, "here we are."

Upstairs, the cop watching Helzer's office made himself scarce at Bryce's nod. As if by tacit agreement, Bryce offered no instructions. He merely led the way past the front reception area into the dead psychiatrist's office, leaving McKenna to shift for himself.

The psychic opted to visit the wrought-iron balcony first. He opened the unlocked French windows, stepping out into a morning suffused with brilliant sunshine. The sky was a bottomless blue and streaked with feathery pearls of cumulus cloud. Though the neighborhood was seedy and semideserted, the empty lot across the street was a riot of lush bougainvillaea and shimmering mimosa trees. Beyond the lot and the dark hump of the levee, the Mississippi looped and coiled like a huge brown snake turned sluggish by the sun.

The silence stretched on, broken only by an occasional car whooshing by below or the rusty groan of a freighter's signal. McKenna felt nothing except foolishness, just like earlier in Fischler's car.

Sensing that the man on the balcony was

frustrated and needed to change mental gears, Bryce took a chance on a question.

"Besides the obvious pun, exactly what does it mean to be aural sensitive?"

McKenna didn't turn around but answered mechanically. "There's an electromagnetic force field, usually bluish in color, that surrounds all living things. It's called different things depending on where you rent your guru —the etheric double, the psychic aura, the spirit sheen, whatever. Wilhelm Reich called it orgone energy and said it was most intense during orgasm. Anyway, the roughly two percent of the population in any country who are psychic sensitive can often spot that aura around other psychic sensitive. Sometimes even around non-psychics. The more potentially psychic the person, the more luminous his sheen."

McKenna didn't add that the psychologically maladjusted, as well as certain highly suggestible normals, displayed a different color aura, shades of amber or red, nor that certain penumbras could interact, exchanging or transferring energy without conscious awareness.

"Oh hell," he finally muttered, turning his back on the view and joining Bryce in the office, "it's just no good, Bryce. I need a drink. Take me home."

Bryce stood in the middle of the room, making no move to leave. "Don't rush it. Maybe—"

"Maybe I could locate water on the moon first," McKenna interrupted hotly. "This so-called precious ability of mine is only good for screwing up my life when *it* wants to."

He had wandered near the chipped, beat-up rolltop desk. The tape recorder still sat there, nothing in it.

Idly, still thinking about the day's first drink, McKenna extended an index finger and punched the play button and his mind became a camera transmitting images onto the screen of his inner eye. He saw a small motorcycle engine propped up by wooden blocks. A boy with his back to the camera proudly pointed out something on the engine. The camera panned back for a long shot. McKenna now saw himself standing in what looked like a garage workshop. There was a stubby Black & Decker drill in his hand, grooved bit twirling madly, whirring and gnashing at the air. The camera jerked again, and now McKenna saw himself sitting on top the struggling, screaming boy. It was Sonny, Bryce's foster kid, and—and, oh sweet Jesus no, the blood, all that blood. McKenna was ramming the drill into the kid's—into his—oh God, no, not his . . .

Bryce was in the act of untubing an English Corona when McKenna uttered a choking cry of protest and snapped his hand back from the recorder as if the machine had just bitten him.

"McKenna, what is it?"

But the other man was already bolting through the door leading to the stairs.

"Just look at the evidence, dammit!"

Lucien Milo smacked his right fist into his left palm. "One, this nutso is hacking off ears, a practice that both sides engaged in during the

Vietnam war. Two, that 'War is our business and business is good' line was a widespread Army and Marine Corps recruit training slogan during the Vietnam buildup. Three, Lab confirms that fiber trace found in Fischler's vehicle is identical in color and material to military camouflage. I'm telling you, Tex, that a predictable pattern is emerging. Concentrate your energy on that list of psychotic vets, not on spiritualist quacks or restaurant owners in Shytown."

Early afternoon sunshine slanted through the jalousies into Bryce's office and laid a quivering grillwork across the toes of Milo's wingtips. Bryce rolled a number two pencil back and forth across his blotter and said, "I still think the Nam angle is a red herring. For one thing, military chic is all the rage again. Half the Joe Colleges and Connie Coeds in the country are wearing stuff that looks like it came from Army surplus stores."

Milo picked a speck of tobacco from one lip and examined it a moment before he wiped it off on his trousers. "Yeah, and hacking off ears is all the rage, too, huh? Welcome once again to 'The Bryce is Right.'"

Bryce was too distracted to put his heart into the argument. On the way back to the Tahitian Palace, a white-faced McKenna had refused to mention what it was he had felt or seen when he touched that tape recorder. He had sworn, though, that it had nothing to do with the Helzer case. So what was it?

"—nother thing," Milo was ranting, "I do not want that nut Reno Morgan nosing in on this case. Either you produce, or we're gonna be turned into errand boys for the feds."

Delbert Baptiste appeared in the doorway, clutching a manila file.

"Speaking of nuts," growled Milo.

Baptiste slapped the file down on Bryce's desk and flashed him a smug grin. "There you go. I knew I remembered that name."

Bryce opened the file. A Xeroxed newspaper photo of Stevie Lasalle smiled up at him. It was a blandly pretty, college yearbook pose. "LOCAL COED BRUTALLY BEATEN IN GANG ATTACK THAT KILLS BROTHER" blared the accompanying headline.

"Happened a couple years before you came here " Baptiste said. "Her twin brother, Keith, was an actor, and she showed up for the dress rehearsal of his latest play. They had just exited the stage door of the Vortex Theater on Royal when they were jumped. Her brother was pronounced dead at the scene. The girl was kept in intensive care for weeks and wasn't expected to recover. It took three of the best plastic surgeons in the country and one more from Paris to reconstruct her face. The scumbags who attacked and raped her were never caught."

For a moment as he scanned the story, Bryce felt as if he had just been kicked in the chest. Milo crossed behind the desk and read over Bryce's shoulder.

"Yeah," Milo said, "we didn't handle the case, but I remember now."

He picked up the photo and scrutinized it. "Well all I can say is, they sure as hell did a good job of putting her back together again, judging from what I saw yesterday."

He dropped the picture back down in front of Bryce and added, "Wish I would have recognized the name when she introduced herself. I was a little hard on the girl."

Baptiste sniggered. "You just said 'little hard on.' Freudian slip, Cap'n?"

The crude but sentimental Milo whirled his squat bulk toward the subordinate. "Baptiste, you fugging lump of dog shit! Is nothing sacred? This girl has suffered!"

Bryce, still staring at the file, missed Baptiste's lame rejoinder. His first impulse was to call Stevie and ask if he could meet with her briefly, but his flight to Chicago left in less than three hours. He still had to pack and make last minute arrangements with Kyla, who would be staying at the house with Sonny until Bryce returned from paying a visit to Ben Davis.

His own words to Stevie returned to him now, cruel and mocking, a brutal proof that he could still occasionally match the myopic stupidity of his rookie days in Houston.

"No doubt you've got some fancy scientific word for your condition. I'd call it a fairly standard case of man-hating."

CHAPTER SEVEN

I'M FALLING BEHIND, THOUGHT STEVIE, AND there's no reason for it. There's just no reason.

No *apparent* reason, she amended as she began walking the last of the eight city blocks between her apartment and the South Central College campus. Above all else, she reminded herself, her scientific training had made her a rationalist. Every effect had its verifiable cause, no matter how remote. Revising her textbook was simply a matter of discipline, like so many other things she had accomplished. But something subtle was now interfering with that discipline.

The morning humidity was low, and she was comfortably cool in a split skirt and short-sleeved cotton blouse. Her hair was drawn back tightly under an oval platinum clasp, emphasizing her widow's peak and the fine slope of her forehead.

She was still a half block from campus when her scalp tingled slightly. The thick knot of hair was suddenly cold and heavy against her neck. She stopped and abruptly looked behind her, scanning the sidewalk.

There was nothing very out of the ordinary, just a scattered handful of summer students— and that ugly man in the shabby, wrinkled, forest-green military raincoat. He seemed to be absorbed in a study of the feminist bookstore's window display. For a moment she started to look more observantly at the unhealthy pale skin and weak-chinned profile.

"I know what you're doing," the volunteer shouted, backing away from her with fear and hatred burning in his eyes. *"You're poisoning my brain!"*

Why did she think she remem—but now he was ducking into the store, his fists hurriedly lumped into the raincoat's pockets, and the impression faded without quite becoming strong enough to alert her conscious memory.

"Okay! That looked real good. For the rest of the period we're going to concentrate on falling and breaking holds. If you didn't find time to read the handouts I gave you last time, please let me know now."

The 16 pupils enrolled in Basic Self-Defense Skills for Women had just finished a vigorous slap drill, eight of them bracing themselves and holding out soccer balls at arm's length while the other eight practiced strikes and jabs and fist-spinning karate punches against them.

Stevie was in an upbeat mood. This class was going well and had been for several weeks since it began. A few reliable male volunteers, led by the enthusiastic towhead, Gary Mullner, had been showing up regularly to serve as aggressors, and they were giving a great effort to keep the training safe but realistic. All of the women were taking the instructions seriously and applying themselves with enthusiasm, and so far there had been no injuries.

One time, during the third semester she had taught the class, a student had gotten carried away and broken a volunteer aggressor's instep in a more-vicious-than-necessary stomp. Stevie had almost given the class up, permanently, but some inner voice urged her to persist. Since then there had been only a few very minor injuries, mostly split lips or bloody noses from errant elbow jabs. This class was so together they hadn't even suffered a minor mishap.

This is a good group, she thought, watching them pair off efficiently into their A and B teams for mat drill. Classes all had their own personalities, and for this one the group karma was just right.

She was feeling better about a lot of things. Stevie resolved to completely revise one entire chapter of her textbook before she left the office that afternoon.

For a moment she thought of her favorite line from Aristotle: "Hope is a waking dream."

* * *

"Enjoy the weather up there, big fellah," the cabbie quipped while he made change, craning his neck to look out the window at his departing passenger.

The Sou'wester was a commodious one-story building made of timbers, stained gray to resemble old driftwood. Out front, a massive battleship-gray anchor was ensconced in the midst of a tiered garden of evergreen shrubs and crushed white marble. It was only about 11 A.M., but already the asphalt parking lot boasted an impressive scattering of cars.

Bryce headed for the main entrance, his eyes burning from jet lag and lack of sleep. The stiff mattress in his hotel room hadn't been much better than sleeping on the floor, plus the couple in the next room had engaged in a noisy sexual marathon lasting into the wee hours.

It wasn't so much their noise that had kept him awake; it was trying to decide whether he felt resentment or envy.

He stopped outside the stainless steel and glass doors to buy a *Chicago Tribune*. One week, he thought, glancing at the date before he folded the paper and tucked it under his arm. One week had elapsed since a psychotic in New Orleans had decided to make life hell for his victims as well as the police.

"One for lunch?" asked the pretty hostess, smiling up at him.

"My name's Bryce. I called Mr. Davis earlier, and he's expecting me."

The hostess nodded, obviously having received instructions already. A few heads turned

130

to look at the girl, then at the tall, loping figure of Bryce as he followed her through the plush dining room toward a lounge at the rear. He sniffed the musty tang of clam chowder and shrimps, scallops and lobster, and noted that the huge dining room was cleverly designed to appeal to the family crowd while the back room catered to those who would rather drink their lunch and seal a business deal. The lounge was identified as The Captain's Cabin on a jagged driftwood sign over twin, leather-padded doors with hexagonal portholes.

"The bar is closed for another forty-five minutes," the hostess explained as she swung the doors open, "so you'll be able to talk quietly in here. Mr. Davis will be with you as soon as he finishes speaking to the chef."

She flashed him a smile that was all pink gums and dazzling white teeth, and Bryce thought of last night's active couple in the next room—and of Stevie Lasalle's sleek body in that nylon knit dress she'd been wearing when she stopped by his office.

The lounge was small but comfortable, with a thick pile carpet, redwood paneling and milk glass chandeliers. The hostess led him to a booth.

"Would you care for something to eat or drink?" she asked as he maneuvered his legs under the table. "Mr. Davis said it's on the house."

Bryce was about to politely refuse when he realized the western omelette and hashbrowns he'd had earlier at the hotel coffee shop had left his mouth and throat parched. He asked for a draft. The girl drew the foaming beer herself and set a cork coaster in front of him, then the tall, tapering glass.

Bryce asked casually, "You like working here?"

"Love it. I started when I was in college. Now I've got my teaching degree, but I'm still in no hurry to leave. Mr. Davis is the best boss I've ever had."

She looked at Bryce confidentially and added, "His bark's a lot worse than his bite. He takes care of his employees. And the tips here are great."

Bryce hated to do it, especially when he had no concrete suspicions against Davis, but it had to be done. The girl was obviously about to leave, so there was no time for anything more subtle. "A guy that successful," he said, "must take a lot of vacations."

The friendly sparkle died out of her eyes. The mixture of curiosity and suspicion which replaced it announced that she had just realized he was a cop.

"As far as I know," she answered coolly, "he takes one a year, like most people. Now if you'll excuse me, customers are waiting."

Bryce sighed as he watched her retreat, her cute little butt wriggling under a tight mauve skirt. He sipped his beer and idly began flipping through the Trib. The headlines were as familiar as a prison menu—another war of words between Washington and Libya, cocaine scandals in pro athletics, radical alterations in Hollywood social life because of the AIDS scare.

His thoughts drifted to the long-distance call he had placed to New Orleans earlier from his hotel room. Baptiste reported that he had completed the initial comparison of Fischler and Helzer's respective patient files. It turned out they had treated five patients in common, a fact which did not surprise Bryce considering that both professionals had practiced in the same East Bank neighborhood. Three of the patients were dead, one was living in Sarasota, Florida, and the fifth was committed to the state mental hospital in Baton Rouge. Baptiste had even called to confirm that he hadn't escaped recently.

Bryce had resisted the urge to place a second long-distance call, but exactly what would he tell Stevie Lasalle if he *did* manage to reach her? That he just happened to be bugging her from Chicago to apologize for being such an asshole? Besides, he hated those damn message machines.

So it's back to square one, thought Bryce. Still musing, he flipped the next page of the newspaper, then suddenly felt as if something cold and wet had just whopped his face.

NEW ORLEANS POLICE RESORTING TO PSYCHIC? screamed a headline at the beginning of the second section.

Bryce had read the story several times before he realized he wasn't registering a thing it said. He backed up and read it again:

> New Orleans (AP)—Local police have enlisted the aid of a reputed psychic in a desperate bid to stem a growing num-

ber of bizarre mutilation attacks which have terrorized this colorful Southern port since last Wednesday.

Wade McKenna, 40, who made TV history by rejecting a lucrative bid to appear on Johnny Carson's *Tonight Show* . . .

Bryce finished the story, mentally kicking himself in the ass. "A growing number," he thought with wry disgust. That sounded lots more ominous than "two." Obviously there must have been a reporter present yesterday in that crowd of spectators around Fischler's car, one who recognized McKenna, and evidently the resourceful scribe had even followed them. The article mentioned a "seamy, drug-infested brothel" called Rudy's Tahitian Palace and euphemistically described McKenna's Incredible Shoneen act, in addition to recounting the grisly *modus operandi* of Johnny Law, the Van Gogh slasher.

Bryce swore in frustration. Baptiste hadn't said anything when he called earlier, but they must know by now. Milo would be going through the ceiling, and McKenna would undoubtedly refuse to cooperate any further, just when Bryce was sure the psychic had seen something yesterday in Helzer's office. For McKenna, the only kiss of death left in the world was publicity, which he knew his ex-wife would see.

The doors swung open and a nattily dressed

black man of medium height and build hustled over to the booth.

"Mr. Bryce? Ben Davis here. Sorry to keep you waiting."

Bryce rose to shake his hand, his left hip smashing into the corner of the table and slopping some beer over the lip of his glass. Davis measured him with a glance and grinned.

"This is a switch. *I'll* have to be the coach while the white boy does the slam-dunking."

Both men laughed. Bryce took in the restaurateur's brocade jacket, cream cotton ottoman trousers and black lace shoes. Ben Davis had a neat mustache and intelligent, piercing eyes the color of copper.

They sat down. Davis offered him a cigarette, then lit one himself when Bryce refused. "Okay. So what's this you mentioned about some kook using my name?"

Bryce quickly filled him in on Helzer's mystery patient. He gave only the pertinent details and reiterated the vast improbability of someone coincidentally making up not only Davis' name but his unit and exact date of service in Vietnam. As the military details emerged, Davis' face lost some of its friendliness and became more guarded.

"So the nagging question," Bryce continued, "is how and why did this guy, whoever he is, get your life mixed up with his?"

Davis shook his head, tapping his cigarette over a cut-glass ashtray with a frosted clipper ship carved into its bottom.

"You got me on that one, Bryce."

"Have you ever been in New Orleans or anywhere close?"

Again Davis shook his head. "Closest I ever been is the one time I spent fifteen minutes at Houston International, changing planes for O'Hare."

"Got any friends or relatives down south?"

"I'm telling you, none. You think all black folks are descended from Mississippi cotton pickers? I never even knew anybody from your city, anybody I can remember anyway. All I know about 'Nawlins' is that we Yankees don't know how to pronounce it right. Add Mardi Gras, the Sugar Bowl, and the Super Bowl, and that's it."

Hoping Davis was not a close follower of the news, Bryce had purposely withheld one question. Now he watched Ben Davis' face closely and said, "Do the words 'Johnny Law rules' mean anything to you?"

For a moment, a moment no longer than a heartbeat, Bryce thought he saw a distant glimmer of fear and recognition in those copper eyes. But it passed so quickly that a second later Bryce wasn't sure he had seen anything except the projection of his own desperation to be right.

"Man, all I know is you're tossing some bizarre riddles at me."

Whether or not he had seen anything in those eyes a moment ago, Bryce believed Davis was— or thought he was—telling the truth. Unconscious of what he was doing, the cop shook some salt into his beer.

"Hey, man," Davis protested, "you think this is the Gobi Desert? You gotta eat salt or something? Or you trying to say my beer's flat?"

Bryce shrugged. "Just a nervous habit, I guess."

"Yeah? Well, it's stupid to ruin good beer. Why didn't you have Sharon give you a glass of water on the side and salt *that*?"

"Then I'd have to drink the beer, and I don't like beer all that much after the first couple sips."

Davis gave him a puzzled look. "Then why the hell order it?"

Bryce grinned. "To be sociable."

"Bullshit, Mr. Policeman from 'Nawlins.' More like, because people jack their jaws more around a man who's enjoying a frosty one. He smells less like a cop that way."

Bryce winced. "I thought it was a trade secret."

"Well, I got nothing to say, okay?"

Davis kept his voice low and controlled. "Look here, Bryce, I got no bitches, moans or groans against nobody nowhere, you catch my drift? I hear some guys squawking about how they suffered all this sad shit in Nam—right?—and now all the dudes that split to Canada are running the country and warming their tooshes in Jacuzzis. Even building themselves a draft dodgers memorial somewhere in Arizona. So who gives a fuck? Me, I don't see any future in dwelling on Nam. I don't think it's the guys who really saw the shit who're doing all that squawking anyway. See, I got a hot tub, too. I got a twin-diesel Chriscraft down at the marina. I got a VCR and a satellite dish and the whole nine yards. Plus I got a kid'll be starting law school at Yale next fall. I like it all just fine, thanks. And I sure as hell got no time for getting pissed at people I don't even have any grudge against."

Davis ground his cigarette out, causing the ashtray to tremble slightly against the table. "I don't know anything about your past or where your head is at, but I think you're a decent guy who's trying to do the right thing. I also think you're sniffing for smoke in the wrong hole. I just want you to understand that I'm not pissed at anybody, 'cept maybe you for ruining a perfectly good glass of beer."

It was clear that Davis intended his remark as a polite signal that the interview was over. In case there was still any doubt, the restaurant owner tugged the sleeve of his jacket back and glanced conspicuously at his watch.

For a moment Bryce suspected he had flown almost a thousand miles for nothing. Then he recalled that brief, faint glimmer of disturbed recognition in Davis' eyes when he'd heard the words "Johnny Law rules."

Bryce dipped two fingers into his shirt pocket and handed Davis a business card.

"This is the toll free precinct number where you can reach me or leave a message twenty-four hours a day. If you think of *anything* that might help us, will you give me a call?"

"Sure." Davis stood up and slipped the card into a soft pigskin billfold. "But don't bother waiting by the phone."

The terrible shrieking was like amplifier feedback magnified a thousand mocking times by the sickness inside his brain. It grated cruelly along Harlan Perry's spine until he woke up, choking back a scream.

"Welcome to Burger Boy," crackled a distant voice rendered sexless by static. "May I take your order?"

Perry jerked upright too quickly and hissed at the quick flaring of pain in his left lower jaw. He was trapped in the murky mental fog between sleeping and waking, and it took a few seconds to remember that the explosions originated from the nearby junkfood palace's drive-thru speaker.

During those brief nightmare moments of waking sleep he reverted to being only Harlan Perry, a sick powerless little wimp who did not possess the ultimate equalizer of the Terrible Crystal. That Harlan Perry would probably die anonymously in this scuzzy upstairs efficiency with its knotted hairs clotting the drains, rancid stink of months-old bacon grease congealing in instant coffee jars, multicolor mold filming the rusty inside of the toilet bowl.

But then Johnny Law's deep commanding voice barked, *"Drop your cock and grab your socks!"* and he came fully awake.

Perry squinted in protest against the bright splotches of late afternoon sunlight sneaking past the slant of the room's Venetian blinds. The first thing his eye fell on was the caramel-colored flystrip dangling in the middle of the room; while he stared, the parched corpse of a fly flaked off and floated down to the linoleum. He shifted his gaze to the wobbly kitchen table upon which reigned the large jar.

A second ear now drifted fetus-like in the hazy formaldehyde solution.

Perry was wearing only olive-drab boxer shorts. He slapped the linoleum with both bare feet and rose from the narrow bed. Automatically his tongue probed the hole left after Fischler's aborted attempt to infect him. He also noticed, frowning, that his headache was worse. His temples were throbbing like he was trapped in a headlock.

But he felt slightly better when he gazed at the velvet-draped Tuaoi; it stood in lone undisputed glory on the upended footlocker beside the table. Thinking about the crystal, however, also reminded him of something the security guard, Wally Cruz, had mentioned at the end of this morning's shift. The museum was performing its annual inventory soon. He would either have to lay off borrowing the crystal until the inventory was completed or . . . Perry's gut fluttered at the alternative. He wasn't quite ready for *that* yet.

Before he actually absconded with the Terrible Crystal permanently, he had to be sure he was its absolute master.

". . . and a Mama Burger with everything but

mustard, ordera onion rings, a large Dr. Pepper . . ."

Perry knew if he slammed the window shut the prickling stuffiness of the room would soon leave him stinking with sweat. Instead he crossed to the footlocker and gently picked up the Tuaoi, leaving the velvet cloth in place. Though the nightmare flashback to the incident with Stevie Lasalle had not recurred since he'd begun reading about and practicing with the crystal, Perry always handled it with the respect due a volatile charge of TNT.

Stevie Lasalle. Scar Baby and her poisoning machine.

"The pretty *bitch* called me a freaky *glitch*," he whispered absently.

For a moment he forgot about his tormentor, instead thinking about that other vision he'd experienced in the museum basement—of New Orleans gutted and dying, cleansed of its cancerous sickness, and him leading its postoperative return to health. He couldn't help a rush of pride when he recalled that soon-to-be-realized glory.

"Welcome to Burger Boy, may I take your—"

Perry's breath quickened with incipient rage. Still holding the covered Tuaoi, he crossed to the Venetian blind and swung it aside a few inches to gaze outside. Below, on the other side of Arno Street, the Burger Boy was jumping with a lively supper crowd. The parking lot was three-quarters full, and waiting vehicles formed a slow-crawling parade around the drive-thru loop.

Perry watched a trio of leather-clad Punks in a Jeep Renegade flirt with the girl at the order window. All three of the Punks were dressed like cheap clones of the Road Warrior, Perry noted with disgust.

Each speaker noise was a clawing explosion inside his head. Perry was about to scream his usual litany of obscenities when he became aware that the velvet cloth had somehow slipped away from the Tuaoi and fallen to the floor.

Had it fallen through his carelessness? No! Perry realized the Tuaoi was notifying him that it was time to test Johnny Law's combat effectiveness over an increased range. Among other recent complications necessitating this, the pretty female PCA with the scar may have recognized him this morning when he foolishly moved in too close.

Staring into the naked crystal was like peering into an infinity of melting, stretching, shifting mirrors. Perry held it in the foreground of his vision, allowing his gaze to flow around it and down onto the sidewalk on the other side of the street. Immediately he spotted a middle-aged pedestrian with a stack of books under his arm, about to walk past the exit of the drive-thru loop.

A moment later came his thin stiletto smile. He had also just noticed, clinging like radioactive pollen to the driver of the jeep, a deep infrared penumbra.

Later, the cop on the motorcycle would swear that he had witnessed a cold, premeditated act of murder, not a mere vehicular manslaughter.

The official report, verified by several witnesses, supported his claim.

Patrolman Fletcher was cruising north on Arno at approximately 25 mph when he heard an engine being revved. He was just approaching the Burger Boy Restaurant at 420 Arno when he glanced to his right and saw a beige jeep containing three white male occupants in their early twenties.

The vehicle was beginning to exit the restaurant's drive-thru. Its driver was intently watching a pedestrian start to cross in front of him, revving the jeep louder and louder until the fanbelt was shrieking. When the pedestrian was directly in front of the jeep, the driver appeared to deliberately sidestep the clutch and mow his victim down, crushing him under all four wheels. The driver would have continued fleeing if his two shocked companions hadn't wrestled him and the vehicle to a stop approximately 100 yards down the street.

But it wasn't that part of the cop's report which most terrified the public and opened an even larger can of worms for Neal Bryce and the BSI. It was what happened (verified by two witnesses in the parking lot) after the agitated cop parked his motorcycle and rushed to the side of the crumpled pedestrian surrounded by his books.

The middle-aged man was obviously killed instantly. His spine and pelvis were crushed, and one side of his skull had been mashed and was oozing brain matter. Fletcher turned away to fight back nausea as the dry heaves threatened him. That was when the twisted corpse abruptly jerked itself up into a sitting position.

Both eyes popped open, and it grinned at him.

"Johnny Law rules!" the dead man croaked in a voice as raw as the north wind in a gale. The cop, who had heard of psychosis but never metempsychosis, couldn't know those words were simultaneously being spoken upstairs in the dingy redbrick tenement across the street.

Then the grinning spectacle from Hell puked up a bubbling clot of blood and collapsed back into a heap, its mad giggle fading away slowly like the long dying whinny of a frightened horse.

CHAPTER EIGHT

"YOU MARK MY WORDS, COWBOY. YOU'RE RUINING a potentially good career in law enforcement by not listening to me."

Bryce glanced up from the manila folder whose contents he was perusing under the glare of a brass desk lamp. Two eyes that were red-rimmed pouches of fatigue swept over Milo's cheap blue acrylic suit and peppermint-stripe shirt. With his black necktie knotted so tightly that wattles of fat were melting over the shirt collar, the squat little cop made Bryce think of a sausage packed too tight for its own skin.

"Didn't know you were into career counseling." Bryce flicked his eyes back to the folder's photocopied articles.

Milo interrupted his nervous pacing to stare hard at the other man. "Well, screw you then! I mean, you really chap my ass. If you're such a goddamn bonehead that you can't see what McKenna is up to, just go right on eating out of his hand. Go ahead, play his game like a sap. Forget that we're supposed to be a team here, Bryce. Right? Just like you conveniently forget to scrape that Texas flytrap off your chin."

Bryce looked up from the folder, closed both burning eyes for a long moment and pressed his fingertips against them. He consciously willed his muscles to relax before he said, "Okay, so let's hear your theory on what McKenna's up to."

"It's not a theory, it's as obvious as a third tit! He's using you—us—for two things: publicity and money. *He* leaked that damn story himself. He's trying—"

But Bryce muttered something unintelligible and swept Milo's sputterings aside with one hand. He returned to scanning one of the articles, reviewing passages he had underlined during his first reading months ago. It was titled "The Color of Personality: Scientific Interpretations of the Etheric Double." Bryce had copied the article from *Proceedings from the Soviet Symposium on Psychic Research*. It was one of the reports cited several times in the Stanford Research Institute's study on Wade McKenna, a copy of which was among the folder's contents.

"Dammit, Bryce, I mean it!"

He glanced up to see Milo brandishing a meaty fist at him across the broad desk.

"You think I'm wearing this monkey suit for my health? I don't like being called on the carpet at Headquarters. You've got that federal cockroach Reno Morgan sucking up to them again. He hates your guts, and you know it. More than he hates mine, even, and that's saying a lot. Now that you've made us national laughingstocks, you think they ain't gonna rake my ass over the coals this afternoon?"

Bryce resisted an urge to pick up the nearest pencil and snap it in two. Instead he said testily, "So what would you like, sir—a thousand push-ups? Or should I just scream, 'The private is a lowlife maggot, sir,' over and over until I drop?"

As usual when he succeeded in getting Bryce's goat, Milo's mood improved noticably.

"Okay," he said. "Forget Reno Morgan. He never bought me a drink, anyway. Look, you get ahold of the girl yet? This what's-her-name?"

"Cheryl Lance. There's no answer to the door or the phone at the address the restaurant gave us," Bryce explained. "The power company confirms that someone with her name has been paying the electric bill. But Patterson checked around with the neighbors and found out she's going with this biker type, and they split town a lot on her days off. I told Patterson to stay on it. Anyway her manager told me she's an exceptionally dependable employee and due back at work at seven A.M. tomorrow."

As soon as the motorcycle cop's story had been reported, an hour after Bryce's return flight to New Orleans yesterday, the detective had attempted to contact the drive-thru employee who had last spoken to the driver of the jeep. It was a long shot, but she might remember something useful. The driver was still in shock, claiming to remember nothing, and was being protected from police questioning by his doctor and lawyer. Neither of his companions in the jeep had been able to report anything.

Milo cut into his thoughts. "What do you think of this talking corpse bit?"

"I don't know." Bryce riffled the pages of the Xeroxed article. "Fletcher's got seven years on the force with an outstanding conduct and proficiency sheet. And two witnesses back him up."

"Yeah, maybe they're not exactly lying, but did they in fact witness what they *thought* they were witnessing? I mean, you've seen chickens when you chop their heads off. They—"

"Fletcher swears this wasn't just a nervous reflex. The body of Candelaria sat up, smiled and even giggled."

"Uh-huh. Listen, we know you're gullible," Milo said, "or you wouldn't be handing out blank checks to a spiritualist quack."

Bryce let the comment pass. He was still thinking of the 47-year-old high school science teacher who had been run over yesterday. Any chance of Francisco Candelaria himself being Johnny Law—one logical explanation for uttering those words—had been eliminated when Baptiste's initial R & I check was compiled. Not only was he a five-time winner of the city's Teacher of the Year award, but he had been emceeing a summer school honors banquet at Lafayette High School about the same time last Monday that Martin Fischler was frightened to death and mutilated.

Bryce gazed one last time at the folder before he rose and turned to a huge laminated city map behind his desk. Bright red thumbtacks marked the locations of Johnny Law's two known attacks, as well as the Burger Boy slaying to which his deadly moniker had been linked.

"So far," Bryce said, "the incidents are limited to the East Bank ghetto. We've got to concentrate our search there."

Milo's grunt implied otherwise. He tucked an unfiltered Camel between his lips, produced his black combat Zippo and leaned forward into its flame. Bryce suspected that the only reason he smoked so much was to show off his lighter.

"Like I said, concentrate on that list of psycho vets."

Bryce turned away from the map, crossed to the Mr. Coffee in a few long strides and checked the level before he flipped it on to warm up. While he waited he tugged the jalousies open wider and felt the hot afternoon sun on his face and chest. Straight ahead of the old precinct building, across the river, Decatur Street's sleaze strip stretched along one flank of the Vieux Carré, a few neons already seductively winking. Visible to his left was the high, arching span of the Greater New Orleans Bridge. If he glanced right and flattened his cheek against the glass, Bryce would see several of the neat gray concrete lozenges comprising the U. S. Coast Guard station barracks.

But Bryce failed to notice the familiar view. Instead he was back in Illinois, watching that quick flare of recognition in the black veteran's eyes at the words "Johnny Law rules." *Well, I got nothing to say, okay?* Nothing to say verbally maybe, thought Bryce, but there was something deep down inside the man trying to claw its way to the surface of memory.

Milo's respectful tone behind him startled Bryce. "Good afternoon, Doctor."

When Bryce spun around, Stevie Lasalle was standing in the office doorway watching him.

For a long moment both men stared, caught off guard by how pretty she looked. Stevie wore a sleeveless taupe blouse tucked into cotton harem pants. Her hair was a lush sable cascade flowing over both shoulders and down her back. The only jewelry was a delicate, triple herringbone pattern necklace of yellow gold.

This time Bryce saw, just below the gold chain, one edge of a long pale scar.

Milo spoke again, awkwardly glancing away from her neck. This stilted, formal manner was a side of his boss Bryce hadn't seen much of.

"If you'll excuse me, Dr. Lasalle, Lieutenant Bryce . . . " Milo waited deferentially for Stevie to step further into the office, then stretched himself out to his full five-foot-seven and made for the door. Some of the old Milo surfaced as he peered back over his shoulder at Bryce and added malevolently, "I have an appointment downtown."

His heavy steps retreated down the hall. Stevie moved closer to the desk until Bryce was breathing the fresh tropical scent of her perfume.

He invited her to sit, then offered coffee,

which she declined almost impatiently. Bryce poured himself some and sat down behind his desk again.

"Mr. Bryce, do you still want my help? I mean concerning your so-called festering brain angle and this—this psychotic animal you're hunting?"

"Of course." He tried to filter the surprise out of his tone. His plan for the afternoon, after the inevitable showdown he was dreading with McKenna, had been to contact her again. "I welcome all the expert advice I can get," he added as a sincere afterthought.

"I felt—" Stevie hesitated and met his gaze more frankly. "I felt that I was unnecessarily rude to you last time we met. But it's unprofessional to let personality clashes interfere between two adults who should be cooperating."

Bryce recognized the opening he had been waiting for since learning the story of her past from Baptiste. He started to speak, but almost as if she suspected the topic he was about to broach, she hurriedly snapped open the Swiss briefcase propped against her chair and offered him a bound sheaf of papers.

"Here's a complete set of copies for all my studies of violent criminals and brain tumors. As I said before, delusions of grandeur enough to be grossly megalomaniacal are often present. I agree with you, Mr. Bryce. The psychotic intensity of the anti-Semitism in the Fischler case and the thirst for ultimate power implicit in the name 'Johnny Law' itself suggest the vindictive holy mission of the acute megalomaniac."

"I take it," Bryce said, flipping through the photocopies, "you've heard about the latest incident possibly connected to Johnny Law?"

She nodded. "It's eerie, but frankly, I don't accept the no doubt exaggerated account about the mangled corpse sitting up and talking."

When he said nothing either by way of agreement or disagreement, she added, "I also read the business about your consulting a psychic. When I realized how terrible this criminal is and how desperate you must be, I was angry at myself for not being more cooperative. I want you to know that my time is yours until this madman is caught. Whatever I can do, Mr. Bryce. I mean it."

"Neal, if you don't mind. And I hope you *do* mean it, because I assure you I'm going to hold you to your offer."

"Neal," she agreed politely, though he noticed she didn't reciprocate the cordiality by inviting him to call her something less formal.

Bryce glanced one more time at the report on aural sensitivity studies, then he swivelled in his chair to examine the trio of red thumbtacks on the map behind him. The chair groaned in unoiled protest as he spun back around again and found the pretty researcher's huge gray eyes.

"So you would say, based on your experience, that there's a good chance this Johnny Law character is in fact suffering from a brain tumor?"

"Nothing is certain without a complete catscan and an extensive diagnosis, but yes, I'd say

152

there's a reasonably good chance in this particular type of case."

"Then let me toss another hypothetical question at you. Assume that we had some . . . unorthodox but effective method for identifying a potential pool of megalomaniacal suspects. Is there a more standard, more valid psychological tool to help determine which individuals are more likely to be acutely afflicted than others?"

Stevie's brow furrowed in sudden suspicion. "Do you mean, a psychological tool that carries more official weight than, say, the irrational guesswork of a local psychic? One of questionable reputation, at that?"

Bryce cleared his throat and occupied his hands by rolling a pencil back and forth across the blotter. "I guess you could put it that way. Remember, this is all purely hypothetical."

"Well, to answer your question, general psychopathology is only a collateral interest, not my specialty, but yes, there are such tools. My research shows that certain types—not all—of brain tumor influenced criminals exhibit a distinctively aberrant pattern on projective personality assessments. True, they share a few traits with the classic paranoid type, especially the persecution complex, but they see a unique pattern of antisocial imagery in Rorschach inkblots, for instance. There is a pattern not matched by abnormals of the schizophrenic or delusional or manic-depressive variety. Likewise, the B-T criminal provides his own bizarre brand of plot twists on a TAT or Thematic Apperception Test."

Bryce raised his eyebrows.

"In the TAT," she explained, "the subject is required to write brief stories explaining what's going on in the accompanying ambiguous illustrations. As a matter of fact I've developed my own brief assessment scale to assist me in the initial screening of B-T subjects confined to mental wards."

Bryce seemed mildly heartened by her response, but he only said, "Right now I'm just playing around with an idea, in case there's no break soon in our investigation and more agressive measures become necessary."

"I'm not the press, Mr. Bry—Neal. Please skip the officialese. Don't you mean, in case there's another attack?"

"Yeah, I guess that's exactly what I mean."

The conversation ceased as abruptly as a spring downpour. The only sounds were an unanswered telephone clamoring somewhere in another office and the whirring of a teleprocessor down the hall in Records and Identification.

Bryce cleared his throat. "The last time I saw you—"

She cut him off, but the faint smile of sympathy suggested that she appreciated the gesture he had been about to make. "To quote some of my favorite advice: 'The Past is a dead thing. Leave it alone.'"

Their eyes met and Bryce thought, My God, she's beautiful.

She could tell that he still wanted to say

something. Her voice was calm but determined when she continued.

"I know what you're leading up to, and I know what you're probably thinking deep down, Neal. You think that what happened to me has got to break me, if it hasn't already. They all thought it would break me, but they were wrong. It didn't break me, and it's not going to."

Her eyes were brighter than usual, but no tears threatened. Stevie's beauty was almost intimidating now in the fierce determination to master the turmoil of her inner feelings.

"Nothing or no one will *ever* break me, I assure you. I'm unbreakable. And believe me, I'm not just some naive graduate student temporarily hyped up on an assertiveness training seminar."

Bryce believed her, all right. At that moment he almost imagined he could feel the force of her will like some palpable energy in the room.

"I'm not thinking anything," he said, "except that you're a remarkable woman and I admire you very much. It might have been too easy," he added, thinking of Wade McKenna's bitter, self-pitying style of coping with tragedy, "to tell life to go to hell."

Stevie snapped her briefcase shut and stood up. Bryce also rose.

"Not as easy as you think, Neal. Idle hands may not be the Devil's playmates, but idle minds sure are. I did try, for a brief time at least, to tell life to go to hell. Both of my parents are dead, so when I lost Keith I literally lost my entire family.

But deep down in my heart of hearts I never wanted to stop believing in humanity. I told myself that other people have survived the ugliness of sick individuals, gone on with their lives and become even stronger for the hell they've endured. If they can do it, so can I. So *will* I."

She was abruptly embarrassed when she realized her voice was starting to climb an octave or two. For the second time that morning she smiled at him, this time a bit less professionally. "Now it's time to pack up my soapbox and leave you alone."

Bryce didn't tell her that she and her soapbox were welcome to cross his threshold anytime.

While he escorted his visitor downstairs, he couldn't help picturing McKenna up there on that garishly lighted stage, cracking one-liners and ramming needles into his palms in a black parody of self-crucifixion. In the narrow hallway leading to the front entrance, they nearly collided with Milo as he emerged from a side office en route to keeping his appointment.

"A thousand apologies, Dr. Lasalle."

Milo gazed melodramatically into her eyes, and Bryce realized the gaze was supposed to seal an eternal bond of camaraderie, not romance. "'Only those who have crossed to Death's other Kingdom . . .'"

His smug little sidelong glance at Bryce was a clear reminder that certain unnamed individuals who had "fed marijuana dogs in Danang" were excluded from membership in the Fellow Sufferers Club.

Stevie stared back, her face a puzzled mask.

Her voice was genuinely curious, not malicious, when she asked, "Have you been taking drugs, Captain Milo?"

For a moment the precinct chief looked like a confused drunk who had just woken up on the pool table. Bryce struggled to keep a straight face as Stevie turned back to him and reiterated her offer of help.

A moment later she was reduced to a blur by the double-glazed windows of the front door.

Wade McKenna swore out loud when a quick trio of knocks interrupted his meal.

"Jesus, can't you studs keep your dick in your pants until a decent hour? Go back one door to your left!"

The voice in the hall was a muffled echo through the door. "It's Bryce."

McKenna slowly leaned sideways to set the greasy carton of red beans and rice down on the floor next to the recliner. For a long moment he was silent, staring at the backs of his freckled hands on the arms of the chair.

"Sonofabitch," he finally muttered, grunting slightly with the effort as he rolled forward out of the chair. The bolt snapped back loudly; a second later he was staring straight ahead at Bryce's chin.

"Sorry," McKenna said, "that I mistook you for a stud."

He turned around and headed back to his chair without otherwise acknowledging the visitor's presence. Bryce paused in the doorway to take in the carton with its gray grease-stained amoebas. Beside it squatted a half-liter bottle of Arrow vodka.

McKenna flopped heavily back into the recliner, noticing the detective's disapproving glance at his liquor.

"Not exactly what the lah-dee-dahs drink, Bryce, but I can't afford cognac anymore. Besides, you know what the man says—I'd rather have a bottle in front of me than a frontal lobotomy."

Bryce closed the door behind him and dropped into the nearby chair, stretching out his long legs and crossing them at the ankles. He was holding the same thick manila folder he'd been perusing earlier at his office.

"Keep hitting the sauce this early, and you're going to have both."

Now McKenna finally met the other man's glance, the jade green eyes livid with resentment.

"Don't lay that phony, big-brother concern on me! You couldn't give a fuck if I drank myself into acute gastritis. I'm just your convenient sap, your decoy. You set me up hoping to scare this Van Gogh slasher into either tipping his hand or retiring early. You dropped the dime on me to the press, boyo."

"That's bullshit."

"No, *you're* bullshit, Bryce, you and your sanctimonious concerned-cop routine. All you want is to cover your own ass between promotions. Meantime, until this blows over, it's costing me twenty bucks a day to make sure the bouncers downstairs keep those press turkeys off my ass. Look —"

McKenna nodded toward a fake leopard-skin leotard dangling from a nail on the back of the door.

"The latest costume Rudy sent up. He's tired of the turquoise tights. But you can just bet your sweet bippy he was delighted to read about me in the papers and get a free plug into the deal."

"Listen," Bryce protested, "you—"

"*You* listen, lieutenant! My cover is blown, but I'm still under contract here. Even if I break it and let Rudy's goons bust my kneecaps, where would I go? This place is at least sleazy enough to scare most of the gossip columnists away. Assuming I could bone up for the bar exam in another state, how would I explain all the gaps on my resumé, the lack of references? As for that teaching job you mentioned, I can kiss that in the ass goodbye, too. Thanks, chum. With shits like you for a friend, who needs enemas?"

For a moment, in his exhaustion and frustration, Bryce could feel anger throbbing in his ears. He stood, moved to the side of the red-head's chair and slapped the folder onto his thighs.

"You're a self-pitying fool, McKenna. If I just wanted to use you for cheap publicity, why have I studied all this until my eyes are crossed?" He returned to his chair near the door.

McKenna looked at the title page of the first article, dealing with the color significance of the etheric double. There were several other articles touching on various aspects of aural sensitivity in certified psychics. Two more studies debated spirit channeling, the controversial, disputed phenomenon of serving as an intermediary between the dead and the living. All of the articles were heavily notated and ink-smudged in the margins from constantly being handled.

"You mean," McKenna said slowly, "that you already knew all that crap you were asking me a couple days ago in Helzer's office?"

Bryce nodded. "I was just comparing notes. I've scanned the titles of your library over there under the cot and knew you were up on this stuff. Use your head. Why would I get Milo on my case and the brass downtown pissed just to play one sloppy long shot?"

McKenna was obviously relenting. "Nah, you're right. The long shot doesn't seem like your style. You'd be more likely to win the game patiently on rebounds and free throws."

"Then we're still working together?"

McKenna fished a beat-up pack of cigarettes from his shirt pocket and shook one out. "All bent to shit," he grumbled, straightening it as best he could and lighting it anyway. Finally he said, "Why not? For one thing, I doubt that the Incredible Shoneen would qualify for unemployment benefits if he's forced to quit here. Besides, every swinging dick between Orleans and Alaska knows by now anyway. Hell, why'ncha just get me one of those t-shirts that says Property of NOPD?"

"Good," Bryce said, tuning out everything but

the first part of McKenna's response. 'Then tell me something, and don't get pissed at me, okay? Just *tell* me. Is it true, like these articles claim, that certain psychotics—I'm talking about the ones who are way around the bend—have a distinctive electromagnetic field color? At least to the eyes of some psychics?''

McKenna nodded. "Sure it's true. But not just surrounding psychotics. It's also possible to spot auras around epileptics and even normal people who would, say, be highly susceptible to hypnosis or an authority figure.''

"What color do *you* see?''

"The range is from light amber to deep infrared, but I can't always see them. For one thing, I have to be sober and rested. Even then I'm usually aware of other psychic sensitives more than crazies.''

"What color are other psychics?''

"For me, always blue.''

"Aren't the fruits as easy to spot as the psychics?''

McKenna looked at his hands. "Maybe. There's sure as hell more of them. But staring at a psychotic's aura is kinda like . . . I can't explain the feeling you get . . . kinda like staring at puke. It's not something you normally do.''

"But when you look at any aura, what do you actually see?'' Bryce persisted. "One article said something about a luminous mist.''

"Sorry, old sleuth, that says it as well as I can. No offense, but you might as well ask me to describe the feeling of a hard-on to a eunuch.''

161

Bryce couldn't resist a brief grin. "Sounds like a pretty flattering description of psychic power, coming from you."

"You're right."

Bryce thought of the East Bank murder yesterday. "Tell me something else. How did Candelaria's corpse sit up and talk?"

"Yeah, I've been wondering about that myself."

McKenna shifted uncomfortably in the recliner, brushing some ashes off his shirt. "I guess I'd answer you this way. There are three possibilities. One, it wasn't yet a clinically nerve-dead corpse, and all three witnesses are full of malarkey. Two, it was a case of psychokinesis. Three—"

"Whoa," Bryce said. "Say again?"

"Psychokinesis. You know—PK. Moving objects with the mind or will or whatever the hell you call that buzz inside your head. Like those show-offs who bend spoons and roll cueballs across a pool table without touching them."

"You're saying—"

"That a corpse is theoretically no different than a cueball. It's an object. So in principle it can be moved by a PK, a psychokinetic."

"Do you think these PK's are legit?"

McKenna hedged. "Let's just say that I've never met one, but I wouldn't leave the neighborhood if one moved in."

"Thanks for settling that question so decisively. Okay, so what about the third possibility?"

"You won't like it," McKenna warned him.

"I don't like spinach either, but I eat it."

"Okay, smartass, the third possibility is that the same influence that moved that corpse also turned the driver of the jeep into a killer."

"That's . . ." Bryce paused.

McKenna grinned and finished the sentence for him. "Crazy? You got it. Crazy and something else."

"I have read something about the evil eye," Bryce finally conceded.

"You bet you have," McKenna said. "The effect's been verified by researchers studying Navajo black magic and the voodoo cults, among others. And the more its victims are prone to believe, the stronger the effect. It would also be consistent with the fact that the first two victims died ambiguously of generalized nervous system failure."

And it might explain something else, thought McKenna, like that nightmare vignette two days ago in Helzer's office. *Could* it have been premonitory? But hell no, how could he ever conceivably commit such a heinous act against anyone, let alone Bryce's kid, a kid he liked, one who'd never hurt him? McKenna knew he was a bitter, even hateful, man, but he also knew the limits of that bitterness and hatred. What he had seen was impossible, a psychotic fancy, not a premonition. It had been maliciously induced hallucination. After all, he argued fiercely with himself, the seeds for such vivid but harmless nightmares were inside all of us. Who hadn't felt it when holding a very young bird or kitten or even a newborn baby—that omnipotent, shivery realization that the power to destroy life is literally in your hands?

Thus ruminating, McKenna missed what Bryce said. "What?"

"I said, do you mind taking a little ride with me after your act tonight?"

"Sounds sinister. A little ride to where?"

Bryce shrugged. "No particular destination. Just cruise around the East Bank, listen to some good music."

His meaning dawned on McKenna. "Cruise around, Yeah, I'm snapping on. And of course you're figuring I'll be mentally hyped and sober right after my act."

Bryce deferred the point by standing up. Again for a moment he was tempted to ask McKenna about that experience Tuesday in Helzer's office, but he decided not to push his luck just yet. His glance fell to the floor and the smudged white carton with its plastic fork anchored in a clot of cold rice.

The sight reminded him of something he'd been mulling over since the wire service story had blown McKenna's cover, namely the fact that one of the people likely to know his whereabouts was Johnny Law himself.

"Listen," he said, "my name wasn't mentioned in that article or on the TV report. You're welcome to stay at my place for awhile. We've got plenty of room. Kyla only cooks three nights a week, but she usually fixes up a casserole or something for the other nights. Sonny's been asking about you. I know he'd be glad to have you."

"Thanks," McKenna said hastily, "but for now I think I'll just hide behind the bouncers."

"Well, the offer's open."

"Thanks again," McKenna said, averting his eyes. "Maybe sometime I'll take you up on it."

Neal Bryce whunked the heavy Sheffield butcher knife down hard and interrupted Sonny to warn "Watch your fingers."

Sonny was rinsing vegetables at the sink and sliding them along the gold-flecked Formica counter to Bryce, who flipped them onto a scarred cutting board; after rapidly and expertly slicing, dicing, or paring them, he tilted the board over a wok and used the duller edge of the Sheffield to scrape each new contribution into the sizzling peanut oil.

It was hard to tell whether Sonny was nodding carelessly at Bryce's warning or just shaking the dark bangs out of his eyes.

"But the Honda Aero 50 is my favorite," he resumed enthusiastically. "The speedometer goes up to fifty, and there's a rack on the rear fender where I could tie a stack of newspapers. Plus—"

"Hand me those mushrooms," Bryce interrupted absently.

The Sheffield whunked down over and over, destroying the soft pale umbrellas. The mushrooms were followed by a bunch of green onions, a red pepper, the bright green wrinkled pods of a handful of snow peas. Bryce added each in turn to the strips of beef Kyla had cut and tenderized for them yesterday. The sukiyaki sizzled and sputtered momentarily when he added a tablespoon of white chablis as the final gourmet touch.

Bryce became aware that he was thinking too much about Stevie Lasalle's tropical flower scent instead of listening to Sonny. He stirred the sukiyaki and said, "You do know—right? —that state law says you have to be fifteen for a license to drive a motor scooter?"

Sonny nodded. "Yeah, but couldn't I maybe just ride it in the driveway?"

The kid's pleading eyes made Bryce grin. "I suppose so, but don't you think the view might get kind of boring? Anyway, how much do these Aero 50's cost?"

Sonny hesitated. "About seven hundred bucks."

"And how much have you got saved up?"

The pause was even longer this time. "About two hundred, I think. Maybe a little more, even."

"Well, how about we discuss it again when you're closer to having the price?"

Throughout the kitchen early evening sunlight was quivering in gold splashes. A brass ceiling fan with wooden blades twirled lazily overhead. Behind them, a dado wall topped by a shelf of unvarnished red sandalwood separated the kitchen from the cool dark shadows of the living room.

Distracted, Bryce was stirring the sukiyaki too

frequently and adding too much soy sauce. He didn't notice that Sonny was watching him more closely than usual from under his curtain of bangs.

"Neal?"

"Hmm?"

"That Wade guy who was in the paper yesterday? He's the same one who did the magic tricks at my birthday party, right?"

Bryce was caught off guard. He had forgotten that the kid sometimes actually read the product he delivered.

"Yeah, same guy."

"Well, why did Scott Liedel's mom call him a sidekick?"

For a long puzzled moment Bryce forgot to stir. Then he laughed. "I think you mean psychic."

The 12-year-old frowned slightly with offended dignity. "No, she said sidekick." His face relented a bit. "I *think*."

Bryce started ad-libbing a lame definition of the word psychic, but just then Sonny remembered something else and cut him off.

"*Un momento*! I forgot. I got something to show you!" He turned the water off, hastily dried his hands on the thighs of his jeans and raced toward his bedroom.

Bryce laid two places at the table and set out the salad and dessert frappé Kyla had prepared yesterday. He poured a cup of coffee for himself, fizzling ginger ale for Sonny.

"*Mira*," said the boy, holding something out across the dado wall. "*Qué* dices, hombre? I got it for two bucks at the flea market. Works just like new."

Bryce glanced at the dull silver purchase. "Neat," he said without too much enthusiasm. "Come on, let's eat. I have to go back out tonight."

"Neat? God, what a boffo! It's totally awesome!"

Sonny brandished the Black & Decker drill like it was a ray gun. "Zap! Take that, Darth Vader!"

Bryce distorted one side of his face like a man suffering a stroke, jerked both hands to his neck and pretended to be dying a grisly death. "Ahharrg . . . !"

Sonny howled a victory cheer and started to dash back toward his room with the drill when Bryce shouted out behind him.

"Don't run with that in your hand! And you know the rule on tools, partner. They go out in the garage, not in your room!"

CHAPTER NINE

HARLAN PERRY CLUTCHED HIS BLACK LUNCHPAIL protectively and swung extra wide to avoid the infection zone of a fellow pedestrian approaching him along Decatur Street.

"Lissenup, people," barked Johnny Law's voice inside him. *"Don't clusterfuck asshole to bellybutton! This area is lousy with Claymores. Spread out in a squad vee and keep at least twenty feet apart."*

Besides his unbuttoned forest-green military raincoat, he wore the blue work uniform he had purchased while living in Houston—the one with his name stitched in red script over the right pocket—and a pair of cream-colored sneakers. They were stained a grungy gray from continually slopping filthy mop water on them. His hair still protruded in sweaty spikes from the previous night's shift. In the wan morning light, his skin was anemic and sickly.

He paused in front of the closed-up Tahitian Palace to read the crude Incredible Shoneen poster. The flamboyant purple letters and the figure lying on the bed of nails seemed to mock him secretly. *We'll put slimy cancerous parasites in your brain yet, Harley boy, oh yes, we will, we'll put . . .*

He scowled and stepped back, tucking the lunchpail up under one arm so he could jam both fists into his raincoat pockets.

Thanks to the newspapers, he had learned exactly who and what The Incredible Shoneen was. More important, he had learned that this extraordinarily talented Political-Carcinogenic Agent had gone undercover in an elaborate bid to interfere with Johnny Law's holy mission of Cosmic Chemotherapy—destroying the infected cells and regenerating the diseased body of society. Of course McKenna would have to be surgically removed, lanced, scraped away.

Unfortunately, the interior of Rudy's Tahitian Palace would be crawling with carcinogens; other PCA's would be planted everywhere, waiting to infect him through the first vulnerable orifice of his body. But he would watch and wait, get to know McKenna's comings and goings, who his friends were. Then . . .

Somebody passing behind him suddenly sneezed and Perry's blood turned into Freon.

Moving swiftly before the assassin's germ cloud could envelope him, the janitor resumed his trek toward downtown. Once again he resisted an urge to don the gauze surgical mask in his pocket. It was too conspicuous in the daylight hours.

As he hurried along, he constantly scanned the surrounding windows for snipers and maintained a wide personal space. His head throbbed with dull pain, but the thought of his victory two days ago at the Burger Boy made Perry dizzy with elation. The long-distance weapons were developing nicely, he decided.

Despite the heat and his coat, goose flesh was crawling up both arms as he savored a momentary foretaste of his greatness. He was rubber-kneed from the sensation of realizing his awesome might, his equally awesome responsibility. Thus exalted, Perry felt flagrantly insulted when he turned the corner toward St. Charles Avenue and encountered the graffiti: MY MOTHER MADE ME A HOMOSEXUAL.

Blurry but still fresh black letters had been spray-painted against the white-plastered wall of an automotive parts store. Below this line was added in a different style and brown letters: IF I BUY HER THE MATERIAL, WILL SHE MAKE ME ONE, TOO?

Cute. Real cute. The kind of garbage men had time for when they were capable of no better service to their country.

But to be fair, he reminded himself, most of them weren't entirely to blame. A high rise emerged into view ahead, glass and white marble twinkling, and he quickened his pace, thinking again of the pretty, scarred slut with the cancer-planting machine.

There was an upper echelon commander! That was clear from her access to the machine and the frustrating security of her living arrangements. But Perry again remembered his long-distance victory last Wednesday; then he thought of that black security guard on duty in the lobby of Stevie Lasalle's apartment building, the one with the deep amber aura.

True, it was only amber, not the throbbing infrared of the jeep's driver. Perry didn't really understand or care about all the subtle nuances of meaning inherent in the color of a person's psychic aura. *The Story of the Terrible Crystal* assured that eventually all colors were subdued by the Tuaoi master's increasing skill. But instinct told him that, for now, the enemy wore blue—blue auras—and his potential allies, red. Amber was somewhere in between. Meaning the smiling security guard could eventually be rehabilitated and enlisted in the great cause of Cosmic Chemotherapy.

Perry checked for traffic and crossed the wide avenue, his eyes narrowing as they fixated on the double glass doors. He selected the cleanest of several benches scattered among the bike racks in front of the high rise, then sat down at the best angle to turn his face away if *she* came or went unexpectedly. Though of course this was Friday and Perry knew, from extended observation, that she always drove her car on Fridays because that was her shopping day.

He also knew that the religious fanatics out front would leave him alone over here. Perry recognized the one who always wore the I'M

GOING STEADY WITH JESUS badge. His acne-pocked face, thought the janitor with a shuddering tingle, would be a hotbed for carcinogenic infiltrators. Hardly what you'd call officer material. Who else *but* Jesus could love such a loser wimp? Maybe there would be time to play with Bible Boy later.

Duncan Hilliard's bristly profile abruptly appeared beyond the glass doors and interrupted his thoughts; Perry's lips formed a thin rictus of a smile as his fingers reached for the chrome-plated snaps of the lunchbox.

Goddamn all of you, he would soon be ready!

Stevie approached her building from behind, guiding the silver Peugot 504 into the sunken parking deck which comprised half of the structure's ground floor.

It was the middle of a Friday morning, and the parking area was nearly deserted. Stevie angled in beside a concrete pylon with her apartment number stenciled on it. She glanced around carefully before she slid out and locked the door behind her. Wearing a cool green dashiki and white kid sandals, she carried a mesh shopping bag.

Despite the parking area's generous fluorescent lighting, ominous shadows blurred the corners. Stevie felt only a momentary dent in the upbeat mood which had started Wednesday during her self-defense class. Then again this morning the class had run like clockwork. The women were developing confidence and a deeper understanding of the notion that effective self-defense included much more than bottom line physical combat. Plus, her constant dread of injuries during contact sessions was so far proving groundless.

She swung her purchases as she walked toward the double blue doors marked TO LOBBY AND STREET. With the class behind her and her shopping completed, the only remaining obligation today was an afternoon lecture at the medical school. Meaning she could—*would*, she amended—devote plenty of time to the next chapter of her textbook revision.

A low-slung Trans Am parked near the exit doors formed a blind side against the wall to her left; no longer even conscious of the evasive precaution, she swung wide to guarantee herself adequate reaction time, if needed. Though she appeared to be looking straight ahead at the door, she was also relying on an acute peripheral vision sharpened by the eye-strengthening exercises she practiced during her *katas*.

Inside the lobby Duncan Hilliard was assisting a wheelchair-bound tenant through the street entrance. Beyond the glass doors Stevie caught a glimpse of the day's flawless blue sky. Outside it was humid, but only a few wispy vapors of cloud drifted over Lake Pontchartrain northwest of the city.

The sight reinforced her good mood. Afraid she might tempt the religious fanatics outside, she didn't walk close enough to the doors to see the scruffy creep in the military raincoat, sitting and staring intently at the entrance. A black lunchbox lay open on his lap.

Again something tried to dispell her good mood, but she resisted its persuasion. Stevie knew that Duncan would stand outside chatting with Mrs. Kruger until a city handicap van arrived for her. Besides, tenants were permitted behind the unlocked counter when the guard wasn't present or on duty.

Only one note was in her slot, and she recognized the paper instantly as one of Dr. Charles Wright's official prescription blanks. The fine angles of her face seemed chiseled even more sharply for a few moments as she unfolded the note:

> *Stevie, You can't run from your past and you can't run from me. If you don't call me soon, I'm going to do something embarrassing like come to one of your lectures and cause a big scene in front of your students.* Get in touch!

Crash, she thought glumly. Her good mood was now officially destroyed, but the anger she felt this time was a little duller, the guilt gnawing at her stomach more acute. Not facing him was worse than irresponsible, it was mean. It would be unpleasant, but she resolved to call him and break it off civilly, if that were possible. If not, at least he would be duly notified that she was not interested.

As she stepped back around the counter, tucking the note absently into her mesh bag, she realized that at least a small part of her present emotional turbulence was disappointment. For a brief moment she had almost hoped the note was from Neal Bryce, police business or otherwise.

My, my, how sappy and romantic we're being, she thought immediately, trying to chastise herself with scorn. They were professionals collaborating to solve a crime, nothing more. Didn't she already have enough problems with Wright? Besides, she was sure that Bryce was one of those arrogant, conceited Texas imports who were insufferably boring and possessive once you got to know them.

She was about to cross toward the bank of elevators when the front doors opened and Duncan was approaching her.

She mustered enough cheerfulness to greet him with the usual smile. "Hello, Duncan. How go things with you?"

"Doin' okay, I guess. Considering what I'm paid compared to *some* people." He passed her brusquely and went behind the counter.

She would have been surprised enough by the lack of enthusiasm in his voice, but the all-too-obvious surliness was a genuine shock. When she tried to search his face, he pretended to be busy with the security log.

She was still staring at him in confusion when he looked up and met her eyes. She paused, waiting, some vague dread quickening her pulse. Why did his white scruff of chin whiskers suddenly make her think of foaming muzzles and rabid dogs?

He winked and flashed his gold-brimming smile. She relaxed her breath and felt the ten-

176

sion fleeing from her neck and shoulders. Stevie realized now that, being preoccupied, she must have missed his irony. She had only foolishly imagined the sullen rancor in his eyes.

He was only joking after all.

Bryce was dimly aware that the Liszt tape had reached the Mephisto Waltz section, his favorite movement on side two. Late morning traffic moved sluggishly in the heat. He was forced to wait through three complete cycles of the stoplight, the Olds' temperature gauge crawling further and further to the right, before he could turn onto Arno Street.

The air conditioner was whispering softly. Outside, heat blurs shimmered over the pavement. The pedestrians were moving in slow motion, many of them with faces obscured by wide-brimmed hats and parasols. The color seemed to bleach from everything, transforming the city into a weird, monochromic lunar landscape.

Bryce, wearing a nylon shirt and cool white ducks, eyed the pedestrians and wondered which one was Johnny Law and which one would be Johnny Law's next victim.

He doubted that the fast-food employee he was about to question could really help him. But he had already struck out with the two passengers in the jeep, and Jim Bevell, the driver, was in an unresponsive fugue state—or so claimed his lawyer. Baptiste had run a thorough R & I on Bevell. His history showed a pattern of moderately aggressive behavior—brawling, mostly, and otherwise disturbing the peace. Bryce knew that at least two counselors at the seafood cannery where Bevell worked had labeled him emotionally disturbed, but not psychotic.

Bryce signaled a lane change and eased around a line of orange road construction barrels. The question that had been nagging him since Delbert's report hit his desk now recurred. Was this the record of a man crazy enough to kill like Jim Bevell had killed two days ago?

Somehow Bryce didn't think so. The record of a potential slime, yes. A wife beater, maybe, or a child abuser. But a pathological killer? No way. Unbidden, McKenna's words leaped forth from memory: *The third possibility is that the same influence which moved that corpse also turned the driver of the jeep into a killer.*

Desperate for any distraction, Bryce noticed that his cigar had gone out in the ashtray. He relit it, but he promptly forgot the panatela and let it go out again as his thoughts shunted off along another track.

The first 'aura spotting' patrol with Wade McKenna, last night after his act, had proven a disappointing trial run. The psychic was in a scratchy mood, as usual, and smelled as if he had sneaked a few quick ones between acts. Whatever the reason, Bryce thought, he sure as hell hadn't spotted any etheric doubles with the distinctive red shade of a raving psychotic.

Bryce flicked his eyes toward the rearview mirror and saw his own self-doubt reflected there. Was Milo right? Was this preoccupation with a so-called psychic just one way of avoiding the fact that this case was stumping him? And wasn't something even deeper bothering him about Johnny Law, something personal, something he couldn't quite face? For the first time Bryce permitted himself to consider the possibility that in a bizarre way he and the psychopathic mad slasher might be soul mates.

He was leaning more and more toward the theory that Johnny Law was using the Vietnam War touches—the recruiting slogans, the sensational ear amputations—as a type of demented wish fulfillment. So in a sense, the cop knew that the man they sought could be suffering an extreme version of a condition which afflicted himself and millions of other normal men honest enough to admit it—namely, vague, half-formed doubts about whether or not they were in fact "men" in the ultimate sense of the word, i.e. combat-tested warriors.

The tape player clicked off and Bryce absently flipped the Liszt cassette, forgetting he had already listened to the other side. Had he tried hard enough to reach the front or had he been secretly relieved when his old man's interference kept him at the rear in Danang? If that were true, it might mean his present profession was just an elaborate ruse to continue fooling himself. After all, in nearly a decade of his brand of police work, he had never once fired a gun in the line of duty except to requalify every six months on a target range. He no longer even carried one, though he was authorized to. Nor had he ever once been shot at.

Ben Davis would understand what he felt

because he had proven himself under fire. Even that bragging old fart Milo had passed the test. And if passing that test means so much to me, Bryce thought, what might it do to obsess a madman like Johnny Law?

Lost in reverie, Bryce was only dimly aware of the busy K-Mart plaza rolling by on his right, the A-frame Burger Boy popping into view just beyond it. Soon, he told himself, he would have to arrange a meeting between Wade McKenna and Stevie Lasalle. Bryce was dreading the potential personality clash he suspected would result, but they had to meet for a brainstorming session.

Bryce was incapable of exploiting their individual talents by himself, and he knew it. Just as he knew that the slasher would strike again.

As he signaled and slowed for the right turn into Burger Boy's parking lot, a brief thought of Ben Davis knotted his stomach in frustration. The vet knew something, but Bryce couldn't prove that and he mistrusted his own hunches. Hunches were McKenna's racket, not a cop's.

Have you ever been to New Orleans or anyplace close?

Closest I ever been is the one time I spent 15 minutes at Houston International . . .

It was still a half hour or so before the usual clamoring confusion of K-Mart shoppers and employees would descend on the Burger Boy for lunch. Bryce unbuckled his shoulder harness and stepped out of the air-conditioned car, the heat radiating off the asphalt already intense. He immediately felt warm beads of sweat crawling through his scalp.

He spotted the car as soon as he started toward Burger Boy's side doors—a familiar Ford sedan with a U. S. Government Interagency Motorpool number on the license plate. Bryce realized immediately that the feds were horning in on him and which particular fed it no doubt was.

As if timed for dramatic effect, the Burger Boy's pneumatic door sighed open and Reno Morgan emerged into the glaring heat.

Bryce watched him pull Foster Grants out of the breast pocket of his tan jacket and slip them on. Morgan was over six foot, large-framed and balding, with a hard, intelligent face that Bryce couldn't imagine ever lapsing into a smile. He knew that his chief reason for disliking the man—besides a run-in they'd had years earlier in Vietnam when Bryce was assigned to the Army's Criminal Investigation Division—was the fact that Morgan sometimes reminded him of his own father.

Bryce quickened his pace to make sure he would cross Morgan's line of vision before the agent reached his car.

"Well, well. Neal Bryce. King of the GI drug pushers and the pride of the Khaki Mafia."

Bryce knew the sudden heat in his face was caused by more than just the weather. That incident a decade and a half ago in Danang, when Bryce had helped a Navy pilot beat a trumped-up drug smuggling charge, still rankled in Morgan's craw, no doubt because the rookie government operative had spearheaded the FBI's aborted case.

"I won't even ask," Bryce replied, "what you're doing here. I mean, turn over a rock and you'll always find the slugs clinging underneath."

Morgan brushed past him, hunching one shoulder and deliberately elbowing the taller man off balance for a moment, but Bryce caught himself and quickly lifted the side of his foot to trip Morgan. The agent seemed to tread water for a moment, trying to recover, before spinning halfway around and plopping heavily onto his can. Bryce chuckled and headed toward the restaurant again.

"Don't push it, rich boy," Morgan shouted behind him. "You're built just like your dick— all length and no muscle!"

The Texan paused, turned around and met the mirror-surface shields over Morgan's eyes. The man had struggled to his feet and was angrily slapping dust off his trousers. Bryce smiled the irritatingly sweet smile he usually reserved for Milo.

"Who would be in a better position to know that than a professional ass kisser like you?" he asked reasonably. "Besides, I never hear your wife complaining about my diameter."

Morgan's jaw muscle bunched into tight knots. He took a quick step toward Bryce.

The goading smile bled slowly from the tall detective's face. What remained was an undisguised mask of contempt and hatred. "Yes?" he invited softly. "You'd like to pursue the matter?"

Morgan hesitated, pointing a thick finger at Bryce. "Enjoy it now, Bryce. You won't act so smug once you get your ass reamed out like Milo did yesterday up on the hill. You dipshits at BSI are screwing this one up royally, and you're gonna lose it. The heavies on the City Council are tired of you jeopardizing the entire city while you play the media hotshot with some washed-up psychic fake. You think—listen to me, Bryce!"

But Bryce had already tossed him a snappy two-fingered salute and was heading for the door.

The fast-food palace featured swivel-mounted orange plastic half-shell chairs that swung out only halfway from the tables. Bryce was forced to sit sideways on one buttock to keep his knees from poking up into the gum stuck underneath the table.

"And that was just about it," the girl concluded. "After I took their order and told them what it came to, I did my usual spiel about telling them to pay for it at the pick-up window. But they never stopped there. I heard the driver gunning his motor like crazy, then the next thing, everybody's all screaming that some guy got run over."

Cheryl Lance sat across from him, sipping from a medium Diet Pepsi and wearing the rust-colored slacks and jumper of the Burger

Boy uniform. She was cute and plump, about 19, with deep blue valleys of eye shadow and a pert little nose. Her dishwater-blonde hair was done in a buzzer cut that swept it to one side of her head.

"What kind of mood did he seem to be in?" Bryce asked. "The driver, I mean."

The girl looked puzzled.

"You know—was he impatient with you, did he kid around or make small talk or anything?"

Cheryl Lance glanced around the restaurant self-consciously. This was her second police interview this morning, and she knew she was the talk of her fellow employees. She was simultaneously embarrassed and thrilled about speaking to a detective, even one that looked funny with his legs all scrunched up like a praying mantis. Actually, she thought, he was kind of cute, if you were into straight-looking guys old enough to be your dad. At least he smiled once in a while, which was more than she could say for the creep who just left.

"Well, he sorta flirted, I guess."

"How do you mean?"

She stared into her Diet Pepsi as if she were reading her cue in the crushed ice.

"You know how we always go, 'May I take your order?' Well, he goes, 'Baby, you can take all I got,' or something like that."

Bryce politely glanced away until her slight blush had passed. "Anything else?"

She shook her head.

"Did he or anybody else in the jeep look strange to you—weird facial expressions, gestures, whatever? Like maybe they were high on something?"

Again she shook her head.

"Was his voice unusual in any way?"

"No. Except maybe," the girl added, "it was kinda deep and loud, 'cause he was shouting into the speaker. I thought maybe he'd get that nut across the street going."

Bryce narrowed his eyes slightly. "What nut?"

"Some guy over there." She pointed vaguely toward the row of tenements across the street. "I don't know which place it is, exactly, but some kook is always screaming at us to shut up. It's the speakers that get him pissed."

Practically herniating himself to do it, Bryce shifted in his chair to look in the direction she had pointed. Through the broad front window he saw a dull red facade broken only by tattered shades, yellowed Venetian blinds and the occasional shabby blanket serving as curtain. The brick walls seemed to ooze a greasy patina of sweat in the heat.

By squinting, he could just make out the peeling decal numerals of the address directly across the street: 421½.

He glanced one last time across the street. Already he was wondering why he'd bothered to copy the address down. That damn speaker *was* loud and raucous; Bryce had flinched himself when he had heard it while walking across the parking lot. Whoever was blowing off steam was probably just some working stiff understandably pissed at missing valuable sleep. Still, there was a chance in a hundred he or someone else across the street might have seen or heard something. Bryce decided he'd make it a moderate priority and have Patterson talk to a few of the tenants.

Scowling at the perverse acrobatics demanded by his chair, he squirmed around to face Cheryl Lance again. There were just a few more perfunctory questions.

Yolanda Davis was pretty in the pale moonlight, her face a smooth ebony glow against the pillow. Peaceful sleep and the flattering moonlight combined to erase the fine network of creases at the corners of her eyes. Only one thought had troubled her while drifting down that slow escalator into sleep, repeating itself with metronomic insistence. Ben's dream was recurring more frequently now.

The huge elm tree standing sentry outside the dormer windows shivered in a cool wind, rattling its limbs like a clumsy, shaggy scarecrow. The leaves fluttered and turned the bedroom into a fantasy chamber of amorphous shadows that moved across the bed and the room's ornately carved Chippendale furniture.

Beside the sleeping woman, her husband was stretched rigid on his back while his terrified face sweat-glistened in the moonlight.

Corporal Benjamin Davis was losing his cherry.

. . . *dead oh God dead, most of his unit are dead but Cherry Boy's M-16 is bucking, exploding, puking spent rounds like sparks*

. . . *atta boy Cherry Boy . . .*

oh God no, dead, most of them are dead but Cherry Boy slaps home a fresh magazine and takes up the slack and kills kills kills, tucks and rolls just like in training because war is his business and business is good

. . . atta boy Cherry Boy, let's fry some slopes . . .

dead oh God dead, most of them are dead but not that white sergeant yelling beside him, lord that boy is pale but he's mean so goddamn mean

. . . atta boy Cherry Boy, just me and you, we can do it but take cover, Cherry Boy you stupid crazy fucking nigger, you want to die . . .

The enemy grenade rolls across his boot and Cherry Boy screams . . .

. . . and wakes up clinging to life, to hope, to the warm comforting breast of his main reason for not putting an end to all this hell sooner.

CHAPTER TEN

IT HAD BEEN MORE DIFFICULT THIS MORNING TO achieve the no-mindedness of *mushin*.

But Stevie finally found the rhythm of pure unmeditated movement. Her bare feet made smooth, slithering noises on the vinyl mats as she advanced back and forth across the simple training room. No movement was wasted when she executed the highly stylized practice forms. She chambered for a roundhouse kick, snapped her foot in a fast delivery, rechambered and delivered a jump kick. Her hands vectored the air in a fast follow-up series of precisely controlled hand chops. Stevie completed the attack cycle with a spinning back fist, then returned down to the mats executing a completely different series of *katas* from the more than fifty patterns she knew.

Her pretty, serene face reflected the stillness of an uncluttered mind. Action was not slowed down by thought, but instead was in a total harmony with it. She was the dancer who had become one with the dance.

But the dance had to end. Her infallible internal clock told Stevie it was almost 8 A.M. and time to get on with the mundane fact of living. Gradually, the usual thoughts began to move once again along the path of conscious awareness.

It was Monday, she reminded herself, the third day since a horrible incident out front had threatened to encroach on her little bastion of safety here on the eleventh floor of one of the most secure apartment buildings in the city.

She untied the knot of her belt, peeled off the crisp white cotton jacket and stuffed it in the wicker laundry hamper. She showered and returned, naked and pink-mottled from the stream of hot water, to the opulent luxury of her bedroom. Stevie crossed to the wide closet and selected a pair of sleek leather pumps and a navy two-piece linen suit.

She dressed, the finely sculpted face preoccupied with something, then checked her appearance in the long oval glass beside her dressing table. Again, as she gathered up her rich, tawny hair, she thought about what had happened out front last Friday, apparently only minutes after she had left again in her Peugot. This rumination naturally led to the thought of Neal Bryce's most recent request.

This afternoon he wanted her to meet Wade

McKenna, that supposed psychic the papers had sensationalized. Stevie's feelings about the impending meeting were mixed. The rationalist in her was angry for wasting valuable time on a probable hoax, time that should be spent on revising her textbook, but the broader, more eclectic scientist in her was curious to examine this supposed freak of mental nature at closer range. Like most specialists in her field, she had already tried to investigate firsthand the boasts of self-proclaimed psychics. But in fact she had not met or observed one yet who she believed was anything more than a clever stage magician in the fascinating but fabricated tradition of Uri Geller or The Amazing Kreskin.

Still musing, one hand trapping the knot of hair against the back of her neck, she turned toward the ivory-inlaid dressing table beside her to grab her favorite hairpin.

She paused, free hand still outstretched over the table, and frowned. Faint puzzle lines appeared at the corners of her nostrils.

Her filigreed silver jewelery box had been moved.

She always kept it at the right-hand edge of the table so she could reach it from in front of the mirror. Now it sat way over on the left edge. She could not remember moving it.

But she must have, she realized, unless she decided to believe in poltergeists.

She went out to the kitchen and opened a can of cat food. Hearing the familiar whine of the electric can opener, Mr. Cat came padding in from the living room. The chubby, dark-striped tabby plopped himself down imperiously in the middle of the tile floor, yawning in a show of indifference.

Mr. Cat had always been more finicky and aloof than some cats, but Stevie noticed that he wasn't brushing against her ankles like he usually did at mealtime. And he had spent more time than usual this weekend hiding under the living room sofa. He didn't usually act weird like this except . . . except on the rare occasions when she had visitors. It was as if someone had been up here recently, but that was impossible. She was imagining things, just inventing ominous signs because she was still jittery about what had happened out front last Friday.

After all, she reasoned as she set Mr. Cat's plastic dish down on the floor, the only other person with access to her apartment was Duncan.

Stevie emerged from her high rise into a day redolent with golden morning sunshine. The humidity had dissipated during the night, and the steady mimosa-scented breeze felt like the cool fingers of a gentle blind person exploring her face.

The fanatics were conspicuously absent today. She fended off a shudder and tried not to dwell on what had happened, but the *Times-Picayune* box just outside the foyer drew her gaze with magnetic force:

POLICE FIND NO CLUES IN FOURTH MYSTERIOUS DEATH

The front page story no longer rated the lead

headline, but she noticed it was still above the fold. Angry at herself for being too curious to pass on by, she stooped slightly to scan the first few paragraphs. There was nothing new except a mention that local FBI officials were watching developments closely and were "eager to assist local law enforcement personnel." The story repeated the address of her building and reiterated that last Friday an itinerant street evangelist had leaped to his death in front of a city bus after screaming, in front of several witnesses, "God is dead and Johnny Law rules!"

Stevie already knew, from the fuzzy photo in Saturday's paper, that the victim had been the *Revelations*-spouting fanatic who wore the I'M GOING STEADY WITH JESUS badge.

Four deaths had been linked somehow to the elusive Johnny Law, and as Bryce had gloomily pointed out to her during his latest request for help, this incident downtown broke the pattern of being confined to the riverside area of East Bank.

But why her building? Like most rationalists, Stevie was particularly troubled by coincidence.

She had straightened back up, tightened her grip on the Swiss briefcase and taken several steps in the direction of the campus when the small hairs on the back of her neck began to stiffen.

She whirled around and surveyed the broad sidewalk behind her. It was practically deserted except for a gaggle of laughing office girls and an impatient mother dragging a small child in each hand. But hadn't someone dressed in green ducked into the lobby of the next building?

Deep below the surface of memory something stirred—an image of an ugly little man with wired eyeballs backing away from her, his face a revolting mask of fear and hatred and insanity. *I know what you're doing to me. . . .*

But the image immediately sank back again into the oblivious realm of the forgotten. Already Stevie's disciplined mind was focusing on the morning's upcoming self-defense class.

"We have a very dedicated crew of aggressors this semester."

Her voice was raised against the vast hollowness of the gym.

"So let's convince them their time hasn't been wasted. And stay safety conscious. You've been excellent about that so far."

Stevie hadn't intended the 'so far' part as a joke, but she noticed several female students and male volunteers grinning a bit self-consciously.

"Any questions before we break for mat drill?" she added. Stevie gave them plenty of time, her huge gray eyes making contact with each of them individually.

A sweatsuited woman in the front row of the bleachers raised her hand. "Should we *kiai*?"

The men had been attending less often, and a few of them looked puzzled.

"*Kiai*," Stevie explained, pronouncing the word key-eye and turning slightly to face the visitors better, "refers to the powerful sound or shout used to unnerve an attacker and embolden the defender. It also helps concentration, and the sharp expulsion of breath will tighten the muscles. A couple weeks ago we debated its use."

She turned again to the woman who had asked the question. "I can't tell you whether or not to use it, Marsha. A good old simple but healthy scream can sometimes distract an attacker, especially at the moment you're starting a particular move. But screaming and shouting also require energy; overdoing them can tire you out and work in your attacker's favor. If you do experiment with *kiai*, be judicious."

The woman nodded.

"Any more questions?"

Silence from both ends of the bleachers.

"Okay then!"

Stevie clapped her hands once sharply, reiterated the safety rules, then delivered her predrill summary. "Remember, you absolutely refuse to be a passive victim. Take control immediately and become the aggressor. Look through your attacker's eyes, not into them, and face him obliquely to provide the smallest possible target. Dodge, feint, attack."

She finished her spiel, then sent them to the mats. For the next 20 minutes she circulated among the struggling couples. She paused occasionally to demonstrate a movement or exchange a word with one of the students. The intramural gym echoed with grunts, the sharp sound of skin slapping mats, an occasional guttural shout or piercing scream as someone practiced her *kiai*.

Stevie was correcting a student's kicking technique when, out of the corner of one eye, she saw the accident happen.

Marsha Kramer, who had asked the question earlier, had suddenly aimed a practice jab at the face of a burly male volunteer who was trying to get her in a hold. A moment later the man was writhing on the mat in agony too convincing to be feigned, pawing at his right eye.

Stevie hurried over to the growing throng around the downed male, fearing a serious injury, but he had been fortunate. Though the eye was bleary and slightly puffy, he reported his vision was fine and the pain already diminishing. He insisted it had been only a glancing blow and probably his fault for ducking into a jab intended for his nose. He also insisted he wanted to continue practicing.

Grateful and relieved, Stevie decided not to drag her soapbox out. Instead, she only reiterated to the others the rule against practicing any type of blow to the eye, adding, "As you can see, care is necessary even when the practice blow isn't intended for the eyes." Then she turned to comfort Marsha and remind her that there was a big difference between being partially at fault and totally to blame. Stevie had learned that, often in a training injury, the guilt of the inflictor was greater than the pain of the receiver.

But the reassuring smile froze on Stevie's lips,

only half-formed. Marsha Kramer was staring at her resentfully. The student's face seemed almost disappointed that her errant strike hadn't caused worse damage. She turned abruptly and helped her partner to his feet without an apology.

Only one person noticed the face watching them through the chicken-wired window of a door at the far end of the building, but Gary Mullner, the muscular towhead in the green body shirt, just assumed it was a curious spectator.

After all, he thought, ignoring his partner for a moment to watch Stevie, who could blame a guy for staring at a woman who looked that good? On top of being beautiful, she really knew her stuff when it came to personal defense skills. Mullner had respected her from Day One.

But then on the other hand, argued an abrupt, intrusive inner voice that startled him, don't you think there's something kind of arrogant and emasculating about the bitch?

The campus was barely out of sight behind him when Harlan Perry realized how tired he was.

He slowed his pace, though his eyes continued to scan the sidewalk for potential assassins. It was a long walk from South Central College to his place near the river, and he hadn't been to bed since his shift at the museum ended at 7 A.M. Again he reminded himself that soon he would have to commandeer a vehicle. *She* had one, didn't she? Then so would he. No war was won by failing to match or surpass your enemy's equipment.

He fell into cadence with the rhyme repeating itself in his mind: "The pretty *bitch* called me a freaky *glitch*."

His work uniform was sweaty under the rain-coat and radiated the stale smell of used mop water. He was tired, so very tired, and the pain inside his head felt like nails piercing the backs of his eyeballs. At times, the fizzing noise trapped in his skull was magnified a thousand times into both eardrums.

The morning was dripping brilliant sunlight, and Perry imagined he was a vulnerable microbe being observed under a giant electron microscope. Light had been troubling him more and more; now he wore a pair of cheap, blue-tinted sunglasses that made him look like some bug-eyed alien from the cover of *Weird Tales*.

He was passing the open stalls of the fruit and vegetable market on Magazine Street when a pretty female employee balancing a wide platter of canapés stepped toward him from the shade of the store's canvas awning.

"Compliments of Maison Lecompte's Produce," she invited with a wide promotional smile made almost sincere by youth.

Cover your flanks, screamed Johnny Law.

Perry held his breath and ducked around her, barely restraining a whimper and protectively hugging his black lunchbox.

Perry soon quelled his fear with the thought that he was becoming better and better at directing the Tuaoi. Now he was even starting to influence the normals, the ones without the amber-to-red auras surrounding them, as the incident in the gym had just proved.

The incident last Friday with the pimply God peddler had been spectacular. But after all, the victim's etheric glow had already been the right color. In one sense it had been like preaching to the converted. Today was a limited success, granted, but also a major breakthrough in the sacred struggle for Cosmic Chemotherapy.

Perry was mildly troubled by something else he had seen in the gym, something he hadn't noticed before about the pretty Scar Baby, but it was forgotten now as he recalled a bit of information the security guard at the museum, Wally Cruz, had mentioned last night. The team which was to perform the museum's annual inventory had already decided to transfer most of the contents of Storage Facility A to their closed warehouse on Decatur Street.

Meaning he would probably lose the—*his*—crystal.

But of course they would never get it. He was ready for them now, all of them. Perry glanced suspiciously toward the huge antebellum and Victorian houses surrounding him and made sure no one was observing him from the hostile, glittering glass eyes of their windows.

One hand cautiously unsnapped the lid of the lunchbox and snaked inside. He brought the Walkman's earphones out and hastily donned them. The hand returned inside and one trembling finger activated the tape player riding beside the velvet-shrouded Tuaoi.

"What's the difference," screeched his metal-lic voice, "between tradition and sick habit? Nothing, really, except that the former usually suggests something sacred and good, the latter something evil and corrupt. In America we no longer have a tradition of leadership. We have a habit! A bad, sick, maggot-festering habit. But like most habits, it can be broken, and at my command!"

Harlan Perry's face was ecstatic as he watched the cars, the buses, the motorcycles, the pedestrians flowing all around him, the busy, vital lifeblood of the city. *His* city. His people, his raw recruits were waiting to be molded into disciplined warriors.

"Remember," continued the mad, shrieking voice on the tape. "Remember, my poor little germ-riddled warriors, that there is safety in numbers when Johnny Law rules!"

"We aren't ignoring any of the conventional angles of inquiry," Bryce assured his two visi-tors. "It's just that, so far, the standard route hasn't been too productive."

Bryce was perched on a corner of his desk, both hands locked over one raised knee. Stevie Lasalle, efficiently pretty in her navy linen suit, sat in an armchair in front of the desk. It was one of those maliciously uncomfortable wood-en chairs with a thin red corduroy cushion that kept shifting around under her. Wade McKenna was leaning carelessly against the back wall of the office, gazing absently through the slanted jalousies and watching the muddy brown Mississippi refuse to give off sparks despite the dazzling sunlight.

Every now and then, Bryce noticed, McKenna would glance at the girl oddly, an ironic smile twitching his lips.

"We know from questioning an acquaintance of the first victim that we're probably looking for a white local. During at least one attack, he may have worn military fatigue pants. He's mutilated two of his victims with a precision-edged instrument similar to a razor blade or scalpel. Besides the name 'Johnny Law' he's left behind a card printed with a Vietnam-era military training slogan. And it looks like a loose time pattern might be emerging regarding the crimes. Helzer, the first victim, was attacked late on June 18th or early on June 19th. The next victim, Martin Fischler, died about four days later on June 23rd. But the last two victims—assuming they *are* victims, which we haven't positively established—have died exactly two days apart—Candelaria on the 25th, the Jesus freak this past Friday the 27th."

"Meaning," put in McKenna, "that he's attacking more frequently, and he's due or overdue to strike soon. In fact, today."

"None of the witnesses have been able to help you?" Stevie asked.

Bryce shook his head. "I've got a man checking with some of the residents across from the fast-food restaurant where Candelaria was killed, but I don't expect much from that. The other Jesus freaks couldn't help me, either. They said the guy just suddenly screamed his line at the top of his lungs and jumped in front of a bus. That's it. Right out of the same can as the school teacher's death, except that this time the victim did the freaking out, not the driver."

"What," Stevie asked, "do you plan to do next? I mean"—she glanced over at McKenna, whom she had just met five minutes ago—"why did you ask us here together?"

"Oh, Bryce is a regular party animal," McKenna said. "He loves to throw strange bed-fellows together and see what happens."

Stevie ignored him. She hadn't liked him from their first handshake, and so far the cynical redhead had done nothing to alter that impression.

Bryce slid off the desk, crossed to the Mr. Coffee and topped his cup. He turned toward Stevie and said, "Did you bring that diagnostic scale you mentioned? The one you developed for spotting certain brain tumor psychotics?"

Stevie nodded, reaching for the briefcase beside her chair and snapping it open. She handed Bryce a folder of papers.

"It's an abbreviated combination of the Rorschach inkblot test and the TAT or Thematic Apperception Test. You realize, of course, that this is no substitute for a complete clinical exam, including a brain scan?"

Bryce nodded absently, towering beside her chair as he examined one of the brief one-page tests. McKenna, too, wandered over to check it out.

"You simply ask the testee to report what he

sees or thinks he sees in these two rows of ambiguous inkblot illustrations," she went on, "then to write or narrate brief stories explaining what's going on in the cartoons at the bottom of the page. Here—"

She pulled another set of papers from the briefcase.

"—are the typical responses of fifteen B-T patients to the second part of the exercise. I'm also giving you a set of normal responses and a set of tests taken by psychotics not afflicted with organic brain disorders. You should study them carefully to learn the pattern differences, which are quite distinct. As you'll notice, the B-T group will reflect a strongly megalomaniacal bent in their responses. Look."

She selected a test randomly, pointed to one of the TAT cartoons. It showed a woman and a man locked in embrace on a sofa, guiltily looking up at a second man who watched, obviously shocked and angered, from a nearby doorway.

"Most normals," Stevie explained, "come up with the obvious. The woman is married to the man in the doorway and has just been caught with her lover. The more creative normals will elaborate a bit or come up with an imaginative alternative to the obvious. But this B-T response is solidly typical."

Bryce read it out loud.

"'The man in the doorway is a very important individual charged with a sacred mission to save the world. The couple on the couch are enemy spies attempting to hinder him. They are pretending to be lovers as a diversionary ploy so he won't suspect their real mission, but God cannot be stopped.'"

"The word 'God,'" Bryce added for McKenna's benefit, "is all capitals and underlined three times."

"Jesus! Fruitcake City," commented the Incredible Shoneen.

"The predominant images they report in the inkblots," Stevie said, "are very unpleasant and visceral. They see feces, pus, blisters, infected wounds, cancerous growths. Possibly this is an exteriorization of what you criminologists so colorfully call their festering brains."

Stevie paused. "What, exactly, are you planning to do, Mr. Bry—Neal? What good is my scale if you don't even have a suspect?"

Bryce dropped the papers on his desk, wandered around to the laminated city map and stared at the four red thumbtacks marking the attack sites.

With his back to the other two, he said, almost as if still trying to convince himself, "It's highly experimental, I realize, kind of like searching for the proverbial needle in the haystack. But it beats sitting on our butts while Johnny Law leisurely selects his next victim."

He turned around again and ran one hand through his curly hair.

"McKenna and I are going to mount roving patrols on the East Bank," he explained. "McKenna—"

He cut himself off, deciding to skip the technical details. "McKenna is going to identify only

204

extremely psychotic individuals. I can't legally require them to take your test, but I can offer them twenty bucks cash for helping a graduate student—me—collect harmless, anonymous data for his dissertation. I'll pay on the spot and claim I need their names and addresses for my receipt book. You'll have final say on interpreting the results. Any potential BT's of the type we're talking about will be tailed and investigated. We'll also assign a tail to anyone who's too emphatic about refusing to take the test."

Stevie glanced at McKenna and looked dubious. "In the first place, I don't understand how you can spot psychotics walking in the street."

Again Bryce noticed McKenna staring oddly at the pretty researcher. The psychic seemed especially amused by her last comment. So far he had shown much less hostility than Bryce anticipated.

"We're going to give it a try," he answered evasively. "We've got nothing to lose."

The technical matters had been taken care of. Now Bryce resumed his seat on one corner of the desk and glanced back and forth between the other two. It was time to open the debate he'd been waiting for.

"What I'm wondering," he said, "is why the last two victims shouted those words—one of them when he was reported to be already dead. How is this Johnny Law character causing that?"

Stevie spoke first. "He isn't, except indirectly. I think media sensationalism about the first two crimes is creating a climate of hysterical suggestibility. Those people only thought Juan

Candelaria was dead when he spoke. And the victim last Friday was a religious fanatic. By definition he must have been highly superstitious."

McKenna had wandered back to the window; sunlight filtering through the jalousies painted a bright gold ladder from his waist up. He spoke without turning around.

"Malarkey. Like I told you, Bryce, Johnny Law might be some kind of PK, a psychokinetic. He can move things or people with his mind."

Stevie whirled in her chair to shoot his back a withering glance. "Not too surprising, coming from a man who preys on the gullible for a living."

Here comes the blast, thought Bryce. He had brought them together hoping to learn something from the dialectical struggle between Stevie's rationality and Wade's intuition. Maybe it would just end in a brawl. But surprisingly, McKenna's voice was patient, almost gentle, when he turned around and spoke.

"On stage I'm a fakeer, not a psychic, and even you should know that the fakeer's ability to block nervous transmission of pain signals is well-documented."

Stevie relented. "Granted. But blocking neural transmissions of pain and influencing dead corpses to sit up are not exactly identical phenomena."

McKenna smiled, a genuine, spontaneous kind of smile that Bryce had never before seen on his face. "That's a typically scientific answer, Dr. Lasalle. I admire science, but I don't admire science's religion of the purely objective and measureable."

The remark threw Stevie. Before she could reply, McKenna looked at Bryce and said, "Don't play dumb with me this time, old sleuth. Just tell me the truth. Have you read about something called the Psychic Ether in your recent studies?"

Bryce nodded. "It's a basic concept of occultism and magic, right? An invisible substance that carries mental vibrations."

"Yeah, exactly. I'm not saying it's real. I'm saying it would be one explanation for psychokinesis, thought control, ESP, thought photographs, the whole psychic ball of wax."

Stevie was staring at Bryce. "And you're the same criminologist who complimented my article in *Review of Neuropsychiatry*?"

"Hey," McKenna said, "go easy on our boy here. There's more to life than just intellect, lady. You can rationalize it away all you want to, but there *are* natural powers. Telepathy, thaumaturgy"—he hesitated as he recalled something unpleasant—"premonitions of danger."

Bryce couldn't believe his ears. McKenna was sounding almost like a true and proud believer. Something in his confident, reasonable tone seemed to be affecting Stevie, too. She was silent for a long moment, her huge eyes matching McKenna's thoughtful gaze.

"I don't deny some of what you're saying," she finally conceded. "When my twin brother and I were, oh, about seven or eight, we used to act out this silly made-up talkshow we called Professor Wiggle-Wobble and Friends. Keith was always Professor Wiggle-Wobble, and I'd always be various friends with whom he had these crazy interviews.''

Stevie paused, as if surprised she had opened up about Keith. "This is going to sound like a platitude from a pulp thriller. Anyway, Keith had this line he'd picked up from some old gangster movie and given to Professor Wiggle-Wobble: 'Move it or lose it, sister!' I'd crack up every time he said it in this goofy, imitation tough guy voice. We outgrew the game soon after that, and I thought I'd forgotten all about it. Then, when I was thirteen, I spent the summer with my grandmother in upstate New York. Keith stayed home because he was in Little League here. One night I was woken from a sound sleep by Keith's goofy Professor Wiggle-Wobble voice saying that line over and over, 'Move it or lose it, sister!' And the room just reeked of gas. My grandmother had baked a chicken earlier that evening and must have accidentally turned the oven back on after the flame was out. She was already passed out downstairs, but I woke her up in time to get her outside.''

Stevie looked at each of the silent men and flushed slightly. "I know it sounds . . . silly. I mean, I know it was just the gas smell that woke me up, not Keith's—Professor Wiggle-Wobble's voice. But the incident *did* happen.''

"I believe you," McKenna said matter-of-factly. He was somewhat distracted as he tried to remember that phrase from Freudian psycho-analysis. What was it—reaction something? Now he had it—reaction formation. It was a defense mechanism in which an unconscious, repressed feeling is expressed consciously as its exact opposite. Thus the burly queer hater secretly longs to stroke another man's penis. Or a powerful but reluctant psychic might become a confirmed rationalist.

He looked at Stevie Lasalle and thought of the background Bryce had provided about her traumatic attack. He realized that was the repressed incident which explained her own massive case of reaction formation. Who wanted to accept second sight if it was capable of seeing ugliness and brutality, too? Well, her secret was sure as hell safe with him.

He tried not to stare at the lustrous blue, two-inch-deep glow surrounding the woman like a halo.

Like him, Stevie Lasalle was psychic.

CHAPTER ELEVEN

"ANYBODY CAUGHT SMOKING, DRINKING OR screwing," said Coach Winslowe, stalking up and down in front of the bleachers, "is gonna find his dingus in the wringer."

A minor strain of nervous laughter rippled through the 60 or so teenage boys seated before him. Behind them, bordering the wide green playing field, fragrant oleanders drooped pretty, poisonous leaves like leather fingers. The Tuesday morning air was still a lambent haze over the field, and the sky peeked through here and there in faded patches the color of cobalt. Parked nearby was a battered green equipment van with the Manzano High School logo on the door.

Coach Winslowe pursed his lips and sent an

amber stream of Red Man splatting into the grass.

"You're here to learn hard-slamming football," he continued, "not to play grab-ass with your buddies. Is that clear?"

"Yessir!"

Winslowe cupped one hand over his ear, leaned forward as if straining to hear better.

"Yes, sir!"

"All right, that's more like it. So get it clear now. I'm the head hancho around here. Anybody who challenges that"—Winslowe brandished a meaty, hairy-knuckled fist the size of a regulation softball—"catches one right in the old snot locker."

He paused again. It remained so silent the boys could hear the stuttering whisper of the automatic sprinklers scattered around the field.

Coach Hamlin Winslowe was in his late forties, a tough, grizzled, ornery ex-Army drill sergeant who had spent three years making life hell for recruits at Fort Polk. During his nine-year stint at New Orleans' Manzano High he had caused the administration some headaches, primarily because of his brutal training tactics, which had elicited angry complaints from parents over the years. But a career win-loss record of 85–14 had also earned him five consecutive Prep League championships and quite a few staunch supporters in high places. LSU and Tulane currently recruited more players from Manzano than from any other high school in the city or state.

"Okay! Here at summer football camp is

where we start weeding out the pussies and the non-hackers. No pain, no gain. Form up at wide intervals for p.t.!"

The boys clamored out of the bleachers, growling fiercely to prove their motivation, and formed several ranks in the grass. Winslowe was about to call the cadence for 50 four-count jumping jacks when he noticed that a kid in the last rank—Tommy Meredith, a sophomore trying to make the team for the first time—was chomping on gum.

A huge purple bubble swelled out of his mouth and popped. The kid tongued the mess back into his mouth and started all over again.

"Man on fire!" Winslowe screamed.

The veterans from last year's team stiffened in nervous anticipation, each one hoping his name would not be the next one called. They knew what was coming.

"Meredith!" the coach shouted.

Roaring, growling and screaming "Douse the flames!," the rest of the boys turned on Meredith and began piling on the frightened youth, leaping, scrabbling and crushing him under their collective weight.

Meredith's breathless grunt was muffled under the squirming mass. He seemed to be shouting from deep underground.

"Off me, get off, can't breathe . . . !"

Winslowe's raw, beefy face was split by a grin. "Fire's out," he called moments later.

The gridders unpiled slowly, peeling off one by one to the sound of Meredith's panicked whimpering. When he finally stood up he was unhurt but badly shaken and blinking back tears of rage and humiliation. Only fear of Winslowe kept him from running off the field.

"Swallow the gum, Meredith," the coach ordered, "before I cram it up your ass. Okay! Jumping-jacks! Ready . . . set . . . "

No one noticed the ugly, anemic, ratlike little man watching from behind the fence at the far side of the field.

Harlan Perry wore his wrinkled green military raincoat and the cheap blue sunglasses that gave him bulging sci-fi eyes. Despite the early hour, the glasses were necessary. Light was bothering him worse now; last night he had even unscrewed the bulb in his refrigerator after its glare pierced his eyeballs like knife points. If he took the glasses off now, he knew it would feel like his brain was carbonating inside his skull.

It was the poison that pretty, scientific cunt had planted in his skull. The battle raged as his system fought it off.

Still watching the group exercise on the playing field, he unsnapped the black lunchbox clutched in his left hand.

If he was successful this morning, Perry promised himself, he would go home and grab a nap, then experiment a little. He wanted to try the Tuaoi's power when it was concentrated on, say, a building instead of just a specific person.

Sort of like expanding his horizons, discovering his potential.

Almost as if the Terrible Crystal realized discretion was necessary, no telltale ruby beam emanated from it this time. But when Perry picked it up, it glowed the deep fathomless red of the Devil's eyes.

Winslowe had just finished counting out the jumping-jacks when he spotted a lone figure loping clumsily toward them from the main parking lot.

" 'Bout goddamn time, Oakes!" he shouted in his bullhorn voice.

The boys glanced behind them and recognized the skinny, clumsy newcomer as Roland Oakes, editor of the school newspaper, *The Manzano Messenger*. Oakes had a crush on one of Manzano's more buxom cheerleaders and had decided that making the team would duly impress her.

"Hurry up, buttlick!" somebody yelled.

"Get the corn cob outta your ass, pukepot!" another boy said. The rest of them erupted in laughter. Coach Winslowe only scowled and launched another blast of Red Man into the grass.

Oakes, looking malnourished in oversized sweatpants and jersey, sheepishly took a spot in the last rank. A thick black elastic band held his hornrims in place. His Puma shoes were conspicuously new.

Winslowe was about to lead the count for deep kneebends when he suddenly realized with crystalline clarity that *Roland Oakes was a maggot, a slimy, cancerous parasite*.

"Man on fire!" he screamed. "Oakes!"

Caught totally by surprise, the kid collapsed

like an empty sack when his growling peers piled on.

Winslowe's eyes glowed with livid pleasure as he observed the tangled, writhing confusion of human limbs, and listened to the snarling aggressors and Oakes' pathetic little mouse squeaks.

The boys, too, were getting carried away in their enthusiasm, those who were able to reach him adding punches and kicks and claws to the weight oppressing Oakes. But at the point where the coach usually yelled, "Fire's out!," he instead screamed, "It's still burning! Douse it!"

Something cracked with a sound like a dry stick breaking, and Oakes' scream of pain rose above the melee.

The scream had a booster effect on the maniacal fervor of the teenagers. Still kicking, punching, gouging, ripping, they immediately took up the chant started by their frenzied coach:

"Johnny Law rules!
Johnny Law rules!
Johnny Law rules!"

Another sharp crack, and something wet was glistening in the grass. Brian Oakes' last thought on earth, before his left arm was ripped from its socket and he blanked out, was that his mother was going to be mortally embarrassed by the shit-stained underwear he hadn't had time to change that morning.

Detective Sergeant Bill Patterson stopped outside the door of apartment 2-C.

The redbrick tenement building was stuffy,

poorly ventilated. The cloying smell of mildew and stale cooking odors hung thick in the air. Under the collar of a knit shirt, his neck was slick with greasy sweat.

He fished a plastic container of Dynamints out of his trouser pocket and shook a few of the little white pellets into his mouth, crunching them thoughtfully. Thank God 2-C was the last unit in this disgusting hole. These people hated cops. Patterson liked and admired Neal Bryce, but this assignment was clearly a dead end. Even if one of the residents *had* noticed something on the day Candelaria was killed, he wasn't about to share it with the law, unless maybe it was the Crimestoppers hot line and they were picking up some cash for their efforts. Hell, the big s.o.b. at the end of the hallway was meaner than a junkyard dog; he thought Patterson was serving a warrant for nonsupport and had almost punched the cop's lights out.

Patterson, who had a mild phobia about bad breath, waited until he had chewed and swallowed his breath mints. Then he knocked on the door.

Nothing. Except that he thought he heard a brief noise like a chair scraping the floor, then a jar lid being hastily screwed on or off.

He knocked again, louder. In the long pause that followed he heard a door slam downstairs and a woman's voice raised in anger. Somewhere a water pipe bucked and coughed, then groaned into silence. But now it remained quiet inside apartment 2-C.

For a moment he smelled something pungent

and chemical, something that made him think of high school science class and fetuses floating in jars. Then the smell blended with the oily stink of the hallway.

Screw it, he decided. Mission completed. Patterson was a fair-to-middling cop when he had something he could sink his teeth into, but before being promoted to plainclothes division, he'd been a uniformed patrolman cruising a black-and-white near Riverbend, one of the liveliest beats outside of the Quarter. This door-to-door canvassing crap, he told himself, was for down-and-out private dicks trying to trace missing husbands.

He removed a pen and a small notebook from his back pocket and placed a final check in the notebook. This was three times now he'd visited this rat hole; he'd be damned if he was going to come back again.

He closed the notebook, dropped it into his back pocket and decided to grab some lunch at the Burger Boy across the street.

Helen Banning began her afternoon shift at New Orleans' East Bank General Hospital in the usual manner. After ten minutes hanging out at the ground floor nurse's station while she caught up on the latest hospital gossip, she collected her patient charts from the duty nurse and began her initial rounds on the post-op wing—answering call buzzers, checking IV's, administering medications, recording blood pressures.

She was in her late 40's, plain but pleasant

218

looking, dressed antiseptically in a crisp white uniform, fine white lisle stockings and spotless white leather shoes. The appearance matched her manner. Her patients didn't know exactly why, but most of them usually felt a little better, physically and spiritually, by the time she left their rooms.

In the busy main hallway the intercom crackled to page a doctor. Two Emergency Room orderlies rushed past her, wheeling a gurney on which writhed a screaming three-year-old boy who had swallowed a forbidden snack of drain cleaner.

Stomach pump and concentrated milk of magnesia to neutralize the digestive track lining, she thought automatically and dispassionately. Sixteen years of nursing had long ago worn the edge off the word 'crisis.' She worked hard and with real dedication to her patients (even the assholes, whiners and creeps, she told herself), but she had also developed the thick skin of a weary combat medic.

The only patient currently in room 107, a four-bed unit, was a 59-year-old indigent bag lady named Arleen Vichot. She had been found unconscious in a warehouse district near the river, beaten and raped. Several hard blows to the side of her head had caused a concussion and, more ominously, detached both of her retinas.

Helen checked the unconscious woman's IV unit, took her blood pressure and recorded it on the chart.

Despite the protective shell of her professionalism, Helen paused for a moment to gaze at the patient. They always seemed so vulnerable in those flimsy medical gowns. The bruises over both temples had turned a greenish-yellow color like not quite ripe bananas.

A tight bubble formed high in the nurse's chest and made it difficult to breathe. Why? But why ask, she scolded herself. You're a nurse, not a philosopher. It was the poor and defenseless who were preyed upon and victimized the most, Helen had learned long ago in this profession.

The surgical procedure for reattaching retinas was new and delicate, and the post-op period more crucial than with many other eye operations. Minute, stainless steel surgical tacks had been used to connect them to the back wall of the eye. The procedure was made even more delicate by Arleen Vichot's age and the fact that she had already received an earlier form of the operation in both eyes. If the retinas didn't heal in place this time, the woman would permanently lose her ability to detect motion and color. The first 48-hour post-op period was so critical that Arleen would be kept flat on her back, heavily sedated and perfectly still. The slightest movement could rip the tiny, fragilely planted tacks loose and float the retinas on a slick of blood.

Nurse Banning was about to leave when she noticed the slant of the Venetian blinds was aiming too much afternoon sunlight across the sleeping woman. She crossed to the window and glanced out briefly across the west parking lot. Visiting hours had begun, and for a moment she watched the steady stream of cars and people. My God, was that guy in the chintzy sunglasses actually wearing a raincoat? She tugged the blinds nearly shut and turned to leave the room.

But she stopped at the foot of the bed as a profound new insight hit her that the non-paying female customer in that bed was a disgusting parasite!

Suddenly, it was all so chillingly clear. Arleen Vichot was a maladaptive cell, a dysfunctional biological unit, a disgusting parasite sucking at and infecting the lifeblood of the body vital.

It was also crystal clear what had to be done.

Her face grim with sanctimonious high purpose, Helen Banning crossed to the head of the bed, raised the sleeping woman by slipping a fist between her shoulder blades, centered the other palm against her chest and slammed her back down into the bed with enough force to make the frame creak. She slammed her over and over, rapidly and methodically, her nostrils flaring with the effort of increased breathing.

And as Helen shook her like a huge rag doll, she screamed a gruesome cadence, applying extra force to the slam accompanying each third word:

"Johnny Law rules!
Johnny Law rules!
Johnny Law rules!"

The first impact tore Arleen Vichot's retinas loose again. By the sixth or seventh blow, the woman's pupils began to fill with a red glow as her eyes started hemorrhaging.

Helen Banning's shouts soon attracted a

roomful of horrified witnesses. Later, the three nurses, two orderlies and one burly doctor it had taken to claw the screaming, berserk woman away from her victim would all swear that Helen Banning had possessed the strength of a demon.

About the same time that Helen Banning was being wrestled to the floor and injected with a sedative, a dark blue Cutlass Supreme was slowly cruising the nearby vicinity of Manzano High School.

The few pedestrians who bothered to glance at the car sometimes took a curious second look. The man driving was tall, curly-haired, modestly good-looking, his eyes pouched with fatigue; the woman riding beside him was a stunning brunette whose finely molded face might have been chiseled by Michelangelo. Slouched in the back seat was a surly-looking redhead who kept to himself and scrutinized each pedestrian they passed.

Suddenly the passenger in the back seat sat up straight and stared out his window at a shabbily dressed fat man who had just emerged from a K & B drugstore. He clutched the driver's shoulder and said something. The driver nosed in toward the curb and parked illegally in a diagonally striped, commercial loading zone.

The driver, a clipboard pressed under one arm, unfolded himself from the car and approached the pedestrian in long, springy steps. He smiled congenially and spoke to the fat man, nodding several times at the clipboard. At first the other man looked around with wild-eyed confusion and tried to ease away, but when the tall university researcher produced a crisp new $20 bill and snapped it smooth a couple times, the fat man's eyes took on an interested glint. He accepted the clipboard and a pen; his face was ludicrous with concentration as he began filling out the questionnaire.

A few minutes later, the driver was carefully keeping the chunky pedestrian in view while his pretty companion hurriedly examined the paper in the clipboard. She finally looked up and shook her head in the negative. The driver grimaced with frustration and turned around in a deserted intersection, beginning to cruise the opposite side of the street.

When they passed the high school again, a white Ford van with CHANNEL 2 EYEWITNESS NEWS painted in blue letters on the side was parked out front. A media pretty boy was interviewing the Cajun groundskeeper who had witnessed the horrible carnage earlier on the athletic field.

The blue-suited glamour boy, radiating the pseudo-concern his profession shared in common with morticians, turned to the camera and said something. The trio in the blue Cutlass were too far away to hear him or read his lips, but they knew that he was probably asking the same rhetorical question as the rest of the city.

When will the terrifying Johnny Law strike again, and what are the police doing, if anything, to find him?

* * *

At first, Jet Simmons had hated the idea of vacation Bible school for teens.

Church was stupid enough, anyway. Some days Jet knew for sure (well, almost for sure, some tiny voice in her head amended) there could be no God. If there was a God, then why had He picked on her when she'd done absolutely nothing to hurt Him? Why, then, had He made her illegitimate and her mother an alcoholic prostitute? Why had He made Jet a ... halfbreed? mulatto? *mestizo*?

The 14-year-old paused halfway across the Jackson Avenue pedestrian bridge to gaze at her arms, left bare by a faded yellow sundress.
The skin was a pale, creamy bronze in the warm late afternoon sunlight. It really was such a pretty color, she admitted in spite of her mood. Why did she have to hate it so much?

But these thoughts brought the other thoughts back, too, and suddenly she was dizzy with sickening fear. Making sure not to glance over the bridge's tubular railings into the wide brown expanse of the Mississippi far below, she quickened her pace.

Instead, she thought about Ms. Wendy Conlin, and the dizzy fear eased away like a bad cramp unknotting.

Once she was across the bridge, the Salvation Baptist Church loomed into view, a massive old structure made of uneven gray stones. Jet knew Mama had only enrolled her in Bible school to keep her out of the way for a couple weeks. She had planned to skip out after that first day, but from the very first minute Jet laid eyes on the teacher, she sensed that her life had changed.

Wendy Conlin, a recent college graduate, taught creative writing at a prestigious private high school during the academic year. But she had grown up poor in the same East Bank neighborhood as Jet. Consequently, she eagerly nurtured the dreams of other kids who were trying to get out. Though she dutifully stuck to the Biblical topics on her syllabus, she made it clear during that first Bible class that she would gladly read and comment on the creative work of any of her students, whether it was religious or not.

Best of all, thought Jet as she turned off onto the flagstone path that wound between the church and the newer Youth Activity Hall, Ms. Conlin had not laughed when she had showed her the pages from the private journal she kept hidden under her mattress. The teacher was excited by her dream of writing poetry and drama and her fervent desire to go to a private girl's college like Sarah Lawrence. She had not even scolded Jet for writing so often about . . . about the other thoughts, too. Instead Ms. Conlin said that suicidal thoughts should not be kept locked inside, that we should "write them out of us."

Jet swerved wide to avoid meeting the creepy man in the long green coat. She paused, one hand resting on the cool metal bar of the activity hall's main door. What was that beautiful line Ms. Conlin had quoted? The one by that weird guy who wrote the story about a man turning into a giant cockroach. "Writing should be an axe for the frozen sea within us." That was it—beautiful!

Her eyes were suddenly hot, and she rapidly blinked back the brimming tears as she entered the cooler semidarkness of the hallway. It felt like a small bird was fluttering its wings inside her stomach. Earlier this afternoon, during class, a smiling Ms. Conlin had asked her to drop by later for a conference about Jet's latest short story. Deep down, Jet was sure the teacher had really liked it. Ms. Conlin had been reading her stuff for the past week, sometimes assigning symbolic A-pluses to show what it would have earned in her honors writing class.

But still, the girl was nervous about this meeting. She hadn't intended it to, but her last story had dwelled so long on suicide.

The wing which housed Ms. Conlin's office was brightly lit by a high row of mullioned windows facing the westering sun. Light glistened off the tile walls and bathed the long bank of slate-gray lockers where the students stored their art supplies. Jet paused in front of a blond hardwood door, hovered diffidently, then finally knocked.

There was a long pause, and she was afraid that Ms. Conlin had forgotten about her. Outside, the bells of the ancient carillon in the church tower announced 5 p.m. by jerkily chiming a stanza of "Onward Christian Soldiers." Jet was about to knock again when the words startled her.

"Come in."

Did Ms. Conlin have a cold? She sounded . . .

different, like she was speaking through a wool scarf. Jet eased the door open.

Ms. Conlin was seated behind the wide metal office desk, doodling on a notepad. The young teacher was pretty in sporty white shorts and blouse with her blonde hair in a ponytail. And though Ms. Conlin still hadn't looked up yet, Jet knew her gray-green eyes were wing-shaped and so beautiful they could have starred in the ultimate eye shadow commercial.

Then she did look up, and Jet felt her arms and legs turn into icicles. Nothing obvious was different, yet somehow the girl felt like she had just glimpsed the face of the snake-haired Medusa.

"Jet," Ms. Conlin said, in that new voice like she had a bad head cold, "those A's I gave you?"

Jet nodded. She was too numb to speak.

"Judging from the pathologically ambitious things you keep writing, I'm afraid you've completely mininterpreted them."

Jet didn't understand what she meant, so she said nothing. Her eyes dropped to the notepad. Now she saw that Ms. Conlin was not idly doodling, but instead writing the same three-word sentence over and over. When she saw the girl trying to read it, she erected a wall in front of the pad with one hand.

"Those A's, Jet," Ms. Conlin continued, "were in recognition of your excellent grammar and punctuation. You are a natural-born secretary, granted. But you have the imagination of a . . . well, let's face it, of what you are —a culturally deprived, marginally schizophrenic mixed breed from the ghetto. And you always will be. Science has proved that personality and life potential are permanently shaped by age three."

For a moment Jet felt like she was standing on a madly tumbling roller coaster. She was back on the Jackson Street Bridge, dizzy and nauseous with fear as the uncaring Mississippi waited to swallow her body, the same bridge she would have to cross on her way home.

As if she could read her thoughts, Ms. Conlin suddenly smiled. The round white pearls of her teeth were actually longer and more pointed than Jet remembered.

"Jet, you often discuss the possibility of suicide in your writing. Frankly, that's an alternative I would consider if I were you. At least suicide gives you the option of cutting short the suffering."

Her stunning eyes drilled into the girl's. "You think about that, okay? And you think about—"

But Jet had choked back a sob and bolted from the office. Wendy Conlin could hear her worn-out cheap sandals making rapid whiplash sounds on the tile floor as she fled.

Disgusting little parasitical nothing, she thought with a warm glow of achievement.

She added one more to the growing column of sentences under her pen. Instinctively, she realized the three words would soon be Jet Simmons' unofficial epitaph.

A pair of huge, shady, moss-festooned oak trees dominated the backyard of the Bryce residence, tall twin sentries with a double-weave hammock stretched between them. Sonny lay in the hammock swaying gently as he flipped through his foster dad's basketball scrapbook. The July day was a typical Delta scorcher, and he wore a swimsuit, mesh tank top, and his straw jipijapa hat with the floppy brim cut off.

The afternoon was waning. Past the end of the street and the busy West Bank Expressway, the descending sun was turning the river into a ribbon of molten fire. Sonny could also just make out, if he bothered to sit up, the tall spire of the Salvation Baptist Church. It rose out of the East Bank skyline just across the river at a perfect angle to the yard.

Neal wouldn't be home again until late tonight. Lately he had been working almost 16 hours a day, not even showing up for the meals Kyla prepared. Sonny knew that some of the kids in the neighborhood were starting to say the police would never catch Johnny Law.

For perhaps the hundredth time in his life, Sonny read a yellowing newspaper clipping about Bryce's selection to the All-Southwest Conference collegiate team. The story made him remember something, and he lay the open, leather-bound scrapbook carefully in the grass, rolling sideways out of the hammock and trotting across the yard to one side of the garage workshop. He stood with his back to the wall, his bare heels pressed against the cool cement foundation. He removed his jipijapa and dropped it in the grass, unleashing a thick black fringe of bangs. Next he lay his right hand flat on his head until the fingertips were poking into the rough stucco behind him. Then, careful not to move his hand, he turned and examined the wall.

His face twisted into an impatient scowl. The fingers were poking right into the pencil mark he had made two weeks ago. He hadn't grown one lousy effing bit.

'Cripes,' he muttered with disgust. *"Soy un muchacho mu pequeño."*

He was measuring himself a second time, just to be sure he hadn't missed a millimeter of growth, when the faint-booming notes of "Onward Christian Soldiers" drifted across the river from the Baptist church's carillon.

Five o'clock, he thought absently. Time to pop Kyla's casserole into the microwave.

He hadn't moved three paces from the garage when an abrupt fluttering, twittering clamor overhead made him stop and look up. The sparrows which nested under the overhanging garage roof had suddenly become agitated. Even as he watched, a half dozen of them peeled away from the building in a ragged formation and hurled themselves at the surprised boy.

"Hey!"

He ducked quickly, feathers tickling the back of his neck, and scuttled to the middle of the yard. Jeez, what was that all about, he wondered, watching the birds resettle under the overhang. They seemed to be watching him, their bright suspicious little eyes wary. But sparrows didn't attack people, did they? Maybe they were hatching eggs or something, he decided.

230

He was halfway back to the hammock, planning to retrieve the scrapbook and go into the house, when a ferocious barking broke out on the other side of the redwood fence which separated their yard from the nearest neighbor's.

Sonny stopped, puzzled again. It was Mia, the Hanchon's friendly old golden lab. Only now she was glowering at Sonny through a wide slat in the fence, her yellow fangs bared angrily.

"What's wrong, Mia?" he called soothingly. "What's the matter, girl?"

But Mia didn't quiet down until Mrs. Hanchon came out and cussed at her. Then the animal slinked off with a growl idling low in her throat, casting malevolent backward glances at the boy.

Weird, thought Sonny. *Muy extraño.*

The last echoing notes of the carillon were wafted to him on a sudden breeze. He was about to pick up the scrapbook when he experienced a brilliant image of the Honda Aero 50 he wanted so badly to buy.

Neal was putting it off because he was . . . probably going away soon, like your real parents did, insisted a mental voice that scared the 12-year-old. He's been gone a lot lately, hasn't he? He's getting tired of you just like your other foster parents did. Who wants a kid who isn't even tall enough to play basketball?

Sonny picked up the scrapbook by grabbing several pages, instead of closing it and gripping the cover properly. He could feel the heavy weight threatening to pull it back down, but he did nothing to prevent the sudden ripping as one of the pages gave way.

His lips formed a tight, mirthless smile when he watched a newspaper photo of Bryce, a younger Bryce leaping through two tenacious defenders to make a lay-up, tear slowly up the middle.

Harlan Perry stood on the broad grassy hump of the levee, riverfront neons winking to life behind him as he stared out across the turgid Mississippi.

The U.S. Coast Guard station was visible just past the tip of the Algiers peninsula on the opposite bank. Coppery streamers of light filled the western sky as the sun fell, but in the east scudding banks of clouds the color of steel wool were threatening to disgorge a summer downpour.

As Perry watched, six canvas-backed troop trucks ground to a stop on the tarmac apron in front of the military installation's transient barracks.

A ragged newspaper clipping fluttered in Perry's fingers, teased into motion by a cooler breeze which announced the coming rainstorm. U.S. ZAPPO REGIMENT ARRIVES FOR SPECIAL TRAINING, said the low-priority headline buried on an inside page. Perry read the brief announcement again:

New Orleans (AP)—Approximately 150 members of the U.S. military's elite interservice antiterrorist unit are to arrive here Tuesday for a special two week course in swamp warfare.

According to a Coast Guard spokesman, the commandos, accompanied by a combined services instructional team, will spend one week at the local Coast Guard station receiving familiarization training in new high tech weaponry. The remaining week will be spent in the undrained, uninhabited swamps surrounding the Intracoastal Waterway southwest of the city, where the commandos will practice small team counterterrorist tactics under live fire conditions.

Perry watched the men climb out of the trucks and form up in front of the transient barracks.

"Pretty squared-away looking troops," growled Johnny Law, *"but have they seen any real combat yet?"*

The first fine needles of rain began to prick at Perry's cheeks. He smiled the stiletto-thin, rotten-toothed smile and ignored the dredge which chugged and farted past as it scooped sediment from the inside curve of the river. His right arm protectively tightened around the lunchbox.

It no longer mattered what color his victims' auras were. He could command anyone now. Johnny Law's new troopers would be seeing some action real soon now.

CHAPTER TWELVE

"THE TWO CONFIRMED INCIDENTS YESTERDAY," Bryce said, jabbing two more red thumbtacks into the laminated street map of New Orleans behind his desk, "at least reaffirm our theory that Johnny Law's home turf is on the East Bank."

His jaw trembled as he stifled a yawn. He turned around to glance at Stevie. His tired face was covered with a blue-black patina of beard. During the past couple days Milo had foregone the usual Texas flytrap jokes, especially now that the precinct captain's own unshaven face was beginning to resemble dusky sandpaper.

"The only known aberration so far in his *modus operandi*," Bryce said to Stevie, "was the incident in front of your building downtown last Friday. But why?"

"Why not?" retorted McKenna, who was slouched against the wall by the window. "If the guy is clever enough to control people like marionettes, why wouldn't he also have the brains to hop on the St. Charles streetcar?"

The other four people in the office ignored him. Stevie crossed her legs, adjusted her skirt over her knees and said, "You didn't learn anything from the people involved in yesterday's"—she hesitated, groping for a word—"yesterday's crimes?"

"Zilch," Bryce said. "The nurse, Helen Banning, was still heavily sedated as of an hour ago when I called East Bank General, but we interrogated Coach Winslowe and most of the boys last night. All they can remember is that they were suddenly full of hate for the Oakes boy. In fact, if it hadn't been for those two ear amputations and the calling cards, we wouldn't even have any physical evidence that there *is* a Johnny Law."

In the silence that followed Bryce's comment, Stevie shuddered and hugged herself against the sudden chilling of her blood. Low in the background, the London Philharmonic was performing a sonata by Beethoven.

"The papers mentioned a teenage girl?" Stevie asked.

"Jet Simmons, age 14. Her body was dragged out of the channel about a quarter mile downriver from the Jackson Street Bridge. Apparent suicide, but since it was the same day and vicinity of the other attacks, we're leaving open the possibility that she was somehow victim number seven."

"Jesus," McKenna breathed, "somebody pinch me. All this can't be happening."

"What about this roving patrol of ours? Do we keep it up?" Stevie asked. "I mean, it seems so iffy and imprecise to me. For starters, not one of the tests I checked yesterday fits the brain tumor pattern of delusional thinking that we're looking for."

Bryce combed his hair with his fingers and measured out a long sigh. He crossed to the front of his desk and perched on one corner. Then he looked at Baptiste, who was seated across from Stevie and stealing sidelong peeks at her legs.

"How 'bout it, Dell? What's the verdict from R & I?"

Baptiste shrugged. "Several of those people checked out definitely whacko, all right. Certified schizos, manic depressives, one even did some time in the slammer for buggering young—" He caught himself, glancing quickly at Stevie. "Sorry. For molesting young boys. I'd say you're on the right track."

Bryce turned to Patterson, who was standing just inside the office door quietly crunching a mouthful of breath mints. "Did you finish talking to those tenants across from the Burger Boy?"

Patterson swallowed and nodded. "None of them saw doodley squat."

Bryce remembered something that Cheryl

Lance, the Burger Boy employee, had mentioned.

"What about the guy on the second floor? The one directly across from the restaurant who likes to scream out the window. You talked to him, too?"

The tall detective was too tired to notice that Patterson's eyes shifted away for a moment. "Sure. He didn't see anything, either."

"Figures."

Bryce fought back a wave of irritation. For two weeks now he had been slamming his head into one brick wall after another. "Did you get the master list of tenants' names and have Dell computer check them against Fischler and Helzer's patient files?"

Patterson nodded again. "Nothing."

This time the plainclothes sergeant was telling the truth. He had dutifully tracked down the absentee slumlord and acquired a current list of tenants at 421½ Arno. Unfortunately, as the result of a slight, one-letter typographical error no one was aware of, the occupant of apartment 2-C had been listed as H. Berry, not the Harlan Perry included in Fischler's records. A human might have noticed the coincidence, but the computer was not adept at making such delicate inferences.

"All right," Bryce said. "Thanks for your time. You two go home and catch some sleep."

After Baptiste and Patterson had left, Bryce rose from his perch on the desk and crossed to the Mr. Coffee, pouring the morning's third Styrofoam cup of coffee.

He glanced at the other two and said, "We don't know who or what Johnny Law is, or how in the hell he's influencing people. In fact, until yesterday there was no concrete reason to believe that he *was* actually influencing people. After all, we were dealing with highly suggestible mental unstables—Jim Bevell, the emotionally disturbed driver of the jeep that killed Candelaria and a spaced-out Jesus freak who jumped in front of a bus. Either or both could have been influenced by media hype."

Bryce paused to take a hissing sip of coffee. He belched discreetly and an acidic taste like corroded pennies erupted in his throat; he reminded himself to pick up some Maalox tabs later.

"But now," he resumed glumly, "that comforting theory is shot to hell. This Coach Winslowe is a mean one, granted. I don't doubt that he likes to play a little illegal roughhouse with his players, but he's definitely no mental unstable. Neither were the boys who"—Bryce hesitated—"dismembered Roland Oakes. And Helen Banning is an RN with a long record of exemplary service, a woman who actually turned down promotions to higher paying administrative positions so she could remain with her patients. Now she's blinded one of those patients for life."

McKenna knuckled one slat of the jalousies open wider and glanced to the right toward the Coast Guard station. Idly, he watched a squad of camouflaged troops, obviously not Coast Guardsmen judging from their snazzy berets, being led through the manual of arms with assault rifles. For one horrifying moment the image faded, and instead he saw himself plunging a madly whirling drill into the eye of a screaming boy.

"Christ Almighty!"

He slapped the jalousies back into place and spun away from the window.

"You know what's the shittiest part about all this?" he said. "We don't know who's on this psycho's side. Hell, even one of us could become one of his murdering zombies."

Stevie rose quickly from her chair and faced the redhead. Despite the turbulent emotion evident in her face, she was strikingly pretty in a sea-green dirndl skirt and white silk blouse. Her hair was drawn back tight in a bun over the nape of her neck.

"Look," she began, eyes snapping sparks, "I confess that after watching you in action yesterday, I have a new respect for you. Every one of those people you identified exhibited evidence of some type of extreme maladaptive behavior. Your ability to spot psychic auras is evidently legitimate. But can't you see that your defeatist, negativistic attitude is playing right into this Johnny Law's hands?"

It was Bryce who spoke. "What do you mean?"

She turned to him. "I mean simply that a healthy, disciplined, confident mind can actually repel hostile forces. Studies have shown that so-called accident proneness, for example, chiefly affects people who lack confidence, people who've made their psyches vulnerable by defeatism and lack of mental discipline. They expect bad luck, and therefore they create it or let it happen to them. That's why much of martial arts training concentrates on quieting the mind and equipping it to deal with hostile forces."

Bryce was visibly impressed by her outburst. Once again he could almost feel the force of her will like some tangible presence in the room.

Stevie turned again to McKenna. "Maybe you are going to worry about this psychotic slave driver enlisting you to his side. You obviously have too little self-respect to believe in yourself. But I refuse to believe that my thoughts and actions can be taken over by anyone."

McKenna, deciding to wreak revenge, looked at Bryce and grinned.

"You were right, old sleuth. She *is* a ballbreaker."

Bryce was trapped. He hadn't actually used that word, but ballbreaker did aptly sum up the gist of a careless remark he had made to McKenna about her.

She glanced quickly at Bryce and saw the guilt on his face. She seemed more amused than offended.

"Is that a logical metaphor, Neal?" She poured him a saccharine smile.

"I mean, as a former athlete, you ought to know. Do you 'break' a ball?"

Bryce gazed back at her with the expression of an undertaker rendering an estimate.

"I wouldn't know," he replied drily. He tried

to make his words as deliberately ambiguous as hers. "I'm not susceptible to that type of injury."

Stevie arched her eyebrows and smiled, glancing at her watch. "I have to be going. I teach my self-defense class in forty minutes."

Wade, still miffed, turned back to the window and muttered, "Yeah, right. Self-defense. Nothing like teaching women to get their little asses in trouble by fighting back and pissing off the attacker."

Once again Bryce stood by for the blast, but once again he was surprised when it didn't come. Stevie merely looked at McKenna's back speculatively for a long ten seconds or so. Then she said, "That woman left you full of hate, didn't she? She must have absolutely shattered your self-esteem. But don't take it out on me, Wade. God knows why, but I actually like you."

Bryce saw McKenna's shoulders stiffen. The psychic whirled around, a scathing rejoinder ready on his lips.

But McKenna never delivered the retort because Stevie had turned at just the right angle for him to be reminded of two things simultaneously—the long thin scar just below the hollow of her throat, and the blue-glowing etheric double that surrounded her and identified her as his colleague.

She's a goddamn gutsy fighter, he told himself, and I've got plenty to learn from her.

"Yeah?" he said quietly. "Well, you oughta know all about it, I guess. You're the big-time research expert. Me, I'm just a two-bit, washed-up freak on the carnival circuit."

"Why don't you admit that to the papers?" said a voice from the doorway of the office, a voice unfamiliar to everyone except Bryce.

All three heads turned as one. A very disgruntled-looking Lucien Milo stepped into the room followed by the speaker, FBI agent Reno Morgan.

After Morgan's crack, Milo was the first to speak.

"Well, folks," he said, in the reluctant tone of a man being forced to publicly proclaim his own mother a witch, "meet the newest member of our investigative team."

Now Bryce noticed the letter in Morgan's hand. The moment he recognized the official seal of the New Orleans Police Department he realized that the document was an enjoining request from Headquarters, petitioning the Feds for assistance in a case normally outside their jurisdiction.

Morgan proffered the letter. "It would appear, rich boy, like your rep as a supercop is on the line."

Bryce didn't bother to accept the letter. He knew it was a slap in the face from Headquarters, an admission that they had little or no faith in BSI's handling of the Johnny Law investigation.

Morgan shrugged, stepped into the office and laid the letter on Bryce's desk. The agent wore a tan, tropical, worsted suit with a burnt-orange knit tie. Even indoors he wore his chrome sunglasses. The shrewd, vulpine face didn't even hint at a smile.

"Here's the sitch, Bryce. You were asked to liaise with us. You refused. Now we're joining the investigation—officially!"

Stevie had immediately sensed the long standing animosity between the two big men. She glanced at Bryce inquisitively.

"Our mutual hate society," he explained, "goes way back to Vietnam. Morgan here despises me because I wouldn't let his slimy organization frame an innocent man."

"You attempted to obstruct military justice, Bryce. You—"

"What I did," cut in Bryce, aiming a withering glance at the agent while directing his words at the others, "was intercede for a Navy pilot. He'd been charged with trying to smuggle a million bucks worth of heroin from Danang to Iwakuni via the missile compartments of his F-104."

"We f und the shit in his aircraft," Morgan said hotly.

"Right. But that pilot didn't know a damn thing about it, Morgan, and you know he didn't. It was his ground crew who had worked out the arrangement with some of their buddies in Japan. They'd pulled the same stunt with other aircraft, too. I had proof of that, but not enough to nail specific individuals. WestPac Command was currently on a big antidrug kick and needed a quick symbolic scapegoat—and coincidentally, this particularly pilot had written an articulate letter to the *New York Times*, condemning indiscriminate selection of civilian bombing targets by the Pentagon brass."

Morgan's cynical sneer was as close as he

could come to a smile. "And this articulate Navy pilot just happened to play basketball a couple years earlier for Rice University, another private college in the same conference as Baylor, your alma mater."

"I wasn't a lawyer. I didn't know that until it came up at the court-martial."

"Yeah, right. And you didn't know he was a rich daddy's boy like you, either, did you? I guess blue blood is thicker than water."

Bryce didn't give him the pleasure of snapping at the bait. He knew Morgan resented him for being a millionaire's kid, for "playing cop" and earning a spot in police lore while Morgan had grown up dirt poor, been forced to settle for a mediocre state college, and was destined to obscurity in the FBI annals. Never mind that Bryce was estranged from his father and hadn't received a cent from him since throwing off the old man's yoke and taking a commission in the Army.

Morgan now said, "Aren't you going to ask for my ideas on this case? I mean, hey, aren't you the cop who's famous for being open to all channels of input?"

"Matter of fact," Bryce replied, "I am morbidly curious."

"Yeah," Milo chimed in. "Me, too. Morbidly curious is kinda like peeking into the toilet before you flush."

Again Morgan's cynical sneer split his face. "When you look in the toilet, Milo, you're just searching for your roots."

McKenna didn't like the guy, but he couldn't

help snorting at the put-down. Milo's jowls tightened, and his face flamed scarlet. He was about to reply when he glanced in Stevie's direction. He swallowed a more colorful retort and settled for a simple, "Go to hell. And watch your talk in fronta the lady."

"You started it," Morgan said, ignoring Milo now and turning back to Bryce. "Our consensus is that BSI is wasting time on the wrong line of investigation. We've been liasing"—here Milo and Bryce both winced—" with Doctor Eugene Gardner, a well-known New York City psychiatrist who does consulting work for us."

Morgan interrupted himself to pull a sheet of notes from an inside pocket of his suit jacket. He unfolded it and reluctantly flipped up his sunglasses so he could see the notes better.

"Gardner has formulated a mass hysteria theory to explain the recent attacks and suicides attributed to this so-called Johnny Law. Gardner calls it a 'wolf-dance' theory. It's like in the Middle Ages, when thousands of people went berserk in Europe and started dancing madly in the streets until they dropped dead from exhaustion."

McKenna snorted again. Stevie showed no reaction,though she had heard of Gardner's work, especially his studies of mass obedience to authority. In fact, she herself had already considered some type of mass hysteria as an explanation and still hadn't completely discarded the possibility.

Morgan scowled at McKenna and continued.

"We believe the real culprits behind this wolf-dance phenomenon are Third World terrorists, terrorists who—"

Morgan faltered and glanced down, reading verbatim from the sheet in his hand. " 'Who are cleverly exploiting both the latent hysteria of the Deep Southern psyche and the unique strangeness of New Orleanians.'"

"Horseshit," Milo said.

"Pure psychobabble," McKenna agreed.

"That's too farfetched even for you," Bryce added. "How much LSD did you slip Gardner before he came up with that?"

Morgan was obviously enjoying himself. He slid his glasses back down onto his nose. The twin mirrors surveyed each of them in turn, pausing at Stevie.

"We haven't had the pleasure of meeting, young lady, but you look very intelligent. What do you think of our theory?"

Stevie, who was still standing by the chair she had recently vacated, stared at him coldly. "If meeting someone like you is a pleasure, then getting six teeth pulled would be ecstasy."

She glanced at her Omega and turned to Bryce. "I really do have to go now, Neal. You've got the number of my office. I'll be there until my three o'clock lecture, then I'll be at home."

She nodded to Wade and Milo, giving Reno Morgan a wide berth as she left the office.

"Nifty little piece," Morgan commented, "but a little too mouthy for a broad."

He looked at Milo. "You weren't so eager to go

247

to bat for Bryce when your ass was on the carpet last Thursday. Now all of a sudden you're siding with him. What gives?"

Milo bit the bullet and muttered, his face pained because Bryce was listening. "I've decided the cowboy knows what he's doing."

"Since when?"

"Fuck you, Morgan." Milo had only been waiting for Stevie to leave so he could express his true sentiments.

"Try it and you'll never go back to pigs, greaseball."

A grim smile froze itself on Milo's lips. He tucked his chin into his chest and swallowed a belch. Then he took a couple more steps into the room and unbuckled the spring-clip holster under his left armpit. He laid the holster and snub-nosed .38 on Bryce's desk.

"You're a big sonofabitch, Morgan, but you're all mouth and no guts. I'm unarmed now. Make your move, numbnuts."

"So the little man wants to play hardball?"

Morgan laughed, a little too loudly, and looked uneasily at the others. Bryce was obviously ripe for a piece of the action himself, but Morgan was pretty sure Bryce wouldn't jump in two on one. The problem was, Morgan had a long history of getting his ass kicked by tough, cocky little men like Milo who had low centers of gravity. McKenna looked on, grinning in anticipation of a good fight.

"Yeah, right. Two against one. That's the way you swamp rats operate."

"You got it, skinhead," Milo said. "One of us

holds you down while the other does the dirty deed. Smart money says you won't be ridin' a bike for awhile."

McKenna did his best not to chortle. Too bad, he told himself, that he couldn't incorporate Milo into his act at Rudy's Tahitian Palace.

Even Morgan seemed unable to top this last one. He edged toward the door.

"That's right," Milo encouraged him. "Just tiptoe on out of here before you get hurt."

"Okay. Have your little laugh, play the heavy. But you assholes are going to be taken off this case. I'll be back."

"Let us know when," Milo shouted after him, "so we can make plans to disinfect the area after you leave!"

McKenna stretched out in his recliner and added another dollop of Remy Martin to his glass; this, he decided, was as close as he'd ever get to heaven, so he might as well enjoy it now.

The chipped drinking glass featured a three-color picture of Captain Kangaroo smiling with avuncular kindness. McKenna, reading a cloth-bound volume titled *Disturbances in the Psychic Ether*, took a sip, then sipped again. As the paragraph he was reading became progressively more engrossing, he set the glass down on the floor beside his chair and forgot about it.

The nauseatingly familiar knock was followed by a whispered, "Lena?"

Wade's cheeks flushed warm with irritation.

"She's got a dose of the clap, Bozo! Go home and get a grip on yourself!"

A gruff voice invited him to perform a certain anatomical impossibility on himself, then footsteps scurried away down the hallway. A moment later McKenna was already absorbed again in the passage he had been reading.

Eyes hidden by the cheap blue plastic bubbles of his sunglasses, Harlan Perry stood on the sidewalk in front of Rudy's Tahitian Palace. He was staring at the man on the crude but eye-catching Incredible Shoneen poster.

Perry recalled that knock on his door last Tuesday and remembered overhearing one of his neighbors mention that cops had been nosing around. This clever Politico-Carcinogenic Agent, Wade McKenna, aka The Incredible Shoneen, was somehow tipping them off.

In the early afternoon sun, Perry's face was as bloodless and pale as corpse flesh. His head throbbed, and beyond the sound of his own voice, he heard a constant gaseous noise like he was holding a glass of fizzing soda pop near each ear.

"Commence movement to contact phase," barked Johnny Law.

Perry glanced around, watching for enemy snipers, before one hand began fumbling in his lunchbox.

Now McKenna was excitedly taking notes and muttering to himself. He had just picked up his drink again when giant, invisible, incredibly strong hands plucked him out of the recliner.

The book clunked to the floor. As McKenna

hung skewered in midair, he stared, horrified, as page after page ripped itself out and burst into flames. He dangled two inches above the cheap carpeting, his feet kicking like a hanged man's. Then invisible biceps flexed, and he was hurled across the room and slammed hard against the opposite wall.

His glass shattered, raining cognac and shards of glass on the carpet. He slumped to the floor like an off-balance sack of meal, ending up in a sitting position against the wall with the wind knocked out of him. McKenna gasped as he tried to find a breath.

He was just starting to win the battle for air when his head was slammed into the wall three times. His face suddenly went rigid with twisted, paralyzed fright and pain. Blood erupted from his nostrils and both eyes bulged, crossing wildly.

The little girl's singsong voice that emerged from him was the same voice that had ruined his career and doomed his marriage on the night of that ill-fated sundowner.

"Three months later all was well;
Six months later she began to swell;
Nine months later out it came;
A redheaded devil with an eye-er-ish name!"

The voice abruptly ceased, and was replaced by an image on the screen of McKenna's mind, an image so vivid and real and immediate that he felt like he was staring through a trapdoor into Hell.

His ex-wife, Judith, was lying naked on a bearskin rug, performing eager fellatio on her new husband. Wade saw himself standing in the background dressed in his fake leopard-skin outfit, ramming a needle through his hand over and over. He was singing in a plaintive, parodistic warble, "Do Not Forsake Me, Oh My Darling."

Now her husband, handsome as a Greek god, was grinning at Wade and laughing, laughing as he ejaculated, laughing as white ropes of his semen erupted from Judith's mouth and turned instantly into marble petals. First it was a deep sonorous baritone laugh that gradually climbed the scale until it became the mad hysterical whinny of a terrified horse.

I mean simply that a healthy, disciplined, confident mind can actually repel hostile forces.

As quickly as it had appeared, the vision vanished. McKenna lay on the floor, gasping, choking back sobs, while white-hot pain throbbed in his head.

What was it he had started to remember . . . something Stevie had said . . . something that had mercifully ended the hallucination. But his brain was a lump of stiff clay and refused to cooperate. It was a full 20 minutes before he attempted to struggle to his feet. During that time he reached a decision.

He didn't know what was happening or the exact significance of the nightmare images he had just experienced. It could have been the malevolent influence of Johnny Law or simply another of those despicable hallucinations he was apparently doomed to suffer for as long as he lived. Already the confused McKenna doubted that he had actually hung suspended in midair. It must have been a hallucination. If it had all been real, why was the book now lying there in one piece, unburned?

Whatever it meant, some inner sense told him it was time to quit his Incredible Shoneen act—contract and Rudy's thugs be damned —and get out of this place. His psyche was trying to tell him something.

He would mention it tonight when Bryce picked him up for the roving patrol with Stevie. Just until he could find another place to live, he would take Bryce up on his offer and move to the detective's house.

Stevie closed the door of her apartment's practice room behind her, dissatisfied with to-day's performance.

The early meeting at the Algiers Police Precinct had forced her to forego the usual morning *katas*. She had delayed practicing until the end of the afternoon, after teaching her defense skills class, delivering a lecture on "Postmortem Evidence of Cerebral Cortex Changes in Schizophrenics," and revising her textbook for several hours at the office on campus. So she knew she shouldn't be surprised that concentrating and emptying her mind had been more difficult than usual.

But more than her lackluster performance just now was troubling her. Stevie forced herself to admit it as she stuffed her white cotton *gi* into the wicker laundry hamper in the hallway; naked, firm breasts bouncing in sync to the taut concave flexing of her buttocks, she headed toward the bedroom.

It was becoming increasingly difficult to— she searched for words—to hang onto her moods, too. She was more irascible lately, more . . . more pessimistic and resentful and just generally bitchy, she decided.

Stevie crossed to the closet and selected a pair of jeans and a gray short-sleeve knit top. She dressed and paused in front of the oak-framed mirror to brush her hair out of its tight knot. Once again her mind wandered to Mr. Cat's strange behavior lately.

He was hiding under the sofa a lot, and twice in the last couple days he'd actually hissed and spat at her. He had always been cool and aloof, even for a cat, but seldom before had he deigned to show any strong feelings, either of affection or anger.

She had only taken a few steps into the kitchen when she paused, listening. She could hear a delicate, fragile tinkling sound like fine goblets clinking together. Her glance rose to the mobile—six delicately carved glass birds linked by strong nylon thread—dangling from the light fixture. She had never heard a draft activate them before indoors, but now they were in slight, jerky motion, as if they had just been agitated by something . . . or someone?

Her skin pricked slightly as she glanced nervously around the spacious kitchen. The countertop electric range, built-in oven and microwave, and coppertone refrigerator-freezer, all seemed to stare back mute but somehow knowledgeable, holding out on her.

My God, she chided herself, I'll have to add paranoia to the pessimism and resentment and bitterness.

She selected a can of 9 Lives from the teetering stacks filling one of the cupboards. Usually, Mr. Cat came scurrying in when he heard the electric can opener thrumming, but there was no sign of him today. Worried, she carried his yellow plastic dish into the living room.

Stevie knew he was taking refuge under the fringed sofa, but from what? She knelt at the front edge, trying to coax him out with the savory smell of the food.

"Come and get it, Your Highness. Pâté de foie gras and beef a la Béarnaise."

She backed away at the animal's warning hiss, puzzled and troubled.

"Okay, big baby, it's out in the kitchen when you want it. I hope you choke, Grumpy."

She stood and turned toward the kitchen. Then her glance swept over the smoked glass coffee table in front of the sofa and she started violently, almost dropping the dish.

The table held only a few magazines—*Vanity Fair, Saturday Review, Harper's, Art Forum*—and the framed eight-by-ten color photo of Keith. The photo sat where it always sat, still upright and undisturbed by Mr. Cat. But the glass face of the picture frame was completely spider-webbed with cracks.

* * *

Halfway across the lobby, Stevie noticed who was on duty at the security counter. Surprised, she glanced at her watch.

"Still here past 3:30, Duncan? I thought you'd rather face torture than miss Oprah Winfrey. Where's Wayne?"

Duncan Hilliard looked up from the *National Enquirer* splayed out before him on the wide Formica counter. His gold caps winked at her when he smiled.

"I figgered you were comin' down one more time today, Miz Lasalle, and that's worth waiting for even if it means puttin' in overtime without pay."

He was his usual friendly, ageing Don Juan self. Again Stevie wondered how she could have believed he had been surly with her on Friday.

Stevie smiled back. " I know you're a notorious flirt, but I thought eight hours a day of it would curb your appetite."

"My age, takes eight hours to work up an appetite," he corrected her, grinning. " 'Sides, you don't see what goes on once I leave here."

"I see," Stevie said with mock seriousness. "The Oprah Winfrey bit is just a cover for your secret life."

"There it is, Miz Lasalle. The story's out now."

He chuckled low in his throat and winked at her. "You'd be surprised what I turn into under a full moon."

Stevie had steered her way around the last potted palm and was about to push through the double glass doors when she remembered that she didn't have her front door key. She turned

256

back around toward the guard.

"Will someone be on duty until the usual time tonight, Duncan?"

He glanced up from the *Enquirer*, his soft brown eyes meeting hers. "You bet. Ol' Wayne's just gonna be a little late."

Duncan hesitated, then added, "Says he had some kind of car trouble, somebody ripped his spark-plug wires off. You believe that one? He's probably just hungover and flinging some bull. When I was his age I had lots a car trouble. And poor old Granny died at least six times a year."

Duncan paused long enough to return her smile, then added, "Anyways, I'll be around if he don't make it in tonight." He winked. "So don't you worry."

Stevie was about to exit when the image of that cracked picture frame upstairs flitted across her mind.

"Duncan?"

Once again his gaze met hers until the prolonged eye contact became uncomfortable for her. "Miz Lasalle?"

But she couldn't bring herself to say it. How could she actually ask him if he were using his passkey to enter her apartment? And why would he damage things even if he were? She must have bumped the picture without realizing it, or maybe it was a sonic boom or . . . or something.

"Nothing," she finally replied, reminding herself to hurry. Bryce and McKenna were picking her up out front in a few minutes. "You have a good evening, and don't work too hard."

Traffic noise assaulted her as soon as she

tugged the door open. At the first break in the flow she hurried across St. Charles, paying no attention to the lone man in the green coat who occupied one of the stone benches to the right of her building.

What was that, she wondered idly, Duncan had been doodling over and over in the margin of the *Enquirer*?

All over the city Orleanians were hurrying home to dinner. The sky directly overhead was still a bright turquoise dome; east, toward the river and the dying light, it was a brassy afterglow. A hybrid perfume of mimosa, bougainvillaea, and oleander sweetened the diesel and gas exhaust smell of the busy avenue.

Stevie kept an eye out for Bryce's blue Cutlass. A streetcar bound for the Quarter rocked and rumbled past her, its windows sprouting camera-wielding tourists. At the sidewalk cafe nearby, more travelers chattered over drinks under gaily colored umbrellas advertising Cinzano and Dixie beer.

A nearby horn startled her, and she heard her name called. Then a green BMW nosed into the curb and Stevie felt her pulse accelerate with nervous tension.

The man who leaped athletically out of the car and approached her was as handsome as he was sumptuously dressed—early forties, razor-trimmed salt-and-pepper hair, a notch-lapeled three-piece suit and silk tie, black open-weave Gucci loafers.

"Stevie!" Charles Wright said, "I've finally caught you!"

"Caught me? I didn't realize we were playing tag," she said coolly.

"Quit hiding behind that hardboiled exterior. You know damn well what I mean."

She felt her face glowing warmly. "Yes, I do know what you mean. I thought I made it perfectly clear when I called you last weekend that I'm no longer interested."

He moved closer on the sidewalk until she could smell his Brut.

"My God, Stevie, how can you just turn your feelings on and off like . . . like hot and cold water taps? What about that night—"

"Look, forget that night, okay? You're obsessed with it, but frankly, for me it was far from memorable."

"I see." Wright gave her the professionally stern gaze he reserved for wayward patients. "The old slam, bam, thank you, ma'am. Only this time *I'm* the ma'am."

Stevie stepped back away from him. "I guess you're just too sensitive for this cruel world." She hadn't intended the sarcasm in her voice, but she had already tried being civil to the guy.

It was at that moment that Wright made the mistake of grabbing for her.

Using a simple aikido move, she pinned his right arm in a painful elbow lock.

Wright grimaced and quickly threw his body off balance to take some pressure off the hold.

"Stevie, let me go! People are staring."

"That didn't matter when you grabbed for me, did it?" she retorted angrily. "But your precious male ego can't tolerate public humiliation from a woman."

"You aren't a woman, you're a—*ahhowch*! Stop it before you dislocate my ulna!"

Stevie increased the pressure until he was forced to either drop to his knees or let the joint snap.

"You leave me alone, understand? Get out of my life and stay out of it."

She stared into the kneeling man's frightened but defiant eyes. One part of herself—the disciplined martial artist—couldn't believe she was actually doing this. Never before had she violated the sacred code of *bushido*, "The Way of the Warrior," which governed all martial artists and sternly insisted that pain be inflicted only in self-defense or the defense of others. Wright was being a nuisance, yes, but clearly he was not threatening her life.

But another part of her—a newer part she had never been aware of before—urged: *Go ahead. Break the respected surgeon's arm!*

For a moment she wavered, ignoring a small gathering of amused onlookers as her will seemed to wrestle with some awesome evil force. Then she heard the voice of her first master, a humble, gracious, humane old Okinawan gentleman who could still neutralize four younger opponents when he was well into his sixties. He had begun every contact session by quoting his favorite line from Shakespeare: "It is wondrous to have a giant's strength, but it is tyrannous to use it as a giant. "

As abruptly as she had grabbed him, she let Wright go. Massaging his arm, his handsome face flaming scarlet as the onlookers stared, he hurried to his BMW and roared off with tires shrieking.

Stevie ignored the others and moved a little further down the sidewalk. Her mind seemed to be a jumble of wildly conflicting emotions. She felt elated, yet somehow ashamed—like a woman who had just enjoyed satisfying sex in a church pew.

For some reason, she mused, she just hadn't been herself lately. Then her mouth went dry with fear when she realized the terrifying implications of that last thought.

CHAPTER THIRTEEN

BRYCE CRANKED UP THE VOLUME ON THE OLDS' tape player. For the next few blessed minutes he was aware of nothing except The Manhattan Transfer.

He was cruising an East Bank warehouse district close to the river, not really sure why he was doing so. Mainly, he suspected, he was searching for an opportunity to mull the disjointed facts in the Johnny Law case. Lost in reverie, Bryce failed to recognize that the block-long tenement creeping by to his right was actually the back of the same redbrick monstrosity across the street from the Burger Boy.

It had been approximately 48 hours, he recalled, since the death of Roland Oakes inaugurated Tuesday's spree of death, maiming and suicide. Suicide, since Jet Simmons had recently and officially been added to the list of known victims.

Bryce had questioned the mother and learned that Jet's last known destination was her Bible school teacher's office. At first Wendy Conlin adamantly denied seeing the girl that day; polite but persistent interrogation, however, soon reduced her to hysterical sobs. She still claimed that she had absolutely no memory of her conversation with Jet Tuesday afternoon, a claim Bryce believed after she had tearfully produced a sheet of scratch paper covered with her frantically repeated sentences, "Johnny Law rules."

She had somehow been used, like the others, but also like the others, she was useless as a source of information on Johnny Law. Even hypnosis had proved worthless.

His window was open, letting him inhale the cool early morning breeze and its tang of river mist. Occasionally, in the brief interstices between the massive old warehouses on his left, the Mississippi flashed into view, a wide, dull expanse of brown just visible beyond the levee. He stopped once to let a squat-nosed Diamond Reo snake its huge trailer against a concrete loading dock.

For a moment before he accelerated again, Bryce's eyes met the truck driver's. The two men stared at each other.

You know what's the shittiest part about all this? We don't know who's on this psychotic's side.

The truck driver smiled, nodding his thanks for Bryce's patience. The cop nodded back before goosing the accelerator.

Once again thoughts began defeating music in Bryce's mind. The roving patrols with Stevie and McKenna Tuesday night and yesterday afternoon had proven to be productive policework, but ultimately useless to the Johnny Law investigation. Stevie had so far cleared every testee from suspicion of brain tumor induced megalomania. Bryce had also encountered several refusals to cooperate. They had been tailed, then a legman assigned to feed Delbert Baptiste enough initial data for a preliminary Records and Identification check.

Thus far their efforts had turned up one outstanding warrant for domestic violence and one former mental patient who had been skipping his weekly mandatory psychotherapy session. McKenna and Stevie were cooperating completely, now sharing Bryce's single-minded urgency to apprehend this elusive and terrifying psychotic. Their belief in the possible usefulness of their aura-spotting patrols had been boosted by analysis of the locations of Tuesday's crimes. The geometric pattern, as well as time and distance between geographic points, supported the hypothesis that Johnny Law might well be traveling around on foot.

Stevie, especially, had committed herself wholeheartedly to this investigation. She had completely abandoned her earlier theory of hysterical suggestibility created by the media. Bryce tried not to wonder again if she were opening up to him more, liking him a little better than she had during that first cool meeting ten days ago in his office.

Christ, she was a beautiful woman.

The street dead-ended at a dirty gravel and tar apron bordering a railroad yard. Empty boxcars, tankers and flatbed cars were scattered like grazing cattle. Bryce whipped a U-turn, wheels chewing gravel, and headed once again in the direction of Harlan Perry's (known to the police only as H. Berry's) tenement.

The pleasant frame of mind induced by recent thoughts of Stevie gave way to an irksome reminder that Reno Morgan was no longer satisfied to share jurisdiction; he was now attempting to have BSI ousted from command of the investigation. Morgan was insisting that the only line of action, in the event of another rash of incidents like last Tuesday's, was to call in the National Guard and enforce a virtual quarantine of afflicted neighborhoods until the terrorists and their accomplices were arrested.

At least, thought Bryce idly as he flipped the cassette, McKenna had finally moved his butt out of that rathole on the waterfront.

Yesterday the psychic had moved into Bryce's second-floor guest room. The detective knew that something besides boredom had triggered McKenna's sudden request on Tuesday. That evening, in the car, he had acted more withdrawn and distracted than usual, though Bryce had detected no signs of booze. McKenna had also moved his head stiffly, as if his neck had recently been injured, but he refused to answer any questions about it.

A housewife in a frumpy, sexless dress was hanging clothes behind one of the tenements.

Bryce watched a pair of damp bedsheets snap in the morning breeze. Unexpectedly, the sight saddened him, making him feel pessimistic in spite of the golden forsythia bushes that cheered up the little postage stamp backyards like gaily waving pompons.

His mind returned to McKenna. Bryce believed in the psychic's powers, though he didn't understand them or know their extent, but he also believed that the seeds of sickness and psychotic insanity were not purely occult. The city itself could produce them. Calling any city a jungle was misleading. At least in the jungle killing was purposeful. Here it was done for kicks, and the older Bryce grew, the harder it became to tell the criminals from the innocent bystanders.

The rear of the tenement at 421½ Arno was growing steadily closer, and Neal Bryce's thoughts continued to grow steadily gloomier.

He recalled something Stevie had mentioned yesterday, one of her instructions to her self-defense students. If they ever decided to yell for assistance during an attack, they needn't bother yelling "Help!" or "Murder!" It was better to holler "Fire!" Property damage was one thing people would bother to respond to. Christ, the whole goddamn country was going to hell in a handbasket.

Bryce realized he was in a foul mood and cranked the music up a tad. But almost as if memory had turned into an invading microbe bent on penetrating and hurting him, it refused to grant him peace. For the first time in a long while he deliberately dwelled on the woman he had almost married.

He had met Kristen at Baylor, a sexy, cute, but not fatuously bubbly sorority girl majoring in English and minoring in philosophy. She was impressive to him, somebody whose interests were exotically different from his own. Later, she confessed to him that she only went out with him that first time to prove her "*a priori* generalization that all jocks are assholes." Apparently, either he had proved her wrong or she had a secret penchant for assholes; by the time he graduated from Army OCS and received his first set of orders, they were engaged. As the top officer candidate in his class he could have picked Hawaii, England or embassy duty in Paris. He opted instead for Jump School and a field assignment in Vietnam. He got the country, but thanks to his father's meddling he didn't get the field assignment.

Kristen, however, was aware of no distinctions between an air-conditioned barracks in Danang and a bunker hellhole in the Que Son Valley. To her and her friends Vietnam was Vietnam, when her fiancé staged out from Fort Benning in the late 60's, but shortly after that it was suddenly a very unfashionable spot in which to have a soldier-lover. Bryce had been in-country for six months before the first sign of a rift surfaced.

Until then, and even afterward, she wrote to him every week with dutiful regularity. He answered regularly even though he knew he had nothing to say to her. They had known each other exactly ten months before he left. Half their time together had been spent wisecracking in the style of their favorite movie stars. The other half had been spent in bed. Then came the letter in which she solemnly informed him that she needed "time to think." These were the same words which he had watched spell agony for some unlucky GI at practically every company mail call. Except that unlike most of them, Bryce had felt secretly relieved when he recognized—with an analytical detachment that bothered him even then—the first stages of their own official cooling out.

Dutifully, while Bryce watched bodybags being choppered in from the front and stacked up at Graves Registration, Kristen continued writing on her expensive, pretty stationery. It was he who finally quit writing, trying to make things easier for her. Her last letter included a lukewarm invitation to "drop by sometime." Bryce did them both a favor and never saw her again.

Maybe McKenna was right, and Stevie was a ballbreaking bitch. But she, too, was right about one thing—the past is a dead thing, leave it alone.

He pinched the English Corona out of the ashtray and relit it, irritated that his fingers were trembling slightly. What was bothering him— Kristen? No, not her. It was the fact that she *didn't* bother him, that's what bothered him. The fact that Stevie had to convince herself, work at believing the past was dead and that she was tough enough to accept its death, while for him the assumption came all too easily. As if inside, where most people had living, breathing, cherishable memories, he had only carefully alphabetized file cards labeled, "Facts from A Dead Past." Not literally dead, maybe, except for his mother, but like her, buried and gone forever.

His father was dead.

Kristen was dead.

The Vietnam War was dead.

Baylor University and the Southwest Conference's classiest zone defense and Criminology 406 with Professor Moran. All were dead.

Angry at himself, Bryce forced his mind to dwell on driving. What was the point of all these whiny memories, anyway? He reminded himself of Bryce's Law: Add nostalgia to a nail, and you're left with a nail.

He immediately began to feel better as he passed beyond the incidental range of the Tuaoi, the Terrible Crystal that Harlan Perry was just then practicing with in his apartment.

Despite the mounting tension of the past two weeks, Stevie was reveling in the morning's laid-back sunshine.

The campus was alive with skateboarders and summer students forming little huddles to play footbag with Hackey Sacks. Birds twittered insouciantly, while magnolia trees lazily rained fragrant purple flowers and dappled pedestrians with fine capillaries of shadow. Stevie was in an upbeat mood, too upbeat to conjecture that such mornings as this all too often end in horror.

The heat was not yet intense, but the weatherman was auguring a day in the 90's with sweltering humidity to match. She had dressed cool in a ribbed tank top, white silk culottes and featherweight Capezzio walking sandals. A delicate, gold rope-chain necklace traced the hollow of her throat; it was not, she had reminded herself a bit too firmly earlier that morning, an attempt to aesthetically offset her scar, which the scoop neck of the tank top left nakedly conspicuous.

A trio of skateboarding males had been watching her approach since she turned off from St. Charles Avenue. One of them, a cute 19-year-old spinoff of Tom Cruise, whooshed past her in an attempt to dazzle Stevie with a flying reverse jump. Instead, his skateboard launched out from under him and clattered into a nearby black marble fountain. The kid landed square on his butt, face flaming as his buddies jeered behind him.

The fall was harmless. Stevie knew she should have enjoyed a laugh at the young Romeo's athletic faux pas. Instead, for some reason she was reminded of Charles Wright, reduced to his knees before her and begging her not to hurt him. And she was reminded, with an involuntary little shiver, of that horribly tempting moment when she had almost snapped his elbow out of joint.

Hell, even one of us could become one of his murdering zombies.

She rounded the fountain, out of which the sheepish undergrad was fishing his skateboard, and passed the unpolished granite facade of the

Fine Arts Building. Now she could spot the east wing of the intramural gym where her self-defense class met. The sun felt good on her skin and made her feel lazy, as if she were immersed in a warm therapy pool.

It was impossible, she realized, not to contrast Wright's possessive arrogance with Bryce's low-key respect for her. Wright could never stop making her feel as if she were a pretty but brainless coed, a valuable adornment to the medical field but not really useful except as a pair of token tits to show how liberal South Central's med school faculty was. But Bryce seemed genuinely fascinated by her work and seemed to respect her and her knowledge.

Did he feel something else, too? Or was she deluding herself, making the classic girl-meets-boy mistake of romanticizing him?

Maybe her initial hunch had been right. The tall, boyishly good-looking cop was just a ruthless jobber, one who was adept at using a wide variety of people to advance his own career and enjoy the ego thrill of an occasional hunt. Despite Bryce's dismal progress on the present case, even that macho creep Reno Morgan had grudgingly recognized his reputation as a supercop.

She was still mulling the problem as she entered the side door of the gym and headed toward the women's locker room to change for class. Out of longstanding habit, her expanded peripheral vision constantly scanned the dimly lit corridor with its double row of recessed doorways.

She had neglected, however, to glance over her shoulder as she entered the building.

The two coeds were dressed alike in floppy-tailed shirts and gaudy pastel sneakers. They interrupted their chat to stare incredulously at the newer-than-New-Wave figure emerging from behind a kiosk. He stared toward the gymnasium door, which was still closing behind Stevie.

They couldn't decide which was more surreal —the long green belted raincoat, the blue bulbous shades, or the putty-colored complexion. The strange apparition moved—marched was more like it—toward the intramural gym, occasionally glancing suspiciously toward the treetops and second-story balconies surrounding him.

A Walkman cassette player hung from the belt of his raincoat, its earphones snugly in place. Whatever he was lip-syncing to, he did not seem to be mouthing song lyrics.

The prettiest of the two coeds brushed her spiked bangs aside and looked at the other. "Spacey, but he's kinda cute."

Her friend nodded. She, too, was still watching the retreating figure. "I wonder what's under the raincoat?" she said in a tone laced with mock innocence.

They both giggled, then headed toward the student union. There was just time for a coffee and some boy scouting before this morning's psychology lecture on "The Myth of Mental Illness."

* * *

"Just a reminder. Please don't forget that we had an injury earlier this week. A minor injury, yes, but the fact that it was minor was just luck. And a consistent philosophy of self-defense, whether in training or fighting for your life on the street, must stress that you resist leaving your fate up to luck."

As usual, most of the women were highly attentive, but Stevie thought the men seemed almost to be staring instead of attending. Some of them even briefly smirked at her, or was her imagination just working overtime? Now she thought she realized what a man in a crowded room felt like when he wondered if his zipper was down.

She was almost sure that one or two of them had surreptitiously poked his neighbor, then glanced toward the wire-reinforced window in the door at the far side of the gym.

So what? Couldn't her ego stand the thought that their attention spans were wandering? Maybe she was becoming too preachy.

But even the likeable towhead, Gary Mullner, she thought, was staring back at her now with something very different from the usual respectful attention.

"The injury occurred," Stevie continued, "because a basic safety rule was violated. Again I remind you that although this is not martial arts training per se, we follow the lead of many such classes in banning any practice of blows, strikes, kicks or jabs to the eyes. Use a mirror or a dummy to practice these possibly valuable moves. Furthermore, no movement you do actually practice here should be carried through to completion except defensive blocks or evasive falls and rolls. Any questions?'

There was a shuffling of nervous feet from the visitors' side, then a sound like one of the men was snickering—or had he just snuffled his nose?

"Okay! Let's have a safe and productive session!"

From the corner of one eye, Stevie saw Lauren Bartlett roll forward and leave the ground in a fast-tucking somersault. It was a daring evasive roll, and the 40-year-old woman had executed it crisply. Stevie felt her face tugging into a smile as she started across the mats to congratulate her. Then Lauren finished rolling and wobbled up on one knee, her face ashen, her broken right arm sticking out at an impossible angle.

It didn't register during those first few shocked moments. Stevie assumed the woman had neglected to flex and correctly position her arm during the fall. Then she saw that Lauren's partner was Gary Mullner and she suddenly realized that she was only assuming that Lauren had botched an evasive roll. She might just as well have been thrown just before Stevie turned around.

She had only covered a few steps, no one else having yet observed the mishap, when Stevie's bleakest suspicions were confirmed.

Mullner leaped to the injured woman's side, ostensibly intent on assisting her. Only Stevie saw him drive a knee hard into his fallen partner's kidneys. The combined pain made Lauren's body jerk like a released bow. She collapsed into slack semiconsciousness.

"Off the mats!" Stevie ordered, stopping just out of striking range behind him.

The big muscular blond turned slowly, his eyes meeting hers. "Just trying to help," he said. His voice was sullen while his eyes remained mocking. He glanced around, as if making sure no other students were close yet.

Then, never taking his eyes off Stevie's, his right fist delivered a short, fast, discreet hammer blow, and the unconscious woman's lips split audibly; blood spurted down her chin, dripping to the mats with a steady tick-tocking sound.

"Off the mats," Stevie hissed. *"Now,* or I throw you off. You touch her again, and I'll consider you a potential murderer."

Mullner measured her offensive posture and realized exactly what she meant by that last remark. He hastily complied, scuttling crabwise toward one edge of the matts.

"It was just an accident!" he insisted loudly for the benefit of the few others now starting to hurry over. But he was still meeting her glance when he—*it*—whispered for her ears only, the voice a rasping wind from some moldering crypt:

"Piss on the martial farts, Scar Baby. Johnny Law is more powerful than your dead Professor Wiggle-Wobble. And he's gonna get you, bitch!"

The room was very nice, Wade McKenna thought, but it definitely lacked the woman's touch. That was one thing he shared in common with Neal Bryce and his foster son—the lack of a woman's touch.

And yes, McKenna told himself, the cheap pun on "touch" was emphatically intended.

He stood in the middle of the guest bedroom, not quite sure how it felt to be in a real home again after so many months in sleazy flophouses. The room was light and cheery, with a blue chenille bedspread, crinkly white stucco walls, a leather settee halfway between the double bed and the slatted doors of the closet. Through an open gauze-curtained window opposite the river, McKenna could see the shimmering, emerald-green rectangle of a neighbor's pool. A redwood deck surrounded it like rust-colored scaffolding.

Without really wanting to, he thought about the twelve-room Victorian revival he and Judith had purchased near Audubon Park; he had sold it for a loss shortly after the divorce.

A bottle of Remy Martin was nestled among the BVD's and nylon socks he'd stuffed into the top drawer of the dresser, but McKenna forced it out of his mind. He liked Neal Bryce, mainly because the cop knew how to show some trust in a guy without getting all preachy and self-congratulatory about it. Bryce would never impose on him, yet Wade knew the detective was glad to have someone around the house with Sonny these days, especially since McKenna and the Vietnamese boy had already hit it off instantly six months ago when Wade had performed his magic act at the boy's birthday party.

The room had double-sash windows on three sides. McKenna crossed to the sill that looked out over the backyard and the pair of huge, spreading oak trees which anchored the hammock. He wore a brashly floral tropical bowling shirt, baggy tan walking shorts and rubber-soled deck shoes. The short but muscular bowlegs were bristly with curly hairs that glinted russet in the sunlight.

He gazed through the window without focusing, still thinking of Bryce. Was something developing between him and Stevie Lasalle? They were somehow too . . . careful with each other, like two people tiptoeing around something they were trying to pretend wasn't there. Wade thought it seemed unlikely, but what the hell? So were Arthur Miller and Marilyn Monroe.

His eyes slowly focused until Sonny came into view below, crossing from the garage to the house. He wore his trimmed-off jipijapa and was looking down to read something as he walked. He looked up only long enough to open the kitchen screen door.

Another fighter, thought McKenna. He and Stevie Lasalle. Why in the hell am *I* so bitter?

"Wade!" The kid's voice reverberated in the stairwell. "Wade, come see this!"

Sonny met him at the foot of the stairs, waving a water-stained but still legible page in front of him. Wade nudged one hard cover up and read the book's title, *A Brief History of Executions and Torture*.

"I found this old book in the garage. Just listen to this. 'The ancient Burmese royalty enjoyed

278

witnessing an especially grisly ritual slaughter. The victim was always given a choice. In the first option, his hands would be tied between his knees and his head held back while slaves, naked except for loin cloths, beat his throat with sticks until it collapsed. The alternative was to have gunpowder packed tightly into the nasal cavities, then lit.' "

Sonny glanced up from the book, his mind rapidly scanning his repertoire of contemporary slang for the appropriate word to express his astonishment. Failing to find one, he simply blurted, "God, man! Do they still do this stuff?"

McKenna bit back his first cynical reply. Instead he only said, 'Not legally, but there's some real sickos in power out there."

"Catch this," Sonny said, beginning to read again. "In ancient China, when a young girl was accused of having sexual inner—intercourse with someone besides her hus—' "

"Give me that." McKenna snatched the book from him. "If Neal says it's okay when he comes home, you can have it back."

Sonny looked disappointed, but stopped short of objecting. Something else had just occurred to him.

"You wanna watch the late movie with me tonight?" he asked.

"Depends what time I get back. Neal wants to borrow me for a little while again tonight. Why? What's on?"

"Paper says it's some horror flick called *I Dismember Mama*."

Wade made a face. "Jezuz, kid, what's with

you? Throats beaten in, blown-up nasal cavities, dismembered mamas . . . Besides, too much television will give you pimples."

"God, that is so lame!" Sonny gave him a pitying look. The look became more sly as he added, "Anyway, it's not TV that's supposed to give a guy pimples. It's something else."

"You kids learn early nowadays, don't you? I didn't know about that stuff until I was 37."

Sonny looked skeptical. *"Vaya! No lo creo, hombre."*

"I only speak English and Ig-pay Atin-lay. What'd you just say?'

"Kinda like 'bullshit.'"

Wade did his best Edward G. Robinson. "You got a smart mouth, kid, yeah, real smart, yeah. Yeah. Keep it up and summa my boys'll be dropping by to see you, yeah. Yeah."

Sonny was heading back through the kitchen toward the back door. "If Neal comes home, tell him I'm working out in the shop."

Wade was whistling, almost under his breath, as he mounted the stairs again. Back in his room he lay the musty old volume on top of the dresser next to a stack of his own books. The top title on the stack caught his eye: *Disturbances in the Psychic Ether*.

He hadn't read that one since the freakout in his old room two days ago. He thought again of the chapter called "Juju Fetishes and Mind Control," with its discussion of C. G. Jung and the nether archetypes. Fascinating stuff, this notion that basic life instincts and creative drives could be converted into their opposites.

He reminded himself to show it to Bryce.

He was still idly whistling. The red hairs on his forearms uncurled when he became conscious that the tune was "Do Not Forsake Me, Oh My Darling."

Out back in the garage, there was a sudden screeching like the scream of an angry jungle cat. Sonny had flicked on his drill.

Andrew Jackson Jeffries—known as Jack the Man to his fellow salesmen—hung the phone back in its cradle and shrugged apologetically at the queer apparition on the other side of the gray metal desk.

"I'm sorry, Mr. Perry, but according to our routine check you haven't established an adequate credit base to finance under our usual 5.9 percent terms. Perhaps with a larger down payment . . .?"

Jack the Man trailed off. He had written this kook off long ago, in fact, from the very moment he had wandered in and announced without preamble that he wanted to buy the all-black Saab Turbo on display out by the lot's main entrance. It had taken Jeffries 20 tough years to rise from being a strike-by-night repo man to manager of Quality Imports, Inc., the only import dealer on the East Bank that boasted a limited edition Ferrari on a revolving dais. And one of the many lessons Jeffries had learned was that you never, repeat *never*, piss off a kook. Just humor them until they find a new hobby-horse.

Again Jeffries took in the dorky sunglasses and facial skin the color of faded mattress stuffing. The kook seemed to be protectively hugging that lunchbox which was not quite concealed behind the military raincoat.

"Actually, I brought the entire purchase amount in cash . . ."

Again that voice that made Jeffries dig his toes into the soles of his Florsheims. He watched with growing curiosity as the bizarre customer pulled the lunchbox into full view and, aiming one cautious glance toward the door of Jeffries' private office, set it on the desk and opened it.

Why not, thought Jeffries suddenly, why the hell not? There were old ladies with millions under the mattress.

Harlan Perry removed a grapefruit-size object with a black velvet cloth draped over it, then placed it beside the lunchbox.

"You know what I want, trooper." Perry grinned, baring the furry, discolored teeth. "Take care of it asap."

He whipped the velvet cloth aside like a magician revealing a mysteriously summoned rabbit.

Jeffries' curious glance rapidly transformed into wide-eyed astonishment. The shimmering brilliance was formless, devoid of lines or planes or angles, yet mesmerized him with its aura of all-pervasive, omnipotent solidity and power. Like two symphonic counterpoints merging into a chord, his mind fused with Perry's. A voice seemed to crawl down beyond the various public masks of his self and scream, "We are one and our cause is holy!"

Jeffries was still staring into the Tuaoi's brilliance as he replied, "I understand and I will obey, Commander Law."

Several minutes later the manager shoved a completed title, vehicle registration, bill of sale stamped PAID IN FULL, and a license plate receipt across the desk. Then he turned to a huge pegboard behind him and snatched a double set of keys off one of the hooks. He dropped these onto the pile of documents.

As the man had leaned across the desk, Perry automatically flinched and turned sideways to avoid his germs. He knew that eventually an audit might expose Jeffries' duplicity, but Perry didn't plan on being in a position to have to worry about it by then.

The respectful manager tore his eyes away from the crystal only when his leader put it away again. "I'll tell one of the lot boys," he said, "to make sure the tank is full for you."

The detachment of commandos snapped off an impressive Order Arms, 150 rifle butts smacking the tarmac like one. Harlan Perry gazed through the tinted windshield of his new Saab and smiled with paternal pride.

Those were *his* boys.

Perry had parked in the last row of an unattended U-Park-It lot, just past the narrowest tip of the Algiers district. He was far enough back from the main gate of the Coast Guard station to avoid arousing suspicion. The area was open, nearly deserted except for occasional traffic to or from the base; there was even more occasional traffic to or from the top-heavy building he could see by glancing over his left shoulder. Perry couldn't make out the small, official sign over the building's main entrance, but he knew the place was the wrong color to be part of the Coast Guard base.

He was in too good a mood to worry about the building for very long. He was ready for any contingencies that might crop up unexpectedly. The Tuaoi Stone and the book explaining its power were both his now. Last night had been his final shift at the museum, and he had craftily remembered to give a week's notice; no undue suspicion should fall on him too soon. Of course the Terrible Crystal and the book would eventually be missed, certainly by the time the inventory team tried to transfer them to the museum warehouse.

But by that time, the city would be his.

Lost in dark dreams of glory, Perry glanced over his left shoulder.

Oh Christ, no!

For a long nightmare moment, panic turned his arms and legs into deadwood. His ears turned hot and throbbed like someone had just cuffed them. Then his thighs closed reassuringly on the lunchbox tucked between them. Its solid presence calmed him.

It was her, Scar Baby, the pretty Politico-Carcinogenic Agent who posed as a scientist in order to destroy the brain cells of the uninfected. Luckily, he had caught on before she talked him into a second zap from her machine.

Now he saw it wasn't just her. The redhead in the tan shorts was The Incredible Shoneen himself, another formidable PCA. And the tall man, the one driving the blue Olds, had picked her up Wednesday night after the incident in front of her apartment building.

Perry watched them enter the building together. He no longer had to wonder what the place was. She was helping the police. The tall guy was a city cop. Johnny Law had obviously proven too much for the government's best secret operatives, if they were openly collaborating with cops.

In his rage Perry was tempted to throttle the steering wheel. He could use the crystal on them now, but the woman had already proved she could resist it better than most others. It might be indiscreet to reveal his presence so close to the lion's den. Last Wednesday he had willed her to injure that overdressed boyfriend of hers who drove the BMW; she had resisted. He wasn't sure if it was her distinctive blue aura, which he could see only when he held the crystal, or something different about the bitch's mind. But she, too, would fall. All of them would. What he had planned for tonight was just a trial run. This would be his first attempt to plant a command that would be carried out later, in the absence of the crystal's direct influence.

His trembling hands opened the lunchbox and groped for the precious crystal. Perry's anemic face fell into a trancelike ecstasy as he focused once again on the formation of commandos.

* * *

285

Calisthenics and close-order drill were complete, and all the required training notices had been read to the men. The crewcut noncom in the crisply starched five-color jungle camis had one last piece of business before the men were issued overnight liberty passes.

"All right, people, lissenup. I know it's Friday and you're all gung ho to pick up a dose of that creole clap out in the ville."

Laughter and a few cheers. The salty noncom raised both hands like a tired old cop stopping traffic. 'Stow that shit! I want to get outta here sometime today."

Staff Sergeant Fanning squatted to an olive-drab shipping crate, resting near his feet on the tarmac. When he stood up again, several men in the front ranks whistled.

"Yeah, you can fuckin' whistle, all right. She's as mean as she looks."

He held the brand-new 9mm. machine pistol high so everyone could see it. Its short barrel glinted blue in the waning sunlight.

"Gentlemen, meet the Honecker-12. Technologically, a direct descendant of the World War II Schmeisser. Supposed to be more accurate than the Uzi and more portable than those South African jobs with the rotary magazines. Only eleven inches long with the stock retracted, and she can kick out over a thousand rounds per minute."

A buzz went through the ranks. Still hefting the surprisingly light weapon by its pistol grip, Fanning snapped the stock into place and worked the breech mechanism.

"We just finished training day three. Next

week, after you complete your classroom instruction, we bust open a shipment of fifty of these little puppies and hit the boonies south of here. DOD wants these weapons tested for accuracy and optimal sector of fire in close combat."

He paused, seeming to concentrate for a moment like a bird dog preparing to point. Only a few men in the first ranks noticed that his eyes glazed over slightly, as if he had fallen asleep without closing his eyelids.

And even those few men stopped noticing once their own eyes did the same.

"Okay then, you'll be seeing more of the Honecker next week."

He squatted, replaced the weapon in its shipping crate and stood back up. "Now, assuming you ladies can get that squadbay squared away for the inspection at 1700 hours, you'll be going out on liberty."

He paused and inclined his head slightly in the direction of the big parking lot beyond the tarmac deck, as if listening. His left hand drifted to the haft of the K-bar commando knife on his clutch belt. Making the movement appear nonchalant, he unsnapped the sheath and slid the wickedly serrated weapon out, wiping its blade along the razor-sharp crease of his cami trousers.

Each of the 150 commandos had an identical knife riding high on his left hip.

"Remember, while on liberty, you are strictly forbidden to remove any weapons from this government installation."

Fanning paused. "That applies especially to

287

smaller weapons"—his fingers gripped and released, gripped and released the haft of the K-bar—"which are easily smuggled past the main gate."

During another pause, the city's traffic roar drifted across the river like the soundtrack of a TV show heard from the next room. A freighter groaned from deep in its iron bowels, bullying its way up the channel.

"I know this warning only applies to a few of you," Fanning continued, "and you know who you are. There's always that ten percent who think they're above the law."

His mouth seemed to struggle against a knowing grin. "You people think about that."

He sheathed the knife in a fast movement, then added before dismissing them, "I think you know what I mean."

. . . atta boy Cherry Boy, let's fry some slopes . . .

dead oh God dead, most of them are dead but not that white sergeant yelling beside him, lord that boy is pale but he's mean so goddamn mean he collects ears and they call him . . .

. . . atta boy Cherry Boy just me and you, we can do it but take cover Cherry Boy, you stupid crazy fucking nigger you want to die . . .

The enemy grenade whunks into the dirt at his feet and Cherry Boy screams at God to have mercy on his soul . . .

Cherry Boy turns into a chunk of ice and waits for the explosion that will rip him to meaty shreds but falling rolling somebody pushing him aside, it's that ballsy sergeant, he knocks Cherry Boy aside, he jumps on the grenade, he hugs it into his guts, his pale blond face turns to stare at him and in that last insane second before the grenade explodes with a muffled shudder the sergeant grins wide at Cherry Boy and bares the biggest buckteeth Cherry Boy has ever seen

Not real teeth but two ridiculously huge shiny white porcelain caps and both of them are perfectly carved with tiny letters alternating in red white and blue and they say . . . theysay

oh Lord they say JOHNNY LAW RULES!

Now he remembers

Them teeth was custom-built in Okinawa and they call that mean motherfucking white boy Johnny Law . . .

Yolanda Davis was wide-awake. Goosebumps raced up her arms in rapid waves as she listened to her dream-muttering husband.

"Johnny Law! They call that mean bastard Johnny Law. They call that mean motherfucking white boy Johnny Law. He saved my ass, Johnny Law rules, but dead, the rest of us are all dead, oh God no, got to write it all down, all dead . . ."

She instantly had recognized the name. Not only had her husband filled her in on Bryce's recent visit, but every major newspaper in the country was now featuring the bizarre Johnny Law case as page one fare.

Yolanda slid open the drawer of a mahogany nightstand beside the bed. She removed the small white business card with the phone number Bryce had left.

Ben had quieted down now. Yolanda waited several moments for her arms to quit trembling, then she reached for the telephone on the nightstand.

CHAPTER FOURTEEN

"HELL," MILO WAS SAYING TO DELBERT BAPTISTE, "if you wanna talk about some wild times cruising in the black-and-white. It's two a.m. and I'm doing the routine patrol through Audubon Park, when I see this '65 Chevy Impala pulled off into the trees. Looks like an abandoned vehicle. Naturally I contact the dispatcher and request a DMV check on the license number, but no stolen vehicle report comes back on it. So next I break out my flash and peek through the back window, and that's when I just about shit my knickers. Some buck-naked broad is in the back seat hittin' it on one a them vibrators, while this guy beside her watches her and pounds his pud. So I—"

Baptiste suddenly cleared his throat and nodded toward the door behind Milo. Three more pair of eyes—Milo's, McKenna's, and Bryce's—swiveled to focus on the woman at the same time.

Stevie Lasalle was nothing short of stunning in a maroon felt beret, white silk campshirt and print jeans that accentuated the long flare of her hips.

The scathing tone revealed that she must have been standing there longer than they'd realized. "Excuse me for interrupting your titillating locker room bull session, Captain Milo."

Beneath the swarthy veneer of beard shadow, Milo's pudgy neck and face flamed scarlet.

"Dr. Lasalle," he said weakly, looking like a teenage boy whose mother had just caught him trying on his first lubricated Trojan, "I—uhh, that is, I—"

Stevie relented when she saw him squirming, unable to resist a brief flash of smile. "Next time maybe I should knock."

Baptiste crammed two knuckles into his mouth to stifle a laugh while Milo's color slowly returned to normal. Stevie greeted McKenna, who was slouching near the window with one hip against the wall, then looked at Bryce. The unshaven, rumpled, hollowed-eyed detective rose from the corner of his desk to greet her.

Only McKenna noticed that the abysmal dejection on the towering Texan's face seemed to lessen for a moment.

Bryce said, "I take it you've heard what went down last night?"

Stevie nodded and stepped around Milo, who obsequiously scuttled out of her way. "I saw it this morning in the papers. I still can't believe it."

"Believe it," Bryce said. "I just got back from viewing every one of the bodies."

"Coffee, Doctor?" Milo offered, eager to atone for his blunder.

"No, thank you. I can't stay."

She looked at Bryce again. "I was in the neighborhood and just stopped by to ask if you could find time to drop by my apartment later this morning. I . . ." She hesitated. "I have something to discuss with you. Privately."

Milo and Baptiste exchanged knowing glances, but Bryce warned them with a glare. "Will do," he said. "What time?"

"Say, between eleven and noon?"

Bryce nodded.

Stevie said good-bye to the room in general and left. A faint, teasing odor of tropical flowers lingered behind like the memory of a pleasant dream.

Baptiste was the first to speak. "'I have something to discuss with you—privately.'" The R & I chief winked at Bryce, flicking his tongue rapidly from side to side several times. "Time for the old slap 'n tickle, hey, Romeo?"

Bryce glowered at him without speaking, until Baptiste grew uncomfortable at the silence and began nervously picking at a button on the sleeve of his sport jacket.

"Sorry," he muttered.

"You sure as hell are," Milo gloated. He was glad to see someone else on the spot after his embarrassment of a few minutes earlier. He fished his combat Zippo from a front pocket and began absently toying with it, clicking the top up and down.

"Okay," the precinct captain said, "enough scuttlebutt. We're supposed to be having a strategy session now, not a circle jerk."

Bryce sighed, tried to scrub the weariness from his face with both hands and sank down into the swivel chair. A freshly typed stack of official crime reports stared up at him mockingly.

During the night a wave of brutal knife murders had left six people dead in widely scattered sectors of the city. They were routine killings this time, the badly slashed bodies leaving no mysteries surrounding the official cause of death, as had been the case with Johnny Law's earlier victims. Nor had there been the gruesome calling cards like those found on Helzer and Fischler.

But the stump of gristle where the left ear should have been on each corpse had announced the handiwork of Johnny Law.

The city, Bryce realized, was on the verge of panic, and that panic would soon evolve into utter chaos—especially if the media came to the same conclusion he had after analyzing the distance between the six red thumbtacks added to the city map behind his desk, as well as the approximate time of attack for each victim.

Even with a car, one man alone could not have committed all those widely scattered murders, meaning Johnny Law now had accomplices.

Milo's voice jarred into the gloomy silence of his thoughts.

"That cockroach Reno Morgan is still pushing this terrorist angle. He's up on the hill right now, trying to get us pulled off this case completely. He's pushing for city-wide curfews, calling in the National Guard, demanding house-to-house searches in what he calls the 'ethnic barrios.' Fucker chaps my ass."

Milo tugged impatiently at the left armpit of his too-tight, cheap white safari suit. He stared accusingly at Bryce. "What's this crap about you flying to Shytown again, cowboy?"

"No crap at all," Bryce said. "It's a fact. I'm flying out first thing tomorrow morning and coming back tomorrow night. I'd be gone right now if it hadn't been for this little spree last night."

Bryce had already been roused from bed and was investigating the scene of the night's first murder when Yolanda Davis' call had been received. As per standard hot line routine, her call had been recorded and played back for him. Her description of Ben's nightmare mutterings renewed his conviction that the Viet vet indeed held a key—if not *the* key—to the identity of Johnny Law. Bryce had returned the call early this morning, speaking briefly with both of them and making arrangements for himself and a police psychiatrist to meet with Davis on Sunday. Though Davis was reluctant, his wife had evidently convinced him he should agree to undergo questioning under hypnosis.

Bryce now recalled something Davis had said

just before hanging up. "Look, man, I'm telling you. I think I know, and I think I *don't* know."

Bryce shifted uncomfortably in his chair. After last night he had unwillingly dug his weapon out of its locked storage box in a closet at home; now one checkered rubber grip of the Browning 9mm. Parabellum pressed clumsily against his left ribcage, a chamois holster doing little to buffer its weight.

"Well," Milo said, his voice heavy with resignation, "you're gonna do what you damn well please no matter what I say, but mark my words, every minute counts now. Once Morgan gets complete federal jurisdiction, we lose the whole ball of wax. Work fast, or you might as well keep right on flying to Cloud Cuckooland and take a long vacation while the media rake us over the coals."

Bryce nodded. For once the wisecracking little Cajun was right.

Milo and Baptiste left to check on something down the hall at R & I. Lost in glum reverie, Bryce had almost forgotten about McKenna's presence until the redheaded psychic nervously cleared his throat.

Bryce glanced up. McKenna had left his spot by the window and crossed to the side of the desk. He proffered a book toward the detective.

"I've been meaning to show you a section from this. After what happened last night, this seems like as good a time as any."

Bryce noted the book's title: *Disturbances in the Psychic Ether*. A chewing gum wrapper marked the spot McKenna meant. Bryce accepted the volume from him and opened it to a chapter called "Juju Fetishes and Mind Control."

"The whole chapter is good," McKenna said, "but for now just read the part I've underlined about Jung and the nether archetypes."

C. G. Jung's most important contribution to human psychology, read Bryce, *was his theory of the Collective Unconscious. According to Jung, this CU contains certain symbols or archetypes (of flight, rebirth, motherhood, tribal unity, etc.) which influence our thoughts and behavior. However, Jung emphasized that these archetypes represent only potentialities: predisposing forms without specific, fixed contents. Thus, for example, the same primordial instinct corresponding to need for social order can be fulfilled by Nazism or Catholicism or Zen Buddhism, or for that matter, Punk Existentialism.*

Bryce looked up, slightly puzzled. "It's interesting, but what—?"

"Keep reading, old sleuth. The best part's coming up."

Obediently, Bryce continued. *Since the precise meaning of these archetypes cannot be fixed or pinned down, some cults of the juju fetish believe that certain evil objects—the Hebraic golem, the American Indian kachina, the famed Tuaoi Stone or Terrible Crystal of Atlantis, etc.— can be used to concentrate psychic hatred. Thus healthy, vital archetypes can be converted into their negative or nether archetypes. Love of life becomes love of death, and the instincts for peace or beauty are transformed into a craving for*

297

*violence and ugliness. This function is said to be
closely related to the occult power of metempsychosis, the projection of the will into the body of
others. This projection of the will supposedly takes
place as a wave phenomenon in the invisible
psychic ether, so that eventually* (here McKenna
had underlined the words twice) *more than one
victim can be affected.*

Bryce finished reading and looked up at
McKenna. For a moment they locked glances,
the only sound a low crescendo from the Vivaldi
tape playing in the background. Bryce absently
plucked his panatela out of the copper ashtray
on the desk and puffed at it, failing to notice that
it had gone out long ago.

Outside, rising above the music, they could
hear a faint singsong cadence as the visiting
antiterrorist unit was marched to morning
chow. Neither man gave the noise a second
thought.

"It would explain a lot," Bryce finally conceded. "It's just that it seems so . . . " His voice
trailed off.

"So absolutely irrational and impossible?"

The detective nodded helplessly, his face troubled.

"No shit, Sherlock. You sound like Stevie. But
what else would you call what's been happening
lately?"

Milo and Baptiste could be heard in the
hallway, arguing as they returned toward
Bryce's office. "I was just offering an opinion,"
protested the voice of Baptiste. "Opinions are

like assholes," Milo's acerbic voice retorted. "Everybody's got one."

Bryce was gazing at his forearms. As the full implication of what McKenna was suggesting sank home, he watched both arms sprout tight little goosebumps.

"Morning, sir," Duncan Hilliard said. "May I help you?"

The double glass doors swung shut silently behind Bryce. He nodded at the mulatto security guard. "I'm here to see Miss Lasalle. She's expecting me. Name's Bryce."

The polite smile slowly faded from Hilliard's face. His liquid brown eyes hostilely surveyed every inch of the tall visitor's frame. Rudely turning his back on Bryce, he picked up the house phone and dialed a number.

"A Mr. Bryce to see you, Miz Lasalle," he announced stiffly.

"Please send him up, Duncan," came the reply.

The guard met his eyes again and both men exchanged a long, uncomfortable stare.

"Go right on up, sir. Apartment 11-B."

Bryce wove his way through a lush superabundance of potted palms to the elevator at the far side of the lobby and jabbed the button for the 11th floor. When he glanced over his shoulder, right before the doors opened, the guard was still staring at him intently.

Stevie was waiting to greet him at her open door; she was without the beret of earlier, and now her hair fell over both shoulders in a curtain of sable curls.

"If that sourpuss downstairs ran a graveyard," Bryce quipped, as he entered, "people would stop dying."

"Duncan?"

Her tone was surprised, but Bryce immediately realized she was distracted by whatever it was she had invited him by to talk about. He gazed around at the apartment's tasteful but austere furnishings.

"Very nice," he commented politely.

She smiled as she shut the door behind him and clicked the deadbolt home. "Don't lie, Neal. You think the place is as hard and bare and cold as my soul, don't you? Most men do."

The remark caught him off guard. His eyes traced the graceful lines of her body and came to rest on the huge, gray eyes.

"I'm not a very religious man," he finally replied. "I guess maybe I've thought more about your body than your soul."

It was her turn to be caught off guard. A few minutes later they were both settled, chastely removed from each other, on a fringed sofa before the low smoked-glass table, sipping steaming cups of coffee laced with Kahlúa. For a moment Bryce's growing exhaustion caught up with him; he yawned by flexing his cheeks instead of opening his mouth, jaw trembling. He was tempted to draw a nearby ottoman closer and prop his feet up on it, but rejected the idea. Stevie was right. The place was too formal to invite such a move.

She still seemed reluctant to broach whatever was on her mind. Stalling to give her time, Bryce nodded toward the photo in its brand-new frame on the coffee table.

"Your brother was a very handsome man."

"Boy," she corrected him without rancor. "He was practically a boy when he was killed, Neal. He had most of his life ahead of him."

He blurted out his next remark without thinking. "So do you."

She shifted sideways to look at him, her cup halfway to her lips.

"What's that supposed to mean?"

"Exactly what it means, and nothing more." But he couldn't quite meet her eye.

She studied him for a few seconds, then decided to let the comment pass.

Stevie took another sip of coffee and said, "Neal, yesterday I was forced to cancel my self-defense class for the rest of the semester."

This time when he met her gaze, the finely etched beauty of her face made Bryce feel like he was flying over the top in a Coney Island roller coaster.

"Why?"

Calmly and carefully, she explained the events of that last class session—the deliberate injuries inflicted on Lauren Bartlett, the way Gary Mullner had continued to hurt her even after she passed out from pain, the chilling, threatening words that had come hissing from his mouth when Stevie intervened.

It was clear that Bryce believed her, but he suspected that he didn't appear as surprised as she expected him to be. Again he recalled the disturbing fact that the previous night's murder-mutilations could not possibly have been committed by one man.

It took him a while to realize she was staring at him.

"How long have you suspected?" she finally asked.

Bryce became intensely interested in the delicate blue pattern of his cup. "Suspected what?"

"Don't be coy, Neal. It's not your style. Suspected that this . . . this whatever he is is somehow controlling people?"

Bryce leaned forward to set his cup and saucer on the table. He leaned back again and shut his eyes, massaging them with his fingertips. The long sigh was a surrender, though he didn't know to whom or what.

"Wade," he replied, "suggested it as early as the Candelaria murder at the Burger Boy ten days ago. But I didn't seriously consider it until this morning."

He explained the passage McKenna had shown him, his own theory about the accomplice or accomplices for last night's bloodbath. She was silent when he finished. Her face was preoccupied, troubled with the effort of pitting a thoroughly rational mind against a thoroughly irrational—yet now undeniable—reality.

Something occurred to Bryce.

"Stevie? This incident yesterday, that's twice now you've been near or involved with the murderer's influence. If our original theory still holds, that the guy's a brain tumor psycho, couldn't that mean you're possibly one of his targets? I mean, could it maybe be someone you've experimented with in your research at the mental hospitals, say?"

"I know what you're doing," the volunteer shouted, backing away from her with fear and hatred burning in his eyes. *"You're poisoning my brain!"*

For a brief moment, as Stevie considered the proposition, something vague and remote and buried stirred in her memory. Then the moment passed and she said, "It's possible, but not very feasible. For one thing, that type of experimentation is already four years behind me. I was fresh out of grad school. Besides, the majority of the people I worked with were either terminally ill or institutionalized for life. And brain tumors couldn't . . . I mean, what would account for the ability to control people mentally?"

Reluctantly, Bryce nodded. "Yeah, you're right. Still, I could have Patterson nose around a little. Do you have a list of their names?"

She nodded. "At my office on campus."

Now Bryce filled her in on Yolanda Davis' phone call and his appointment to meet her husband tomorrow for interrogation under hypnosis. When he mentioned the police psychiatrist, she interrupted him.

"Neal, may I go with you instead?"

At his surprised glance, she explained, "I'm really quite good at hypnosis. I am. I studied it in France as part of my research on electrical changes in the brain during altered states of consciousness. I've successfully hypnotized dozens of people."

Seeing him consider, she added, "I do feel involved in this thing, Neal. I want to help. I haven't done you any good so far."

He rose from the sofa, towering over her. "Okay. When Wade and I pick you up tonight for our patrol I'll let you know the confirmed flight time. But don't be so sure you haven't done me any good."

It took her a moment to realize that the remark was personal, not professional. She didn't expect the sudden quickening of her pulse or the slight difficulty of inhaling the next breath smoothly. Bryce, smiling inwardly, watched her set her cup down and rise too quickly. She did a poor job, he decided, of pretending to have missed the point of his remark.

As she saw him to the door, she said, "I can't help dwelling on something Wade mentioned— that we can't be sure exactly who is on this Johnny Law's side."

They were side by side at the door. The two locked glances, her comment so unsettling that they were forced to don nervous, foolish smiles. Once again Stevie felt something ethereal and remote and portentous stir in her subconscious.

"There it is, Miz Lasalle. The story's out now." *Duncan Hilliard chuckled low in his throat and winked at her. "You'd be surprised what I turn into under a full moon."*

* * *

304

Harlan Perry's bloodless face was the color of new putty in the apartment's muted light:

He had drawn the Venetian blind tight against the late morning sun, allowing him to remove his sunglasses. One of the military recruiting posters had come loose and was peeling away from the kitchen wall like a flap of dead skin.

Perry sat at the rickety Formica table, gazing into the one-gallon jar.

He thought again of the young enlisted commando who had just stopped by, as per his crystal-transmitted orders, to deliver the night's combat booty. He was a good man, thought Perry with a twitching smile of satisfaction, a squared-away trooper. The entire unit was a formidable fighting machine.

"War is our business, and business is good!" screamed Johnny Law.

For a moment the smile wavered as needlepoints of red hot pain stabbed the back of his eyeballs. His battle against the cancerous growth that bitch had deliberately planted in his head was growing fiercer every day. But her assassination attempt had failed. Just as the attempt, by her and the rest of the government's Politico-Carcinogenic Agents, to infect and destroy society would fail.

Perry's smile widened. Recently, undetected in his new Saab Turbo, he had followed Wade McKenna and that tall cop to a house on the West Bank. Now he knew where they were staying. He also recalled Stevie Lasalle and thought of the mulatto security guard in her apartment building. Soon, goodamn all you bastards, soon it would be time to commence the final movement to Contact Phase.

Perry gazed at the velvet-enshrouded Tuaoi in the middle of the table and reminded himself that though it meant traveling light and deserting much of his personal gear, he would have to leave soon. Any day now the museum would notice the theft.

A small yellow notepad lay beside the Terrible Crystal. On the top sheet had been drawn a crude map of New Orleans and the outlying, undrained backswamps southwest of the city. Dotted lines emanated from the swamps toward the bridges and ferries connecting the most populated sectors of town. Perry had labeled the map, in neat block letters, OPERATION COSMIC CHEMOTHERAPY, PHASE ONE.

Acting impulsively, he picked the jar up in both hands and gave it a few shakes. He smiled with almost childish glee as he thought of those clear plastic, water-filled paperweights with their drifting snowflakes; then he set it back down and watched all eight of the wrinkled ears settle lazily in the lambent glow of the formaldehyde solution.

It was going to be a topnotch job, Sonny thought with anticipatory pride.

He shook his head a couple times to flip the dark bangs out of his eyes. Then he slipped the long plank of unvarnished red cedar into the vise and clamped it down tight.

He was bent over a nicked and scarred workbench which protruded from the back wall of

the garage. A 75-watt bulb with a green metal
shade hung directly overhead, its extension cord
snaking back toward the wall plug near the side
door. Tin bins behind the bench housed a
confusion of nails, screws, washers and odd
scraps of wood. A 10' miter saw was attached to
the far end of the bench by a bar clamp. Within
easy distance nearby were also a belt sander, a
foot-powered lathe and a cog-belt planer.
Sonny's refurbished Honda engine was propped
between heavy wooden blocks near one end of
the workbench.

"Eso mismo," he muttered with satisfaction
when the cedar board was placed exactly the
way he wanted it.

Recently, Sonny had discovered a box in the
garage containing all of Bryce's sports trophies
—football, basketball, track—dating back to
the Texan's college and high school days. Since
his foster dad's birthday was coming up in a
couple of weeks, Sonny had decided to make
him a stained shelf for mounting them more
ceremoniously in the house.

He had just finished rechecking the angle of
the cedar when he thought he heard the side
door moving.

Sonny spun quickly around. He had left the
door open for ventilation. Now he couldn't tell,
from the blue wedge of afternoon sky peeking in
near the top of the frame, if it had been moved.

"Wade? Is that you?"

There was no reply. He felt foolish listening to
his own voice bounce back from the empty
corners of the garage.

There was nobody there.

God, he admonished himself, what a paranoid bubblebrain!

When he turned back around, his eyes rested for a moment on a shellacked wooden plaque which the last owners of the house had left hanging on the wall. An old Balkan rhyme was inscribed on it,

Even a man who is pure in heart,
And says his prayers by night
Can become a wolf when the wolfbane blooms,
And the summer moon is bright.

Dumb, he thought.

Sonny picked up his Black & Decker drill and snapped it on, its banshee screech suddenly filling the garage.

CHAPTER FIFTEEN

"JUST PROMISE ME THIS, BRYCE. IF I OFFER YOU A cold beer, you won't ruin it by salting the damn thing!"

The two men exchanged a grin, Davis' intelligent copper eyes twinkling. It was his only day off of the week, and the restaurateur wore faded jeans and a pullover shirt with a creased linen jacket. Introductions had officially been completed several minutes ago and his wife had discreetly disappeared; now he fingered the neat dab of his mustache and once again bestowed an approving glance on Stevie.

"They sure grow 'em pretty down there in bayou country," he said after looking over his shoulder with exaggerated caution to make sure Yolanda was well out of earshot.

He led them through a long hallway with wainscoted walls, making some polite small talk about the unseasonably cool weather and their flight. Davis conspicuously ignored the portable tape recorder and small electric metronome Bryce was carrying as well as the medical jump kit dangling from Stevie's left hand. At the end of the hall he paused before a set of carved, rosewood doors. The doorknob and hinges were old-fashioned solid brass.

"This is where I count my money," he quipped. "I'll feel safer here."

He ushered them into a plush, spacious den. Three of the walls were dark Honduran mahogany inlaid with teak parquet panels; the fourth was lined with tall walnut bookshelves alternating with varnished oil paintings. The carpeting was so thick it seemed to heave up against their soles as they entered.

"It's beautiful," Stevie said approvingly. She gazed slowly around the room.

"Not bad for a high school dropout," Davis conceded with offhand pride.

He nodded toward a scrolled secretary against the nearest wall and Bryce crossed to it, depositing the metronome and tape recorder.

There was an isolated knock before Yolanda Davis entered, looking far more nervous than her husband.

"Anyone like some coffee or refreshments before you get started?" she asked.

Her offer was politely declined all the way around. Ben came nearer and kissed her quickly on the neck. "It's gonna be all right, honey,"

310

he assured her. "You just make sure the kids lay low for awhile, okay?"

The door shut behind her and an uncomfortable silence ensued. Bryce exchanged a brief glance with Stevie, awkwardly clearing his throat.

"I want to thank you again, Mr. Davis, for agreeing to cooperate. I have absolutely no authority to force you to do so. I take it you understand that?"

"Yeah, I understand." Davis shrugged, nervously fingering his mustache again. "Hell, I don't like being connected in any way with this psycho who's offing people in New Orleans."

He paused to smile at Stevie. "Sorry. In 'Nawlins.' Yola told me what words I was screaming the other night. And I *am* connected to him somehow, or he wouldn't have used my name when he visited that shrink he killed. I'm tired of holding this goddamn thing down inside me, whatever it is."

Davis glanced again at the livid white scar visible beneath the hollow of Stevie's throat. "Besides," he added, "I guess I ain't the only one that's lugging around a shitty memory or two."

Davis took an audibly deep breath and slapped his stomach with both hands like a man finishing a good meal. "Okay. What do you want me to do? Lie down on the sofa and talk to Doctor Freud?"

Stevie smiled. "We want you comfortable, but not falling asleep. Have you got a favorite chair?"

"Does Dolly Parton sleep on her back? Course I got a favorite chair." Davis crossed to a floral print wingback chair near the slate fireplace and settled in.

Stevie unzipped the jump kit she was still holding. Davis' copper eyes widened slightly when she removed a plastic-sealed hypodermic syringe containing a premeasured isotonic solution. Bryce had wheedled it from the police psychiatrist at her request.

"Thiopental sodium," she explained. "So-called truth serum. It might predispose you to cooperate better under hypnosis, though I'm not banking on it."

There was a crisp snapping sound as Stevie broke the sanitary plastic seal. "Technically," she continued, "it's illegal for me to administer this without an M.D. to supervise. I guess you know that. We don't have to use it."

Davis shrugged again and grinned at both of them. "That's okay, lady. I grew up in Cicero over on the West Side." He winked at Stevie. "There's been a few other illegal needles poked into me."

Stevie found a vein in his right forearm, swabbed a spot with alcohol-soaked cotton and injected him.

"First," Stevie said, her tone soothing but authoritative, "let's get you relaxed."

Unceremoniously, she knelt beside the chair and placed a hand on his abdomen.

"I want you to breathe from your diaphragm, not the top of your lungs. If you're doing it right, you should feel your stomach rising, not your chest . . . that's it, take in air from lower down. Make it feel like your stomach is a basketball being inflated. Good . . . good. Now slow down and take a little longer to exhale than you do to inhale. That's it . . . not the top of the lungs, but way down in your stomach . . . slower . . . slower . . . good."

She nodded at Bryce and he crossed to the secretary, activating the battery-powered metronome's amber light signal. Stevie had preset the tempo dial so the unit would flash at one second intervals.

"I want you to watch the light and only the light."

Her voice was soothing, even gently seductive.

"Watch the light and listen to me. Ben, can you remember a time in your life when you felt relaxed—I mean *totally* relaxed? Happy, at peace with the world, no troubles, no bad memories? Just relaxed and glad to be alive. No, don't look at me. Watch the light."

After a long pause, Davis answered slowly. "Yeah, I can remember a time like that. On the beach at Mazatlan. Me and Yola went to Mexico for our honeymoon."

"Good," Stevie said. "Think about Mazatlan and let yourself relax, let your muscles grow slack and heavy. The sun is warm on your skin, Ben, the sand is warm beneath you. The waves are making a soft, gentle, lapping sound that is lulling you, relaxing you, draining all your tension. Your muscles are heavy, Ben, incredibly heavy, and you've never felt so relaxed and in harmony with the world. But don't close your eyes. Watch the flashing light.''

She nodded again and Bryce depressed the tape recorder's play and record buttons, carrying the unit closer to the chair without crossing into Davis' line of vision. Bryce had already briefed her about the direction of the questioning.

Without altering the tone of her voice, Stevie said, "When did you join the Army, Ben?"

"January '67."

"Where did you go through basic?"

"Fort Knox. Then infantry training at Fort Jackson."

"When were you sent to Vietnam?"

"June '67."

"To what part of the country were you assigned?"

A long pause. The light blinked on and off. The tape recorder made a faint scratching noise. Stevie repeated the question.

"Ben, to what part of the country were you assigned?"

"The South . . . the Mekong River delta."

"What was it like there?"

Another long pause. Then, "I had it pretty easy after. . . . '' Davis trailed off. His voice remained calm but wooden when he resumed. "After that first month in-country."

Sensing that she should approach obliquely, Stevie said, "Let's skip the first part. What was it like after that first month?"

"Because of what happened they kept me at a reinforced firebase in the rear. It wasn't too bad there. Some VC snipers, a few artillery strikes by

314

the NVA regulars. They didn't send me out on . . . on no more patrols."

Stevie took a long breath. They were approaching the critical denouement, the unknotting.

"Ben, what happened during that first month?"

Silence.

"What happened during that first month, Ben?"

"I was assigned to a rifle platoon. I was still a cherry boy. Couldn't even walk in that damn elephant grass yet. I still didn't know hardly none of the guys. During my first action we . . . they say we was ambushed hard by a division of NVA. They caught us in a pincers movement. Finally got some air support from the firebase and they retreated. I don't remember everything. They say the whole platoon was wasted 'cept for me. . . . "

A line of sweat broke out on Davis' forehead, his pupils dilating with fright. Stevie was familiar with time regression in hypnosis, so she wasn't surprised to notice that his grammar and pronunciation were regressing, too. More closely approximating the dialect of the young Black GI from Chicago. But she felt the nape of her neck tightening when his right hand rose off the arm of the chair, index finger crooking over and over reflexively as it took up imaginary trigger slack.

"It's okay, Ben, it's o-*kay*. It's not happening now. You're only remembering."

Stevie turned away for a moment to regain

control of her own agitated breathing. Then she turned toward the veteran again and said, "Tell me what happened during that ambush?"

She was forced to repeat the question. Davis began writhing in the chair and started panting like a frightened animal. His face was an ebony mask of glistening sweat.

Stevie grabbed his left hand and held it in her own. "I'm with you, Ben. I'm right here."

Only later would the woman for whom the past was "a dead thing" question what next emerged from her sincerely and spontaneously. "You've got to get it out. It's hurting you too much to leave it buried so deep."

Still he refused to speak. She looked pleadingly at Bryce but he shook his head, mouthing the words, "Keep going."

"Tell me what happened during that first ambush?"

Stevie almost leaped at the hideous growl which rose from deep in his chest.

"War is our business, and business is good . . . kill!"

Stevie's eyes were suddenly silver with tears. She whirled on Bryce. "Neal, I'm torturing him! I can't do it—I just can't!"

Her face crumpled. Bryce set the recorder on the marble mantle of the nearby fireplace and grabbed her by both shoulders.

"Look, dammit, you've got to keep going. You're the one who insisted on coming with me. He knows something, Stevie. You suppose I'm enjoying this any more than you are? But if you think this is cruel, what about what Johnny Law

did to that school teacher, that little girl he sent
leaping off the bridge, that high school kid who
got ripped limb from limb? Last time he killed
six people, Stevie. How many next time? Now
snap out of your shit and conduct yourself like
the tough professional you're supposed to be. Or
is all that just the act of a weak, frightened little
girl?"

Her huge gray eyes snapping sparks at his
taunt, she jerked out of his grip and turned to
Davis again.

"Ben, there's still something you're not telling
me about that ambush. Tell me, Ben. Let it come
up out of you now and it will never ever have to
frighten you again."

Davis arched away from the chair and his
body went rigid, as if from electric shock.

"Dead, oh God, dead! Most a them dead, but
not that white sergeant beside me, lord that boy
is pale but he mean so goddamn mean, he
collects ears and they call him Johnny Law! They
call that boy Johnny Law, the mean
motherfucking white boy. He save my ass, say
Johnny Law Rules right on his big buckteeth!
But now he dead, too, the rest all dead, oh God
no, got to get it all down in my journal, all
dead. . . ."

With a massive shudder Davis collapsed back
into the chair, his chest heaving with sobs.

Ten minutes later, after Davis had wept most
of the trauma out of his psyche, Stevie knelt
beside his chair and said gently, "Where is that
journal, Ben? May we see it?"

"Can't." His voice was thick, blurry with grief.

"Why not, Ben?"

"Don't have it."

"Did you lose it in Vietnam during the battle?"

"No. Not in Nam."

"Did you give it to someone?"

"No. Kept it awhile, then threw it away."

Bryce's upper lip was white with tension. He stood immobile beside the chair, straining to catch every word.

"Why?" Stevie asked. "Why did you throw it away?"

"Didn't want . . . didn't want to remember. I was the only one who knew. Couldn't handle that."

"Where did you throw it away?"

A pause as Davis frowned with the effort of remembering. The amber-blinking metronome was a lurid neon pulse in his copper irises.

"Back in the States. It was in my handbag, along with a spare uniform, my dogtags, everything 'cept the clothes on my back. I stuck the whole bag in the trash. Lotsa guys getting out was doing that, just stuffin' 'em in the trash."

"Where in the States, Ben?"

"The . . . airport. I wasn't planning on doing it. I just got the idea when I saw this Marine ahead of me toss his seabag away. The airport employees was digging them out again. Right after I tossed mine, I saw this ugly little punk of a janitor drop his broom and run over to dig it out. I thought, hell, he could have it. I was sick of uniforms and war and the Army."

"Which airport?"

"The airport in . . . Houston."

Despite the potential breakthrough Davis' confession represented, Bryce felt like kicking himself in the ass. He had missed the Houston clue during his interview eleven days ago with Davis at the Sou'wester.

Stevie stood back up and turned to the detective. Her eyes, still bright with barely contained tears, dwelled accusingly on him. Anger seethed just beneath the surface of her words.

"He must have repressed it. He repressed almost all of it because it hurt too much to remember—the sergeant called Johnny Law, the diary . . ."

She trailed off and turned her face away so she wouldn't have to look Bryce in the eye. "Is that enough, or do you insist that I torment him some more?"

Bryce's heartbeat quickened as his own anger surged to match hers. "What are you talking about? He may have just given us the clue to the murderer's identity, for Christsakes. Somebody got hold of that journal. Okay, sure, we still haven't figured out how Johnny Law is doing his—his mind control thing—but with any luck we'll have a list by tomorrow morning of every janitor who worked at Houston International when Ben passed through there."

"I'm sure that'll be just dandy for your bruised policeman's ego, won't it? Now you can lord it over Reno Morgan. But maybe, just *maybe* you'd be a little more sensitive to other people's problems if just once in your pampered life you'd ever had to really suffer!"

Once again Bryce couldn't prevent that momentary feeling like something sharp lodged inside his esophagus, that discomfitting realization that the psychotic Johnny Law suffered only a sick and wildly exaggerated version of Bryce's own doubts and insecurities about the war.

"I'm sorry," he said, his voice heavy with bitterness, "that I didn't die in Vietnam so you could really admire me."

"Neal, wait! I didn't mean—"

But Bryce was already hurrying out of the room to find Yolanda Davis and ask her where the phone was.

"All right, people, quit the grabassing and lissenup! Be ready to move out at oh-five-hundred tomorrow. First stop is the armory for weapons issue. After chow you draw your field gear, then form up on the tarmac for final deployment inspection. Any questions?"

Staff Sergeant Fanning stood several feet higher than his men, straddling the turret of a camouflage-painted, all-terrain assault vehicle. He surveyed the three platoons of commandos standing at ease and clad in five-color camis that matched the vehicle. Even at his present altitude, he didn't notice a few yardbirds in the last rank. They were ripping open their C-ration boxes, digging out the cellophane-wrapped B-1 Units which contained the chewing gum and cigarettes and packets of fudge.

Several men had been excused from formation to serve as a loading party for the swamp-fire exercise which was scheduled to begin the day after tomorrow. They clambered on and off the line of assault vehicles stretching out behind Fanning, stowing inflatable rubber rafts, cases of naphtha flares and rocket-propelled grenades.

"All right."

The noncom bent down and slapped the turret beneath him. "Maybe the most brilliant among you have already figured out that we're also gonna be testing a dozen of these new vehicles. These're Commando V-150's, manufactured by General Electrics, a diesel-powered, all-terrain assault vehicle capable of 88 kilometers per hour on open land."

He paused, then added, "Designed for swamps and marshes as well as close combat under built-up urban conditions. The gun is a 20mm., 6-barrel Gatling capable of busting 3,000 caps a minute."

A murmur stirred the ranks.

"That's right, gentlemen. Between these V-150's and those state-of-the-art burp pistols you're being issued tomorrow, we're gonna set up one helluva righteous wall of firepower."

Fanning paused again to cock his head slightly, like a man trying to detect a far-off sound in a stiff breeze. Then he rotated 90 degrees until he was facing the nearly deserted parking lot just past the main gate. He could see the black Saab Turbo and barely make out the shape of a man behind the wheel.

He nodded. When he turned back toward the men, his eyes blazed with the eagerness of a rampaging hussar.

"Remember! You men wear the red beret! And what is red the color of?"

"Blood!" screamed 150 voices as one.

"Stop," McKenna said. His tone was almost bored. "I see one."

The man he was pointing at was exiting a greasy spoon on South Front Street near the river. As Bryce whipped the Olds in toward the curb, he only had time to notice the bubbled sunglasses; odd, he thought, considering it was almost completely dark. Then the man passed under the pale sickly glow of a streetlight, and Bryce noticed the long military raincoat and the dark lunchbox tucked football fashion under his arm.

Without comment Stevie reached across the seat to hand him the clipboard with its pad of phony questionnaires. Relations between the two had been strained since returning from Chicago earlier that evening, though a mutual sense of urgency ensured their cooperation. As Bryce had feared, there was no way to get the required information telexed from Houston International before tomorrow morning at the earliest. Despite the exhaustion of their round trip flight and the ordeal with Ben Davis, they had agreed to a brief aura-spotting patrol. So far the results had once again been frustratingly ineffectual, but knowing that Johnny Law was due to strike soon, the trio had opted to take the only kind of action they could think of.

Bryce parked under a streetlight. He had just gripped the door handle when the odd little man locked glances with him.

The detective felt cold sweat prickling his scalp when Stevie caught her breath and said, "My God, he looks familiar!"

The man had been heading toward a line of parked cars on the other side of the street. Now, as Bryce swung out of the Cutlass and hurried toward him, he suddenly whipped an about-face and disappeared in an alley between two warehouses.

Bryce's long legs covered the distance to the alley in a few fast strides. Overhead, the last lingering light of day left a saffron afterglow in the sky. He could see the man's shape diminishing toward the river.

"Halt!" Bryce shouted, knowing the university researcher gig was up. "Police!"

Gravel crunched under his shoes as he raced through the alley. The hoarse sound of his panting echoed off the high brick walls on either side, blood pounding in his temples.

He was within twenty feet, closing the gap rapidly, when he realized the man was fumbling inside the lunchbox.

A gun, thought Bryce. Without breaking stride, he reached under his sport jacket and clawed the Browning 9mm. parabellum from its holster.

He was about to shout "Halt!" again when he abruptly slowed down, stopped and began to feel foolish.

He couldn't believe he was making such a gung ho ass of himself. At worst it was some dockside lowlife with an ounce or two of pot he was about to pitch.

Never even suspecting that his mind had just been changed for him, Bryce watched the man disappear into the inky darkness at the base of the levee. The cop holstered his weapon and returned to the car. He didn't notice the Ford sedan parked behind him until he was about to open his door.

"It's official now, rich boy," Reno Morgan said, stepping out of the surrounding shadows and thrusting a letter toward him.

The agent managed to look gloating without quite breaking into a smile. "You're off this case for good."

CHAPTER SIXTEEN

STEVIE RAISED THE STRAIGHT, LIGHT, LETHALLY honed scalpel until its razor-fine edge gleamed in the glare of the bedroom's blue porcelain lamp.

She guided it toward the fine ridge of callus at the base of her left index finger, caused by constant rubbing against the handle of her briefcase. Carefully, deftly, she peeled off a sliver of dead skin as thin as a fly's wing.

Good. The instrument was sharpened to perfection. It would cut clean and quick, do the job efficiently.

She slipped it back into the vinyl instrument case lying open on the bed and tucked the case into her jump kit. Stevie had taken the instruments home with her after last Friday's dissection lecture at the med school instead of returning them to her office on campus, as usual. She would need them again this afternoon to finish her seminar on structural malfunctions of the cerebral cortex.

She had just finished showering and had donned her chartreuse satin bathrobe. Yesterday's back-to-back flights and the ordeal with Ben Davis had left her tired, overwrought and out of synch.

Stevie confronted herself in the mirror. This morning made it several times now in the past week that she'd missed her precious morning *katas*. Deep valleys of fatigue under her eyes made them look even wider, making her seem deceptively naive and vulnerable and afraid. As for the thick mass of belligerent hair, all she'd had time for these past few days were quick shampooings on the run, then a cursory comb and brush, letting it settle like a rumpled sable cape over her shoulders.

In the midst of these literally vain ruminations, she realized she hadn't seen Mr. Cat since she had returned to her apartment last night.

She had come home exhausted from the fruitless patrol, then tumbled into bed without looking for her pet. Now she remembered that she hadn't seen him since early Sunday morning, a full 24 hours.

Mr. Cat was aloof, but not reclusive. Why hadn't he curled up on the foot of the bed during the night, as usual? At least been in to greet her by now?

He was nowhere in the living room, including

under the sofa. Barefoot, robe whispering against her thighs, Stevie padded across the soft floral patterns of the Persian rug, then the cooler solid oak floor between the edge of the rug and the east window. She snapped the latch back and swung the window wide open on the day. Below, miniature people and vehicles went about their business oblivious to her. Ahead, the river was a brackish, sluggish snake, swirling through the city while ships inched along its spine like crawling centipedes. Already, before 8 A.M.., the day was sticky, overcast, breezeless; thunderheads were massing over the Gulf in thick dark columns, and Stevie knew it was going to be one of those days that felt like an unventilated steamroom.

One of the spuming thunderheads was suddenly livid with fine white veins of lightning. Stevie caught her breath and spun around.

The living room was empty.

Of course it was empty.

Why wouldn't it be, she asked herself reasonably. She resumed her search.

"Here, kitty-kitty. C'mere, Mr. Cat! Front and center, Your Highness."

A quick search revealed that he wasn't in the bathroom either. The only remaining rooms were the kitchen and her *dojo*, but this last was always kept closed against him. She headed for the kitchen.

Stevie was sure his food bowl would be empty, but she was surprised when the first glance showed it to be brimful. The surprise turned to cold shock when she realized that the food in Mr. Cat's bowl was raw ground beef, still pink and lean and fresh.

She never gave him ground beef, didn't even have any in the apartment.

Blood throbbed in her temples as she slowly approached the bowl, still feeling more confused and disoriented than frightened. Who could have fed Mr. Cat so extravagantly, and why? Whoever it was didn't realize how finicky her pet was. Mr. Cat wouldn't touch any food unless it was cut or balled into little bite-size pieces.

She picked up the bowl. In the glare of the overhead light, something inside the meat glittered and caught her eye. Granules of sugar? She squinted and examined it more closely, probing with a cautious fingertip. Her entrails turned into a solid chunk of ice when she realized.

The glittering stuff was very finely ground glass.

Whoever had gotten in knew that cats weren't equipped to chew their food well. He also knew that even just a little of that deadly glass powder would painfully lacerate Mr. Cat's guts once digestion had started.

Fear tightened her scalp. Now she wasn't quite so sure that none of the food had been eaten. But she was convinced that Mr. Cat, if he was even here, could only be in one room—the *dojo*.

Someone had entered her apartment, no

doubt while she was in Chicago yesterday. The thought kept her heart knocking hard against her ribs as she retraced her steps through the living room. Stevie was halfway to the hallway which led past her bedroom, ending at the mat-converted spare room, when she paused, glancing at the draperies over the north window.

The draperies were closed, cutting off the view of City Park and the I-10 causeway threading its way over Lake Pontchartrain. It was just as she had left it, except that the cord had been cut off. One badly frayed end dangled about six feet over the floor.

Cut off . . . why?

Maybe because someone is waiting in the dojo to strangle you with it.

No!

She was letting herself panic, losing her grip on reality. Stevie made a conscious effort to regain control of her breathing. Then, remembering to ease the tense muscles, she finished walking to the closed door.

Time seemed to pause as she stood there, hand poised over the knob. The door was solid wood, expertly hung, with a spring mechanism. She knew it would ease open quietly. Still, she found herself irrationally wishing for the protective sibilant whisper of Keith's Professor Wigglewobble voice, telling her if it was safe or not to open that door—just as the voice had warned her of the gas leak on that night so long ago.

But that's mere regression to childhood, she scolded herself, denying reality to cower behind a defense mechanism.

She turned the knob, and the door swung open.

The room was dark, its only window blocked by a bamboo screen. She switched on the light just inside the door.

No!

Oh, dear merciful God, no!

Stevie jammed the edge of one hand into her mouth and tried unsuccessfully to choke back the scream.

Neal Bryce massaged both closed eyelids, combed his curly hair with his fingers, stood up from behind the desk and absently popped another antacid tablet.

"Sonofabitch," came a mutter from down the hall in Records and Identification, where Delbert Baptiste was computer-searching the telexed data which had just arrived from Houston. "Son of a *bitch!*"

Bryce was listening to *The Magic Flute* and didn't quite make out the muttered curse. He was also thinking of Stevie Lasalle, thinking about what she had gone through behind that theater a decade ago, about the truth of what she had told him yesterday. He never *had* really suffered, neither for himself or anyone else. For all that she knew, he didn't give a good goddamn about his fellow man. Hell, for all *he* knew he didn't.

"The man you want is named Harlan Perry."

Bryce blinked several times, focusing slowly on the doorway. Baptiste, his face split by a triumphant grin, scuttled in trailing the folds of a computer printout. Milo followed him, protecting the errant folds of paper like a maid guarding the tail of a chiffon gown.

"What?" Bryce blinked stupidly and leaned forward to turn down the stereo's volume.

Milo said, "A mind like a steel trap! The man's telling you that your little excursion to the Windy City paid off. I think we found our boy!"

Baptiste flopped the sheaf down on Bryce's desk and jabbed it with a stubby index finger. "The man you want is named Harlan Perry. Worked as a custodian at Houston International Airport during the same time Ben Davis passed through there. His name is also in Martin Fischler's patient file. Had a root canal done about five years ago. Same man—Social Security number checks."

Baptiste, relishing his role as harbinger, paused dramatically before adding, "And the address listed here is located right across the street from that Burger Boy."

Bryce stared at the columns of data and started to object, but Baptiste had anticipated him.

"Yeah, I know. Patterson already got us that tenant's list and we checked it, but look."

Bryce took in the fatal typographical error—Berry for Perry—without comment. He looked at Milo.

"Morgan says I'm off this case. What do you say?"

Milo shrugged and kept his expression carefully noncommittal. "Who am I to challenge The Nation's Finest?"

Bryce knew that this bit of low-key sarcasm was as close as he'd get to an official sanction. But he also knew there was nothing native Orleanians like Milo hated more than outsiders trying to run their city. It was a longstanding island-bastion mentality. And when push came to shove, Milo could overcome even his lifelong, knee-jerk hatred for Texans. He considered Bryce a fellow islander, albeit a defective imported model, in the struggle against Reno Morgan and his non-islanders. Bryce realized, as did Milo, that it was too late to turn this new information over to the Feds. Morgan, committed to finding his Third World terrorist ring, would simply shelve it and prevent BSI from pursuing further leads.

Whatever was done, Bryce knew it would have to be done on his own—and done quickly. Reno Morgan's state of siege scenario was now being enacted. Late last night the Governor of Louisiana had reluctantly agreed to send in the National Guard. Six battalions were due to arrive later that day.

"There's something else," Baptiste said as Bryce was heading toward the door. The R & I chief smiled with childish delight, almost reluctant to spill this last dramatic secret.

Bryce sighed and shook his head in exasperated defeat. "Well, what is it, for Christsakes? Or should I play three guesses while Rome burns?"

"Just this: 'Member how you wanted me to go

through that list Stevie Lasalle provided us of the names of her experimental subjects? Well, I just checked Perry's name against it. Her records show that on April 15, 1982, she issued him a check for five dollars. All of a sudden this dude's name is popping up all over."

The cord from the living room drapes had been tied to the *dojo's* ceiling light fixture. Something raw and red and glistening was dangling from it, slowly twirling in the slight breeze caused when Stevie opened the door.

Her heart eased down out of her throat and back into her chest. Whatever it was, it was not Mr. Cat. She could see that now. Stevie moved a few feet closer until she realized that it was an uncooked filet mignon, tied awkwardly around the middle.

Something bumped into her from behind. The startled protest died in her throat when she spun around, almost kicking an indignant Mr. Cat. He brushed against her ankles again, yawning sleepily and demanding food. The tabby must have been shut in the *dojo* all night—shut in by whomever had come and gone yesterday. Somebody obviously had used a key to enter the apartment. It could have been one of the security guards or someone else who managed to copy the master key. Stevie resolved to violate her rental agreement and bribe a locksmith to change the locks, but first she would call Neal.

She was still thinking, still looking cautiously around the unfurnished room, when Mr. Cat arched his back in a fight-or-flight crouch.

She watched him stare in the direction of the

kitchen, spitting and hissing. His pupils dilated with fright until both eyes resembled large black watermelon seeds. Then cold sweat broke out on Stevie's face when she heard the unmistakable tinkling of the mobile in the kitchen.

It was no longer a matter of someone who had come and gone. Someone was with her right now in the apartment.

"Rest assured that you have discovered my command post too late. Soon, very soon now, the inexorable Wheel of Fortune begins a giant down swing, and marks a New Apocalypse for the great diseased body of civilization. Presently the bloodsucking parasites and slimy cancerous growths hold sway. But I alone am a strong cell, and I alone can regenerate the diseased body. In America now we no longer have a tradition of leadership. We have a malignant habit, a bad, sick, maggot-festering habit! But like any habit, it can be broken, scraped away like any tumor, and at my command! JOHNNY LAW RULES!"

Once again, with the grating voice silent, the tape began to hum like an open mike. Bryce clicked the cassette unit off. His face was pale, slick with sweat in the rank stuffiness of the grungy efficiency. There had been no response to his knock, but the worn bolt had yielded quickly to the edge of a plastic credit card.

The ransacked appearance of the hovel suggested that it had been left in a hurry. Then he had discovered the cassette player reigning in the middle of the kitchen table with the Memorex tape lying invitingly beside it.

Now Bryce stood rooted to the kitchen linoleum, his slowly revolving head a camera recording impressions—the Vietnam-era recruiting posters plastering each wall, the 40mm. shell-casing ashtray, the hand-lettered sign on the refrigerator proclaiming ONE BULLET, ONE ENEMY. When he finally moved he had to duck around the dried-up flystrip dangling in the middle of the room, dotted with dead flies like shriveled raisins.

The tape proved that this was the one-time home of a madman, but Bryce needed more than circumstantial evidence to prove he was *the* madman.

He cautiously nudged the door of the corner closet open. Hanging from a nail on the back of the door, each encased in rubber to silence their clinking, was a set of dogtags. Bryce cocked his head to read them: DAVIS, BENJAMIN AUGUSTUS. RA2519720. The only other item in the tiny closet was an olive-drab vinyl handbag that Bryce recognized instantly as standard issue to Army recruits during the Vietnam War.

He hitched his trousers, knelt, then straightened with a grunt and smacked his head hard against the closet's back shelf. Cursing and massaging the sore spot at the top of his skull, he carried the handbag back to the table and unzipped it.

He found the diary first. A faded, fake-leather volume labeled simply "Personal Record." Bryce flipped one cover open and spotted the clumsy printing: Davis, Private B. A. RA2519720, 'G' Company, 2nd Battalion, Third Infantry Training Regiment, Fort Jackson. Begun April 9, 1967.

Next the detective fished out a three-hole spiral notebook neatly labeled by a different hand: KNOWN AND SUSPECTED POLITICO-CARCINOGENIC AGENTS (PCA'S). He flipped it open, brows knitting in confusion at the first entry he spotted: TRADE WINDS FRUIT COMPANY, SAN JOSE, CALIFORNIA. Then he discovered the official Air Force letter signed by Lydell Helzer: "Dear Mr. Perry, This agency regrets to inform you . . ."

He also spotted, taped to one page, Stevie's yellowing classified ad soliciting participants for an experiment to measure changes in brain electricity. And the notebook's latest entry was AGENT WADE MCKENNA, AKA THE INCREDIBLE SHONEEN. Perry had added in parentheses, "Have some fun with this one before liquidation."

A folded rectangle of paper fluttered out of the notebook and landed on the table. Bryce ironed it flat with the side of his left fist. It was an employee paycheck stub, made out to Perry, recently dated and issued by the Municipal Museum of Natural History. His pulse quickened. Since Perry had apparently deserted his digs, it was unlikely he still worked for the museum, but any lead was valuable now, and someone there might hold the clue to his present whereabouts.

Or even to his incredible, inhuman power.

The small yellow notepad Bryce next extracted from the handbag seemed blank at first. Then he noticed faint indentations in the top sheet, made when something had been written and sketched on the sheet above it. Eyes narrowed to slits, turning the pad at oblique angles under the glare of a naked bulb overhead, he barely made out some dotted lines heading from the bottom left toward the top right corner of the sheet. Then he deciphered the barely discernible impressions of the words OPERATION COSMIC CHEMOTHERAPY, PHASE ONE."

It meant something crucial, Bryce knew, but what? With all that he had discovered here today, he still lacked two vital components—incontrovertible physical proof that Harlan Perry was behind the recent assaults, and any kind of clue as to how he was actually executing the attacks.

It was then that he spotted the newspaper clipping, wadded into one corner of the handbag. He gouged it out, straightened it and read about the two-week training course for the highly elite U. S. Zappo Regiment visiting New Orleans.

Bryce didn't make the connection until he neared the end of the piece.

> . . . remaining week will be spent in the undrained, uninhabited swamps surrounding the Intracoastal Waterway southwest of the city, where the commandos will practice small team counterterrorist tactics under live-fire conditions.

Bryce recalled his theory that one man couldn't have committed the multiple killings last Friday without accomplices. He also thought of those dotted lines on the notepad, running from southwest to northwest, and suddenly he was afraid that he knew what OPERATION COSMIC CHEMOTHERAPY, PHASE ONE was all about.

He felt his face sweating. It was impossible. He wanted to grab all this evidence, take it to the Feds and force them to listen. But all he would likely accomplish was getting his own butt suspended without pay for disobeying his superiors and failing to relinquish jurisdiction in this case.

No, he had to act fast and on his own. According to that article this was the week of the swamp-fire exercise, which would also explain Perry's desertion of the apartment. Leaving all this incriminating stuff behind might imply that he was too insane to reason. It might just as well, Bryce decided, mean that his plans were too grandiose to allow him to worry about something as inconsequential as cops.

He had to check on Perry at the museum, then warn Stevie and Wade.

To satisfy his curiosity on another point, Bryce paused at the window to tug the Venetian blinds open. Yes, this was the window directly across from the Burger Boy.

The thunderheads he had spotted earlier had edged in closer to the city. Jagged fibers of lightning became eerie white neon skeletons trapped in the clouds. The muttering of thunder was growing gradually louder, like the din of a nearby drunken party increasing into the wee hours.

Bryce turned from the window and crossed the room in several giant strides. Later, he never

338

did figure out exactly why he paused again, paused to open the dirty enamel cupboard over the sink. Maybe it was because it was already ajar several inches, piquing his curiosity.

He heard the rumbling, rolling, sliding noise just in time to duck out of harm's way when the large object came tumbling out. There was a glass-shattering crash when it struck the floor, liquid splashing his shoes and trousers. Bryce cursed, then recoiled in horror and kicked savagely. He kicked over and over, making sure he got rid of the wrinkled white human ear that had washed up onto his shoe like some beached fragment of hell.

A quiet mind feels no fear.

Stevie stepped carefully around Mr. Cat and into the hallway, repeating the line from her training meditations.

A quiet mind feels no fear.

Your will is a fist and you can clench it.

Terror was what men preying on women always banked on, she reminded herself as, barefoot, satin robe pulled tight to prevent its telltale whispering, she reflexively lowered her center of gravity and moved silently toward the living room. They had faith in their usually correct assumption that the female victim will be paralyzed by fear, made inert by lack of mental and physical preparation, unassertive and timid by virtue of the simple fact of being a woman.

Something thumped in the living room, and she took the same advice she had given Ben Davis yesterday. She began breathing slowly from her diaphragm, desperately trying to induce the fully observant, mindless dexterity of *mushin*.

But this was the real thing, not training.

Thump!

Someone or . . . some *thing* was waiting for her out there.

She could no longer identify the noises. She no longer tried. One moment her mind teetered on the brink of panic, the next it seized control like a disciplined warrior for whom the threat of death held no sting.

She passed the closed bedroom door and edged cautiously past the bathroom. It was still humid from her recent shower, the air outside the open doorway like warm wet fog on her face.

She stepped into the living room. Duncan Hilliard was relaxing comfortably on the couch, waiting for her.

Except that he was also standing by the door exposing his penis, also grinning at her from the middle of the room, also waving at her from the kitchen as he defecated on the cool tile floor.

The apartment was full of Duncan Hilliards. She didn't realize that they, like the bizarre noises, were all illusory until she felt the very real hot breath on the back of her neck.

"Howzit goin', cooze?" said Duncan's voice behind her.

Time meant nothing during the next immeasureable moment. Stevie wasn't aware that the framed photo of Keith on the coffee table had spun silently around, facing her. Nor was she aware of the sudden penumbra of ghostly blue light which sheathed it. All she noticed was a strange, disembodied voice repeating words she delivered every semester to her self-defense skills class:

"Always be prepared for one of the most effective and disabling strategies your attacker can use—surprise strangle attack from behind known as the garrote."

Mental gears clicked as the proper movement was named, and what happened next fulfilled the aesthetic ideal she had trained for. Stevie did as little as possible.

Cold steel had barely touched her neck when, at the last possible moment she crossed both arms in front of her at the wrists and shot them up and over her head in a powerful cross block. Hilliard's encircling arms flew apart. The steel rebar—a 15-inch whip of thin, hard, twisted metal used to reinforce concrete parking curbs —slashed through the air as it flew from his hand.

Without wasting a second to calculate, Stevie dropped to the floor and rolled onto her left side, looking up and backward at Hilliard. As she had done thousands of times before during *kata* drills against imaginary opponents, she slid her right foot behind the heel of his nearest foot and pressed her instep against it to brace his leg; her free left foot launched a strong thrusting kick at his kneecap. The patella popped loose with a sound of gristle snapping, and Hilliard toppled like a house made of cards, gasping at the incredible, fiery pain.

Stevie rolled free and quickly rose to a defensive crouch. She knew she had disabled him for any renewal of the attack. As she cautiously watched him, pulse thudding in her head like twin earaches, she gratefully noted that the other Duncans had disappeared.

But in the midst of huddled agony, Hilliard looked up at her, grinned the old grin and flashed his gold teeth.

"Looked just like a rotten melon, didn't it, Sis? Just like a big old rotten melon."

Stevie's face crumpled in terrified grief as she backed slowly away. It was unmistakably Keith's voice. And while she watched, so mesmerized by fear and disbelief and revulsion that she couldn't look away, Hilliard's face was transformed into Keith's. It began to melt, cave in, deform itself until it resembled the bloody, pulpy mess she remembered from that night in the alley.

Something warm tickled her left leg, and she was dimly ashamed when she realized that she had just soiled herself. The hellish mask leering at her from the rug abruptly transformed itself once again and became a familiar acne-pocked face.

Outside, muttering thunder gathered itself into an explosive roar.

"Woe, woe, woe to the inhabitants of the Earth!" warned the voice of the dead religious fanatic. "Johnny Law rules!"

The next explosion of thunder turned Stevie's scream into a silent movie parody.

CHAPTER SEVENTEEN

WALLY CRUZ LIVED JUST OFF FRONT STREET ON THE East Bank, a bleached-gray clapboard with one of its louvered shingles hanging by a single hinge. But a pair of well-groomed chinaberry trees saved his place from the naked appearance of squalor.

Bryce, still unaware of the hellish ordeal Stevie had just survived, rolled to a stop out front. He tamped his panatela out in the ashtray, unbuckled the shoulder harness and unfolded his long body from the Cutlass. After leaving Perry's apartment he had visited the museum. He had garnered very little about the elusive murderer from the uncooperative daytime supervisor, although he had finally been given Cruz's name and address and informed that the security guard had shared the graveyard shift with Perry.

Early afternoon humidity thickened the air and plastered his shirt to his back. Thunder still advanced closer to the city like approaching artillery fire. Gray clouds roiled overhead, and the chinaberries in Cruz's front yard were waving the lighter side of their leaves into view. It's going to storm like hell, Bryce thought idly as he followed the cracked and buckled concrete walk toward the house.

The owner of the dwelling, taking advantage of the steady breeze that had sprung up to signal the storm's arrival, was watching a portable black-and-white TV on the front porch. Seeing the tall man approach from the street, he struggled out of a weather-beaten porch swing and ambled to the front stoop.

"Howdy," he called amiably.

The swing's rusted chains screeched rhythmically behind him and Bryce shuddered, thinking of the mad voice on that cassette tape.

"What can I do for ya?" the man added.

"Wally Cruz?"

The chubby man nodded. "In the flesh. 'Less you're a bill collector."

"Haven't worked myself up that high yet," Bryce assured him, stepping onto the porch and flashing his badge.

Cruz was drinking Colt .45 from a 40-ounce bottle. He wore rumpled chinos, a plum-colored t-shirt and house slippers with broken-down heels. A hairy white pot belly peeked out between trousers and shirt.

Seeing the badge, Cruz self-consciously set his malt liquor down on the porch railing and reached out to snapoff the TV.

"Look," he began nervously, "I don't know if you got a warrant or not, but you're welcome to search my place. Go ahead, tear it apart. I never touch a thing at that museum, swear to God I don't. I'm a lazy sumbitch, f'sure. That's why my old lady left me. But I'm honest. You ask anybody, they'll—"

"Take it easy," Bryce said. "I'm not here to bust you for anything. What're you talking about, anyway?"

Most of the nervous tension drained from the guard's face.

"Christ, I thought you was here about that doohickey. Some artifack is missing from one a the storage areas at the museum where I work." Cruz mopped his glistening forehead with a sleeve of his t-shirt. "God Almighty! Scare a guy, why don'tcha? So what *can* I do for you?"

Giving only as many details as he felt prudent, Bryce explained his interest in Harlan Perry.

"You worked with him," Bryce concluded. "What was he like?"

"Ol' Perry?" Cruz crooked an index finger and tapped his right temple a few times. "Well, like Sonny Crockett says, that dude has left most of his groceries at the market."

"What do you mean?" the cop pressed him.

"Well, he was a strange little fucker. Never had much to say. Just walked around with them damn headphones on all the time, muttering to hisself. The one night I did get anything out of

345

him, he went rattling on about how the world was divided up into producers and parasites, or some shit. And that last couple weeks or so before he quit, he lugged his damn lunch bucket with him everywhere he went, like I was gunna steal his chow or something."

"Lunch bucket?" Bryce instantly recalled the encounter last night. "A black one? One of those old-fashioned barn-shaped jobs?

" "Yeah, you got it. Why? You know Perry?"

Bryce ignored the question. He realized now that his thinking had been manipulated last night—and by none other than Johnny Law himself. Now something else occurred to him.

"You mentioned a missing artifact. What is it?"

"You know . . . " Cruz trailed off, his fleshy brow wrinkled in speculation. "I never thought about it much till you brought up the lunch bucket, but he could've easy stuck it in there. Guess I shoulda been more on the ball."

Bryce couldn't keep the impatience from his tone. "He could have stuck *what* in there?"

"Ahh, that missing doohickey. Called a Twaddy Stone or something like that."

Bryce's face tensed. During the plane flight yesterday he had carefully read the chapter called "Juju Fetishes and Mind Control" from the book Wade had given him Saturday morning at the precinct office.

"Do you mean the Tuaoi Stone?" Bryce spelled it out. "The so-called Terrible Crystal?"

"You got it. That's it. Nobody's even sure exactly how long this doohickey's been missing.

All they know is it was swiped sometime between the last inventory and whenever they went to warehouse it. I figger they must've suspected Perry. But the thing is, I hear this crystal's only a cheap fake. Ain't nobody really sweatin' about it. They was planning on mothballing it anyhow."

Bryce was hardly listening. He had to contact the museum again and get more information on that "cheap fake." What he was thinking was impossible—insane, even. But insane or not, it fit the known facts. He recalled that the legend of the Tuaoi maintained that once the crystal master achieved virtuoso status, only his death could free his psychic slaves.

Again Bryce thought of that clipping about the commandos and that crudely sketched map labeled OPERATION COSMIC CHEMOTHERAPY, PHASE ONE. He decided to cut this interview short. If he was right, there wasn't much time.

"Thanks. You've been a lot of help. You think of anything else, leave a message for me." Bryce handed him one of his cards.

The sky over most of the city had grown even more grainy and opaque, and the atmosphere was electrically charged with the imminence of the storm. Bryce was halfway back to his car when he looked up and spotted Stevie's Peugot as it turned in behind his car. When he got a closer look at her face, he covered the rest of the distance to her at a run.

Bryce wasn't sure what he had expected, perhaps that the cold, indepenent loner would

347

fly into his arms, sobs wracking her body.

Instead, she slid slowly out from behind the wheel in a parody of dignified composure, but her vacant, shell-shocked eyes made Bryce think of what battle-weary grunts in Nam used to call "the thousand yard stare."

"Neal," she said, her voice weak and tired, "I'm—I'm glad I found you. Milo told me you'd be here."

He stepped closer, aching to touch her, knowing she wanted to be touched, knowing she was desperately searching for the words she needed.

When she flinched back, he said angrily, "You just simply refuse to admit that you need anybody, don't you? Ms. Total Control. What happened, Stevie? What is it?"

A little moan of terrified agony escaped from her, and she rushed into his arms, almost knocking him off balance.

Bryce folded her against him and felt the warm supple give of her femininity. He kissed her hair and soothed her while Cruz gawked from the porch, forgetting to turn his TV on again.

The sobs diminished to pathetic little hiccups while she explained about the attack earlier that morning at her apartment. Bryce's jaw tensed in anger directed chiefly at himself. He had chosen to visit the museum first instead of warning her about that page he'd discovered in Perry's notebook.

And Wade McKenna was home alone with Sonny. Bryce recalled the line, "Have some fun with this one before liquidation." But no, unless Perry's strange powers included omniscience, he couldn't know where the Incredible Shoneen had moved to.

"Where's Hilliard now?"

Stevie's reply was muffled against his chest. "I called the police. He's being booked for illegal entry and attempted assault."

"Listen," Bryce said gently. He tipped her chin up until he was gazing into the huge, teary gray eyes. As briefly as possible, but leaving nothing pertinent out, he explained what he had discovered earlier that morning at Perry's apartment. Her eyes widened when he mentioned the ad she had once run soliciting subjects for an experiment measuring electrical changes in the brain.

"I remember that. It was my very first project after returning to New Orleans from grad school. But Harlan Perry . . . Harlan Perry . . . the name just doesn't register."

"Remember last night?" Bryce coaxed. "That guy I chased, the one you thought you recognized?"

For a long moment her pretty face remained blank. She sniffled and dabbed a Kleenex at her eyes, self-consciously moving out of his protective arms.

"Oh my God, *now* I remember him!"

Memory clicked and her words came in a tumbling rush. "His brain showed such an odd printout on the EEG that I requested his permission to schedule him for a cat-scan. He was practically hysterical in his refusal, as I recall. There was nothing I could do. I mean, his type of printout could have been caused by several factors, including a mild epileptic seizure. I just I oh, damn, how could I have been so dense?"

"To quote one of my favorite people," Bryce said, " 'the past is a dead thing, leave it alone.' Maybe you were too adept at following your own advice.' "

She nodded, miserable. "Don't rub it in right now, okay? Just tell me what we do next?"

"I'm still figuring that out, but our options are limited, considering that I'm officially off this case."

He quickly filled her in on what Cruz had told him about the missing supposed replica of the Tuaoi Stone. After what she had just witnessed and experienced in her living room, she was now far less skeptical about the possibility that a juju fetish was behind Johnny Law's frightening powers.

"Time is our worst enemy right now," Bryce said. "I've got a lot of groundwork to do. For starters, getting information on those commandos and their itinerary. That means counting on Milo to pull some strings for me and help us circumvent the feds."

"What can *I* do?" Bryce had never seen Stevie so close to looking like a helpless, frustrated little girl. "I'm the one who helped botch this thing by not remembering Perry sooner. I want to help you, Neal."

"Maybe you can. But for now just stay away

from your apartment. Are there a lot of people around your office on campus?"

She nodded.

"Good. Hang around there until I call you. It might be pretty late, though."

She caught at his sleeve as he was about to turn away.

"One second, busy cop. I've been meaning to tell you—meaning to say I'm sorry for what I said to you at Ben Davis' place. That was stupid of me. I wouldn't want you different in any way."

He was composing a suitably light reply when she stretched up on tiptoes and kissed him, full on the lips. Her mouth was warm and slightly salty from a stray tear or two still drying on her lips. He felt the full weight of her breasts as she pressed into him.

When the throbbing blood rushed into his penis, bulging it in an erection, Bryce started to discreetly ease himself back. Then some inner voice persuaded him to go ahead and let her feel his body's response to hers. She did feel it, and she made no attempt to pull away.

His pulse was still thumping in his temples when the first National Guard troop truck rolled past, canvas tarp flapping.

The young pfc driving stared out his open window at the couple getting it on near the curb. Bryce met his glance, then felt the fine hairs on his forearms stiffening. The trooper seemed to grin malevolently, knowingly, cunningly.

A cracking explosion seemed to shake the gray dome of the sky apart. Then the first huge spikes of rain began hurtling down at the city.

Harlan Perry rolled the driver's window down and breathed the clean, cool, mimosa-scented night air.

The afternoon rain had cleared away the humidity and washed the dust from the streets. The stately live oaks he had parked under towered over the West Bank suburb like shimmering canopies, painting the nearly deserted street and nearby houses with wavering, slithering shadows.

And the summer moon was bright.

Perry glanced again toward the California bungalow to his left. The driveway and portcochere were empty, the house enshrouded in a cloak of darkness except for the few downstairs windows that glowed like unblinking yellow eyes. In the sterling moonlight slanting through the Saab's window, Perry's face was dull black from sepia dye. He wore his floppy bush hat and full combat fatigues.

And goddamn all you bastards, he was ready!

Perry knew it was time to strike. Soon, very soon, he would rendezvous with his men near Bayou Barataria south of the city. Dull embers of fury still burned inside him because his mission to take out the pretty Scar Baby earlier had failed. He had left the job up to the mulatto security cop, but obviously the Tuaoi's power was weaker when he relied on intermediaries. This time he would ensure victory by vanquishing his enemy himself—and anybody else unlucky enough to be inside that house with him.

He flung the lid of his lunch bucket back. A stray shaft of moonlight struck the Terrible Crystal and illuminated its brilliant, fathomless, coruscating depths.

Sonny sat cross-legged in the middle of his bed and carefully laid a strip of Scotch tape over the torn photo in his foster dad's basketball scrapbook.

Funny. He couldn't remembering tearing it.

Sonny was only dimly aware of the muted murmurings reaching him from the living room, where Wade was watching TV. Glossy car and motorcycle magazines were scattered everywhere. For visitors the bedroom always felt claustrophobic from the backlog of outgrown or broken toys, games and sporting equipment which Sonny stubbornly refused to throw away or at least move into the garage. Over the head of the bed, Luke Skywalker and Darth Vader engaged in a staring contest.

And beyond the window's white curtains, the summer moon was bright.

Idly, patting the tape into place, Sonny wondered when Neal was coming home. He lay the scrapbook lovingly aside and started flipping through an issue of *Cycle World*. He wasn't sure exactly what made him glance toward the open doorway of his room.

Wade was standing there, smiling an odd, crooked little smile at him.

"I hear," said the freckled redhead, still leering, "that you've got a reconditioned Honda engine out in the garage. Can I see it?"

". . . and all I gotta do," Sonny chattered excitedly as he led McKenna through the kitchen toward the back door, "is keep my eyes open for the right frame and mount my engine on it. Neal says I can drive it around the driveway until I get my license."

Behind the boy, McKenna's lips twitched spasmodically and his face was like an elastic mask that constantly stretched into different, contending expressions—rapt interest one second, bitter scorn the next. Intelligent, ironic affection now gave way to dull loathing, then transformed into something indefinably more terrible.

Deep within his psyche, down at the primordial level of tribal consciousness known as the archetype, the battle raged.

His mind was a camera transmitting images onto the screen of his inner eye. He saw a small motorcycle engine propped up by wooden blocks. A boy with his back to the camera proudly pointed out something on the engine. The camera panned back for a long shot. McKenna now saw himself standing in what looked like a garage. There was a stubby Black & Decker drill in his hand, grooved bit twirling madly, whirring, gnashing at air. The camera jerked again, and now McKenna saw himself sitting on top the struggling, screaming boy . . .

"—cause in Louisiana," Sonny rattled on, reaching for the doorknob, "they got this stupid law that you gotta be fifteen to drive a motorcy—"

"*I mean simply,*" Stevie said, "*that a healthy, disciplined, confident mind can actually repel hostile forces. Maybe you are going to worry about this psychotic slave driver enlisting you to his side. You obviously have too little self-respect to believe in yourself, but I refuse to believe that my thoughts and actions can be taken over by anyone.*"

Sonny was opening the door, spilling a shaft of bright yellow light across the moonlit backyard, when McKenna spoke behind him.

"Just a minute. I'll be right with you."

His voice was wooden, mechanical, and if Sonny had glanced into his eyes at that moment, he might have made a mad dash to one of the neighbors. But he only nodded obediently as Wade added, "I've gotta make a quick phone call."

Stevie was half-heartedly revising a section of her textbook when the phone on her office desk suddenly jangled.

She started and sucked in a sharp breath, the pencil leaping from her fingers. She waited a moment for the lump in her throat to dissolve before she plucked the receiver from its cradle.

"Neal?"

A long pause while she felt her heart thumping.

"Neal, huh? Tell me," said the male voice, "have you and Bryce finally got around yet to doing the old in 'n out, in 'n out?"

For a moment she didn't understand; then,

when the caller's meaning dawned on her, she couldn't believe she had heard him correctly.

"Who is this?" she demanded.

"C'mon, sweet nips, let's party down. Oh, wait, I forgot. You yuppie sluts don't party, you 'network.'"

Despite the computerized lifelessness of the voice, Stevie thought she recognized it now.

"Wade? Wade McKenna?"

Another long pause was punctuated by brief moans of grief. "Stevie? Stevie? Help me. I'm trying, Stevie, help me, oh Jesus, help me"

She felt her flesh recoiling from the touch of her blouse. His voice had sounded more normal this time, though dreadfully pained. "Wade? Wade, what is it?"

"You better—better tell me more about how the—how the . . . mind the mind—LISTEN, CUNT!—how the mind can repel hostile forces . . ."

"Wade, what's wrong? What are you talking about?"

His abrupt burst of laughter was harsh in her ear and made her flinch. "You still haven't snapped to what I'm telling you, sweet skivvies. I'm trying, you stupid mutt. Tell me more about how my mind—how my mind can fuck you in your nice tight little asshole, huh?"

For a moment her confusion was replaced by a hot wave of anger. He was falling-down, stinking drunk. That must be it.

"Get your mind out of the gutter and make some sense, or I'm going to hang up," she threatened.

"Yeah, you just go ahead and do that, slutbox. But I'm home alone with Bryce's kid—savvy?"

In that horrible second she *did* savvy. Hundreds of tiny needles prickled her scalp, and the palm pressing against the phone broke out in sweat.

"Wade, listen, I'll talk to you. I'll talk as long as you want, okay? I'll—"

"How's chances for a little bitta nooky? I mean, you're not exactly the most horrible hog I've ever seen. You suck dick?"

"Wade, listen to me. The mind *can* repel—"

"Well, we don't have to get all in a snit now, do we?"

"Wade, the mind can—"

Heavy breathing was followed by, "Deeper, Daddy, deeper! Ram that porker into me." The harsh laugh, a brief pause, choking sounds, as if McKenna couldn't breathe. Then his voice became more nearly normal. "Tell me, Stevie. I'm trying, but he's getting stronger in me, you— you sleazy piece of twat."

"Wade, listen to me. In the 1950's a man named Wolpe—"

"Wolpe, Wolpe, Wolpe!" screamed the voice. "Whoopee, whoopee, whoopee! Guy who invented the fart cushion, yeah?"

"—a man named Wolpe wrote a book called *Psychotherapy by Reciprocal Inhibition*, and—"

"C'mon, baby, can the chitchat and let's make like the two-backed beast, let's do the ol' maximum interface, let's—"

"*Listen*, Wade! Wolpe revolutionized clinical psychology by proving that so-called anxiety could not exist when the muscles are totally relaxed."

"Well up my petticoat and in to my junction! I didn't know that!"

Stevie tried to ignore him, only wanting to keep him on the line long enough to plant the basic idea in his mind. "Reciprocal inhibition, one condition blocking another, works for the mind, too," she continued desperately. "You can stop certain thoughts, block them if—"

"What's about six inches long," said the voice, "and when you squeeze it white stuff squirts out? First clue: It's *not* a tube of toothpaste."

Stevie fought back a mounting sense of panic. She saw now that her effort was useless. "Wade, where is Sonny?"

"Out in the kitchen playing with his little pee-pee."

"Listen, Wade, part of you wants to help, understand? That's why you called. Now, tell him to run away and go stay with a friend, okay?"

"Sure, I'll do that." She could hear him shouting away from the telephone. "Hey, kid! There's a dizzy broad on the phone says you should run away from home, go mooch off a friend!"

"What's he doing?" Stevie demanded.

"Going out the door, chickee, just like you wanted. Now we got the place to ourselves, what say we—"

Hope surged inside her. "Wade, I'm coming over there. Wait for me. But tell me, *is* Sonny leaving?"

"You calling me a liar, bitch? Didn't I say he was? Didn't you hear me tell him?"

Then thank God, thought Stevie. She pulled the city phone directory closer and, fingers trembling violently, searched the West Bank listings for Bryce's address.

"Wade, how far is he going? Tell him to run, Wade!"

"Run, Wade!" she heard McKenna's mocking voice shout. "Run, Wade! Oh, run!"

"How far is he going? Where is he now?"

There was an unbearably long pause before the sly inhuman voice finally answered, "It's too late, Scar Baby. He's in the garage."

Then the line went dead.

"That was sure a weird phone call," Sonny said when Wade stepped through the garage door. "Who was it?"

Wade laughed and shut the door behind him. Sonny thought he noticed him drop something into his pocket.

"Ahh, just my ex-wife goofing around. She's still in love with my ass."

His freckled face formed a lopsided grin. As he looked around the garage, he broke into a softly whistled strain of "Do Not Forsake Me, Oh My Darling."

In the stark light of the green-shaded 75-watt bulb, he took in the long workbench projecting from the back wall. The red cedar trophy shelf, now freshly stained, was leaning against the vise. Tools were scattered everywhere, and colored pictures of Yamahas and Kawasakis and classic Harleys covered the wall above the bench.

"Here it is," Sonny said proudly, kneeling down past one end of the bench. The dull-silver, finned engine was propped between solid wooden blocks. "Only paid five bucks for it and another twenty to get it running. Want me to kick it over?"

But McKenna appeared not to hear the question. Instead he edged closer to the bench.

Idly, he patted the 10″ miter saw clamped to it. Next he picked up a rubber mallet, gave it a cursory glance, set it back down, then did the same with a level and a heavy Phillips screwdriver. Finally he picked up the Black & Decker drill and, after glancing around a moment, a long extension cord. He plugged the drill into the cord's socket, then knelt, kneecaps cracking loudly, to plug the cord into a wall socket beneath the bench. He moved slowly, almost reluctantly.

"You know what, kid?" Wade's voice was nearly normal again, though strained. "Everybody nowadays thinks they're different, that they're somehow out of it, but they don't know shit. *I'm* out of it. I'm a goddamn certified freak, that's what. Not worth a rat's ass to anybody."

He stood back up and gazed, eyes narrowing in slight confusion, at the drill balanced in his palms. Woodenly, his lips repeated the words: *You can stop certain thoughts, block them . . .*

"You're not a freak," Sonny said vehemently, "You're a magician. Magicians are neat."

Again the lopsided grin flickered across

McKenna's face. His right index finger twitched against the drill's trigger, making it whirr on and off briefly. When he spoke, his voice was more alien, even menacing.

"Magic? Oh yeah, magic's okay. But I mean, haven't you ever wondered what a revolving drill bit would do to . . ."

He turned to face the 12-year-old and stepped closer. "Say, a human eye?"

Sonny stepped back a pace or two, an uncertain smile on his lips. He said with nervous good humor, *"Pues, eres loco, viejo.* You're crazy!"

"I'll give you crazy, punk!"

Wade suddenly flicked the drill on, leaped forward and plunged the whirling bit until it made contact. A split second later, moist, gelatinous clots of goo were splatting against the pegboard over the workbench.

It's too late now, Scar Baby. He's in the garage.
The words formed a fatal litany in her mind as Stevie bore toward the river trying to urge more speed out of the Peugot's sedate diesel engine. As she had feared, Bryce was gone when she had called for him at the precinct office in Algiers. Rather than waste more precious time trying to convince someone else, she had decided to go it alone.

Now she was racing along the Lower Canal Street border of the French Quarter; despite the relatively late hour, drunken groups of reveling pedestrians forced her to slow down and play footsie with the brake pedal. She swore and swerved dangerously to avoid a mule-drawn surrey laden with gawking tourists. To her left, the Quarter's ornate wrought-iron balconies flashed by, interspersed with splashing fountains and cobblestone streets.

She was still halfway between Chartres and Decatur Street when she spotted a National Guard checkpoint dead ahead, near the edge of the International Trade Mart. It was here that two of the bodies had been discovered after the killing-mutilation spree three days ago. Swearing again at the delay, she swerved hard onto Magazine Street.

Too late now, taunted the voice in her head. *Way too late, Scar Baby.*

Sonny howled with shocked but appreciative laughter as Wade pulled the twirling drill bit out of the open can of lubricating grease on the workbench. Gooey amber clots of the stuff were clinging everywhere.

"Hey, *hombre*! You're gonna clean that crap up, not me!"

Sonny laughed again and flicked a speck of grease out of his thick bangs as he added, "God, what a space cadet!"

Wade, his face twitching wildly as it ran the gamut of conflicting emotions, paused to cock his head toward the street. He seemed to listen for a minute before fixing a glassy-eyed stare on the boy.

"That's it. Time's up. Now it's me *and* you, kid. He says it's gotta be you first, then me." Again his finger twitched on the drill's trigger as he slowly inched closer to the boy.

Sonny, convinced this was all a crazy but weirdly funny game, teased him. "Go ahead, Darth Vader! Stick your particle beam in my eye. I dare you, chicken!"

"Shut up!" Wade screamed, his face wildly distorted. Stevie's words were a jumbled confusion in his mind: *Reciprocal inhibition, one condition blocking another, works for the mind, too . . .*

"Dare you, chicken!" Sonny flapped his arms like wings. "Bwak, bwak, bwak!"

Wade was only two feet away from him now. With a wild howl of rage, he squeezed the drill back on and lunged forward again. At the last moment before the gnashing bit would have chewed into Sonny's eyeball, Wade, his face reflecting a supreme effort, swerved the drill down into his own right thigh.

With exploding force, his agonized scream reverberated in the garage.

Sonny's jaw fell open as he gaped, wide-eyed with shock, at the bloody chunks of meat now clinging to the bit, turning it into a shish kebab skewer. Then two things occurred almost simultaneously. He glanced out the garage's only window and noticed how brilliant the full moon was. Next, like it was a magnet attracting his gaze, he stared at the shellacked wooden plaque on the wall over the workbench:

Even a man who is pure in heart,
And says his prayers by night,

Can become a wolf when the wolfbane blooms,
And the summer moon is bright

He dropped his glance to McKenna's wired eyeballs. The redhead leered, moved closer and said in the gravelly inhuman voice, "Finally caught on, eh, boyo?"

Sonny spun around and leaped for the door. It refused to budge. He groped for the skeleton key that was always left in the lock. That's when he realized that it was the key McKenna had dropped into his pocket, after locking the door behind him.

"Cross my heart and hope to fart," sang the man as he approached, limping and bleeding, the hole in his pants leg showing a pink blossom of gore. The drill's extension cord trailed behind him like a long, coiled black worm. "Cross my heart and hope to fart, Time to tear Chink Boy's eye apart!"

His pupils huge with fright, Sonny backed away, almost mesmerized as he stared at the bloody drill bit. Then his head bumped into something made of metal on the wall behind him—the cover of the fusebox.

Panting like a dehydrating animal, Sonny whirled around and clawed the box open. He threw the main power switch, plunging the garage into almost total darkness except for the shaft of moonlight slanting through the window on the opposite wall. His breath rasping in the blackness, he yanked out several fuses and flung them toward the far end of the garage.

"Pretty smart for a rice burner," whispered

the voice, practically in his ear now. "But you're still going to die."

A shrill laugh trailed off like the whinny of a frightened horse.

Sonny cried out and made a mad dash toward the window. He was halfway there when an incredible pain seared into his right hip and he cried out again, sprawling spread-eagle on the concrete floor and sliding a few more painful inches. Too late he realized he had forgotten about the heavy, foot-powered lathe near one end of the workbench. When he tried to stand, hot pain lanced through his right side. The hip must be broken, he thought desperately. Even if he managed to smash the window out, he doubted that he could climb through quickly enough.

He finished crawling to the wall and huddled against it, just outside of the moonlight splashing through the window. Harsh, labored breathing was growing closer in the darkness.

"I got a hammer, gookboy. I'm gonna smash your fucking Vietcong head like an eggshell!"

Hot tears sprang from Sonny's eyes as he huddled tight against the wall, waiting to die.

An explosive shatter was followed by the window fragmenting into hundreds of shards of glass.

"Sonny!" It was a woman's voice. "I'm a friend of Neal's! Can you hear me? Are you here? Run to the window, Sonny! Hurry!"

Sobbing with fear and the unbelievable pain in his hip, the boy pulled himself up and limped sideways to the broken window.

"I'm hurt!" he gasped. "I can't climb out!"

A moment later small but strong hands gripped him under both armpits, and he tried to assist as they yanked him out into the cool night air, lowering him gently to the grass.

"So what, bitch?" screamed the man in the garage. "You can't stop me from killing myself! I'm gonna ram this drill bit into my *own* eye and poke that sonofabitch all the way into my brain!"

"No , you aren't," Stevie answered in a commanding voice. "No, you *aren't* because of reciprocal inhibition, remember? Remember, Wade? The mind can repel hostile forces. It *can*, Wade!"

There was a long suspenseful moment when Stevie could hear nothing but her own heart pounding and the boy crying softly in the grass beside her. Somewhere a dog howled, and from the East Bank traffic noise reached her in an airy murmur. It's too late, she told herself. Oh God, it's too late.

Too late, Scar Baby. Too late!

A pair of loud metallic clunks startled her as McKenna tossed the hammer and drill to the concrete floor. There was a choked cry from the dark interior of the garage. When he spoke, it was in his own voice, tired, and weak, but his own natural voice.

"Christ, girl, am I glad you're here."

During another long silence Stevie fought the sudden trembling relief that turned her calves into water.

"I knew there was some reason why I liked a cynical old grump like you," she said through

366

the shattered window. "You held him off, Wade! Do you realize you just resisted the man everyone's looking for? You beat Johnny Law! You care about people a hell of a lot more than you let on, don't you?"

The voice that answered was genuinely elated despite its exhaustion and pain. "Yeah, I guess I do. I really do, don't I?"

Caught in the emotion of the moment, none of them noticed the black Saab easing away from the curb out front. It was just one more insubstantial shadow slipping into the darkness of the night.

CHAPTER EIGHTEEN

ONE OF THE MOST POPULAR FEATURES WITH DIE-hard, adventuresome tourists visiting New Orleans is the Bayou Sunrise Cruise.

This five-hour voyage features a diesel-powered replica of a sternwheeler steamboat; it sets out from the Mississippi's Canal Street dock for a cruise through the Intercoastal Waterway and the surrounding bayous south of the city. Unlike the more decadent, frilly cruises, offering jazz bands, drinks, and dinner dances in the afternoon and evening, the more Spartan sunrise trip includes only a wholesome breakfast, with plenty of *café au lait*, and embarks promptly at the ungodly hour of three A.M. Even so, it is usually booked to capacity.

About midnight on the same July night that Stevie yanked Sonny through the broken window of his garage workshop, a deckhand was preparing the *Tom Sawyer* for her next cruise. First the young Honduran swept the deck clean. Then he unfolded canvas deck chairs and lined them along the bulwarks. Finally he put clean place mats on the tables in the dining area aft of the vessel, including candles in rosé globes and a complimentary book of matches featuring a full-color illustration of the *Tom Sawyer*.

He paused for a moment in the midst of his labors to watch a Japanese freighter gliding up the channel, harbor lights winking on and off like lazy fireflies.

Christ, he thought, gazing longingly at the huge international carrier. Those were real sailors, not a bunch of Disneyland *maricones* wiping tourists' noses. He was sick of this boring shit, the same old routine day in and day out, handing out mosquito repellent and pointing out the occasional alligator to oooh-ing and ahhh-ing visitors from Illinois and Iowa and New Jersey.

He sighed and shook the next clean linen tablecloth into place. He wished that for once—Mother of God, just once—something really exciting would happen in his life.

Shortly after midnight an exhausted Neal Bryce entered his house, then froze in the doorway.

Stevie Lasalle was asleep on the sofa; across the room from her, McKenna was curled up on the lounger, snoring heavily.

They both started awake at the same moment. McKenna stood, winced with pain and limped a few steps in Bryce's direction, favoring his bandaged thigh. Bryce stared at Stevie and read something ominous in her face. Without a word of greeting he crossed the living room to Sonny's bedroom and flung the door open, flipping the light switch.

The messy, overcrowded room stared back, as empty and forlorn and abandoned as a cup of cold coffee. The bed was unoccupied except for Bryce's old basketball scrapbook and a copy of *Cycle World*.

Bryce spun around. "Where is he?" he demanded, glancing from one to the other.

Stevie stood up and rubbed her eyes. Her hair was a tumbled confusion of sable curls, her face still puffy with sleep. The imprint of a cushion had left a faint red grid on her right cheek.

"It's okay, Neal. He's okay. He's at Kyla's for a little while until. . . ."

She trailed off, unsure how to finish the sentence. Until when? She went on to explain that she and Wade had taken him to the hospital to have his dislocated hip set. Gently, while Wade stood in the middle of the room refusing to meet Bryce's eye, she explained what had happened. She emphasized Wade's heroic struggle against Johnny Law's inexorable power; she told about his all-important warning phone call to her and how he had held off as long as possible, even injuring himself in his struggle to avoid attacking the boy.

She finished speaking. Wade, still unable to

face the detective, said, "I won't blame you if you stomp my ass, old sleuth. Bring a guy into your house, treat him decently, and this happens."

Bryce was silent for a long moment. "No, it's my fault," he finally said.

He told them about finding Wade's name on Harlan Perry's hit list and admitted that he had recklessly assumed the psychotic didn't know where McKenna was staying . Bryce then raised the rolled-up papers clutched in his right hand.

"Since I left Stevie today at Cruz's place I've been digging up information and equipment. First I contacted a military PR officer for information on the location of those commandos. Then I hit the library and made these photocopies from a detailed Army Corps of Engineers map of the area they're occupying. It shows routes through the swamps that are traversable by four-wheel drive vehicles."

Bryce stifled a yawn and sank wearily onto the sofa Stevie had just deserted.

"I haven't been able to contact Milo and the others in person," he went on. "Reno Morgan and the National Guard have commandeered the BSI Precinct office as their temporary command post on the West Bank. Milo did, very reluctantly, manage to procure the equipment I requested—jeep and some weapons. The stuff is waiting at the central motor pool and armory downtown."

"Wait a minute," Stevie interrupted. "Are you hinting around that you're planning on going into those swamps alone?"

Bryce ran his fingers through his hair and stared at his feet, face deadpan with exhaustion. "That's about the size of it. According to the information available on this Tuaoi Stone, the only way to negate Perry's commands at this point is to take him out. Period. And I've got to get that damn crystal back."

"That's insane!" Stevie protested. "You—"

Bryce held up one hand to silence her. "It's the only way. Besides, a larger force would only attract attention and wouldn't stand a chance, anyway, against the kind of firepower those commandos can muster."

Stevie and Wade exchanged a glance. "Look," McKenna argued, "we're going with you. We've been a team so far, haven't we?"

"Besides," Stevie chimed in, "you're acting illegally, aren't you? At this point you're no more authorized than we are."

Bryce didn't have the energy to object in the face of their obvious determination.

"Okay," he conceded reluctantly. "Okay, then. But we'd better catch some sleep because we'll have to leave in a few hours. Perry could move those troops toward the city at any time now, not to mention the National Guard who're patrolling all over with loaded weapons."

McKenna mumbled a weary good-night and limped upstairs to his room.

"Take my room," Bryce told Stevie. "I'll sleep in Sonny's. Come on, I'll show you where it is."

He escorted her upstairs. They lingered outside the door of his bedroom, suddenly as shy as a pair of adolescents. Bryce cupped her face in

373

both hands, tilted it and gently tasted her lips.

"Sleep tight, pretty lady," he whispered.

He was on his way back to the stairs when she softly called his name.

"Neal?"

He turned around. She was holding the bedroom door open invitingly with one hand, unbuttoning her blouse with the other.

"I know you're tired," she said hesitantly, "but I don't want to be alone tonight. And . . . it's what we both want anyway, isn't it?"

She didn't need to add what they both already knew. This might be our last chance.

He swallowed the thick lump in his throat and nodded, returning to the doorway and pressing her tightly against him.

"Oh God, yes," she murmured.

Then the door was shutting gently behind them and, for a little while at least, there was no Johnny Law threatening to destroy the city, no impending death for the three of them, no world at all except for the selfish little world they made for themselves.

The first roseate traces of dawn were streaking the eastern sky when the *Tom Sawyer* entered the remote bayou country west of the Intercoastal Waterway.

Murky water was churned into pure white foam as the sternwheel slapped at it, sending out ripples that made the floating water lilies dance and bob crazily. Along the cutaway banks, mangroves marched on stiltlike roots, and bald cypress trees formed an almost impenetrable wall. Spectators standing with elbows perched on the boat's gunwale peered intently, trying, in the ghostly light, to discern which half-submerged logs were in fact drowsy alligators.

A dapper tourist in a silk suit was taking photos with a Nikon. As he focused for his next available shot, the camera's lens shattered and the Nikon jumped out of his hands.

At first, the Honduran deck hand pouring coffee from a silver pot thought someone had thrown a string of firecrackers overboard. Then, one by one, the trio at the table he was serving crumpled like boneless rag dolls. Obscenely bright scarlet blood spurted from their bullet wounds.

Screams of terror formed a backdrop for the unrelenting bursts of fire directed from the tree line along the bank. The hidden Commando V-150 assault vehicle's 20mm. Gatling stuttered without pause, the six rotating barrels spewing rounds at the rate of 3,000 per minute. The wall of slugs shattered bones, ripped clothing to shreds and slammed bodies around like bowling pins. The gunner concentrated aim on the stern-wheel for only ten seconds, enough to completely pulverize the boat's wheel and rudder. The *Tom Sawyer* began to swirl crazily in mid-stream.

Some passengers panicked and jumped overboard. They were picked off immediately by troops emerging along the bank, machine pistols barking in their fists.

The unbelievable destruction was over in less than two minutes. As the last weapon ceased firing, all that could be heard were the groans of the wounded and dying still remaining on the floundering boat. A thick pall of acrid cordite hung low over the bayou.

Harlan Perry, outfitted in full combat regalia, his face sepia dyed, emerged onto the bank and surveyed the battlefield. Beneath the black dye his cheeks flushed with victory.

His face creased into the familiar stiletto-thin smile. All this death and destruction had been wrought with only one squad and only one assault vehicle. The rest of his men were deployed further north, poised at the edge of the swamps, ready to converge on the hapless city as it stirred to life for a new day.

Now Perry was glad he had kept one squad behind as a mop-up team. He should have known the government would send this troopship, disguised as a steamboat but actually loaded with crack PCA's, to ambush them from the rear.

He turned to his radioman. "Relay the order to the main body to commence final movement to contact phase thirty minutes after sunup!"

For the first time, he seemed to become aware of the dying groans out on the bayou. He fumbled to open a waterproof, rubber bag clipped to his cartridge belt. Then both hands rose before him in a gesture of offering. He lifted the black velvet cloth away from the Tuaoi.

"We take no prisoners!" screamed Johnny Law.

Even in the murky half-light, the multifaceted crystal shimmered like quicksilver. He raised it up until it was level with his eyes. Squinting, he stared into it, through it, beyond it to the ravaged hull of the *Tom Sawyer*.

A thin, intense magenta beam radiated from the Tuaoi. With a sudden flapping explosion like a gas main going up, the steamboat replica burst into bright orange flames that brought a lurid, premature daylight to the swamp.

Shortly after three A.M., Neal Bryce, Wade McKenna and Stevie Lasalle left New Orleans on Barataria Road, heading through the outlying swamps of Jefferson Parish.

Bryce slowed for a moment when they passed the abandoned Saab Turbo. It was probably just some Joe Citizens playing nocturnal gator poacher, he decided, and he quickly forgot the vehicle.

The murky indigo of the eastern sky was softening to a pearly luminescence when, following the detailed Army map, they turned off into a little-used network of trails webbing the backswamps. Milo had procured a rugged Jeep Renegade with a rollbar, two jerry cans of gasoline clamped over the rear bumper.

Wade rode in the cramped backseat; propped between his knees was an Ithica Police Special pump-action shotgun. Curled beside him on the seat was a canvas clutchbelt with a half-dozen fragmentation grenades clipped to it.

Bryce was inching the jeep along a precariously narrow spine of solid ground, bayous flanking it on both sides like overgrown irrigation ditches. Suddenly they heard distant firing break out. A moment later the first terrified screams reached them, faint and muted by the thick interceding layer of moss-dripping oaks, cypress and tupelo gums. Then, ominously, the screaming abruptly stopped and early morning silence settled down over the swamps like a heavy quilt.

Bryce and Stevie exchanged a wordless glance. Before leaving his house Bryce had donned gaitered boots, khaki trousers and one of his old fatigue shirts with sleeves lopped off at the shoulder. He now wore the Browning 9mm. and its underarm holster on the outside of his shirt. They had made a quick stop at Stevie's place before leaving town, Bryce accompanying her into the building. Stevie had changed into a brown wool sweater against the damp chill of the early morning, jeans and waterproof hiking boots. Her hair was swept back in a simple ponytail.

"What the hell?" McKenna said as the last dying screams gave way to the unnerving silence.

Heedless of the water traps pressing in on both sides, Bryce pegged the accelerator, and the jeep's rear tires chewed up twin furrows of skunk cabbage and sharp-toothed saw grass. Stevie and Wade grabbed the rollbar and hung on for dear life; they jounced wildly along the overgrown trail, branches swiping at them, the headlights illuminating an occasional raccoon or possum scattering in panic before them.

They broke past a thick, high ridge of swamp azalea and spotted a dull orange glow over the neighboring bayou. A few minutes later they sat in shocked silence near its bank, watching the last glowing embers of the *Tom Sawyer's* burnt-out hull settling into an aquatic grave. Bodies floated everywhere like charred driftwood. The charnel-house stink of burnt human skin and hair hung thick in the atmosphere.

They looked on, horrified, as a grinning alligator glided into the midst of the carnage to select its breakfast.

"Christ," McKenna groaned. "Sweet Jesus jumping Christ!"

"Neal, what are we going to do?" Stevie glanced nervously around them. In the ghostly half-light a spidery mist hovered over the water, an amorphous grave shroud.

"Obviously we can't do anything here," Bryce replied grimly, "I say we run without lights until we catch up with Perry. We've got to kill him and stop the influence of that crystal, or those commandos are going on into the city."

While they were talking Bryce noticed a flock of spoonbills settling on the bank just ahead of them.

Now the birds suddenly scattered in panic, and the tall detective felt his face break out in cold sweat as he realized why.

"Take cover quick!" he shouted to the others. "Make for the tree line and bring the weapons!"

McKenna grabbed the shotgun and grenades and stumbled out of the back, following the other two. He was only 15 feet away from the jeep when it exploded, the casualty of a direct hit by a rocket-propelled grenade fired from the hidden assault vehicle.

Staccato bursts of machine gunfire opened up, ripping clots of damp earth loose all around their feet as the trio raced for the cover of nearby cypress trees.

They made it and collapsed in a heap, huddled together behind a large fallen trunk; the assault vehicle was partially visible about 40 yards straight ahead now that they had penetrated the tree line behind which it was hidden.

It lurched slowly toward them, a huge, camouflage-painted beast, relentlessly crushing the shrubs and smaller trees under its giant tires. The withering fire had temporarily ceased.

"They can't get a clear line of fire because of the bigger trees," Bryce explained. "They're planning on flushing us out."

He had already unholstered his parabellum. It seemed ridiculously tiny and ineffective, considering the behemoth military monster now bearing down on them. He nodded at the shotgun McKenna was clutching and said, "In case they have to climb out of that tin can, can you fire that thing?"

McKenna, his face white as virgin snow, swallowed with difficulty. "You kidding? My parents wouldn't even let me have a BB gun."

Bryce seized the gun, pumped it once and flicked the safety off.

"It's ready to fire. You've got five shells loaded and ten more in the pouch on that web belt. Reload the magazine through this opening. Pump it each time you shoot. Don't worry about aiming, just point it."

Bryce unclipped the pouch of spare shells and

dropped them beside McKenna. Then he rolled over onto one side, wrapped the clutch belt and grenades around his hip, rolled onto his other side and fastened it.

"What are you doing?" Steve demanded.

"We've got two choices," Bryce said, peering cautiously over the trunk to check the vehicle's progress. It was rumbling steadily closer, mechanical bowels whining. "We can stay here and wait to die, or we can go on the offensive. The only vulnerable spot on that assault vehicle is the gun turret. I'm going to try to lob a grenade under its lip. If we take the Gattling out, we might stand a chance. Otherwise . . ."

He didn't bother to elaborate on the alternative.

"Neal, no! That's insane! They'll kill you."

"What's insane," Bryce answered, "is just lying here while they get closer. The jeep is destroyed, pretty lady. They've got us now."

He unclipped a grenade, jerked the safety pin ring and kept the safety lever held tight against his palm. As he started to rise, planning on breaking for the nearest tree and leapfrogging from trunk to trunk, McKenna said behind him, "Hey, boyo, let's do this thing right. John Wayne always said, 'Cover me!' "

Despite the fear drenching his body in sweat —or perhaps because of it—Bryce grinned. "John Wayne," he said tersely, "couldn't do a Texas accent worth shit. And you, Shoneen, couldn't cover your own ass with a blanket. You just save those shells in case . . . in case of whatever."

The next second he was gone, dashing for the

nearest cypress with the grenade clutched tight against his chest.

The first exposed area was only about 15 feet across, and Bryce, apparently catching the vehicle's crew by surprise, covered it without incident. But as he raced for the next tree the big Gattling opened up, bullets zipping through the leaves and saw grass all around him. Wood chips rained in his face as he dove behind the cypress. The bucking monster was awesomely close now, momentarily halted as it maneuvered sideways around a thick stand of trees.

Bryce decided to take advantage of the vehicle's temporary oblique angle. He broke from cover and made one last, long-legged dash toward the V-150.

The gun's vulnerable turret was about nine feet above the ground at the front of the mammoth vehicle. There was only one discouragingly small opening where the Gattling's barrel and breech mechanism protruded through the armor plating. Bryce knew that if he missed that opening, he was dead meat. They were all dead meat, like those corpses floating in the bayou— Stevie, Wade and thousands of people back in the sleeping, unsuspecting city.

His body coiled like a spring, arced in a graceful curve and untensed as he raised his right hand in a high overhand motion.

The big 20mm. gun swiveled toward him.

Bullets fanned his cheeks as Bryce released the fragmentation grenade and dropped to the ground, rolling clear. It sailed high and seemed to hang suspended in midair for an agonizingly long moment. Then it dropped toward the turret —and missed the opening by less than an inch, bouncing off the lip of metal.

It bounced again and finally clattered inside the turret.

Not a swisher, Bryce thought gleefully as he rolled with desperate haste toward cover. Not a swisher, sports fans, bounced off the rim, but made it, goddamnit! Made it!

The huge assault vehicle exploded and shuddered like a dinosaur shaking off some nettlesome pest, the 20mm. Gattling's barrel snapping free. For a moment the beast continued to move forward, then ground to a halt as a secondary explosion inside incapacitated the drive shaft. Next came a hectic string of muffled shots as the ammo belts detonated, peppering the crew inside. Their agonized screams were brief.

"Kick ass and take names, old sleuth!" a triumphant McKenna shouted behind him.

Let Harlan Perry be in there, too, Bryce prayed. As he unholstered his parabellum and cautiously approached the smoking vehicle, he failed to notice Perry and Staff Sergeant Fanning when they stepped out from behind a fat oak tree on his blind side. Fanning drew a silent bead on him with his Honecker-12 machine pistol.

The shotgun roared, rattling the leaves with scattered shot and completely missing the pair near the oak tree. But McKenna's shot warned Bryce. He broke into a zigzagging run back toward the fallen trunk, realizing Stevie and Wade were defenseless against that machine pistol.

McKenna pumped awkwardly, fired again, pumped and missed, pumped and fired and missed again. The shotgun was useless at his present range. Seeing the commando aiming at Bryce again, he realized the detective wouldn't make it without a few more precious seconds. McKenna leaped up from behind the trunk and pranced about in front of it, still favoring his injured leg.

"Hey! Over here, cumbag! Free shot!"

Fanning went for it. The machine pistol stuttered briefly, and Stevie and Bryce watched in horror as slugs stitched a neat line of holes across the psychic's chest and flung him in a backward somersault. He was dead before he hit the ground, a crumpled, bloody heap.

Bryce covered the last eight feet to the trunk in a headlong dive. He was just on the verge of dropping behind cover when one of Fanning's rounds hit him just left of his spine, shattering a rib and lodging in his lung.

Stevie cried out as a thin trickle of blood erupted down his chin. She jerked his long legs behind the trunk just as another fast stream of bullets chewed into the wood, chipping relentlessly away at it.

It felt like a spike was being driven into his chest as Bryce managed to straighten himself out behind the trunk. His breathing was rapid and shallow, and a bubbly mixture of phlegm and blood produced a simmering noise in his throat. Another burst of withering fire, and the top edge of the trunk was splintered.

The pair advanced closer, Fanning first, Perry behind him clutching something in a rubber bag. Another burst and one more inch of the trunk's top edge was pulverized.

Groaning at the incredible pain, Bryce rolled to the far edge of the log; dark, blurry waves of unconsciousness threatened to engulf him. The pair was only 40 feet away now, closing fast.

When another round of slugs battered the trunk, Bryce heard Stevie's muffled cry of fear. Toying with them, Fanning sent a random burst of fire into Wade's dead, crumpled body lying out in front of the fallen cypress. It shimmied and writhed in a grotesque parody of movement.

Bryce ignored the driving pain and flying splinters of wood; he rested his parabellum against the chewed-up top edge of the log.

The Browning made a single, insignificant noise against the racket of the machine pistol, but Fanning dropped to his knees, a surprised frown spreading slowly across his face as blood fountained from the middle of his battle tunic. Then he tumbled forward as if his bones had suddenly gelled.

Perry immediately plunged one hand inside the waterproof rubber bag. A moment later, there were at least 50 Harlan Perrys approaching the log.

Bryce emptied his pistol at the multiple images advancing toward them, but it was like plinking at ghosts. The last thing he remembered, before the dark waves finally washed over him and he passed out, was the shrill, spine-tingling laugh like the whinny of a frightened horse. It surrounded them in a reverberating echo, as if the trees all around them housed speakers.

He's dead, Stevie thought numbly as Bryce's face slumped into the damp ground. Oh God in heaven, he's dead, and I never once told him I love him.

Ten feet from the log, the multiple images of Harlan Perry disappeared. The frightened woman listened in shock as his shrill voice blasted all around her.

"New Orleans is officially under siege. It's just me and you now, Scar Baby!"

Again there was the horrid laugh from hell. Then Stevie was left alone in the eerily silent gray light of the swamp.

Waiting . . .

Federal Agent Reno Morgan hung up the telephone on Bryce's desk and aimed a gloating look across the office at Milo.

"Johnny Law is well overdue to strike, but absolutely no incidents were reported during the night. I told you I knew what I was doing. Those terrorists are afraid to make a move now that we're fighting power with power."

Milo gave him a sour, disgusted look, but turned his back without comment, pouring yet another cup from the Mr. Coffee against the back wall. Secretly, he was worried about Bryce. All he knew was that the Texan had picked up a jeep and some munitions from the central police armory and motor pool a couple hours earlier.

"Hey," Morgan called behind him, "why not make yourself useful, little man, and round us up some chow?"

His ears flushing with anger, Milo spun around, sloshing hot coffee on his fingers. His free hand drifted down to pat his crotch.

"Here's your chow, asswipe. A nice thick tube steak."

The corners of Morgan's mouth twitched with barely contained rage.

"You sawed-off Cajun crackers are funny, aren't you? Regular little stand-up, greaseball comedian."

Morgan scratched a telephone number on a pad and rose from behind the desk. He picked up his chrome sunglasses and tucked them into the pocket of his green plaid sport jacket.

"I'm going to grab some breakfast at the Napoleon Cafe on Chartres. Number's on the desk. Stay right here until I get back."

"Where the hell you think I'm gonna be?" Milo replied sullenly. "This is *my* precinct."

The sun was up for only 30 minutes, a dull-glowing saffron sphere just over the horizon, when Morgan exited the Algiers Precinct building. A National Guard corporal clad in fatigues and a helmet stood just outside the door, sliding a magazine into his .45 caliber pistol.

"Unload that weapon and put it away, trooper," Morgan growled. "Who do you think's in charge here?"

"Johnny Law rules," the soldier answered promptly before he raised the .45 and fired a bullet into Reno Morgan's brain.

Stevie lay teetering on the feather edge of panic, listening to the ghastly, inhuman sounds emanate from the swamp. There was still no visible sign of Perry in the hazy early morning light.

Desperately she fought to regain control of her breathing. Without that initial control, she knew she would never achieve the quiet mind of *mushin*.

Her mind rallied for a moment, and she saw the plain white index card taped over the practice mirror in her instructor's *dojo*. It contained a passage from the ancient *Nichomachean Ethics* of Aristotle, and each student read it before every practice: "The magnanimous man does not run into trifling danger . . . but he will face great dangers, and when he is in danger he is unsparing of his life, knowing that there are conditions on which life is not worth having."

Slowly the debilitating panic drained from her muscles, replaced by a dull ache of anger and determination. Now the bizarre noises had stopped. The preternatural post-dawn silence seemed oppressive and portentous. She rolled nearer to Bryce, then felt a brief rush of hope. He was still breathing. Stevie ripped a strip from the bottom of his shirt and folded it into a crude bandage. She used his belt to secure it over the bullet wound in his back, stemming the flow of blood.

Slowly, cautiously, her adrenaline-boosted senses on full alert, she rose from behind the felled tree to meet her enemy.

It almost seemed as if she could hear beyond the silence now, hear insects scuttling under the fallen leaves, hear the fragile water hyacinths opening their petals in search of the sun. But she failed—or more accurately, was unable because of her own psychological defense mechanisms—to notice the ghostly blue sheen now surr unding her body in an ectoplasmic blur.

Abruptly the whinnying laugh split the silence, surrounding her and mocking from all directions. Her body automatically assumed *hachiji dachi*, the open leg stance, as she scanned the trees and shrubs around her for some sign of Harlan Perry.

The laughter grew closer, louder, still louder, threatening to destroy *mushin*. She strained her eyes even harder as she tried to determine the exact direction it was coming from.

The blue aura glowed deeper, not only surrounding her but also the dead psychic's bullet-riddled corpse.

Stevie stepped over the downed cypress and started to move around Wade's body without looking down at it. She was too busy scanning the nearby trees.

Like a jerked marionette, McKenna's corpse abruptly struggled to a sitting position, one arm raised to point behind her. Stevie froze as the dead man's face broke into a hideous smile. The lips twitched spasmodically; then, in a hissing whisper, the voice of Professor Wiggle-Wobble warned, "Move it or lose it, sister!"

Both eyelids flapped up with a sound like elastic snapping, and in their dead surfaces she saw Johnny Law reflected, right behind her.

The corpse collapsed again in a heap. Stevie sucked in a sharp breath and dropped to the left just as an intense ruby beam exploded the tree directly ahead of her. When she shot to her feet again, facing him and assuming the cat stance, she was once more surrounded by at least 50 Harlan Perry images, all grinning the rotten-toothed grin as they closed in on her.

Fear and anger both deserted her as Stevie's mind retreated before *mushin*. She began performing the ritual, highly stylized *katas* designed for defense against multiple attackers—kicking, slashing and jabbing. The mocking laugh intensified as her blows simply passed through thin air, but she refused to stop, knowing that one of the images had to be the real Harlan Perry.

Then, she wasn't sure exactly when, she began to wonder why she was fighting so hard. She began to realize how easy and sweet and wonderful and right it would be simply to die.

How wonderful it would be to give in to her new ruler!

Again Wade's body jerked to a sitting position. This time Keith didn't disguise his voice as Professor Wiggle-Wobble of their childhood games.

"Don't lose it now, Stevie!" urged the dead lips. "Your friend Wade is a channel, and I'm using his aural body until it dissipates. Stevie, you're a together lady, but you have to accept it. The past *isn't* always a dead thing. Here's what I looked like that night . . . remember?"

Wade's leering death mask melted, transformed into the bloody, pulpy, shattered visage of Keith—Keith as he had watched, dying, on the night she was savagely beaten and gang-raped.

"Goddamnit, girl," Keith bellowed, "you're letting that worthless piece of sewer slime ride piggyback on your mind? I've been with you during all these years. Stevie, you know what to do! *Do* it! Watch close now, and you'll see your clue."

All the Harlan Perry images snarled angrily. All fifty raised the waterproof bags up to the face level. But the searing red beam emanated from only one of them, striking the corpse full in its face and melting the skin.

Stevie uttered a sharp *kiai* and snap-kicked, her toes catching the bag solidly and knocking it from Perry's hands. It flew in a high arc and landed in the soupy ground at the edge of the bayou, promptly sinking out of sight.

The spectral images disappeared. The rest was over in five seconds. Stevie whirled, turning her back on Perry as if to flee; instead, she bent forward, dropping both hands on the ground to support herself. She kicked up and backward, kicked through, not at, a perfectly executed *kakato* as her boot heel exploded against his jaw. She spun around at the same time he did, driving a vicious elbow jab into his right kidney.

Perry shrieked hideously, then dropped to the ground unconscious.

Stevie remembered what Bryce had emphasized. Johnny Law's commands could only be countermanded by his death. Acting quickly, before she could have second thoughts, she leaped high and brought all her weight crashing down on one knee against his cervical vertebrae. There was a sound like a wet stick snapping when she destroyed the trunkline of nerves leading into his brain.

Perry's legs kicked spastically for a few seconds. A moment later Johnny Law—the scourge of New Orleans, master of the Terrible Crystal, collector of ears—was dead.

Stevie couldn't realize then, as shock set in and glazed her eyes, that the assault vehicles racing toward the city were already slowing down and stopping and that the commandos were climbing out with dazed, confused, shell-shocked looks not unlike her own. Nor could she know that the National Guard troops already in position to strike were voluntarily removing the magazines from their weapons.

All she could do was flop down to the damp earth beside Bryce and cradle his head in her lap. She would still be there an hour later when a motor-launch crew, dispatched after the *Tom Sawyer* failed to make routine radio contact, would discover her.

Epilogue

COREY WEBSTER CAUTIOUSLY POKED HIS HEAD OUT from behind a cypress and checked the clearing.

It was empty now. Nothing was disturbing the fading daylight of the swamp except the serenade of the wind in the trees and the static buzz of insects.

He moved further into the open, the tattered streamers of his blue shirt fluttering in the chilly breeze. The faded words stenciled across his back were barely legible in the dying light: PROPERTY OF LOUISIANA STATE PENITENTIARY, ANGOLA.

He flexed his cramped, aching muscles, stiff from hours spent huddled behind the cypress head. The search party was definitely gone, he decided. At first, when he stumbled across them, the convicted murderer had been convinced they were looking for him. But soon he realized something was wrong—no dogs, no choppers—and these cops, if they *were* cops, wore no uniforms and appeared unarmed. Besides, since when did you search for escaped prisoners by turning over logs and probing into the mud with wooden poles?

Webster strained his eyes in the grainy twilight, glancing around. No, they hadn't been looking for him. All these wood chips and chewed-up trees—some hairy shit had come down around here.

He thought about that tall dude with the curly hair, the one playing the highbrow music on his ghetto blaster. He had moved gingerly, favoring his midsection as if he'd recently been hurt. And that beautiful fox hanging onto him wouldn't let him make a move without her help. Probably fucking each other's lights out. Neither one of them had paid much attention to the short, fat guy who was obviously in charge, pissing and moaning about the mud screwing up his shoes.

Well, whatever they were looking for, they hadn't found it today. Meaning, Webster decided, that he'd better haul ass from this area in case they returned tomorrow. He'd find a farm and maybe steal a vehicle, then get himself a hostage. But first he was going to wash at least the outer layer of crud off his body.

He moved stiffly toward the sluggish water of the bayou. He paused for a moment to listen to the wind in the trees and saw grass. He felt blood throbbing in his palms and shivered for a moment, recalling the stories his French-descended grandmother used to tell about were-wolves who supposedly roamed the swamps in search of victims.

The ground became less stable as he neared the water, and his feet splattered in the soupy mess. He bent forward to splash his face, sinking up to his ankles.

Something seemed to wrap itself around his left ankle, and he cried out as he jumped back.

He jerked his foot up out of the muck. At first he thought the shapeless, muddy blob dangling from it was some kind of weird reptilian para-site. But when he kicked it loose, it lay harmless-ly inert on the ground.

Cautious, his dirt-streaked, unshaven face tense, he picked it up and rinsed it off in the water.

It was a rubber sack with self-sealing water-proof flaps.

He pried the dripping sack open and reached inside. Webster felt a book and something else, something cool and hard and smooth to the touch. A moment later he was curiously examin-ing the brilliance of the multifaceted crystal balanced on his palm.

Despite the rapidly waning light, it seemed to glow with an inner energy of its own. For a moment his right hand and arm tingled numbly, as if they had fallen asleep.

He sensed something, something he didn't yet understand, something primitive, something like incredible, deadly power.

The cracked lips creased in a smile.

Slowly, heart palpitating with excitement, he withdrew the book. He was still trying to make out its title when the words suddenly seemed to shake themselves loose out of the trees overhead.

"Move it or lose it, boyo!" warned a disembodied voice in an affected Irish brogue.

Corey Webster barely had time to feel his scrotum shrivel in fear before the writhing mass of water moccasins swarmed over him, entangling his legs, sinking their teeth into him in a dozen places to inject their deadly poison. The hideous scream of pain and disgust and indescribable terror went unheeded in the lonely twilight of the swamp.

He staggered under the weight of the squirming pit vipers. As he fell his arms reflexively shot out, launching the book and crystal well out into the bayou, where they promptly sank.

Only the soothing whisper of the wind remained and a hollow, spectral laugh that died out with the last feeble rays of the blood-red sun.

It lurked beneath the tribal burial ground — an ancient evil yearning to unleash unholy terror on an unsuspecting world!

TOTEM

By Ehren M. Ehly
Author of *Obelisk*

A golden hawk fell from the sky, ushering in a storm of terror, as the sleeping dead began to stir beneath the earth. Deaf to the hawk's strangled cry of warning, the workmen continued to uncover the ancient evil that lay hidden within the Indian burial ground; they unwittingly unleashed an unholy force on an unsuspecting world. For they had angered the Ancient One, and his appetite for revenge could only be satisfied with the souls of those who had disturbed him from his eternal rest. Only one woman could stop him, one woman rich in the knowledge of the old ways, one woman prepared to make the ultimate sacrifice at the bloodied base of the totem....

__2746-1 $4.50US/$5.50 CAN